For Malachi.

Sorry I used some of your real-life lines in this book.
I couldn't resist.

PROLOGUE

"Morning, Miss Sage."

Sage choked out a laugh. "Why, hello Mr. Sato. Why the formality of this fine morn'?" She walked into the small sitting room where George sat in his favorite armchair. A scrub jay perched in a giant oak, chirping at the man who fed him scraps through the giant window.

George looked more tired and thinner than usual, his skin like the weathered pages of vintage picture books he loved to collect. He had always been a small man, but these last weeks had aged him differently. The sickness settled in his bones.

"George," Sage said, setting the tea tray down on the cluttered coffee table. Why did they call it a coffee table when neither of them liked that filth? "I think we need to take you in—"

"No—"

"Just to get things checked out. Nothing crazy."

"Sage. My dear, sweet friend—"

Sage smiled, but it felt forced. "Don't try and butter me up, old man."

"I'm tired." This was an admission of something. George prided himself on not being tired. Prided himself on being able to find that extra reserve of energy. But not today. The confession looked to have winded him because he stared out the window unblinking for several seconds before beckoning Sage over. "Come, sit and drink some tea with me. Tell me about that new game. The one where you run around and pick things and garden. We should have had a garden. I would have started the seeds and your young body could have done all the hard work." He laughed at himself, which turned into a dry cough.

Sage rolled her eyes. "You know how much I like outside and dirt and—" she shivered. "Bugs."

"It would have been so fun to see you try," George said. "Drink some tea with me."

They chatted about their favorite teas. They talked about books they enjoyed from his massive library. She made him laugh with a terrible pun. He told her how much he liked watching her play her little computer games. How much he liked her. Loved her as a granddaughter.

She told him how much she loved him too. And then she watched her old friend finally rest his eyes.

1

SAGE

"Thanks for letting me stay with you," Sage said, unlocking her car and depositing Squash, her elderly chihuahua, wrapped in a pink blanket, onto the front seat. The old girl did a rather ungraceful step over the console to her passenger seat (ever the passenger princess) and flopped down on the blanket. Poor thing.

"Of course." Tavy gave Sage another hug. "You sure you don't want to stay another few days?"

Sage sighed and looked out onto the well-manicured lawn of Tavy's mini-mansion. She thought of George's house and the chaotic lawn of weeds, crumbling flower boxes, and overgrown bushes.

"No, I better get home," Sage said. "It's time." And she couldn't impose on Tavy's family any longer. It just felt weird. And Squash, the chihuahua who really had no business being alive at her age, liked the old house with the massive fireplace and creaking stairs. It was her home too.

Tavy nodded in understanding. She was always empathetic like that. "Call me if you need anything."

"Will do." But she wouldn't. Sage was the suffer-in-silence type. No need to bother anyone with her problems.

The drive to the outskirts of town would take her fifteen minutes max. It was a small road leading to the edge of the small town where a row of houses over a century old backed up to old oak trees and forest. Her neighbors were far away because the houses were made back when people cared about things like privacy and space.

Sage had planned to use the drive as a "meditation moment" or whatever Tavy's toxic positivity parents had encouraged her to do. "It will give you a moment to calm your mind, push the sadness away, and breathe in your new life," they had said.

As if grief was that simple.

As if the human mind could simply shut off.

Still, it was worth a shot. She nearly closed her eyes before realizing that despite knowing the road to her home like the back of her hand, it was best not to test that theory completely.

Her phone rang. Well, that *meditation moment* was short-lived.

"Hey girl," Lily said. "How are you holding up?"

"As good as can be expected," Sage said. "How are you?" It seemed like the right thing to ask. It was clearly the opening Lily needed.

"Pretty good. We've been busy with marketing your appearance at the competition. I don't want to push you, but do you have any idea when we can expect you back on your regular streaming schedule? Jared made some social media posts. They don't explain much, just that you had a death in the family and are taking some time away from streaming to attend the funeral and be with family sort of thing."

Jared was her social media manager and he *loved* drama. It made creating content easier, apparently. To be fair, he had grown all of her social media platforms quite a bit over the last few months despite writing stupid captions. What does "Cap, no printer" even mean?

Sage let out a long sigh and rubbed her temple before turning down the long country road. "I think I'll be back sooner than later. I need to get into the rhythm of things again."

"No pressure," Lily said in a voice that conveyed that, *actually yes,* there was a lot of pressure to get it together.

Lily was the owner of LilyTech, a tech company that specialized in creating gaming accessories and set-ups for women. Sage, being on the smaller side, was a great asset to the marketing team. She used all of their gear and controllers, with specifications for women's hands. The new boost in sales at LilyTech could be attributed to Sage's recent streaming success. Lily had taken a risk by sponsoring the young gamer with low subscriber numbers and it had totally paid off. Sage knew it too. And Sage felt like she owed the company for taking that chance on her. Plus, she really did want to get back into a rhythm of life. Death had a funny way of interrupting things.

"No. I want to get back into it. The algorithm will

appreciate it, and to be honest, I could use the mental break. And I want to get better for the competition," Sage said.

"Glad to hear it."

Sage couldn't blame Lily. She had a business to run after all. And Sage, despite considering Lily a sort of friend, knew she was ultimately a marketing tool for the company and Lily needed to get her ROI.

"Now," Lily said, putting on her business voice. "Let's chat about that stalker."

Sage huffed (because Lily wouldn't be able to see her roll her eyes in protest). "You're giving that guy too much credit."

"We take your safety seriously," Lily said.

Sage also knew it would make for good headlines. LilyTech would write articles and post about how one of their female gamers was being targeted by rogue fans and appeal to women's rights everywhere. Sage couldn't blame them. It was a good marketing tactic, especially because it was true.

When men had stalkers, they were more like crazy fans. When women had stalkers, they were dangerous. Unfortunately, the police didn't think so.

"You're just saying that because that's what the cop said." Sage slowed the car to let a group of bike riders pedal across the road, cringing at the obscenely short biker shorts that left so very little to the imagination.

Sage had tuned out Lily's lecture (still scarred by the thighs so blindingly white she might be forced to test the theory of driving home blind) but she jumped back into the conversation when Lily went on a verbal rampage about the hypocrisy of the detective in charge.

The detective filing her report was a piece of work. He had looked at Sage and said—with all the energy of a moose stuck in the mud, "It's just a piece of paper with words on it. If I filed a complaint for every hate comment, I'd run out of trees."

But it was more than some words on a page. And it wasn't just a comment here or there. It was a letter taped to her car. One slipped under a hotel room door during a conference. They were graphic and intense messages from a "fan." Sage was nervous that this "fan" may very well end up on her doorstep one day. The police didn't take Sage seriously, commenting on how her line of work put her in a vulnerable position. Like it was her fault.

"I hired a security company," Lily said.

"Not this again," Sage said. It wasn't the first time they talked about this.

"Unfortunately," Lily said in a way that indicated it was not actually unfortunate at all. "It wasn't a question. And, as your boss, I outrank you here. The last letter was outright vile. I wouldn't be able to sleep at night knowing that this guy, somehow, knows where you live."

That was the most eerie part. The last letter had been taped to her mailbox. He had been standing in front of her house. *Her home.*

The walls were closing in. "The last letter was a few weeks ago, and I haven't been at the house for a week. I'm sure everything is fine. It's more than likely some 12-year-old kid who gets off on scaring people. I probably even played a match against him and that's what started it all."

Lily wouldn't let it go. "You might be right, but you could also be wrong. I hired a security team. It's my cousin's company actually. They do a lot of protection work, mostly government employees. They are above this type of situation but they're willing to help me out."

"Seriously," Sage said. "I'm fine. I really want to focus on streaming, diving back into the game, and getting ready for the competition. You said so yourself, it would be good to get my face out there more. Plus, you want me to test the new headset before the competition anyway. My subscribers will want to see that."

"Yes," Lily said, clearly exasperated. "You can do all of that *with* extra security at your place."

Sage turned down her driveway, slowing over the gravel and eventually coming to a halt in front of the house. Sage's stomach flipped. Her blood ran cold and goosebumps ran up her spine. "Actually Lily, security sounds like a fantastic idea."

"Is that sarcasm? Why the sudden change?" Lily couldn't keep the excitement from her voice.

Sage stared at the two broken windows. "Because I think somebody broke into my house."

As it turned out, someone did break into the house. The cops were called, and there really wasn't much for them to do after Sage discovered that nothing was actually missing. They took down the report of a busted door, a broken window (courtesy of a brick with crude messages written in red letters all over it), and a ransacked cabinet. They commented that she should get some cameras (obviously she was going to do that now) and then the authorities left as quickly as they came.

Lily called back, hours later, and informed Sage that security was sending an agent overnight who would be there first thing in the morning. Lily offered to pay for a hotel for the night and highly encouraged her to do so. But in the end, Sage just wanted to lay in her own bed, in her own space, in the house that felt closest to a home she'd ever had.

And that's exactly what she did. Sage and Squash made the trek upstairs to their space—tea in hand for Sage, a peanut butter treat for Squash—and settled into the plush blankets and lit the most citrusy-smelling candle possible. She didn't sleep much, or at all, really. Squash had lost her marbles—and hearing—years ago and had no idea of the looming danger and was able to sleep so peacefully that Sage had to check that she was still breathing—twice.

Despite the air of unease, Sage was still relieved to be home. Even with the letters and break-in, she could finally relax a little. Breathe for a moment. And that's when the tears came. The past week had been an emotional roller coaster. She let herself be sad, cuddled in bed, listening to the sound of the popping candle and a snoring Squash.

When hours ticked by and it was clear the only one getting sleep would be Squash, Sage got up for another mug of tea. She puttered around the house and did a quick clean. The house smelled like home. Like a little bit of rain and pine, some dust, old books, and citrus. Probably because she had her favorite pink lemonade candle in every corner of the house. If the old, creaking wood ever ignited, the house would go up in flames, smelling a lot like a county fair lemonade stand.

Sage dusted and started to box up some of George's things and put them in his room. She couldn't bear to pack up the chess game they had been playing though. George was a fanatic and insisted on teaching Sage, and, despite her grumbling, she grew to enjoy the game even though she was abjectly terrible at it.

"Why'd you move the knight?" George had asked her during their last complete game.

Sage had shrugged. "He seemed sad to be missing the action. Plus, the horse is pretty."

He'd snapped up her knight two moves later.

"How can you be so strategic in your shooter game and yet so scatter-brained with chess?" George had asked.

Sage had only laughed and made another terrible move.

Now Sage looked at the chess set and frowned. She gathered the remains of George's life from when he had gotten sick—his medications, electric blanket, and water bottles, and put them in his room. She wouldn't dare touch anything inside his space. Not yet. Not for years. There was no need. The house was plenty spacious and had two guest rooms on the first floor anyway. Her room and her office were upstairs. George instead the ladies of the house get the top floor for privacy. And Sage was the only lady.

And Squash.

It was around two in the morning when Sage decided she had done enough tidying. The house really did feel like hers. George had an eclectic collection of knickknacks, but it was tasteful. He was an antiques dealer, buying and selling rare paintings, vases, and clocks.

The house felt lived in and loved. It was a little moody but it felt like it could be the setting of some mystery novel. Antiques hid everywhere, along with cozy blankets —George and Squash both hated being cold—and the art was eclectic. Once George had come home from a walk, smiling wide as he presented Sage with the newest piece to add to the mosaic on the wall.

"What on earth is that?" Sage had asked.

"Couldn't tell you," George had said. "The artist was on the street corner, using what I have to assume was illegally obtained spray paint considering he looked to be about thirteen. Neat, huh?"

"It's giving me a migraine but I can't stop staring at it," Sage said.

"Art," said George. "One of life's greatest mysteries."

Speaking of mysteries, she turned her attention to the broken glass by the front door. She had left that task for last. Maybe it was subconscious, but to clean it up meant the problem was over. And as much as Sage wanted the issue to be resolved, she couldn't shake the feeling that there was still some monster lurking in the darkness.

Lily had said the security team in the morning setting up the cameras would also fix the window.

"Get yourself together," Sage scolded herself. Squash looked at her from her spot on the couch. "I'm not scared," she told the dog as she taped cardboard over the open window. Squash looked unconvinced. But to be fair, Squash, in her old age, looked more like a potato than anything else.

The fatigue was trying to settle in Sage's bones, but she kept herself busy with sweeping up the glass and glaring at the woods. She squinted at the tree line behind the house. Every branch waving in the wind may as well have been a person trying to get her attention.

Still uneasy, Sage did the one thing that helped her escape this world: she joined another.

Headset on, mic at the ready, Squash in her lap, and a cup of tea by her side, she was ready to log in to her corner of the internet. Her Twitch stream slowly and steadily gained new subscribers and her retention was off the charts. Sage tried not to get too excited, but she had been almost able to make streaming her full-time income, but now that George had left her the house, it was actually doable. She might even be able to start a little savings account. And deal with taxes. She wasn't sure how that was going to work now, but that was a problem for another day.

As soon as she went live, Lily sent her a text.

LILY: Good to see you getting back to
your old self.

Sage rambled like she always did when she played. She explained what she was doing and when the chat asked to see Squash, she was more than happy to lift the old pup from her curled-up spot on her lap in front of the camera, where the chat went wild. Squash had unintentionally become a huge part of Sage's brand.

She played *Welkin Wall* until dawn came and chased the shadows and monsters away.

2

LEO

Leo Camaro was in that great stage of life where he had endless energy and the body to keep up with the desire to constantly be on the move. Sure, that little spat in Afghanistan wasn't *ideal*, and the medical discharge from the Marines post-training accident (and the subsequent "who am I if not a Marine" mental break-down) allowed him just enough experience to land a job in a rather elite security agency.

Totally normal.

A brute was a brute, his father liked to say, so may as well get paid for it.

This was not the job his father was expecting Leo to take, which made it all the more fun. He appeased his highly decorated veteran of a father with, "It's a job while I study for the MCATs and apply for med school."

But that was two years ago and Leo still hadn't applied to medical school despite having pretty decent MCAT scores. He continued deferring, saying he wanted to bump his test score just a little more before applying. It was true.

Sort of.

Leo liked this job fairly well. It allowed him to still be that disciplined guy, carry a gun, and serve others. The jobs were long and tedious, but the likelihood of getting to fight someone was enough to hold his attention. The pay wasn't bad either. And he liked to travel and see the country (it had grown on him and was the excuse he continued to give his family when they asked him to settle down, which was a monthly occurrence).

He had just come off a job and was heading into the office to drop off reports and get his next job assignment.

"Leo, my boy!" Jenson called from his office. That man really did live and breathe efficiency. Leo had only been in the office thirty seconds before he was called in for his next assignment briefing.

"What do you have for me?" Leo asked. He'd been at the Sentinel Security Agency for a year and a half and his last job nearly did him in.

"That eager to move on?"

"Afraid Mr. Congressman will change his mind and want us back," Leo admitted. Mr. Congressman was a child stuck in a 66-year-old's body and Leo, despite having enjoyed the location and the random bar scrap he'd been able to put out, was rather excited to leave that piece of work behind.

"If the congressman decides he does want to extend his security, Chandler can handle it. I have a solo job for you."

"Without Chandler?" Leo asked. "Alone?" This was news.

"That is what the word solo means. Chandler thinks you're ready for a solo job. This will be good testing waters for you. If the job goes well, we can officially call your training complete."

The idea of not having to be the "gopher" of a team was appealing. And progressing and improving was a personal high for Leo. Bettering himself in all aspects of his life was essential to his values. And sure, maybe he didn't want to stay at the agency forever (or maybe he did) but always being the low man on the chain would slowly drive him insane.

This was good news. The agency had taken a chance with hiring Leo so young, and Leo knew it.

Now to put it to the test.

"I'm ready. Give me the portfolio and I can be on my way tonight," Leo said. He was a professional at living out of a suitcase now.

Jenson laughed from behind his desk and slid over a paper portfolio (some things were still old-school with this guy in charge). "I figured you'd say that. Go on and book your flight. See you back here when this is over."

Leo grabbed the thick folder of paperwork and flipped through the first page. His stomach dropped. "Sir, is this right? It says Hollandsway, Oregon?"

"That's correct. Is that a problem? I thought it would be good news, Mr. Never Takes Time Off." Jensen laughed. "Plus, I thought you'd like anywhere other than D.C."

Oh, this was going to be *rich*. He had literally, hours

ago, told his mother in no uncertain terms that he would not be able to take time off to come home for the annual family reunion because he was on a very special security detail.

Leo forced out a laugh. "Guess I can pocket that living stipend. Dear old Dad and Meddling Mother will be tickled pink to have me back in town." He tried to come off sarcastic and not at all bitter. (He failed.) He was already planning on crashing with his sister.

Leo had worked hard to stay out of that small town and now he was back in it for, he checked the portfolio, six months. Six months? That was on the longer end of the spectrum.

Jenson seemed to be enjoying this. "The job should be fairly straightforward. Wanted to give you something light for your first solo. Chandler might need some help with tech support, so let him know if you have the downtime for that. We'll compensate you," Jenson said, shuffling paper around and prepping for the next meeting.

"Sure, no problem." As if money were the issue here.

Leo considered asking if there was another assignment. People could do that, appeal assignments due to personal reasons or whatever, but he didn't want to miss out on a chance to do his first solo job, especially if his reason was "Hey, sorry, I don't really want to be in the same town as my parents right now. No, they don't scare me." (Not much, anyway.)

The opportunity for a solo job might not come around again for a while, or worse, they might think he was inflexible and too emotional for the job.

Leo strode out of the office, smiling at the secretary as

he dropped off his receipts and got busy booking a flight during the Uber to the airport.

Leo only took real stock of the situation when he was seated on the flight, heading back home. "Home" sounded too familiar. Too cozy. His mom had nearly thrown a fit of excitement when she heard her "baby boy is coming home tonight!"

He had to talk her off a ledge. She was already threatening to throw him a "welcome home party" which was really just another excuse for her to host something.

"This is for work, Mom. Simmer down for a little bit until I get my work squared away." Leo hoped she'd heard him through the buzzing noise of the airport. "I'm staying at Tess's place." He did not need his mother hovering. Tess was probably off on some pilot job anyway, her apartment was vacant most of the year.

"She's in town, hon," his mother said. "For that wedding she's in! I can't believe I'll have all my little duckies back home!"

"Okay, love you, about to take off."

It was a small white lie. He just needed to call Tess to warn her that he would be crashing with her.

She answered on the first ring. "You'll have to beg."

"Excuse me?"

Tess snorted. "Mom already texted me. So, baby brother in town, finally?"

"You know I'm older." They had been arguing that point since they could talk, and despite trying as hard as the twins could, their parents refused to tell them their birth order. "And yeah, I'm crashing at your place. Leave a key under the mat."

Tess laughed again. "Sure thing. I'm only in town for a few more days. Then I'm gone for like a month and then will probably be back unless another job comes up or something so the place is yours."

This was good news. "Sweet. Thanks. I think I'll actually have some downtime but I'll know more once I get the Subject situated."

"Oooh Subject. Fancy. Do I know him?"

Leo couldn't tell if she was genuine or being sarcastic. It didn't matter. "Can't say. I'll call you when I land."

"Have fun mister big shot."

Leo rolled his eyes. "Bye."

Once airborne, Leo flipped open the portfolio and scanned the pages, doing preliminary research on his new Subject.

Name: Sage Moon

Sage. That name seemed familiar. He knew of two "Sages." One was an acquaintance from high school a few years below him. Another was a dude from his grade (who later moved) who then turned into a professional ultra-runner. Neither with the last name of Moon. He continued reading.

Age: 23

Occupation: Online Gamer, Streamer, Influencer

Leo rolled his eyes so hard they scratched his brain.

A streamer. He shuddered.

An influencer. He grimaced.

Leo pictured a young woman with blue hair, talking like she had just gotten a lobotomy, wearing a low-cut shirt, and busy promoting whatever green powder was paying her that week.

Day to day: Subject spends most of her time in her home on the outskirts of town. She owns the home. Subject spends hours online playing games for a virtual audience, making money through viewership, sponsorships, and merchandise sales.

Leo rolled his eyes. A YouTube star wannabe. Another chick flashing skin online and guys paid her all while she thought it was because she had some skills people want to watch. Sure, if a woman wants to do that, that was her prerogative—but don't tell anyone it's the gaming that pays the bills when it's really just a pretty face.

Threat: Subject has been receiving strange and threatening letters delivered to her mailbox or left on her car. The general thought is this might be a delusional fan. Miss Moon has several scheduled appearances (in-state and out-of-state) in preparation for a big competition in Los Angeles.

Hiring notes: The sponsor for Sage Moon, LilyTech, hired protection. If there are concerns, please reach out to Lily or Jared at LilyTech. See attached note from Lily-Tech. "Please send someone younger and who may be able to blend in on social outings with Miss Moon."

Miss Moon's calendar of events and planned outings were also attached. Nothing too crazy over the next few months. Events like "Tech Con." And "*Welkin Wall* Panel" and "Meet and greet." Looked like she was staying local for the holidays as well, which was probably a good thing for Leo. He'd be able to have Christmas at home. His mother might actually have kittens when she found out the news. Too bad he was allergic to cats.

Apparently all of the events were a big lead-up to the

massive gaming competition for the game *Welkin Wall*. Leo had heard of *Welkin Wall*, not that he had time to play. Well, he did, but Higher Pursuits (like studying and running and cold plunges) called to him, and to be fair, *Welkin Wall* was *hard*. It was technical. But if he was given hours to squander away, he was confident that he could get good at it too. But he had better, more meaningful things to do. He couldn't allow himself to grow stagnant and waste time on games.

Leo continued scanning the pages of the portfolio. Jenson had called ahead and got cameras set up. Easy. All Leo would have to do is check that the cameras were set up correctly, introduce himself, and wait. Protocol didn't demand 24-hour surveillance unless the Subject asked for it or some new development occurred.

Leo skimmed his list of regulations he would present to the Subject and spent the rest of the flight gearing up to face his mother and father after avoiding them for the last year.

The landing made him nauseous and the pilot, in his singsong voice, assured everyone that everything was okay despite the turbulence. Leo hoped it wasn't an omen for what was to come.

Once Leo's feet were firmly on the ground, he picked up his rental (a new 4Runner) and made his way toward Tess's apartment. But instead of stopping to drop off his things, as he initially planned, he made his way to the outskirts of the small town.

Leo scanned the long road, driving slowly through the neighborhood. The Subject's house was in the old part of town and the street was narrow and giant trees lined the sidewalks, mature beasts towering over the few people out walking their dogs. October was quickly ending and the leaves were falling, covering the sidewalks and wooded trails with a carpet of orange. A warm feeling came over him.

Was this nostalgia? He pushed that feeling away. He needed to remain focused.

He pulled into Miss Moon's driveway and glanced at his watch. 4:00. He had made great time considering the travel day. He'd be home in time for dinner. His stomach growled in agreement.

Leo marched up the steps. They creaked under his weight and he took note of the boarded-up window (the portfolio had mentioned a little break-in). He knocked on the giant wood doors and stepped back. He appraised the house. It was old, but it was massive. It could also use some work. Serious work. The large wrap-around porch sagged in some places, the yard was overgrown, and it could do with a fresh paint job.

He knocked on the door again and this time he heard a muffled, "Coming" and footsteps.

And when the door swung open he was faced with the last person he had ever expected to see again, a person he was certain he'd successfully blotted from his memory. But there she was, standing right in front of him.

"Wait, you?" he asked, already knowing the answer.

She slammed the door in his face.

It was going to be a long and uncomfortable six months.

3

SAGE

These UPS guys were *relentless.* Sage couldn't remember the last time she ordered merch, but she supposed it was one of the packages of shirts or stickers that had been delayed. Squash slept through it. Of course, she did. Some guard dog she was.

Sage glanced at her watch. Just after four. Dang, what a terrible wake-up call—she had been peacefully napping on the couch.

She struggled to get off the couch and rolled to the floor. The perils of being wrapped tightly in a mountain of fluffy blankets.

"Coming!" she called when there was a second knock. She glanced down at her attire. Shorts, slippers, and one of her merch shirts, pale yellow with orange and pink squashes all over. It would have to do.

When she swung the door open, she was faced with a tall man. He wore black jeans, boots—very practical for the rain that was trying to break through the clouds—and a simple gray T-shirt with an athletic jacket over the top. Maybe Columbia or Patagonia, no, it said Sentinel Security on the chest.

"Wait, you?" the guy asked. His voice was slightly deeper, but not by much. He had filled out and could grow a proper beard now, but she recognized him despite the years gone by.

So, Sage did the only rational thing and slammed the door in his face. "Go away."

"Sage?" the guy said again.

Oh, she knew this guy, alright. It was no mistake. And based on the slight confusion on his face when he saw her, he was well aware of who she was too. She squeezed her eyes shut and balled her hands into fists so tight she thought her nails might cut her skin. She took a deep breath and held it, willing her heart to stop racing. "I said go away." Sage managed to say it with only a small quiver in her voice.

"Afraid I can't, Ma'am. Under the strict order of Lily. I am here to outfit your house with some new security measures."

"Already have cameras," Sage said, yelling at the door which was really unfair because the poor door had just been slammed so hard into the frame it had made the hanging photo next to it shake and go all crooked. Now it was being subjected to Sage's screams. The old oak didn't deserve the abuse.

"That's what I am here to check out," Leo said. "Among other things."

"Tell Lily I don't need this," Sage shouted as she walked to the couch. Squash was awake now and curious and about ready to walk off the couch and tumble down to the ground. Blind little fool.

The door opened and Leo Camaro strode in like he owned the place. "Lily said you'd be resistant but I assured her I would not be in your hair."

Sage scowled. "I'm fine!" She already had her phone out, ready to call Lily. "I don't need security anymore. False alarm."

Leo looked at the broken window and the brick with crude messages written in marker sitting by the door. What? It was a good doorstopper.

"Clearly you have things totally under control," Leo said, nudging the brick with his foot.

Sage knew she was beaten, but she had other solutions. "Yes, fine. I could use the help. Could you give me the number of your boss or manager or whatever? I'm requesting someone new."

Leo rolled his eyes. Gosh, he really hadn't changed. He was still that high school jock who thought every rule was more of a guideline to be bent.

"Look, I know you don't like me but I am who you've got. Our security agency is very well established and booked out for years. It's me or no one. And no one isn't an option. So, it's just me."

"Glad to see your math skills have improved. Find me another warm body to fill your spot. It can't be that hard."

"I seriously doubt you have any idea how elite the agency is. We provide personal protection for politicians and celebrities. Heck, even visiting ambassadors and royalty. I literally went on tour with Journey last fall."

"Well don't mind if I stop believing that lie."

Leo quirked a smile. "Funny."

"I beg to differ," Sage said. By the time she looked at her phone, Lily had already texted her.

Sage groaned aloud and Squash poked her head out of the nest of blankets for half a moment before disappearing again.

Lily also sent a gift card for coffee. Darn that businesswoman. Clever how she failed to mention Sage's childhood bully would be the guy watching over her. If Lily didn't actually pay a decent amount of Sage's income and if she wasn't as no-nonsense and pushy, Sage might have half a mind to leave the sponsorship. But it wasn't worth it. Not at this point anyway. And security wasn't all that bad considering the strange things happening.

But Leo Freaking Camaro?

This was her house. Her home. Her domain. Sure, she wanted to suddenly become invisible, but this was no time to fall apart.

Sage leaned against the couch and looked Leo up and

down. She was surprised to find him holding the brick, reading the crude messages.

"This what came through your window?" he asked.

"Yeah, probably just vandals. You know how kids get with a full moon."

"There hasn't been a full moon in weeks."

Sage sighed. "Right."

Leo smirked, clearly aware that Sage had caved. "Heard from Lily?"

Sage glared at him. "I'm going back to bed. Do what you need to do. Don't mess anything up. Just check the cameras. They are just outside cameras, right?"

Leo nodded. "Looks like all you'll need are some outdoor cameras and one in your driveway. I can monitor them from my own place."

"Great." Sage picked up Squash from the couch.

"What in the world is that thing?" Leo asked, pointing at Squash.

"My dog..." she said. "How many times have you been hit in the head? Dogs go 'bark' and cats go 'meow' in case you forgot."

"That is not a dog. That is a creature conjured up by some eight-year-old's drawing of what they think a dog might look like if they've never actually seen one."

"Shut up. She's just an old girl." Sage petted Squash just as she made a noise that sounded a lot like a muddy squelch mixed with the wheeze of a smoker. Great.

"You have an alien masquerading as a rat."

"Just check the cameras and go." Sage kissed Squash's head. "Don't listen to that mean man."

"No leaving just yet. Have a seat." Leo plopped onto

the couch and got comfortable. Too comfortable. Was he trying to frustrate her? Did their history mean nothing? Didn't he feel the least bit awkward? Even sorry? Just a little?

"What could you possibly need?" Sage asked, fighting a yawn. The all-nighter and midday nap didn't do much in the way of helping her relax.

"A few answers to some questions, but mostly I just need to go over the safety protocols," Leo said in a tone that sounded like he'd done this a hundred times before. Bored. Formulaic.

How often did people need protection?

Sage stomped over to the couch opposite Leo and sat, crisscrossing her legs, snuggling Squash under her chin.

Leo grimaced. "Most people use pest control for rodents."

"Her name is Squash."

"Is that what happened to her?"

Sage did not need to hear the slander against poor little Squash (who, yes, was squashed by a golf cart when she was young but that was before Sage had adopted her but Leo did not need to know that information). "Just tell me what you need to tell me so you can get out of my hair."

Leo dusted off imaginary hairs. "With pleasure." He cleared his throat before asking, "Why the name change?"

"New identity of sorts," Sage said.

Leo pulled out his phone and tapped on it for a moment. "I just sent you an email with a list regarding your safety concerns. This is not a bulleted list of argu-ments we must hash out. It's not a discussion. I am informing you of the protocols and you need to abide by them if we are to both remain happy about the situation."

"Glad to know we're on the same page." A terrible thought struck her. "Wait, you aren't staying here, are you?"

Leo's eyes widened a fraction. Good. He was uncomfortable, at least a little. "No, that won't be necessary. Yet."

"Yet?"

"Will you let me get to the list? It's all explained there."

Sage pulled out her phone and opened the email. It was a rather long list, but fairly logical.

1. Security cameras are to remain on, twenty-four hours a day, seven days a week, and there are no circumstances in which they will be turned off. The feed goes directly to Agent's secure computer.

2. New locks must be placed on the front and back doors. Agent is the only person to have the spare.

3. Subject is to allow Agent to share locations via phone app until the job is complete or threat is eliminated.

Threat eliminated? That sounded ominous. "Aren't you just here to protect me from the big bad wolf, not, you know, track down the big bad wolf?"

"Yes," Leo said. "In a sense. But it's easier to provide proper protection when we know where the big bad wolf is hiding out."

Sage was not convinced her "protector" had the mental fortitude to tell the difference between a wolf and a sheep. Everyone was prey to a guy like Leo. Everyone was weak and, therefore, inferior. Fitting that Leo found himself a job that put him in a position of power.

She hated being powerless. "Is the whole location-sharing thing necessary?"

"This is not a debate." It was as if he'd been waiting for her resistance, the admonishment was practically hanging off his tongue.

"Whatever." Sage continued reading.

4. Subject is not to deviate from the Calendar of events. Any updates and additions to the calendar must be sent to Agent at least 24 hours ahead of time.

5. Subject may venture out on solo expeditions, but only at the permission of the Agent. It is assumed agent will join the Subject on all outings unless otherwise stated.

6. When traveling, Agent and Subject will stay in adjoining rooms and adjoining rooms only. No exceptions.

7. When traveling, Agent will sit on the aisle seat of the aircraft. No exceptions.

8. Agent will handle all travel details, including (but not limited to) airfare, driving, car rentals, hotels, and other accommodations. Subject is to discuss preferences beforehand.

"Why 'Subject'? Why not 'client' or person or just a name?" Sage asked.

Leo shrugged. "Subject is accurate. You are a thing we study. We get to know you better than you know yourself so we can anticipate danger and how you react to it. Then we can be looking for problems before you step into them."

She did not, in fact, understand any of this nonsense. But maybe that was why Leo was scowling at Sage so much. She was just a complicated problem to him.

9. Subject will provide the agent with a physical lock and passcodes to doors.

"I don't have a key," Sage said.

"What on earth?" He looked on the verge of diving into some sort of lecture so she cut him off.

"It's this specialty key. Fancy and old." She pointed at the thick door. "See? Fancy. Anyway, the doorknobs and locks are from like the late eighteen hundreds so it takes a special kind of lock guy to make a copy."

"Lock guy?"

"To make a copy. Actually four. He'll be done next week. So, I just lock it from inside at night," Sage said.

"That is the most ridiculous—"

"Hush, I'm reading."

10. In the event that the Agent deems it necessary to have 24-hour surveillance of Subject, cohabitation must be accepted by Subject without complaint. Agent will make themselves scarce and not interfere with the subject's day-to-day activities.

11. In any event, should the agent request to move the Subject due to security risks, Subject must acquiesce to the change of plan provided proper accommodation will be made for their work and life to continue as relatively as normal.

12. Accommodations may be granted by the Agent (within reason) to create an atmosphere of comfort, safety, and security.

"Oh great," Sage said, pointing to the word accommodation. "I have this terrible fear of elevators. Got stuck in one at the mall when I was twelve and now I break out in hives thinking about them. No elevators."

Leo cocked his head as if he was deciding whether she was serious or not. "I think we can accommodate that little issue."

Sage wanted to remind him that elevators were the smallest of issues here but kept her mouth shut and continued to read.

13. Subject must be aware and accept the fact that all Agents are trained and approved to conceal carry a firearm in each state and have all the proper licensing to carry on all premises.

"Any questions?" Leo asked.

"When can you leave?" Sage tucked Squash into the blankets, stood, walked over to the kitchen, and put the kettle on. She tried not to be embarrassed about the fact that it was nearing five in the evening and she was essentially wearing her pajamas. But hey, her castle, her crown. And in this case, her crown meant wearing fuzzy slippers.

"I'll leave when I check out the cameras and get some answers from you."

"I'm an open book," Sage said, ignoring the fact that Leo sauntered into the kitchen and leaned against the counter like this was the most comfortable setting in the world. Sage fumed. She wanted to intimidate him. Make him squirm and feel all sorts of angry and flighty like she did right now. Instead, she just asked, "Tea?"

"I'd rather drink toilet water."

"I can arrange that easily. Unlimited supply actually."

"Are you always this welcoming?" he asked with a

smile that almost seemed genuine, but there was malice lurking beneath it. A hint of "dead eyes" that let Sage know that this was not at all fun for him either.

"What do you want?" she asked, pulling out the jars of tea and settling on some chamomile. With lavender. What else could relax a person? Maybe a shot of NyQuil to knock her out.

"What is your sleep schedule like?" he asked.

Sage snorted. "I sleep when I'm tired—"

"I'm really not looking for sass," Leo said, rubbing his temple. "I've had a long day of traveling and I just want to go home and sleep."

"I'm being honest. I don't have a bedtime if that's what you're wondering. Every day looks totally different. I kind of go where the wind blows me, and right now it's blowing me toward a cup of tea, extra sugar, and cream."

"Are you allergic to anything?" he asked. "Medications, food?"

"Why is that part of your preliminary questioning?" Sage brandished a teaspoon at him with the force of a sword. "Shouldn't you be out there getting that big bad wolf or whatever?"

"That is where you are mistaken," Leo Camaro said it so lowly that Sage leaned in to hear. "I am the big bad wolf. And I'm on the hunt."

Sage shivered. The dramatics were not necessary. "Didn't know you were into nursery rhymes, but carry on."

Leo rolled his eyes and crossed his arms. "You said you thought it was just a vandal."

"Right." Sage deflated. Of course, it wasn't a vandal,

not with the messages scrawled on the brick. But it was a nice thought. "Not allergic to anything."

"Any idea who is behind this?" Leo asked in a tone much softer than he had used before. He had his arms crossed over her chest and he was still leaning back against the counter, looking far too at ease in her kitchen.

"No," Sage said. "Honestly I don't."

"For some reason, I believe you."

"How gracious." Sage poured steaming tea into her mug. "Now check the cameras so I can get on with my life."

"I sent you a text. Don't forget to share your location with me before I leave or I'll be forced to come back in and bother you some more."

"Please don't," she said, already hitting the "share location" button. Why did it feel so intimate to have someone know your whereabouts at all times? It was like sharing a jacket and not giving it back. She wanted to make him feel that level of awkwardness, or more than anything, see if he had the capability of feeling awkward, so she said. "I want you to share your location with me too."

He scoffed and shook his head.

Interesting, Sage thought. So, there was a level of intimacy and strangeness about sharing something so simple with a near-complete stranger. She pushed. "Why not? I want to see if you're off at the bar drinking the night away when you're supposed to be babysitting me."

Leo shook his head. "Glad we agree it's babysitting, especially since you're acting like a child."

Sage stomped her foot, like a child. "Just do it."

"I don't have to."

"Rule ten states accommodations can be made. Per the Subject's request. Right now, I am the Sub." Leo wrinkled his nose and it took half a beat before Sage added, "—ject. *Subject.* Quit laughing." Sage's ears were burning. "Look. I am asking for accommodation or are you actually going to force me to make an official complaint."

"Good grief you are a child. Worse, *a Zoomer.*" He pulled out his phone.

Sage shrugged. "I am neither Gen Z nor millennial. I am that strange in-between place. Did you do it?"

Leo took an exaggerated bow. "Yes, Miss Moon. The accommodation has been met. Am I also to tie your shoes for you?"

"Now who's acting like a child?"

"Still you. Don't you know sugar is bad for you?" Leo asked just as Sage was heaping yet another teaspoon of brown sugar into her mug. She made a show of dropping in the sugar. Of course, she was assigned the health nut guy. He probably thought strawberries had little viruses in the seeds and could block a colon or something. What next? A lecture about the perils of Cheetos? She did not need any more negativity in her life.

"Is there anything else?"

Leo sighed, staring at her tea as if it were poison. "I'm sure there will be. But now that we have made the official introduction—"

"Reintroduction," Sage said, cutting him off. She wanted him to know that there was no chance that she had forgotten who he was and what he had done.

"Right. Now that we have officially made contact and

you are aware of the guidelines, I can go check the cameras."

Sage turned and walked up the stairs, calling over her shoulder. "Do what you need to do and then leave me alone."

"Whatever you say, kid." The door slammed behind him.

Kid? *Kid*? The guy was a handful of years older than her. Three, if memory served her right. It was hard to forget the face of someone who humiliated you. Sure, it happened eight years ago, but it still didn't mean her cheeks didn't heat with embarrassment when she thought of it.

Pull it together, Sage.

So, the idea of her high school bully just waltzing around her oasis, her safe haven, her home, was *not* an ideal situation. But neither were bricks flying through her windows.

She rubbed her eyes and stretched. She needed to get out of her head. And the best way to do that was to jump into a game. She opened up *Welkin Wall*. It was the game she had been invited (and financed by LilyTech) to compete in. It would be the first competition she'd attend as a certified competitor, not a spectator.

She had just enough subscribers on her platforms to make her barely relevant, but enough viewership to provide her with just enough income streams too. And fans. People who genuinely enjoyed watching her play and her commentary. She did several streams a week. About half were her playing *Welkin Wall*, and the other half were cozy games that were more conducive to chatting and general commentary. Last livestream she had gone on a tangent about the best types of pasta and her subscribers ate it up (pun intended).

Sage put on her headset, trying to relax her jaw and muscles. Leo Camaro shook her up. And he shouldn't have.

She logged into the game, gripping the controller with unnecessary force, and entered the game. She opted for a random team this time. There were pros and cons of team play versus individual play.

Welkin Wall was like any other first-person shooter, but the difference was the fact that gravity wasn't a thing in this game. There were structures and figures and ways to attach the avatar to areas. Essentially, it was like a puzzle you had to play as well as a shooter game. And the fact that there could be a sniper targeting you at any angle—above, below, any side—was a unique challenge. It was like swimming in open water and a shark coming out of nowhere to get you. It was adrenaline in small doses.

Sage tried some new maneuvers and gameplay, still trying to find a way to attach to the armor of other players and bounce back. She tried (and failed) a few times and grew frustrated. So did her team. She got ribbed a lot by the other players and eventually threw off the headset and played solo for what felt like a few minutes. But a quick glance at the clock informed her that it had been two hours.

She leaned back in her chair and stared out the window. The fall colors greeted her, leaves fluttered by, and the sun was setting.

That's when she heard the yelling.

"What the hell do you think you are doing here?" a deep, but familiar, voice rang out. "I'll call the cops on you!"

"Me?" the other voice yelled. "You're the one walking around here naked. I'm gonna call the cops on you!"

Ah. So, Leo Camaro had met the neighborhood nudist, Filbert. Yes—like the nut. Hazelnuts. Or in this case, just a plain pair of nuts flapping in the breeze.

Sage sprinted down the stairs, still wrapped in her blanket, Squash in one hand, and tore through the back door and onto the porch. Sure enough, Filbert was out on one of his nature walks, wearing just his signature yellow rain boots, and Leo was out walking toward the edge of the property.

"What is going on?" she yelled, running toward Leo. "Are you threatening Filbert?"

"Who?"

"Filbert." She pointed to the very old (and very naked) man now walking toward them.

"I've always called them hazelnuts," Leo said. Then he gestured wildly to the naked man. "And in this case, a good old-fashioned nut case!"

Sage shrugged. "He's always been a free spirit. He walks this trail around here between the properties. It's all private land so when he uh—"

"Forgets his pants?"

"Yeah. That." Sage cleared her throat. "It's not a big deal." She grabbed Leo's arm and pulled him back. It was a strange thing to voluntarily touch someone. It felt like electric shocks over her body. He took a few steps back.

"Look," she whispered. "Filbert has some problems. Mr. Sato and I have called Adult Protective Services, but they don't do much. Filbert has some caseworker who comes by to make sure he's okay and has groceries. Other than the occasional jaunt in the woods, he's fine, I guess. He wouldn't hurt a fly."

"Look here kiddo—" Filbert yelled, brandishing a stick he'd picked up from where the forest was trying to overtake the backyard. "If you here are the one giving Sage problems, I will cut ya!" Filbert turned to look at Sage. "You alright? I'll cut him down." He swung the stick and nearly knocked his own head with it.

"Thanks, Filbert," she sighed. "But I'm okay." Despite seeing Filbert (*all* of Filbert) often, it never did feel normal. "This is Leo Camaro. He is running security here."

Filbert relaxed his grip on the stick. "So that's why you were on the ladder?"

"Checking the cameras. Do you need me to take you back—"

"Nope!" Filbert turned and started back the way he came, waving the stick over his head. "Getting breezy so I'm heading in."

Sage closed her eyes and turned back to her house. Filbert was right. It was getting cold and her slippers were soaked from the damp grass and mud. The blanket wrapped around her did little to stave off the wind. And Squash was shivering.

"The hell was that?" Leo asked, taking a few strides to catch up to her.

"I just told you. That was Filbert."

"Well, I know that now!" Camaro said. His nose was slightly red, likely from the cold.

"How long have you been here? Seriously, how long does it take to check cameras?" she asked, walking into the house. She needed tea. And dinner. Her stomach grumbled and something told her that Leo would turn his nose up and make some snide remark about pizza bites. She didn't need to give him another reason to think she was stupid. Or maybe she did. Then he'd leave and she'd get another agent.

She went for the pizza bites in the freezer and tossed them in the microwave.

"I've been here for almost two hours."

"Huh, I thought you would have left a while ago."

"Did you seriously not see me, quite literally on a ladder outside your office and bedroom window? I was fixing the shoddy camera work for hours. No wonder you've got some baddies on your tail."

She slammed the freezer shut. "What is that supposed to mean?" She poured tea (as angrily as someone could) into a cup of ice. Then she had to wipe up her mess (because if one was to pour tea angrily it meant splashing it all over the place) which only made her more frustrated.

Leo rolled his eyes. "I just mean that you being completely oblivious isn't exactly conducive to a safe environment."

"And yet you stand here and make comments like that. Clearly, you are not picking up the signs of this rather hostile situation." It took all her willpower not to throw her tea in his face.

"Relax," he said.

Everyone knew that the word "relax" did the very opposite. You want someone wound up tight and crazy? Tell them to relax. Instead of telling Leo Camaro this reality of life, all she said was, "I am relaxed." She was imagining what it would be like to magically triple in size and throw him out of her house by his shoelaces.

It was a relaxing two seconds of disassociation.

The ding of the microwave cut off whatever he was going to say.

She could almost hear George Sato admonishing her for being rude. "Food is what brings people together," he'd say. Well, what if she wanted this guy out, huh? What then, Mr. Sato? Then George's disappointed face flashed across her mind. *Fine, George. You win.*

Sage cleared her throat. "Do you want something to eat?"

Leo looked at her measly plate and then the cup of iced tea in her hand. "No thanks," he said. Then he had the *audacity* to wrinkle his nose at her pizza bites. The monster.

Still, it was a relief. She didn't want to share her meals with someone who couldn't appreciate decadence when he saw it. And these pizza rolls were name-brand. Pure bliss.

"In the unlikely event that I will have to come stay with you, will you have a spare room for me to use?" Leo asked, eyeing the plate of pizza rolls like they were some amoeba trying to come to life.

It was her turn to scoff. "Give me some warning. Most of the rooms need airing out." That was an understatement. Several rooms were essentially shrines and storage rooms. One of her favorites was what she and George called the "art room." It was one of George's favorite things to do: collect art. The uglier, the better.

"Well, hopefully, it doesn't need to come to that. I have no desire to sleep with ghosts."

"Yeah, same." Her eyes lingered on his for a moment too long because he looked at her differently. Like she was a puzzle, and she didn't want him solving her.

"Well, thank you," she said instead of *please leave* like she wanted to.

"Miss Moon." His voice was deep and commanding, but there was a softness to it. "I don't know how you are emotionally handling this whole situation right now, but I know that sharing your life with a stranger hired to keep you safe must feel awkward, especially with our rocky past. But please know that I will respect your privacy and this is only a precaution."

Sage took a deep breath. "I don't like any of this. I just want to be left alone."

"I hear you."

"But I'm fine," she said. She took a swig of the tea and pretended it was the strong stuff to give her liquid courage. "Things are fine." Maybe if she told herself that lie enough she'd actually start to believe it.

"If you were fine I wouldn't be here. But for now, I'll leave you to it." Leo took a few strides to the door before he paused and turned back to face Sage, which was unfortunate since she had stuffed several pizza rolls in her mouth and was certain she looked like a troll consuming its plunder.

"Sage, it's an odd name."

"Mother was a hippy," she answered. "She named her other kid Cherry."

He shrugged. "That's not so bad."

"He hates it."

Leo wrinkled his nose. "Fair enough. Where is he?"

"Prison," she answered.

"Free-spirited?

"Icarus."

"What about your mom?"

"High as a kite, floating around somewhere." Sage hadn't seen her since she was sixteen when Sage dropped out of high school.

"You seem pretty nonchalant about it."

"I am." For the most part. Sage had to be. But she was more annoyed than anything that she had to justify her detachment from her family to a complete stranger. She put on her brave face. "You see, I don't find the past haunting me. If anything, it's a pinprick in the fabric of my life and time just keeps pulling me further away."

His face changed. "Some people prefer ghosts. At least you can face a ghost head-on."

He was the ghost of her past. "Is that what you believe?" she asked.

"We all have ghosts that want our attention," he said. His voice was sincere.

"Good thing I don't believe in ghosts."

Leo shook his head just a fraction, eyes boring into hers, all but saying "And yet I'm standing right here." The moment passed and Leo laughed, exaggeratedly looking around him. "Yes. A good thing you don't believe in ghosts considering this haunted mansion you have." Then he smirked and the momentary tension was gone.

"Leave my home alone. I like it."

"I'll be in touch."

"Goodbye," Sage said, walking up the stairs, pausing until she heard the front door close and his car pull out of the driveway.

4

LEO

When his Subject opened the door, Leo wasn't sure what to expect, but a young woman wearing purple slippers so fuzzy they made her feet look four times as large and wearing a scowl was not what he had anticipated. The familiar face didn't ever let her scowl drop the whole time he was there, and the only thing that distracted from the furrow in the young woman's brows was her awful shirt (that pumpkin print should not be allowed to exist) and her little rat-dog thing. Her couch was covered in plush pink and purple blankets. It was like a cotton candy machine exploded and the furniture was the primary casualty.

Just his luck.

And luck had always been on his side. Why leave him now?

He had pressed on with the whole first meeting checklist, and gave his spiel on safety and checked all the boxes he was supposed to. And he was rather pleased with himself that he managed not to (totally) bumble his way through it, which was quite the feat considering he had broken out in a cold sweat due to the flood of (unwelcome) memories that tried to drown him.

He handled that like a champ.

His stomach was in knots.

His heart beat irregularly (probably trying to kill him and put him out of his misery).

She was extremely uncomfortable to be around, and he had no one to blame but himself.

So, what did a total idiot do to avoid the onslaught of high school memories trying to weasel their way into his "let's replay this over and over" part of his brain? He worked.

Despite how relatively easy it was to check all the cameras (the Filbert incident not included—it would take him days to recover from that sight), this job was going to test his limits.

Instead of dwelling on this present storm of events (he glared at Sage's house in the rearview mirror), Leo opted to ignore the whole Sage dilemma and berate himself instead.

Leo was kicking himself for not reading the case file more closely. The name had felt sort of familiar, but not enough to spark his memory of *that* particular incident. To be fair, most of high school was a blur to him. Between chasing girls, playing football, the long weekends away partying and skiing on the mountain, and just trying to graduate made the day-to-day life of high school turn into one fuzzy memory.

A fuzzy memory that turned into fuzzy slippers that were ready to kick his butt.

He should be grateful despite this turn of events. Normally bodyguards stayed in the house with the Subject. Lily had mentioned that Sage might be resistant to that idea and to start slowly. If other incidents occurred, then he could pull out all the tricks. Lily was quite commanding. "My girl's safety is the biggest concern," was a mantra she often repeated in her emails.

They'd catch this stalker guy trespassing and that would be it. Job over. He'd be able to monitor the cameras from afar and accompany his Subject to her public appearances. In the meantime, he'd get to catch up with his friends and sister (if she ever answered his texts—he needed to debrief with someone!).

No better time to procrastinate than the present. He called his sister for the hundredth time.

"Good grief, why are you so obsessed with me?" she yelled into the phone.

An unhappy Tess was better than no Tess. "You're alive!" Leo said.

"Of course, I'm alive you nitwit. What do you want? A ride from the airport? When do you land?" she asked. Ever to the point she was.

"I'm already here. Where are you? Let's get dinner. I have crap to unload on you."

"What a weird way to ask about joining girl's night. I'm at The Hook getting wasted on sushi. You in?"

The timing couldn't be more perfect. Girl's night it was. "I'm literally pulling into the parking lot now."

"For real?" She hung up and not two seconds later

came barreling out of the restaurant and into Leo's arms for a hug only twins who had not seen each other in nearly a year could share. Then she pulled him inside and ordered another round of sushi. Leo had crashed enough girls' nights in his lifetime, so he didn't feel too bad about adding another to the list, but no one seemed to mind. He knew most of them from his high school years. Jules, Tess's best friend and the bride, was always around the house growing up.

"Good to see you again," Jules said. "This is my cousin Danny."

"Nice to meet you."

"So why on earth are you looking like a down dog and what has made you decide to take a job here?"

Leo, through mouthfuls of sushi and authentic wasabi (none of that pasty stuff), explained that he had been asked to squeak in a last-minute (solo) job that happened to be in town. He also scolded Tess for not having her phone on when he had tried calling for a ride, but she brushed that topic away and gave death glares at her friends.

He'd have to unpack that later.

"So, is it a creepy boyfriend?" Tess asked.

"Boyfriend?" Leo shook his head and settled into the booth, sipping on a crisp water with lemon. "Possible stalker. More than likely a couple of kids who vandalized her house."

"And she wanted a bodyguard?" Danny asked.

"No," Leo answered. "No, this chick has a career in gaming and live streaming. She has a sponsor and everything. It was the sponsor that forked up the cash to hire me."

"Hold up!" Tess said, pointing her chopstick at him like a weapon. "You're the one protecting Sage Moon?"

"Uh, how'd you know that?" Leo was not in the mood to explain in front of an audience. Tess didn't count. She knew the history.

Tess rolled her eyes. "I, unlike you, have social media and keep up on things—"

"And yet you don't turn on your phone."

"Whatever," Tess said, pushing the wasabi around her plate.

"And social media rots your brain!" Leo said. "Seriously, get off that nonsense."

Tess just rolled her eyes. "But Sage seems to be doing really well for herself now."

Leo rubbed his temples. "I didn't know she had changed her name—"

"*No,*" Tess looked from Leo to Jules, horror growing in their eyes. "Leo, please tell me you didn't—"

"Just show up to her house having no idea who she was?" Leo asked, sarcasm dripping in his voice. "Yes. That is *exactly* what I did."

Jules let out a bark of a laugh. She just shook her head and shoved his shoulder. "You are a total jerk. Everyone knew you did it. I can't believe you weren't expelled for that crap. "

There was no use justifying it, but Leo tried. "I was a senior. They just wanted to see me graduate..."

"Absolutely false!" Tess said, slamming the soy sauce

on the table like some sort of gavel, calling the gaggle of girls acting as jury into order. "The secretaries and principals were in love with you, Mr. Charming. You talked your way out of that. Gaslit everyone. No one important was totally sure who did it, but everyone knew it was you."

"I am a jerk," Leo said, hands over his face.

"Yep," Jules agreed.

"You're in deep trouble," Tess laughed. "I cannot believe this is happening to you. I call it justice finally served."

"Will someone please explain what the heck you're all talking about?" Danny asked. "Is this some kind of inside joke?" She poured some water into their glasses as she talked.

Leo bit his lip, shook his head, and stared at the wasabi. It was as green as he felt.

"He was a jock and a jerk all through high school," Jules said in a way that only friends could.

"Still is," Tess added. Leo shot her a glare. He did not need her commentary right now. "So," Tess continued. "It was our senior year, and he just liked to be a menace to society. A prankster. Always causing trouble. Nothing major. One day he thought it would be funny to sneak into the girl's locker room while they were all out on the track running laps and steal this poor girl's clothes."

"Look," Leo said, trying to defend his horrid actions. "She was an odd kid. Just a little strange, and, well, you heard the song. She smelled of cigarettes and all that other essential oil crap. Very hippy and 'new age.' Just weird and I—I knew it was wrong. I *still* know it was wrong. But I took her clothes and hid them outside."

"You're a real jerk," Danny said, clearly still not under-standing the severity of his actions. "So, she had to wear her PE uniform all day instead? So, she smelled like sweat and the gym instead of tea tree oil? Boys make no sense."

Tess softened a little after seeing the shame pouring off of Leo. "No," she said quietly. "It was worse than that. I heard about it later from the gym teacher, but this girl, Sage, didn't have a uniform or she'd forgotten it, so she had to use the school's spare. The teacher had a rule that the spare had to be returned to her office *before* you could go change. It was a humiliating experience. Literally standing in your underwear and bra and handing over sweaty shorts and t-shirt, but I think they did that so people wouldn't forget their uniform, you know?"

Leo gulped. "Yeah, so when this Sage girl got back to the locker room before she discovered her clothes missing due to my uh, involvement, she gave her uniform back to the gym teacher."

"So, then what?" Danny asked, still not under-standing.

"She had no clothes!" Leo said.

"Yes, I am well aware of that. So did she have to borrow some from the lost and found or—"

"You have to realize this girl was shy," Tess interrupted.

"Yeah," Jules said. "She was a new kid, clearly from a rough background—" she glared at Leo.

"What do you want me to say! I was an idiot." Leo turned to Danny, trying to rush the ending of this horrible story so they could move on. "Basically, from what I later heard, she was embarrassed and confused and didn't really know anyone. I guess she stayed in a bathroom stall, to do what? I don't know. Maybe search the locker room for clothes or something but it was late and—" Leo swallowed. He was gonna be sick. What the heck had he been thinking back then? He was about to experience eating sushi in reverse.

"Basically," Jules said. "She stayed in the locker room long enough for the school to lock her in."

"Oh no..." Danny whispered.

"It was a Friday," Tess said. Her earlier amusement at Leo's discomfort was long gone, likely feeling a fraction of how awful he was currently feeling. "So, this Sage girl literally spent Friday, Saturday, and Sunday night in the locker room until the janitor found her early Monday morning."

"No..." Danny looked mortified.

"Yeah," Leo said. "I was horrible. A jerk who just wanted to stir things up."

"Poor girl," Danny whispered. "She didn't have a phone?"

"Guess not," Tess said.

Leo cleared his throat. Was it the wasabi making him hot? Oh no, that would just be the utter humiliation and shame. "But things seem to be fine for her now. She's got a house and a job playing video games. Living every teenage boy's fantasy."

"Yeah," Danny said. "I guess so. But at least you had a chance to apologize."

Leo couldn't hide the guilt on his face.

"Oh Leo," Jules admonished like a very disappointed older sister. "Please tell me you apologized."

"We didn't even talk about the incident..." Leo admitted. He had meant to, instead he just talked about how weird her name was like some idiot.

Jules smiled brightly. "Well, maybe this is a chance for you to apologize and patch things up?" Ever the optimist.

"Maybe," Leo said. In truth, it happened just weeks before graduation and he really hadn't given the incident more thought. But now? He wondered how Sage had coped the rest of the year, hell, even the rest of high school with that unfortunate story attached to her.

The night continued on. Leo changed topics and caught up on all that was going on in the lives of his friends, the new jobs Tess was looking forward to, Jules's wedding, and the strange feeling of being back in town. It was like old times, and Leo wondered why he'd spent so long away.

Tess pranced into her little condo, showing Leo to the guest room. Just a bed, dresser, and beige sheets and blankets.

Perfect.

"I have two towels. You can have the smaller one. Generous of me, I know. I also have not gone grocery shopping yet. No rent needed other than your famous popcorn." Tess tossed him the rag masquerading as a towel.

"So generous," he murmured.

His body ached. A long travel day and scaling up ladders to check the camera work had made him stiff. His knee throbbed and it was like a ghost of the past coming back to haunt him. Funny. There were a lot of ghosts today.

A hot shower and a warm bed would be a one-way ticket to dreamland.

Too bad the train had left without him.

The jetlag should have caught up and knocked him out. He was full of great food (thanks sushi) and his body was tired, but Leo's mind buzzed as if he'd had espresso beans for breakfast.

Leo couldn't push the image of that fifteen or sixteen-year-old he'd subjected to his personal brand of torture out of his mind. She looked nothing like that now. As a teen, she wore baggy clothes that reeked of hippy stuff, her hair was always tied up, not that anyone ever saw it since she always wore a hat or hood. Her eyes were dead then like she slept only when forced. Now? She was, despite her rather juvenile approach to life, pretty. Geeky and immature in some ways, like wearing those awful slippers.

Leo groaned. The pit in his stomach wouldn't go away.

Leo opened the app on his phone from bed, the screens lit up. He had mounted several cameras outside to monitor the perimeter of the property, but he also had some angles (from the outside) to point into her office, living room, and even her bedroom. It was shady, but it was necessary. It was his first solo and he would leave nothing to chance. He'd emailed her the form with locations and information about the cameras. She likely had opted not to read them, assuming they were all outdoor cameras. Which they were, just some happened to point inside.

He watched as Sage paced the living room. There was a roaring fire and she knelt in front of it, poking it with a stick. Then she stood and paced again. Then she went to a box and began wrapping things up and packing them away. Then she paced the room again.

It was a strange comfort to know that he wasn't the only one with a lot on their mind this night.

5

SAGE

The days passed in relative peace post Leo Freaking Camaro storming into her life. She let him know when she went out for her weekly grocery shopping. After a quick call where Camaro interrogated her about her shopping habits, he allowed her to go solo, deeming the supermarket secure enough and not a threat. What a gift.

"Buy some coffee for when I'm over next," he'd also said.

She did not.

Okay, so having a bodyguard—security agent?—was weird. What did one call their little shadow with a gun? Whatever Leo Camaro was—it wasn't *so* bad. At least the random notes taped to her mailbox and the door stopped. And hey. No more broken windows. (And yes, it was convenient that he had fixed her broken window too...) Maybe there was something to having extra security measures. She even put a "Caution, Dog on Premises" sticker on her back door. It was a nice touch but Leo only scoffed and said, "The only thing that rat is good for is giving anyone in the vicinity some incurable disease."

Squash grumbled from the couch. What a ferocious beast she was with her fleece puppy pajamas.

Leo texted her every morning, checking in and asking if anything happened in the night. She always sent back a one-word answer of: no. Short and to the point. Maybe he could read two-letter words despite all the head injuries he was sure to have sustained from high school football. He would always respond with "carry on" and carry on she did.

Sage was busy making steady progress on *Welkin Wall*. She also went into her cozy gaming mode and would get all cozy and play through *Breath of the Wild* and other more chill games with her Patreon subscribers. They would chat and relax and she'd show off Squash and her new puppy jammies. It felt like the nights before George died, when she would stay up late once she got George comfortable in bed.

She managed to pack away some of George's things and placed them in neat stacks in his room. It felt like a shrine of sorts. Things she wasn't willing to part with. Things that were only George's and would not belong in any other home. But she couldn't have them living in this home just yet. It hurt too much to see his things staring at her. It was like a whisper of a friend you'd never hear the voice of again. No, packed away nicely and stored in a room that was bound to collect dust over the next few years was perfect. *Totally normal.*

"It's called coping," Roz had said when Sage called her in tears about the illogical situation of it all.

"They're just things!" Sage sobbed. "Inanimate, ugly, perfect little objects that make me cry. I'm in tears because of a stupid little vase with cherry blossom flowers painted on it." Sage glared at the offending item. She sniffed. "I am reduced to a puddle of water when I see the last painting George picked up."

Tavy and Roz had come over and helped her—making sure it was during a time Leo had never dropped in on her because she did not feel like opening that can of drama with her friends right now. They'd go feral if they realized Leo Camaro was her babysitter.

It was weird knowing there were eyes all around her house. She glared at the cameras when she walked by just in case Leo was watching. She said hello to Filbert (making sure to keep really strong eye contact) and went on a few walks because she promised Tavy she would try. "Sunshine and exercise are good for you," said the college athlete. She was such a mom friend. Sage loved that about her. And Roz came over a few times and blasted music while she dragged Sage from her bed and helped her clean up the house and get rid of all of George's old medications and medical paperwork. Her only two friends in the world were the best anyone could ever have.

Friends were like ice cream on a hot day, one could never have enough.

Speaking of ice cream...Sage's stomach grumbled as she looked up from her computer. She had been lost in the world of *Welkin Wall* for a few hours and snacks were the only thing that could bring her back to reality.

She looked at the clock. Noon. Now was a great time for breakfast. To be fair, anytime was a great time for breakfast, especially when Franko's flapjacks were concerned.

It was only after she had driven the two miles to Franko's that she thought about texting Leo where she was. Not that she needed permission, obviously. She was already halfway through her first hot chocolate and a stack of flapjacks were on their way when she thought about it again. She should at least let him know... But by the time they had argued about the safety of pancakes, she would have eaten her fill and be on her way home. It was a small breach of the contract, was all. No big deal.

The first bite of the buttery, gooey pancakes was bliss. The next bite brought back memories of her and George and their weekly pancake outing.

The third bite nearly choked her when a voice boomed, "What in the flapjack are you doing here?"

"Camaro?" she asked but with the pancake stuck in her throat it came out more like *"Creee?"*

He slid into the booth across from her, stabbed a pancake off her plate—off her plate!—and shoved it in his mouth. He brandished a fork at her. "You have a lot of nerve sneaking out."

"I wasn't sneaking," Sage said, eyes watering from the recently dislodged pancake piece in her throat. She downed her hot chocolate and asked Martha for another from across the room with her eyes. Martha knew the look.

"Deciding to *not* tell me your location *is* sneaking," Leo said. "And choosing the most inconspicuous spot in the diner is also suspicious."

"I was not being suspicious," Sage whispered in a tone that sounded rather, well, suspicious. But it was his fault. She didn't want to make a scene and Leo was bound and determined to perform. "I was just getting breakfast in my usual booth."

It was weird having a usual booth, at a usual café, without the usual person.

"Well, if it's a usual occurrence, why isn't this little event on the calendar, hm?" Leo looked rather smug and while Sage looked for the right words (she bought herself time by shoving as many pancakes in her mouth as possible) he ordered himself a fat stack of flapjacks too.

"So," Leo asked, sipping a mug of coffee that had been placed in front of him. "What's your excuse?"

"I forgot."

He looked at her like he knew she was lying. Time to turn the tables.

"How'd you know where I was?" she asked, brandishing her own fork at him this time.

"That's for me to know and you to deal with the repercussions."

She tried to kick him from under the table but he caught her foot in his hand. "Ah, ah," he tutted. "I think a time-out would do you justice. I hate that you resort to violence."

She tried to kick him with her other foot but he caught that one just as easily. Leo shook his head. "You'll get much further with me if you use your words."

Sage just mumbled and tried to jerk her feet away. Leo's grip was firm.

"Say please," he said.

Sage blushed and tried to jerk back, harder this time. It failed. "Please," she mumbled, only because she didn't want him touching her anymore. Was it growing hot in here? Were all guy hands that big and strong? Seriously, was it hot in here?

Leo seemed unphased by the whole...incident. Yes, that's how she was going to catalog it. Foot incident. Okay, now that just sounded weird.

Sage stirred her cup of fresh hot chocolate Martha dropped off. "Seriously, how'd you know I was here?"

Leo shrugged and smiled at Martha who brought him an enormous stack of pancakes. He drizzled half the syrup bottle over them. "I saw your car on the way to your house."

Now why did that feel like a lie?

"Please go away," Sage said. "I want to eat in peace."

"No." Leo shoveled down the gooey mess. "You lost 'eating in peace' privileges when you forgot to tell me you wanted to eat in peace."

"I'm telling you now!"

"Don't get huffy."

"Huffy!" Sage crossed her arms over her chest and glared at him so hard she thought the weight of her stare would push him away. Unfortunately, the lump of Leo remained.

"Why are you wearing pajamas?" he asked.

"That's it!" Sage tried to scoot out of the booth but Leo

stopped her with his leg, effectively blocking her path. "You are a child."

"You're the one wearing pajamas to lunch."

"It's breakfast for me and what's wrong with my shirt?"

"Other than it's giving me a migraine, nothing at all."

To be fair, it was a strange shirt. It was a pastel purple tie-dye background with little images of squashes (the vegetable kind) forming a giant image of Squash (the dog kind). It was almost a design that came alive, like some sort of optical illusion. The more you stared at it, the dizzier you got.

"The adoption agency where I found Squash sent it to me."

"It's ugly."

"Now it's my favorite shirt."

"No wonder you're single with that type of nightwear."

Sage poked at his leg still blocking her path to escape. "They're not pajamas. And who says I don't have a boyfriend?"

"Because no man or woman alive would allow you to go out in public like that. Even your dog has more fashion sense than you."

Okay, well, he kind of had a point. But little did he know that Squash was back home sporting a very similar look with her own tie-dye pajamas. It was cold after all...

"I have fashion sense!" Sage argued more with herself than Leo. "I actually have to go to events and stuff. I know how to look cool and presentable. Gotta stand out from the rest."

"Love, you're a lady among a sea of men who live in their mother's basements and have never heard of shampoo. You're already standing out. Which is why I wanted to talk to you before I had to go out of my way to lecture you about breaking the rules."

Sage poked at his leg again. "Consider me good and lectured, *love*. It shan't happen again." It probably would.

"Have more pancakes."

"No thank you."

"My treat. We have things to discuss and I have a feeling you will be better behaved in a public space with your belly full ."

Sage could feel herself growing red. So red she might turn purple. Maybe she'd match her shirt. "You are the worst!"

"Screaming, scolding Sage. I do love alliteration. What else can we add to this list?"

Sage smacked his knee.

"Slappy. Good work," Leo said, a goofy grin on his face. He leaned back against the booth like a man without a care in the world. Like this was a normal breakfast (fine, it really was lunch) date.

She contemplated climbing over his leg but decided she would die of embarrassment right here on the diner floor.

"Fine!" Sage said, leaning back into the booth. "Since you've decided to force your presence on me, let's get this over with."

"Sassy. Way to keep on theme."

She could practically feel the wrinkles forming

between her eyebrows. And what did he mean by "things to discuss?" Things about, you know, his job protecting her? Or things of the past? Was he going to apologize? Of course not. He was like an ostrich, forever burying his head in the sand. "Ugh, what do you want?"

"Look, I just wanted to go through the Livestream schedule you have so I can try and pop into the chat and check out some of the messages. Thoughts?"

She sighed and rubbed her temples. "Thinking about ostriches at the moment actually. And to answer your question, I don't really have a schedule. I mean I have a few standing times but that's part of the fun of doing what I do. I decide when to do it."

"Like the bird?" Leo asked, clearly annoyed. "Why don't you *decide* when you're going to do it and let me know."

"Why though?" Sage asked, fully prepared to give him a million excuses as to why she couldn't give him her online schedule. Why did it feel strange having this guy join the chat? Was that embarrassment bubbling up in her chest? No. No, that would not do.

"I just want to get an idea of the hostilities surrounding you. Look for clues."

"You're no Hardy boy."

"No, he's a Camaro," a distinctly familiar voice said from behind Sage. It made her jump and splash her hot chocolate down her front.

"Destiny Baker?" Leo asked, standing quickly (finally removing his leg), and giving the woman a giant hug.

"Long time no see," Destiny said. "What on earth are you doing here?"

"Just here for Jules' wedding. What about you?" Leo asked.

Destiny had conveniently overlooked Sage (literally) and hadn't noticed her yet. In order to make her escape (unseen) she'd have to slide under the table and out between their legs. Destiny was blocking her in. She didn't think it would work but was already sliding down the booth seat when Destiny looked down at Sage.

"Hi," Destiny said. "I'm Leo's friend Destiny."

"Cool!" Sage took the opening and stood, briefly shaking Destiny's hand, and made her way around the pair. "I'll let you two catch up."

Destiny was more than ready to take the offer and was halfway seated by the time Sage made it to the door, and for a moment, Leo looked conflicted about staying. She made the choice for him by quickly texting him.

SAGE: I'm going home. I'll email you my stream schedule later.

She flew past the trees that lined her cute little street. It really shouldn't make her stomach clench. But how could she not remember? Sage had sat next to Destiny in Geometry class for an entire year! She let Destiny copy her homework the whole time! And sure, time had passed, but not like an eternity.

Sage pulled into her driveway, marched into the house, and did the only thing that could make someone feel better when they knew logically they had no reason to be sad. She ate some chocolate, cuddled Squash on their favorite couch in her office, and turned on her

favorite movie obsession. Right now, it was Drew Barrymore's *Ever After.*

She was just getting to the good part (the prince
chasing after the thief) when Leo barged through the
front door. She heard him calling her name. She groaned
loud enough for him to find her.

"Am I interrupting?" Leo asked as he walked into her
space.

"Go away, I'm working. The contract states that you
cannot interrupt me during my working hours unless
there is a security risk."

"You're not working."

"And you're not here for a wedding."

Leo sat in her office chair, testing it out and rolling
around. "This is nice. Guess you'd need something fancy
since you're sitting around all day. And hey! I am working
undercover. Can't let the town gossip know I am here for
work."

"I fail to see how that is a problem at all. And I don't
sit around all day!" Sometimes she ended up horizontal,
like now, before being rudely interrupted. "Just don't
embarrass me in the chat."

"What could I say that could *possibly* be more cringe
than what is already there?"

Sage sat up, abandoning the movie. "Okay, first off, no
one says cringe anymore. Unless you want to be religiously attacked for being an elder millennial completely
out of touch."

"I don't care," Leo said.

Sage shrugged. "You might more than you think."

"What can a bunch of strangers on the internet say to

make me self-conscious?"

A lot, actually. Sage pushed the insults that cut deep to the back of her mind, because try as she might, she couldn't push them out.

"I'll email you the schedule like I said I would. You didn't have to rush out of your reunion."

Leo shrugged. "Did you know she was a cop?"

Sage shook her head. But that didn't really surprise her. All the mean girls liked some sort of power job.

Leo sighed. "But now I actually gotta figure out an excuse for being in town longer. The holidays are a good excuse. Speaking of. Any plans I should know about?"

Sage's stomach dropped. She had always spent it with George. The last six years. "Not much. Just local."

It was hard to determine if Leo looked relieved or annoyed with the revelation. "Okay, let me know as we get closer where you'll be."

Maybe she could spend it with Roz. Or Tavy. No, Tavy's family always went to the coast for the holidays.

"Will do," Sage said, flopping back down on the couch, grasping for the remote with one hand and scratching Squash's ear with the other. "Now can you go? I have important work to do."

"Right." The sarcasm was thick on Leo's tongue and she wanted to smack it right off of him but that would require getting up and untangled from the blankets. It sounded a lot like effort so instead she turned and gave him a good glare which he promptly ignored.

"I'll leave you to it. I'll even lock up when I leave." He tossed her a key. "I took the liberty of picking these up."

Sage fiddled with the strange key in her hand. It

looked like a normal key but two sizes too big. The teeth looked more like jagged incisors. "Thanks." She set it aside as if it were going to bite her.

"Don't work too hard. Wouldn't want you breaking a sweat."

She threw a pillow—a squash-shaped one of course—at him on his way out.

6
LEO

When Leo's mother had insisted on throwing a "small get-together" for Christmas Eve, he hadn't expected the entire family in the state to make the trek out there. But here they were, all eager to chat with Leo and Tess who had both been notably absent the last two Christmases due to work conflicts.

"It's so good having you home," his mother sauntered by and grabbed the empty cup from Leo's hand. Ever the hostess. "Be a dear and help me with the ice, would you?"

He unloaded more bags from the garage into the tray on the counter, busy keeping the oysters cold. He snagged some smoked salmon and stuffed it in his mouth before another person could intercept him to chat about the glory days, his job, or really anything else. Tess had the right idea, she was busy listening to Aunt Geraldine talk all about her cats. No one wanted to interrupt them out of fear they might be drug into the conversation, so Tess was free of personal questions for the next hour or so. Smart woman, even if she had to hear about Fluffy and her fleas.

Leo heard the telltale bark of his father over the cacophony. "Betty!" There was a pause. "Betty, I'm coming to get you! He's right here. I promise he's not in prison." Leo's father stormed into the pantry Leo had been hiding in and beckoned him to the phone. "He's right here, Betty. Look, Leo is gonna talk to you." He held the phone to Leo, whispering, "She's in the checkout line at the store trying to buy thousands of dollars' worth of gift cards because someone told her you were in jail and needed them. She's beside herself."

Leo snatched the phone from his father's hand, swallowing down the last bit of Swiss chocolate Tess had the nerve to hide. "Aunt Betty?"

"Leo, is that you?"

"Yeah, it's me, Aunt Betty. When are you getting here? The party is just getting started."

"Thank heavens," his great aunt Betty's voice cracked. "They knew your name. The person from the jail. What a coincidence. They even knew your birthday and where you went to high school. They said you needed the cards for the food and stuff in jail! They said you were really embarrassed and needed to keep this secret and—"

"Aunt Betty, it's a scam. People do that now. Were they going to have you mail the cards somewhere?"

"Yeah." Aunt Betty sniffed. "They emailed me all of this stuff and I couldn't reach you because they said your phone was impounded."

"Did you try?" Leo asked, running a hand through his hair. Who would try and scam a little old lady? The scum of the earth, that's who. "I have my phone right here in my pocket. Where are you? I can come pick you up. I want to see these emails."

And that's how Leo, on Christmas Eve afternoon, became a super sleuth and spent the next two hours backtracking the IP addresses and learning on the fly how to get the name and information of the would-be swindler.

Aunt Betty sat next to him on the loveseat in the den the entire time, gripping her iced chardonnay with such force Leo thought the glass could shatter at any moment.

"To think I almost gave them everything I had," she mumbled to herself. Then she'd get on the defensive. "You know I'd do anything for you and Tessie," she said, squeezing his arm. "Even if it meant keeping it from your parents."

"I know, I know."

Eventually, after a "Please save me" look to Tess (which she ignored twice), Tess came over and ushered great aunt Betty toward the food so Leo could finalize the (he'd admit) haphazard detective work. But the job was done.

He even got the guy's address. After a short call to the police station (and fine, he threw the Agency's name around too—they were well known after all) it looked like Mr. Scammer would be spending Christmas Eve in jail.

Leo handed off the information to his father who would no doubt pursue the full extent of the law for his aunt. He clapped Leo on the shoulder, "Well done, son. I was hesitant about you being so antisocial on the computer over there, but to actually find the guy? Color me impressed."

Tess overheard and piped in. "Ironic that you call computer work antisocial when it literally connects the whole world but okay."

Dad rolled his eyes. "You know what I meant."

Leo laughed. "Yeah." But no. No, he didn't. He was beginning to realize just how big the world was when he jumped into some of Sage's streams. There were people from all over the world tuning in to watch her play. It was overwhelming, to say the least, but Sage looked totally at ease with the audience, which could be numbered in the thousands watching her. Could he ever be that calm under pressure? He didn't want to find out.

His brain hurt. He had definitely gone the roundabout way of backtracking everything, and he was lucky he had the tech from the agency to do it. But goodness he needed a nice cup of espresso and some oysters to ease the pain in his eyeballs.

He couldn't help but glance at the app to check in on Sage. She was at home, streaming. It was a little sad to think about...but then again she'd told him Roz was coming over for their annual Christmas Eve tradition and she'd be fine.

He checked the cameras. She sat in her office, babbling to the camera, a smile on her face, looking totally at ease in her world. If only his father knew how she made money, he'd have kittens, which would be great because it would give him and Geraldine something in common to talk about.

Leo found himself wandering the kitchen and his mind whirled. If he *had* to get Sage a gift, what would it be? To know someone is to be a good gift-giver. Leo prided himself on being a keen observer and therefore an excellent gift-giver. He got Tess nothing, which she loved. She was always awkward regarding gifts and grand gestures, often feeling uncomfortable with the attention. So, he gave her the gift of expecting nothing.

She got him a bigger towel.

He had given his mother a string of pearls, her favorite, the exception being four black pearls in the middle of the strand, one for each of the people in her family. She cried. But to be fair, she would have cried if he'd given her a candle (he would have gotten her a cranberry-scented one because she liked the color more than the scent). See? He knew her.

He got his dad a new golf bag, one that was more ergonomic for that shoulder injury still bothering him.

But Sage? He could go easy and get her tea, but that just felt so...plain. The woman had an entire cabinet dedicated to the leaves, he doubted another addition wouldn't mean much. He couldn't get her any tech stuff since she was very particular and really got everything she wanted from LilyTech.

He could get something for her animal thing. He shivered. Absolutely not. That would be accepting it's claim that it was a pet and not some creature conjured from a nightmare. (But if he *had* to get it something, he'd get the animal a spiked vest so it wouldn't be carried off by vultures—see? A great gift giver.)

Sage still remained a mystery to him. Not unusual. So why did he find himself suddenly ready to solve a mystery?

74

7

SAGE

So. Christmas. That time of year when people spent way too much money on people and way too much time surrounded by their great Aunt Bettys. Sage assumed everyone had an aunt or two named Betty.

Normally Sage and George would spend the first week of December doing all the Christmas decorating and shopping (George loved any excuse to add more eclectic décor to the house and shopping was his passion) and then they'd spend Christmas morning together making tea, playing chess, and exchanging gifts. They'd make cider and drink more tea and end the night with some of George's most expensive whiskey, all in front of a roaring fireplace, of course. George loved the holidays. He loved the snow, the decorations, the lights, and Christmas music.

Christmas felt a little more gray this year.

So what? Christmas was going to be different, and she vowed only to cry a few times throughout the ordeal.

Luckily for Sage, she only had to shop for two people (and Squash).

Tavy was classy, and she came from money. Like *money,* money. So, Sage had to get more creative when it came to her gifts. Luckily, Tavy was painfully practical, so Sage got her fancy Bluetooth headphones with a custom monogrammed case. She was sure Tavy would gush over the case more than the actual headphones, which was just the sort of thing sweet Tavy would do. She'd also write a thank you note to send about two weeks later, despite Sage telling her that it was always unnecessary and that she was wasting a stamp.

For Roz. Well. Roz was a firecracker. She barely graduated high school and flunked out of community college, but she managed to get pretty well known for being an amazing artist. She started out designing stickers and invitations, and started doing portraits. Weddings were her bread and butter and she often did family watercolor portraits. Naturally Sage gifted her with a waterproof backpack, perfect for storing her things on those days when she wanted to paint in the park.

Their usual tradition was to spend Christmas Eve brunch together before all of their family events took over. But Roz was out of town with her new boyfriend. Sage wanted to hate him, but he spoiled Roz relentlessly and, despite being skeptical at first, Sage had to admit he was pretty nice.

Tavy, sweet Tavy, offered for Sage to come over and join her family for Christmas dinner but Sage said she would rather eat a box of rocks than have to sit through a fancy dinner with her parents. Tavy asked to join her at the rock-eating party. It had been a short laugh between them, but spending Christmas alone was the better end of the deal than having to spend it with Tavy's posh and peevish parents. *Look who's good at alliteration now?*

All of this led to Sage sitting in her much cozier living room (she had tried to liven it up a tad and moved most of the boxes of antiques to George's room) and watching *Lord of the Rings* and sipping on some tea. All things considered, it was the cozy and quiet night that she needed. No stream chats to talk to. No games to play. No social media posts to make or photos to take. Jared had come by weeks ago and had taken a million photos of her to "batch content." Whatever that meant. All Sage knew was that he ended the session with his signature "Everything is perfectly peachy" which was a sign that he was at least going to leave her alone for a few days.

All Sage had to do was relax and be merry. And she was until the thought of tacos entered her mind.

Tacos were delicious.

Tacos could definitely be considered a Christmas Eve tradition.

Tacos could be the start of her brand-new solo Christmas Eve tradition she was starting this year. At this moment, actually.

The thought of tacos could not be ignored. She bundled up Squash (who looked positively squeamish at the mention of a car ride) and left her snoozing on the couch as Sage searched for her keys.

Taco Bell was a quick five-minute drive away. Seriously, how could someone hate small towns when everything you ever needed was within such a quick driving distance?

"Because some people like more than two restaurants and want to see Target every once in a while," Tavy said when she was leaving for college in the big city.

"Well, I have a target in my sights tonight," Sage said to herself, thinking of tacos, and she stepped onto the porch. "Holy Crunchwrap it's cold."

Sure, she could run back in and grab another coat. She looked at her slippers (pink bunnies with ears) and considered some more practical shoes, but a glance at her phone pushed her to the car. There was no time! Christmas Eve hours listed had Taco Bell closing at nine. She had about half an hour to get there and grab the goods, and she was not going to be one of those customers that showed up a minute to closing.

If only she'd known what was to come. She would have worn boots instead.

It was cold and trying to snow. The rain that fell turned into this slushy mess that wanted to call itself snow but it was really more thick water that froze to the ground. Other people might have called it ice. Locals of the valley referred to this as "slush" that would later turn to ice and then be labeled as frozen rain, because that was, apparently, very different than ice. Or so George had told her, and who was she to distrust a man with 80 years of weather experience?

Still, the heater in the car worked like a charm and she pulled out onto the empty roads and five minutes later into the drive-through, which had no line. No surprise there.

That's when she realized she'd forgotten her wallet.

"Take Apple Pay?" she asked the man working.

"Not at this location. But in Hurley they do."

Sage was not about to drive half an hour to the next town over for tacos when she could go home and grab her wallet like a normal person. She told the man just that.

"I'll be here," he said with a sigh that reeked of boredom. "And just so you know," he gestured between them, "None of this is normal for Christmas Eve."

"Ba-humbug then," Sage said with a smile. The scent of fake Americanized tacos (that really had no business marketing themselves as tacos) was getting to her.

The man laughed. "Don't be late. I'm closing up shop here in about fifteen minutes."

Sage needed no more prompting to peel back out onto the road and make a loop toward home. The timing was going to work out perfectly.

That was until a mouse ruined everything.

Yes. A mouse.

One of the perils of the incoming cold weather was that little critters would occasionally take up residence under the hoods of cars and in the engine areas. Sage actually wasn't entirely sure where they crawled to get warm, but in any case, this one crawled right up through her heater vent and flopped right into her lap.

She handled the stowaway with surprising grace.

She screamed, swerved, and drove with her knees all while trying to keep one eye on the road and the other on the mouse scrambling up her sleeve. She flung her hand into the window where it just knocked the mouse back onto her lap where the scene repeated itself.

"Get off, get off!" she yelled at the mouse who was not handling the situation with much logic either.

Sage rounded the corner fairly well before she slid out on some of the frozen slush. When she landed in the small ditch, both hands were free to properly smack the mouse away. It landed on the seat next to her and looked a little dazed and confused.

"I'm sorry little dude," Sage said, looking for a napkin, book, newspaper (but who read those anymore) really anything to help keep the furry thing at a safe distance. Still, Sage leaned in slightly closer to check that it wasn't foaming at the mouth or anything. It wasn't.

At least she wasn't going to get rabies.

Bubonic plague? Maybe. Or was that from a rat?

Was this just a small rat?

Before her stream of questions could properly take on the form of a raging river, blue and red lights flashed in the rearview mirror.

"Just great," Sage mumbled, kissing her scrumptious tacos goodbye. She doubted the drive-thru guy would wait up for her. It felt like she was standing up a date.

A tall, lean officer with piercing blue eyes tapped on her window. Sage only had a moment to glance at him before returning her attention back to the mouse. Or rather the empty seat where the mouse *should* have been.

Sage squealed when she felt it run over her feet and she kicked. Except it wasn't the mouse (probably) it was just one of the bunny ears on her slippers tickling her ankle. *Right?*

"Miss?" the officer said, a stern look on his face. His breath fogged up the window. "Roll it down please."

The *please* sounded more like a warning.

Sage was quick to obey and plastered a smile on her face despite the thundering in her chest. Was it because she was nervous about the officer or because she just fought for her life against a mouse (and won—barely) while driving down an icy road?

The wind kicked up and blew frigid air into her car, vanishing the remaining warmth of the heater. Sage shivered. "I'm okay," she chuckled. The ditch was rather small and she was certain she had four-wheel drive and could get out. But to be fair, she thought all cars had four-wheel drive. They all had four wheels after all.

"I am not so much worried about your safety as much as the safety of others when you are behind the wheel," the officer said. He looked so familiar. He had a fair mustache that wasn't totally full but it was distracting enough that Sage really couldn't place the face. Kind of like he took some leftover straw and hay from the Halloween décor of months past and taped it to his upper lip.

"Right," Sage said. "You won't believe what—"

"License please."

Sage cleared her throat and rubbed her hands together. "Well, I was actually on my way back home to grab my wallet since I—"

"Have you been drinking?"

"What?" Sage wrinkled her nose. "No! I was just on my way back from picking up tacos."

"I don't see any." The officer made a show of peeking into the car.

Well, this was not going well. Her eyes darting

around, looking for the vanishing mouse likely didn't help her situation.

"Please step out of the car, Miss." The officer took a step back and allowed Sage to open the door about two feet before it got stuck in the mud. Still, it was just enough room for Sage to slip out but she paused and asked. "Is this really necessary? I don't want to ruin my...shoes." If one could call them that. They didn't have rubber soles. They were pink and plushy and about to turn brown and soggy. "Please?" she asked.

"If you refuse to get out and take a field sobriety test I will be forced to take you in," the officer said, jangling the cuffs on his belt for emphasis.

Sage, smartly, decided not to tell him that taking her in would also require her to vacate the car. She took one last glance around the car, hoping the mouse would show itself. It continued to hide, the cheeky thing. She mentally informed the mouse that she would be using its hide to repair her soon-to-be ruined slippers, hoping her fuming frustration would reach the mouse.

It did not.

Sage sighed and stepped into the mud. It squelched under her feet and she stumbled the three steps onto the road. It was not a busy street, and even less so at this hour, but she was still uneasy about standing on an icy road, in the dark, with a stranger.

To add insult to injury, her stomach rumbled again, protesting about the lack of Christmas Tacos.

"What's your name?" Sage asked, trying hard to sound extra sober even though the only thing she drank in the last month was tea and the occasional water (you know, for health).

"Officer LaBrant."

"Seth LaBrant?"

"Do I know you?" Officer LaBrant asked, reaching around, and grabbing a flashlight. "Please close your eyes and touch our index finger to your nose."

"We went to high school together. This is all a really funny story if you'll—"

"Now do it with your other hand."

"Okay," Sage said, still keeping her eyes closed. "So, there was this mouse that got in my car and it totally freaked—"

"Open your eyes and please walk toe to heal in a straight line until I say stop."

Sage froze (figuratively and literally). She pointed down the dark and sleet-covered road. "I'm afraid I'll fall on the ice."

"No ice. Just a few paces unless you'd rather come in for a breathalyzer test." The officer crossed his arms over his chest.

"This is ridiculous," Sage said, crossing her own arms over her chest, more for warmth than anything. It was freezing and the wind was blowing and it looked like it was going to start slushing again. She already felt a drop land on her head. "You haven't even asked me my name. Can I please call someone?"

"That won't be necessary," the officer said. "If you pass the walking test, you're free to go."

Sage looked at the car stuck in the muddy ditch. Sure, it wasn't a big ditch, she pretty much rolled into it, but even she knew her tires wouldn't get any traction with the goopy mud. It just wasn't frozen enough. Instead, it was like really cold, slimy, quicksand. She looked at her now mud-covered slippers, already resigning herself to the fact they couldn't be salvaged.

On with the walking in a straight line show.

Sage took two steps before falling backward like a cartoon character on her bum. She groaned and gingerly stood up just to fall again.

"I thought you said there wasn't any ice!" Sage yelled at LaBrant who was busy watching with a halfhearted attempt at concealing his laughter.

"There wasn't. Temperatures must have dropped."

Sage couldn't prove it, but she was fairly certain that was not how icy roads happened. Well, they *did* happen like that, but not in the span of two minutes.

"Look!" Sage pointed to her open door. The light was still on (she hoped the battery wouldn't die as it was known to do). Sitting in the yellow glow of the car, right on the top of her steering wheel, was a little mouse. She swore it waved at her.

"What am I looking at?" LaBrant took a step toward the car but immediately stopped when his boot hit the mud. He pulled his coat tighter around him when a gust of wind whipped by.

"The mouse!" Sage turned around just as the mouse did its vanishing act. That's it. She was making mouse slippers. Someone had to pay for her new slippers, and it was going to be that sneaky squeaker who had the nerve to ruin her taco night. She wanted a pound (or ounce in this case) of flesh!

The lights of the cruiser illuminated what had to be snowfall. Long gone was the slush. LaBrant raised an eyebrow at her. "It's Christmas Eve. I'm giving you a warning. Now drive safe."

"I doubt I'll be able to do that with the car stuck in a ditch."

The radio in the cruiser buzzed with some robotic voice and Sage could practically see LaBrant's ears twitch. "It'll pull out fine. Just use your flashers until you're on the road." As he spoke, he backed away and entered the cruiser, slamming the door behind him. He sped off into the night, red and blue lights still flashing, leaving Sage in the dark. Even the moon seemed to dim, hiding behind the clouds in secondhand embarrassment.

Sage swore she heard a tiny mouse laughing.

8

LEO

The party was still in full swing. Some lady his mother knew hugged him more than once and gushed over how broad-shouldered he was. His sister hid in the corner, drinking what was likely to be spiked hot chocolate. She was so dull with her answers to questions, despite her very exciting line of work, that people eventually gave up talking to her, saving her from numerous backhanded compliments. It was the smart play and Leo could only hold up his drink (apple cider, he didn't drink) in a mock salute. She gave him a wink.

It was stuffy in the giant room. The vaulted ceilings made the chatter of the dozens of people echo around him and it all felt too sweet. Fake. Sickening. Like eating a piece of rich chocolate cake and wanting to stop because it was making you feel ill, only to be force-fed the rest of the cake.

His salvation came in the form of a phone call.

"Sage?" he asked, taking the call (which had saved

him from a chat with his other aunt Betty—his mom's side this time).

"Hi," she sniffed. "I kind of need your help but I want you to know it's because my normal people are out of town and this is me scraping the bottom of the barrel here but…"

"But…?"

"But I'm humbling myself and need you to come get me. My car is stuck in a ditch."

As if he needed proof, her heard a tire spinning out in what was likely six inches of mud.

"Most people, when needing a favor, phrase it like a question, not a demand."

"You're paid to help me."

"To protect you." Leo finished his cider, already gathering his keys and looking for his mother (who blended in too well with all the other fake blondes with gaudy red sweaters) to make his quick "I have a work thing" goodbye.

"Is your life in danger?" Leo asked.

"Well, it could be. I'm considering hitchhiking."

"No one would pick you up. You'd be like a mouse on the side of the road, they'd drive right over you."

"I don't ever want to hear the word mouse again. Just come and get me, okay? See, that was a question."

Leo gave up on finding his mother and instead made his way to the door. For as cheeky as Miss Moon was being, she didn't exactly sound the surest of herself. And he didn't like the idea of his Subject being out in the dark alone.

"Wait, aren't you supposed to be with Roz?" he asked

as he slid into his 4Runner. Was that snow? Were they really going to get a white Christmas? Here? In the valley? Leo couldn't remember the last time he'd had a white Christmas. Maybe ten years ago when they opted to spend Christmas in Switzerland.

"Roz had something come up."

Something told Leo that if he'd been able to make eye contact with her, he'd know she was lying.

"Liar," he said anyway without his proof.

"Do you need my address? I'm on Raven Road."

"I've got it," Leo said, pulling up her location on his phone. "I'm twelve minutes out. Are you actually safe?"

"Yes," she mumbled. "Except for the rat in my car terrorizing me."

"You said her name was Squash."

"A real rat!" she yelled. "I should have called an Uber."

Leo snorted. "Why didn't you?" He turned on the setting which alerted him when she left the house because this was going to be a common occurrence.

There was a big pause before she mumbled, "There were none out on Christmas Eve."

"Well, Uber Leo to the rescue. But don't think you're going to get out of me berating you about how you neglected to let me know where you were. I expect you to be quiet and listen to me rant for a solid two minutes."

She hung up. The audacity. As a passenger, she is already well on her way to a two-star rating.

He saw her hazard lights in the distance and wasn't surprised to find her car just as he imagined he would: six inches deep in mud on the side of the back road.

"How'd that happen?" he asked when he parked and

stepped out next to her car. It was far enough off the road that it wouldn't be a danger to others, other than the fact that it was a startling eyesore. Seriously. A yellow Subaru probably from the seventies simply didn't work with the stunning wooded area around them.

"I slid out," she mumbled, not meeting his eye, and she stepped out from the car and stumbled up the small incline.

"On a straightway?"

Sage threw her hands up. "Fine! You know what? I went out for tacos because they sounded delightful and then a stupid tiny mouse that looked cute but was actually evil crawled up out of the depths of hell into my lap and so yeah. I kind of did a weird little move trying not to get my eyes scratched out. And I ended up in a ditch. And your stupid friend LaBrant didn't help anything."

"Seth was here?" Leo asked. "I haven't seen that guy in years. We kind of kept in touch for a while but not recently. Why didn't you ask him for a ride home?"

Sage shook out her muddy slippers, accidentally kicking one off and she was forced to do a rather undignified hop over and slide it back on. Seriously, what was she wearing? He had gone from a Hampton-like Christmas party to a slumber party in twelve minutes.

Sage threw up her hands. "The only place he was willing to drive me was the station because he thought I was a drunk driver or reckless driver or something. I didn't have my license on me anyway. I forgot it. I was heading home to grab my wallet so I could get those darn tacos!" She glanced at the phone. "But they've been closed for twenty minutes by now."

"Please for the love of everything good and holy, please don't tell me you were getting Taco Bell on Christmas Eve?"

"Can I get in? It's freezing!" She stomped past him and to the 4Runner, hopping in, getting her muddy feet everywhere.

"You were!" Someone had to be feeling low, like rock bottom, to ever crave Taco Bell, but on Christmas. That's just...sad. "Where's your coat?"

"At home. Now can you take me back?"

Leo didn't need much prompting. It was cold. The wind was making the trees dance like waves on the sea and the snow bit at his face. "Taco Bell?"

"I happen to like it." Her stomach rumbled. She reddened (which was peculiar but Leo had other things to worry about and filed that little image away for later).

"No one in their right mind likes Taco Bell. So why the pajamas and slippers?"

"It's like nine-thirty. It's cozy."

Leo snorted. "That's like your everyday uniform."

"I do own jeans actually. And I do have a sense of style, but I wasn't exactly planning on seeing anyone. This whole thing is a mess."

"Like the one you're making." Leo pointed to her muddy feet. "Gross."

She just groaned and turned up the heat. Leo felt a pang of guilt. No. Pang was too much. He felt the barest stirring of guilt. She had been out there cold and alone for who knows how long before she gave up and swallowed her pride enough to call him. Still, it was dumb to be out in this weather anyway.

He turned on the seat heater.

They rode the rest of the way to Sage's house in silence and he had barely rolled to a stop when Sage jumped from the car. She slipped on the mud and fell flat on her butt.

"Watch the ground, it's slippery."

Sage stood and scowled at him. "Goodnight." She stomped toward the house, stumbled on the uneven stairs, and slammed the door behind her.

Except it wasn't. Definitely not for her. And not really for him. The idea of returning to the stuffy party made his insides churn. Going back to that party was like being a wolf stuck at a tea party.

Leo balked at himself. He actually wrinkled his nose. Did he just compare himself to a wolf? Yikes. Maybe he was still that arrogant teenager inside.

He shook his head. "Well pop a red hat on me and call me Santa," he mumbled to himself as he pulled out of her driveway. Let Operation Save Christmas commence.

He was in and out of the store in less than thirty minutes. He must be insane. Or just desperate to escape his parents.

But he was a grown man. So, it must be the former.

He hopped out of the 4Runner and nearly face-planted in the mud. "Good lord," he hissed, shaking the slick mud from his boots.

He didn't bother being quiet (or knocking for that matter) and got straight to work once he washed his hands. With the sound of water running from upstairs, he assumed Sage was taking a much-needed shower.

The rat-dog did nothing to alert her of his presence.

It was another fifteen minutes before Sage came barreling down the stairs with a golf club raised over her head. Thank the heavens for the high ceilings because this crazy lady had no spatial awareness. She wore a matching pajama set of shorts and a button-down long-sleeve. It was an obnoxious purple cloud print. And slippers. This time a fuzzy pink pair. Did this woman only own slippers too? How many did a person need? Though he had to admit they were practical. He was wearing just his socks (he took his muddy boots off by the door, he wasn't a total jerk) and his feet were beginning to feel the kiss of cold.

"What are you doing?" Sage asked once she slid around the corner to find Leo in the kitchen. She still kept the golf club raised which made Leo a tad nervous.

"Merry Christmas Tacos."

"What?" She lowered the club ever so slightly, craning her neck to see what Leo was cooking on the stove. "Is that carne asada?"

"And another pan of chicken. And a pot of beans in case you're vegetarian."

"Wai—you made this?"

Leo nodded and started dishing up a plate. "Don't give me too much credit—"

"I would never."

"It was pre-marinated. I just had to cook it."

All things considered, Christmas tacos turned out pretty good. He twisted off the cap of a Martinelli's bottle and filled a mug. He gave her a mock salute. "Feliz Navidad."

She finally set the club aside and raised an eyebrow at him. "Why?"

"Because tacos sounded good." It was a lie. He'd rather have the smoked salmon and pot roast his parents had back home. But he'd die before he admitted that he preferred her company over theirs tonight.

Sage reached for a plate and loaded up her tortillas, avoiding eye contact. Either she was really hungry, embarrassed, or saw through his lie and didn't feel like pressing him about it. He wasn't sure what kind of salsa she liked so he got green and red. (She preferred green—the best option.)

They ate on the couches in front of a roaring fire.

"You make that?" Leo gestured to the fireplace that looked like it belonged in some palace. An entire family could probably live in it.

Sage nodded. "I love a good fire. And tea. And now tacos." She stuffed her face. "Thank you," she said and quickly looked into the fire. "These are good."

"Do you always cause trouble?"

Sage rolled her eyes, clearly relaxing a bit now that she had food in her stomach.

Mental note: keep snacks on hand so the Subject doesn't hop on a quick trip to Crazy Town.

"I have been nothing but easy for you. This is a cushy job for you, huh."

"I guess you're right," Leo admitted.

"Is that why you're here then? Feeling guilty that your babysitting project has been too easy?"

Leo laughed. "Avoiding my parents."

She raised her eyebrows.

Now why had he let that slip?

"What about you?" he asked. "No fun family traditions?" If he was forced to think about his parents, so was she.

"Don't know who my dad is. Mom hasn't called in like two years now. And my brother is in prison. He's probably having the best time out of everyone. You know the inmates do Secret Santas?"

"For real?"

Sage nodded. "I sent him a book hollowed out to fit this fancy chisel I got him."

Leo choked on his taco.

"Kidding." She flashed him a smile and he was surprised to find that she had a nice smile with straight teeth. It was gone just as soon as it came. "I sent him a book, no chisels or pickaxes, and some chocolates."

"He send you anything?" Leo asked. This was either going to rub salt in the wound or make sweet memories.

"Guilt."

Salty.

"Well, I'm no expert on family relationships, but the holidays are better spent around friends. Where are yours?" he asked.

Sage took a long time chewing her bite like she was mulling over the answers. Tension melted away and she leaned against the couch. Clearly she settled on some sort of version of the truth. It was easier to relax when you didn't have to make up lies on the spot.

"I have a few close friends. Most are away at college. If they do come home, they have things to do with their families. We had plans but they fell through and that's okay."

It didn't sound okay.

"I'm dodging my parents. They are trying to set me up with every one of their friends' daughters. Think it'll keep me home more."

"Sounds like a solid plan. You'd have to quit the agency though."

"Yeah, that's not gonna happen. I've put in too much work to let it go now."

"You were in the military, right?" Sage asked almost cautiously.

"Served three years before a bomb took me out. Screwed up my leg so bad they just let me out on medical discharge. I took my MCATs and stuff with the idea of applying to med school, just haven't yet."

"Why?" Sage asked.

Why, indeed. Pressure from family? Needing an escape? Who knows?

"Don't know," he finally answered, which was both a lie and a truth. "But since we are interrogating each other, it's my turn to ask some questions."

"How was *that* an interrogation?"

Leo shrugged. "I just wanted a change of subject."

"Way to be vague."

"Hush," Leo said, mentally opening the list of questions he'd accumulated for her over the last few weeks. "What's with the rat?" Not what he meant to ask but the question burned in his mind.

"I used to work at an animal shelter as my first job. She was there for as long as I was and when I quit, I took her with me. I didn't have money for adoption papers so I just...you know...took her. No one cared. They were probably relieved."

"Wow, your first crime was rodent robbery."

Sage threw a piece of her tortilla at him. "Not my first crime—and no, I will not elaborate."

What a pity. "And she is a dog!" Sage yelled. "What kind? I don't know."

"Probably too afraid to find out and discover she's half—"

"Squash, attack!" Sage commanded.

The rat-dog mustered up the strength to stand from its spot beside Sage and let out a pathetic gurgle followed by the squeak of a fart. Then the poor animal promptly laid back down in the nest of blankets. (Or it simply died, Leo couldn't be sure.)

Sage looked down at the pathetic thing. "She used to be more ferocious, back when she had all her teeth."

"Next question," Leo said because he was not going to dignify that ridiculous claim with a response. "How much do you make?"

"Rude. How much do *you* make?"

"Hey! This is actually important. I need to know if there is a monetary threat at play here."

Sage shrugged. "I inherited the house." Well, that was news, wasn't he supposed to know this? Why wasn't it in the file? "Lily pays for all the travel expenses and tech I need to go to the events they want me to. Plus, a stipend of like two grand a month. Plus, random income from streaming. I think I make a percentage of merch sales. It goes into my savings account."

"So, you're doing pretty well."

Sage nodded. "LilyTech really made the difference. I used to get paid from George but now…"

"Tell me about that. Did he leave you the house? What did you do for him? Was he your grandpa? Is that why everything in here looks…"

"Well loved?"

"I was going to say old as hell." Because yes, things looked well-loved but the decor? The art? It reeked of museum, gothic, but then there were flashes of pink everywhere. Quite the juxtaposition. A deep maroon wallpaper with a faded floral print that served as a backdrop for old paintings and vases really clashed with the green and yellow couches covered with pink and purple throw blankets.

Sage bit her lip and stood up. She grabbed their plates and walked to the kitchen, setting them loudly in the sink. Leo followed her.

Sage climbed onto the counter with surprising grace for someone wearing what were essentially clouds on her feet. She rummaged around a cabinet. "Tea?" she asked.

"I would rather die."

She shrugged like that wasn't the worst thing in the world and took the whistling kettle from the stove. She used loose-leaf tea, which was a classic sign of a tea snob.

Leo rolled his eyes.

Sage rolled her eyes.

They were going to get dizzy with this form of communication.

"Any family? Other than George?" He really didn't know much about his Subject and that was on him. He should have been creating a more complete profile instead of golfing with his dad and dodging his mom.

"No," she said, pouring something vanilla-y into a mug. "Just George. He was an antiques dealer. Mostly paintings and pottery. He came from Japan with some incredible things and made a name for himself. George always dreamed of going back but never did. He'd been collecting and selling for years. Then he got sick and I came into his life."

"As his nurse?"

"As his housekeeper actually. Then cook. Then his driver. Then a live-in helper and friend. He was a boss who turned into a friend who turned into family."

"Care to elaborate?"

"No. All you need to know is that he left me his home when he recently passed away." Sage grimaced.

"I'm sorry for your loss. So you were a companion for him?"

"That makes me sound like a dog."

Leo laughed. "You could use one of those."

"I have one!" Sage pointed at the pattern of Squash's face printed on her t-shirt.

It was Leo's turn to grimace. "A real one. A guard dog."

"I have you." She cocked her head and opened her mouth to sassy something but then closed it. Then it looked like she lost the mental battle and said it anyway. "Bark, mister watchdog. Rollover! Down. Leave it!"

Cheeky thing. "Funny. But I don't bark. I bite." Now why had he said that?

Sage's face reddened. Ah, so *that's* why he said it. Still

got that stupid boyish charm. Any quippy response was cut off by a loud *thud* and glass shattering.

9

SAGE

The glass shattered, Sage shrieked, and Leo bellowed, "Get down!" He hurled his body in front of Sage and pushed her behind him, reaching for a weapon in the back of his pants and cursing quietly. The sound of screeching tires followed after a heartbeat.

Was her heart beating wildly because of the adrenaline? Was it because of the piercing noise of brick hitting glass? Was it thundering in her chest because Leo stood inches away from her, his broad shoulders shielding her from the danger? Was she struggling to breathe because she was scared or because of something...else?

No. It was obviously the loud noise that spiked her adrenaline, not his large hands pulling her firmly, yet gently, behind him and shielding her from another incoming attack.

Most definitely the loud noise.

Sage straightened, trying to put on her logical "I'm not afraid" face.

She supposed the one good thing about having a bodyguard (other than the large hands and broad shoulders that could act as the occasional wall) was the fact that he acted like a personal assistant when things went south. He was the one who called the police and informed them of the brick going through her window. He was the one who chased a car down the street—barefoot, in his slacks and sweater, which was hilarious—and got a partial license plate number. He also coordinated getting a tow truck for her car.

The police took their sweet time coming over, surveyed the scene, took photos, drank some hot chocolate Leo had offered them, and spent hours taking her statement, then Leo's. The paperwork was tedious and she was reminded that she had done this song and dance just a few months ago. Couldn't they simply copy that report and change the dates?

After a moment of silence, Sage surveyed the broken glass strewn across the living room. Sage went to work cleaning up the mess, locating the brick that smashed the window—"Get out" written in red letters because what was a brick through a window without a threatening message on it? She cleaned while Leo used the guest bath to wash his muddy feet.

A glance at the clock told her it was nearing five in the morning. "Merry Christmas to me," she muttered to herself.

Leo emerged from the bathroom looking haggard and tired. "Everything looks to be in order. You know, other than the busted window and smashed mailbox they hit."

"Fantastic. Glad to know the Agency is doing a bang-up job of—"

"Who do you think threw it?" Leo asked.

"I don't know!" Sage snapped. She rubbed her temples and closed her eyes as she talked. *What on earth is happening?* "Isn't that what you're here for?"

"I am here to protect you, not to be your private investigator."

"Surely one of your cameras picked up on what happened."

Leo was already flipping through his phone, probably an app or something that held all the security footage.

"That's what's strange." Leo slammed the phone down. "I already explained it to the cops but the camera picked up *nothing.* It was like it was a ghost. No flicker, nothing. Just a still camera. The wind must have moved it. Or it shifted with the sagging gutters because the camera was showing a very clear video feed of the sky. I told the cop as much."

What good was having security if it didn't actually secure anything?

"How does it taste?" Sage asked.

"What?"

"Failure."

"Disgusting." He seemed to mean it. Or maybe his mouth always puckered that way.

"Huh. Very fancy cameras. So fun that you interrupted my day to set them up and they didn't even work." Sage's heart was thundering despite the hours gone by. She tried to play it cool. She was fairly certain she failed when her voice quivered on the last word.

"They work," Leo said, letting go of a long breath. "They are all working fine except the one we needed."

How had the evening gotten away from them? Had they really been up all night dealing with this?

"Pity." Sage poured herself a steaming mug of something full of chamomile and all the good "calm your nerve" herbs. "Well, as you can see, I am fine. You're fine. We're all fine. Police have the report. You can go." She just wanted to be alone to deal with this, not have this guy scrutinizing her every move. Not like she would sleep though, but it would be fun trying until the anxiety crept in and made her pace in circles.

Leo let out a bark of a laugh and it startled Sage. She jumped and spilled her tea. "That's your laugh? You sound like a seal. You should give people a warning so they don't jump out of their skin." She glared daggers at Leo.

"Very hypocritical of you to say considering your shrill voice could burst an eardrum. And you're not fine."

"I am not shrill!" Sage said shrilly.

Leo made a show of wincing at her. "Oh look, you called the rat with that whistle of a voice."

Sage gasped and sloshed the rest of her tea over the mug as she sprinted to the couch where Squash was determined to tumble down and look more like her name. "Caught her just in time," Sage said.

"Should have just let her fall. Put her out of her misery."

"Vet says she's fine. It's all just cosmetic, uh, issues." Among other problems, but he didn't need to know that.

"The word you are looking for is damage. Cosmetic damage. Disfigurement."

"She's always looked like this." Sage pet Squash and she let out another small squelch.

Leo looked at the animal with a mix of pity and wonder, which, to be fair, was acceptable considering by all accounts the pup should have crossed the rainbow bridge years ago.

Leo tapped the counter like he had just come to some sort of major resolution. "Tuck the animal in for the rest of the morning. You and I are going out for breakfast."

"No thank you." Some resolution.

"My treat. Christmas brunch—"

"At five in the morning?"

"Whatever. We can call it a business meeting then. We have things to discuss and I have a feeling you will be better behaved in a public space." He clapped his hands together, making a show of finding his keys. "I'm thinking of the Country club, my family has a membership to. They always had the best Christmas brunch. Their pancakes were to die for and I can't remember the last time I've been to the restaurant. And heck, my clubs are still in a locker. We could hit some balls."

"I said no."

"I said this is a mandated meeting. As per rule number eleven."

"This isn't a security risk."

Leo bent and picked up the brick from the floor. "Hi," he said in a high-pitched cartoonish voice, shaking the brick. "My name is Major. Major Security Risk."

She could feel her face going purple. "You are the worst!"

"See?" Leo said. "I highly doubt you would use a tone like that at The Valley Club. You'd hate to draw so much attention to yourself...which is ironic considering your streaming habit."

"The Valley?" So maybe he had found a bone to throw her. She hated that she sounded so eager but this was an elite club just twenty minutes out of town where all the big cheeses went. You couldn't even eat there unless you were a member and that probably cost more than her grocery budget for the year.

Leo nodded. "I love that place. Our family has a membership. Put on some clothes and let's go." He paused and stared her down. "*Real* clothes. No sweatpants. No jeans. This is Christmas after all. It's a nice place. Let's see if you can play the part."

"Of all the—"

"They have a tea collection that will blow your mind."

Sage snapped her mouth shut. "Fine." She stomped up the stairs and went through some mental gymnastics trying to figure out what to wear. She didn't want to go in overdressed or too underdressed. She supposed she would try to match Leo in his attire. He said he came from a Christmas Eve party last night when he picked her up. She still couldn't believe she'd been up all night with Leo Camaro.

This was *not* how she imagined her first "sleepover" with a boy to go.

She opted for a black skirt, tights, and a pair of very practical waterproof boots. A Christmas sweater paired with a raincoat also seemed reasonable. She tied her hair back with a clip into a faux updo. It looked like a mess but it was intentional. The girls would get it. Leo wouldn't but she didn't care. Her stomach grumbled.

"Wow, she does own more than just pajamas," Leo said.

She stomped down the porch steps, rolling her eyes at Leo as she went. "Just unlock your car."

"It's a 4Runner," Leo mumbled. "Because there is a difference between the little jalopy that looks inches from death, just like the rat, and my SUV."

"Whatever. Just show me how the heated seats work." Sage didn't even slam the door behind her, even though she was tempted to.

They rode to The Valley Club in silence.

Okay, so maybe—*just maybe*—breakfast was a good idea. As Sage ate another plate of pancakes (What? They were sourdough pancakes so they were healthy, maybe...) she felt herself relax a little.

"Okay so now that you are looking more human," Leo said. Sage gave him her best glare. "Never mind," Leo said, taking a drink of his fourth (fourth!) coffee. "You still look like a gremlin despite actually wearing real clothes for once, but you have food in your belly so I suppose I can begin my interrogation."

Sage scoffed, shifting under his eyes, scanning her from head to toe. "Knew you were Jekyll and Hyde. Good cop and bad cop."

"Exactly." She hated the self-satisfied smile he wore.

"Carry on," Sage said, refilling her cup of peppermint

tea. They were actually not the first people in the massive dining room despite the outrageously early hour. Apparently Christmas golf was popular and the hostess had squeezed them into a little table near a window overlooking the course after Leo sweet-talked her a bit. "I am probably going to have the same answers I gave to the cop, which I assume you already know due to all your research."

Leo shrugged. "I'd like to hear it from you. And I ask different questions."

"Whatever you say, Mr. Cop-Wannabe."

Clearly that irritated him. He bristled and his jaw clenched. "Who do you think is behind this?"

"Of all the questions," Sage grumbled. She sipped her tea unnecessarily loud and long. "I don't know."

"That's not an answer. Give me your best guess."

"Lily thinks it's someone not wanting me at the gaming competition."

"Okay, let's start there. Explain the competition to me."

Sage rolled her eyes. She had to stop doing that, it was giving her a headache. But she couldn't help it. The macho turd in front of her had something about him that induced excessive eye-rolling and there was nothing she could do about it. She would send him the bill for her migraine treatment later. "I'm sure it was in the file sent over to you. Or you can do your job and do a quick Google search to figure out that answer."

Leo stabbed at his bacon with unnecessary force. "I know what it is. But I'd like to hear it from your mouth. You have a unique perspective. The competition is being marketed as the top 25 ranked players fighting it out from ground zero for first place."

Sage scoffed. "In the most simplified terms, yes."

"So, simplify it in your own words."

"*Welkin Wall* wasn't that popular. It's been on the market for several years, but there were some glitches and bugs that people were too annoyed to deal with. And it's actually pretty hard. Most experienced gamers struggle with the mechanics at first. It's not a very beginner-friendly game, so yeah, the top players, really the top players in anything, are gonna be really good. Like playing professionally for years kind of good."

"And then there's you."

"I guess. I kind of came on the scene randomly. I found the game and really fell in love with it. I mostly liked cozy games, still do, but this one is just so fun and I got obsessed with it and before I knew it, I was ranking, which was apparently a big deal."

"Why was it a big deal?"

"Because the top people playing the game had been the top-ranked for years. It was strange. Normally there is movement and whatnot but not this game. The top ten rarely changed, and then I accidentally burst in there and my small gaming channel exploded, and in came this whole new influx of players to this game."

"You shook it up."

"I guess. I was just having fun. George liked to watch me play. Even tried it a few times." Sage couldn't tell if the lump in her throat was from fond laughter or tears she was holding back. Either way, she didn't want to show any kind of emotion to Leo. It felt too personal, and she wanted nothing more than to keep him at a distance.

She needed to get a grip.

What she really needed were more pancakes.

"How did those top ten players react when you busted through the ranks?"

Sage shrugged. "Like normal sore losers, I guess. Like it ignited a new passion for the game, which only made me enjoy it more. I like competition in that way. So, the ranks were constantly changing and I was having a great time. I guess a lot of people were having fun watching too because the biggest gaming host created this event and I was invited along with everyone else."

"Any particular player you think could be a threat?"

Sage laughed. "They're all men with a decent platform. They all scare me."

"Elaborate."

"They can insinuate a lot about me and their fans will believe it. I don't have that kind of power over guys."

"Okay..." Leo looked completely confused. Typical boy. Was she going to have to spell it out for him?

"Okay, so if a nude leaked of me and a nude leaked of Rizzo, I'd be forced to make a public apology because someone else violated my privacy and stole my images, but Rizzo would be applauded for his boldness, he'd be able to laugh it off."

"Do you have nudes floating around out there?"

"No!" Sage shuddered. "But the fact that you just assumed I did is *some* of the prejudice female players are hit with, especially with the new wave of AI fakes."

"I don't need all those looks. I am a feminist, women deserve equal pay and opportunity and you've got it."

"Yes, but I get sexually harassed every time I try to do my job."

That made Leo shut up. "Yeah, I did see that."

"See what?" Sage asked, suddenly embarrassed.

"I watched your stream the other night. Some of the comments were...intense."

"And vile, disgusting, and rude."

"Yeah," Leo said, rubbing the back of his neck.

"I have some moderators that jump into the chat and can remove those comments when I can't, but some still slip through."

"But they are just comments. Stupid people. Stupid guys who live in their mother's basement with nothing better to do. Is there someone out there that you think could take it further?"

Sage thought for a long minute. "Crickets might. I mean, he is all talk, because, well, that's all he can do through a computer screen I guess, but he's the most vulgar. He's also been accused of cheating so I guess he has a lot to prove during this competition."

"But he doesn't know where you live?" Leo asked.

"Theoretically, no one should."

Leo sighed. "And yet a brick went through your window. Twice."

Sage gripped her mug. It still sent shivers down her spine. Someone was outside her window. It was creepy. "Yeah. So, what went wrong with the cameras?" Time to turn the tables.

"Regular technical issues. It was only one camera,

unfortunately, it was the one we needed. Nothing fishy other than high winds and unfortunate timing." Despite his nonchalant words, his shoulders tensed, his lips thinned, and a crease formed between the eyebrows.

"So, you aren't an iPad kid after all?" Sage laughed more at herself than anything, but she had been quite annoyed that the first ten minutes of their breakfast consisted of Leo just fiddling with a tablet. Not that she wanted to talk, but *good grief,* the tech addiction really did span all generations now. Then she had to laugh at herself because she probably spent more time in online worlds than in real life.

Still, it was rude at breakfast.

He pursed his lips and clenched his jaw again. Maybe that's why it had always looked so chiseled. Leo Camaro had been a very angry teenager. Made sense he was equally frustrated as an adult. People don't just stumble into peace. "Let me do my job so you can do yours. Do you have a boyfriend?"

"Wouldn't that be in the file too?"

"People lie."

"I don't lie," Sage lied.

"If you want to sell it, you have to use your eyes. Don't look away. Actually believing your lie would help too."

"Ugh, whatever. No boyfriend. Just a bunch of friends. Some local, some at the college like an hour away." She made sure to keep eye contact this time because she wasn't totally lying. There was a guy. Jason. He was a quick fling that never went anywhere because they connected online and did *not* have any chemistry in the real-life setting. He didn't take the hint very well and it took a very strong phone call from Sage basically saying "Dude, there's no way I can go out with you again" for him to stop calling her. But even now he still hit her up.

Leo had ordered more bacon and eggs and Sage followed suit and decided to see if she could stuff in a few more pancakes. Leo looked cool despite his disheveled appearance. An effortless sort of style with slightly messy hair, clothes tailored to him but with an undone quality, like the top two buttons of his shirt popped open—What? She wasn't looking, they were right at eye level, was she not supposed to notice the base of his neck or something? —and leather shoes that were sure to cost more than a month's wages but simple and classic. Sage couldn't help but feel self-conscious. She had dark circles under her eyes that could make a raccoon jealous.

They ate in silence and when Leo paid ("I insisted we go here") he decided to take a small detour to the driving range. Moments later a basket of golf balls and his clubs were delivered to their spot.

"What are we doing here?" Sage said, looking out at the green rolling hills. She crossed her arms over her chest. "Are you just gonna hit some balls or something?"

"That is precisely what I am afraid of. I have decided for this next conversation, instead of giving you the urge to whack away at my, uh, bits, I figured I'd give you a different target." He handed her a golf club. "It's called a club. People use it for hitting golf balls, not would-be intruders."

Sage blushed, remembering how she must have looked running down the stairs with the club acting like it was a sword. "I don't really want to hit things right now."

"We have more to discuss and I figure it would be safer for me to give you a target to swing at instead of just me."

So he could read minds now? "What are we talking about that makes you think I need some sort of violent outlet?"

"First off, golfing should not be violent. It's an art. Second, it's time to go over some rules. Get a plan in order," Leo said.

Sage's stomach dropped. She didn't want things to change. She took the club and swung at a ball, missed, tried again, missed, and finally hit it about two feet in front of her. "Carry on," she said through gritted teeth, already lining up another ball for what was likely going to be a sad sort of slaughter. Why was this so hard?

"First thing's first," Leo said, clearing his throat and taking on a more serious tone—and three giant steps backward. "Things are going to change."

"What are you talking about?"

Whack. Miss. *Whack.* Miss. *Whack. Whack. Whack.*

"Try putting your hands closer together," he said. "Quit holding the club like a baseball bat."

Whack. Miss. *Whack.* Hit. Wow, at least a few feet of distance this time. Pretty good considering she thought she may have dislocated a shoulder because she was swinging so hard. Maybe Leo had been on to something. It was much easier to tackle uncomfortable topics when she could hit something at the same time.

"Nice," Leo said. "How do you feel about four-star hotels?"

Panic gripped Sage's stomach. "What do you mean?" *Whack. Whack.* She tried to ignore the stares of other actual golfers.

"I mean we need to get you out of the house for a while, maybe even town. Let things cool off."

Whack. Hit. "I'm not leaving my home."

"Be reasonable."

"I am!" *Whack. Whack. Whack. Whack. Whack. Whack. Whack. Why wasn't she hitting anything?!*

"Quit abusing the poor club and use your words. Tell me why you are so gung-ho about staying put," Leo said.

"You can't be 'gung-ho' about something if you want to stay put."

Leo just stared. "When I told you to use your words, I should have been more specific and told you that I wanted you to be *useful* with your words."

"Ugh!" *Whack. Whack. Whack. Whack.* Kick. She faced Leo. "I just lost someone who was pretty much my only family and I can't just pack up and decide to live out of a hotel for a few months. Look, it's taken me years to feel comfortable *anywhere*. We moved around a lot as kids. Literally a new place every few months. Usually left town when the rent couldn't be paid. This is the longest I've ever lived in one place. I'm just not ready to let that go."

Leo took in a deep breath, pausing for a moment and just as Sage turned to obliterate another golf ball, he whispered, "I'm sorry for what I did."

It stopped Sage cold.

"No. No, you're not," she said. *Whack.* She didn't want

to give him room to talk. She faced him again, vowing not to break eye contact. "You're only feeling guilty right now because I gave you a *sliver* of honesty and you didn't like what you heard because you realized you might have something to do with my problems. Save your apologies for when you mean it." *Whack. Whack.* Hit. *Whack.* Hit. That memory haunted her and he was just a living reminder. And now he wanted a free pass? A reason to "forgive and forget" and move on? Absolutely not.

"Sage I—"

"Don't." Sage's voice gave no room for argument. She was low and firm and that one word was all it took for Leo to shed his false concern and go back into business mode.

"Alright, well, I can see why you don't want to move. Plus, I assume your gaming setup isn't exactly mobile. And I don't know if there is a hotel around that would allow a rat to come with us."

"She is a dog! She's just been through some stuff." At least they could at least go back to arguing like normal.

He ignored her. "I'll follow up on the plates of the unknown car. I'll get more cameras by the driveway, the company will be happy to sign off on that. Oh, and I'm moving in."

Sage thought she handled the news brilliantly because she only screamed "Like hell you are!" instead of picking up the bucket of golf balls and hurling them at him like she wanted to.

"What is wrong with you?" Leo hissed, making a polite "I'm sorry this woman is unhinged" gesture to the few golfers staring.

"What is wrong with me?" Sage scoffed. "What is

wrong with you? How can you think that I would accept that? How can you think that I would appreciate having my space invaded, especially by *you*."

"Still holding grudges?" Leo rolled his eyes. "Your safety is on the line. Grow up!"

"You're the one with the fake apology!"

"Look, I said I was sorry, what more do you want?"

"For you to actually mean it! Now leave me alone."

"What are you doing?" Leo asked, stepping in front of her, but the phone was already to her ear.

"Calling Lily."

"She isn't going to do anything. There is literally no one else that is available to do this job at the company."

"Of course, you would say that. At least let me hear it from Lily's mouth."

And Lily let her have it. It was rude to call early Christmas morning complaining about the fact that Lily had hired the "best agency out there" and she told Sage under no uncertain terms that she was not to give the agency a hard time. "They are the best, Sage, and I will not allow you to walk around with a target on your back. End of discussion."

Sage hung up the phone, defeated. Still, maybe she could win this war of attrition with Leo. "Please," she said. "I'll follow your rules perfectly. Please. I don't want you in my space."

Leo considered this for a moment. "Every rule? Perfectly?" He ran a hand through his perfectly messy hair, starting to look as exasperated as Sage felt. It was a small comfort to know he was a human capable of emotions and not a total sociopath.

Sage nodded. "Everything."

"Then fine. I won't stay at your place—"

"Thank you—"

"But if there is another incident of *any* other kind, then I will be forced to move in. It's not up to me, it is the company's protocol and I'm not about to get fired to spare your feelings."

"Good to know some things never change," Sage mumbled.

"Yeah, I can see that. Do we have a deal?"

"Deal."

Unfortunately, part of that deal was allowing Leo access to her home anyway, but at least it was just to set up certain security measures and patrol. She was exhausted and as soon as she got home she bid Leo farewell and went up to her room to try and sleep, ignoring Leo's cry of, "I'm still going to be around today you know, to set up the cameras, so don't attack me with a stick."

How dare he accuse her of holding a grudge? The wound was old and scarred over now. So why did she feel like it was starting to bleed?

10

LEO

Okay, so that could have gone a million different ways. Instead, Leo just had to open his big fat mouth and apologize. And she called him on his crap.

But Leo *was* sorry, but more like sorry that it happened. More like an "I'm sorry I accidentally forgot to bring a side to the potluck" kind of sorry. The sorry to make the apologizer feel better. Instead, he felt worse. Much. Much worse.

So, he did what any self-respecting man would do: he dove into work with a furious passion and tried to block out any emotions trying to creep in.

He was calm. He was rational. He was detached. He was a professional and shouldn't have his stomach in knots over this.

He apologized and that's that. It's up to her. It was no longer his problem. Except *she* was his problem. A little tricky task that was turning out to be more of an issue every day.

Leo shook his head and got to work. He'd been complacent and she was put in danger because of it. Having a job so close to home, heck, in his hometown, had made him a little lax in his normal routines with Subjects. But to be fair, this was a different type of job. As much as he liked the idea of being home and spending time with family, this might be too much. It was definitely not worth the hassle of...emotions.

One phone call and it would all be over. In retrospect, there was so much hope in that thought.

Jenson answered on the first ring. "Leo! How's it going?"

"I'm gonna be blunt, Jenson. I can't do this job for you."

Jenson was notoriously no-nonsense but also fair. He might be willing to make some concessions. Maybe send out another guy. He could swap jobs with someone.

"Look," Leo said. "I have a history with this Subject. I didn't know it beforehand. I guess she changed her surname. It's been years but it has been creating some issues."

"Have you been creating the issues?"

"What? No," Leo said. If anything, he considered himself rather gracious considering everything. He even apologized! "She's just been emotional and difficult."

"So, this job is too hard. Is that what I'm hearing?"

"No!" *Yes.* "It's just that I think she would be much more comfortable with someone else. Someone like Tony or something. Maybe even Lisa."

"Comfortable?" Jenson took on a surprised tone. It made Leo worry. "If you wanted to make sure she was comfortable, you could take her to a spa. Maybe you should have joined some hospitality job if you are so concerned with making people *comfortable.* You want a job at a hotel, Leo?"

Leo sighed. "No Jenson, I don't want a job at a hotel."

Jenson laughed. "Good, because I'd hate to lose you." He took on a more serious tone. "Look, I know this isn't your favorite type of job. I can look into switching you with Arnaz, but his job is probably worse than what you have. He's on the road with a scummy Politician trying to outrun some domestic violence charges."

Leo cringed. Those jobs were the worst. Not only was it notoriously difficult to protect someone on the road, but when you were absolutely disgusted and appalled with your Subject, it was pretty hard to be willing to protect them from what they deserved. At least Sage hadn't done anything to warrant the vandalism. Leo sighed. "Never mind. I can work through this."

"Thought as much. Glad to hear it. I specifically put you on the job. because I knew this would take some more tech skills. Just focus on getting your job done and it'll fly by."

"Yes, sir."

And that was the end of Leo's fanciful thought of getting out of this job. Leo finished setting up the new cameras and said hello to Filbert who was busy walking in the breeze (only wearing boots).

"Howdy partner," Filbert said. He also carried an umbrella and used it like a cane. "How goes it with our Miss Moon in there? I didn't think she'd be taking on another job so soon. What ails you? Arthritis like George? Just plain lonely?"

Leo straightened the camera and then looked up at Filbert (working very hard to maintain solid eye contact so he wouldn't accidentally see the dangly bits flapping in the breeze). "I'm not a patient or client or whatever. I am just here to help Miss Moon out while she gets ready for a gaming competition."

"Pretty funny, all that stuff."

"What's funny?" Leo asked.

Filbert stared at a bird as it flapped by while he talked. "Miss Moon is just as much a recluse as George was. They really liked each other. They went on walks often. Never did understand why they decided to be so bundled up though. They needed to let things breathe to get the full benefits of an outdoor walk."

"Right," Leo said. "But what's funny?"

"Oh, just that Miss Moon is still there. I thought George's son would be in town to help pack things up. He always seemed like a motivated young man. Figured he'd sell it or something. He's been eying that place for years."

The hair on Leo's neck stood up. "Eying it for years?"

"Fil?" someone yelled. "Fil! You out there again?"

Filbert gave Leo a lopsided grin, twirled his umbrella, and took off.

How was everyone so nonchalant about this?

Leo got a lovely view of Filbert's backside while a new thought crept into his mind. Why hadn't Sage mentioned George's son before?

Leo pushed down his rising frustration. The cold

December air sent a chill down his spine. He looked down at his rather strange attire. A button-down shirt from last night's Christmas Eve party, khaki slacks, and his work boots he'd stashed in his car.

Leo walked inside and pulled out his phone, checking his email for a response to the plates he'd sent in. He plopped on the soft couch, jumping back to a stand when he felt something under his bum. He pulled away the blanket, hoping he hadn't just flattened the rodent. It was just another wadded-up blanket. How many did she have floating around this place? He was in serious danger of being suffocated every time he walked into this mini-mansion by the blankets and throws she had stashed all over the place.

He sat again and threw a blanket over his lap. Even a man got cold outside on a December afternoon and occasionally needed (he glanced at the blanket) a ladybug-patterned knit throw to keep him warm and happy.

He pulled up the email. The news was less than ideal. It was a simple rental car. He made a mental note to head over to the rental agency to try and get lucky and get a name attached to the car. Some agencies were painfully by the book and protected the privacy of their clients too well. Others would bend the rules a bit to help a woman in distress. Leo was hoping this company was the latter.

There really wasn't much to go on with this case. Leo had to stop his train of thought and back it up. This wasn't a case to be solved. He didn't need to find out who was behind this. He just needed to make sure Sage Moon was safe. But the best way he could ensure her safety was to figure out who was behind this. Alright then, let the sleuthing commence. He, not for the first time since starting this job, felt a bit like Sherlock Holmes. Scratch that. He was more like a Hardy boy, stumbling upon a mystery where nothing made sense and the main character was insufferable.

Seriously. He had *apologized.* Why couldn't she see that he was sorry? He needed to get a handle on the "having emotions" situation. He apologized. She refused to accept it. Time to move on.

The trees still held on to a handful of leaves, refusing to let go of the October season. He half forgot it was Christmas and expected to find jack-o-lanterns and pumpkins littering the porch.

Speaking of, the rat-dog, Pumpkin, Squash, Gourd, or whatever it was called was busy pacing the top of the stairs looking pathetic. More pathetic than usual.

It was shaking and Leo assumed the sad wheezing coming from the rat was a whine. He felt bad for the thing. Maybe it was hungry? Must be hard to eat while missing so many teeth. Leo couldn't ignore the poor thing and stomped up the stairs to retrieve it.

The rat-dog allowed Leo to pick her up, and when Leo tried to feed her some cheese from the fridge. The rat-dog couldn't look more disinterested. Instead, it looked forlornly at the back door.

"Alright, Scruffy, I'll take you out."

The rat-dog bolted out the door (as much as the ancient thing could—it was more like a hobble with a tail wag) and tripped down the back steps into the yard where she quickly did her business.

"Squash!" Sage's shriek made Leo jump.

"Good grief, woman. Your voice could cut glass!"

"Shut up!"

Leo made a show of glancing at the windows to make sure they were still in one piece. "What's your issue? I was just letting the thing out to the bathroom."

Sage ignored him and stumbled down the steps with as much grace as the rat-dog (which was none). She wildly flapped a blanket she had pulled from around her shoulders and waved it in the air, screeching "Shoo, shoo!"

"Is it back?" another voice asked. Of course, it was Filbert in all in finery. "See it?"

Hadn't Leo already seen enough?

"Not yet!" Sage answered as if talking with a naked man holding an umbrella in her backyard was totally normal. "But I didn't get a chance to look before this guy let her out!"

"Bad move, mister," Filbert said seriously. Filbert opened the rainbow umbrella and joined Sage in flapping around in the yard. "Is she done?" Filbert asked, pointing to the rat-dog with his boot.

"I think so," Sage said, scooping up the scruffy dog in her arms. "Thanks, Fil. Better move on before Dennis finds you. Kind of hard to miss the umbrella."

Filbert closed the umbrella and tipped an imaginary hat at the dog and then at Sage. "Right-o!"

Sage stomped past Leo who was glued to his spot on the porch. What in the otherworldly ritual did he just witness?

"Care to explain what that song and dance was about?" Leo asked, following Sage inside.

She rounded on him and stomped her foot, which was quite the juxtaposition of her carefully petting the rat-dog between its ears. "There are hawks out there, big ones. She held her hand over the animal's crooked ears as if to censor the next words from her dog. "Just last week the old neighbor down the street lost her cat to one of the big birds. Up and took it away. So, excuse me for caring!"

"You don't need to be afraid, no animal would even think of eating something so diseased."

"Go away." Sage spun on her heel and marched to the front living room, depositing the decrepit thing on the couch while she went to light the fire. Turns out "lighting" was now a switch and she flicked on the fireplace.

"And here I thought you were going to have to work for something."

Sage rolled her eyes. "It's gas."

"Well excuse you."

"The fireplace, idiot! It's a gas fireplace. And I *do* work."

Leo walked to the kitchen, making himself right at home. He hated tea, but he thought he saw some hot chocolate packets hiding somewhere in the cabinet during his earlier raiding. He heated some water while he talked. "Sure, you work, if you call monetizing that face of yours work."

"Here we go again." Sage joined him in the kitchen, clearly ready for a fight. Good. He was getting antsy and was more than a little perturbed about her conveniently forgetting to mention that George had a son who wanted the house.

Sage hopped up on the counter and pointed a finger

at him. "I work hard. I worked hard for George and I figured out how to get my little brand set up myself and actually make a go of it. You're just jealous."

"Jealous that I don't have days to sleep away and a game to rot my brain."

"You wouldn't be saying that if you knew the first thing about the game."

Leo crossed his arms. "I'm not here to argue if Mario or Luigi is better."

"Luigi."

"I agree," Leo said. He pulled a mug from the cabinet. Why did one person need so many mugs?

"And I don't sleep the day away." She pointed to a tin. "Pull that down, will you?"

He reached to the top shelf and pulled out the tin. It smelled of citrus and sweetness. It smelled of Sage. The person. Leo sighed. "You have slept more since I've taken you on as a Subject than you have been awake. And get off the counter, that's rude."

"So is insulting someone's line of work."

Was she raised in a barn or something? "It's still bad manners," Leo mumbled.

"So is not offering a person a cup."

Leo rolled his eyes and pulled out another mug. Since when did he become so juvenile? He needed to be the professional here. So, like a gentleman, he mixed up his hot chocolate and sipped it loudly before asking, "Care for some hot chocolate?" He really thought he did well sounding civil.

"Tea sounds lovely," Sage said in a tone that did not indicate that it was a lovely idea at all.

Leo stepped out of the way of the stove. "It's all yours. Once you have your beverage, meet me in the living room. We need to have another chat."

Sage grunted in what Leo decided to interpret as a "sure thing" and he went to wait by the fireplace, hoping her tea would cool enough not to scald him should she decide to chuck it at his face.

Eventually, she curled up on the couch next to the snoozing animal. At least Leo hoped it was sleeping, the rat-dog could very well have died and they could both be none the wiser considering how closely the animal toed the line between life and death.

"What is this about?" Sage asked.

"Why didn't you tell me George had a son?" Leo asked.

She sipped her tea, unfazed. "George doesn't have a son."

"That's not true. Filbert said—"

"Let me stop you right there. Filbert has lost all his marbles and he spends most of his days looking for them. George doesn't have a son. Doesn't really have any family. He has a nephew somewhere. He was supposed to come out last year when George was going downhill but he never did. I think his name is Soto or something."

"Could he be behind the vandalism?"

Sage shrugged.

"Very helpful," Leo deadpanned.

"What?" Sage asked. "I'm not sure what to tell you. I doubt Soto knew much about George. They rarely talked. George had a brother, but he passed away like a decade or more ago. Everyone is still in Japan. They run a glass manufacturing plant, I think. I really don't know who is behind this. I genuinely think it's just some high school kids doing this crap on a dare or maybe they know what I do and think it's funny to shake me up."

Leo downed the rest of his hot chocolate. "On that note, I'll be off. I have a car rental to track down."

He stood and was on the verge of passing right by where she sat when a sudden urge came over him. She was nervous. Clearly not sleeping. Anxiety tinged her features.

He paused next to her and put a hand lightly on her shoulder.

"What are you doing?" Sage asked, staring at his hand.

"I am attempting some sort of reassuring gesture."

Sage snorted. "I'm fine." She looked up at him. It was a platonic type of touch. Less than that. And yet, she didn't move his hand.

"You're safe here. I have a lead with the rogue rental car, and nothing is going to happen to you."

She blinked quickly and looked out the window. "Just let me know what you find." This time she took his hand and pushed it from her shoulder. "Consider me reassured."

Only now *he* wasn't. Was he seriously so touch-starved that the barest skin-to-skin contact made him erupt in goosebumps?

For a moment he allowed himself to dwell on the feeling of her hand on his.

. . .

A few days later Leo found himself in Sage's shower (the *guest* shower). He'd come over early, waking Sage in the process (oops), and declared he would be cleaning out her gutters. They were expecting heavy rain, and he was rather concerned the gutters, filled with leaves, would flood and ruin the cameras. It was a decent reason. Really, he was just bored out of his mind and needed a job to do. However, that backfired when the dilapidated gutters collapsed, drenching him in the sludge of rotting leaves. He must have looked pitiful because Sage offered him a towel and ushered him into the guest shower, only choking on her laughter twice.

His mind wandered to Sage as he showered, as it often did, and he had to slap himself back to reality. She was his *Subject*. The Job. The Assignment that would get him out of dealing with nepo-baby protection jobs and into the White House. Or congress. Or wherever he wanted to be. *Wherever that was...*

He had a full lather of soap in his hair—and, therefore, his eyes—when an ear-shattering scream pierced through the sound of the running water.

Quick as lightning, Leo sprinted out of the shower, slipped, and skidded into the doorjamb (that was going to leave a bruise) then stormed into the kitchen to find Sage bent over the kitchen sink, running water over her bloody hand.

"What happened?" Leo asked, searching for both a weapon and intruder.

"I cut myself bad!" Sage cried. She looked at him and her eyes went wider. "Why are you naked!"

He covered himself with the nearest object—her pink teapot resting on the counter. "Covered" was a generous term. He did the best he could. It was an average-sized teapot and Leo prided himself on being well above—the rest of his thought was cut off by his eyes burning as soap dripped into them. "I thought you were dying!" he said.

"I might be!" Clearly the whole naked man with soapy hair in front of her wasn't as big of a concern as her hand. To be fair, Leo assumed she had seen quite the share of naked man in the form of Filbert. And Leo couldn't help but be a little perturbed that Sage didn't at least give him an ounce more attention. He was not one to compare, usually, but come on! Him versus Filbert? There was much more to appreciate and she clearly didn't have a chance to admire his chiseled chest and toned traps.

He traded the teapot for a hand towel and peered into the sink.

"You might need a stitch or two but it's not that bad," Leo said. It was all talk. It was a gory mess likely in need of six or eight stitches. A slice along her pointer finger down to her palm. No need to panic her more.

She turned to Leo, face whiter than snow. "I'm going to pass out." And then she did.

Luckily he caught her, mostly, trying to guide her to the floor, maintaining the sliver of dignity the micro towel gave him before giving up. He used it to wrap around the sliced finger. The cut was deep and went through her nail. He laid her head gently on the floor and elevated her hand, knowing she'd come to in any moment.

She did about four seconds later. "Why are you

naked!?" she whisper-yelled, darting from his chest hovering over her to her hand which he also held over her.

"I was showering!" he seethed. "Which one normally does naked. Sorry my package has distracted you from the obvious issue—"

"We don't need to talk about your little issue right now, we have bigger problems to worry about!"

Little issue? Bigger problems? "How dare you—"

"The blood is soaking through the towel. I've cut my finger off, haven't I?" She was going ghostly white again.

"It's still firmly attached," Leo said, still not over the whole "little issue" comment.

"I'm going to pass out again!"

She did.

The next time she regained consciousness the scene was exactly the same, only this time Leo took control.

"Clearly you have an issue with blood." She turned green at the word blood. "I swear on everything holy and good if you throw up on me right now I—"

She passed out again. When she came to (seven seconds later) her eyes darted from his face (still hovering over her—his slightly above average package hidden from view at this point) and the blood-soaked towel wrapping her finger (that was still firmly attached).

"Don't look at the blood. It's a gnarly scratch but a few stitches and you'll be good as new."

She nodded and after some coaching, Leo managed to get Sage sitting up, back against the cupboard. He kept her occupied with applying pressure to her finger and he ran to the bathroom, not bothering to take a moment to find another towel to hide his backside as he sprinted from view. He could already feel the soap drying on his neck and shoulders. He rummaged around the drawers in the guest room and pulled on the first pair of jeans and tee shirt he could find and managed to even find a pair of socks. He was putting them on, bouncing on one foot when he slid back to the kitchen. "Still conscious?"

Sage nodded feebly, looking a lovely shade of green. "I don't feel so good."

"You don't look so good."

"Rude."

He hauled her up to her feet and walked her to the door (but not before grabbing the empty teapot on the end of the counter on his way out). The ride to the ER was fairly calm considering Sage had a total meltdown.

"I'm going to barf."

"Here." He thrust the teapot he had been clutching into her good hand. "Aim well."

"This is my favorite teapot! I can't—" Oh but she did.

She closed the lid like it was a dainty little thing once she had finished expelling her guts. "I'll never be able to look at this the same way." She held it at a distance as if it were going to explode.

He wanted to ask if her new aversion to that particular teapot was due to the contents it now held or the fact that it had been a poor shield to his dangly bits earlier but he wisely kept his mouth shut.

Sage still looked a lot like her name, though more pale than green as the minutes ticked by. Once they arrived, he got her checked in and back with a doctor in under five minutes. A bloody towel was usually a fast pass to the front of any line.

"They're going to stab me," Sage whispered.

"You did a great job of doing that yourself."

"With a needle!"

"I guess you could call it that. Doctor said six stitches and you'll be good as new. She's even going to numb it for you. Isn't that nice?" Leo held her arm in his more to ensure she didn't bolt than anything else.

Sage looked ready to pass out again. "With a needle."

He nodded. "That's generally how it goes."

"I hate needles," the last word came out more like a squeak.

"I know," Leo said. He held her good arm and stroked the top of her hand with his thumb. Were hands allowed to be this soft?

"What if I just pass out and then they do it when I'm not looking?"

"Or here's an idea, you can just *not look.*"

She was a kaleidoscope of shades of green and white. Like a watermelon on shrooms.

"I can't do this," she said, staring at the wound and breathing fast. She was going to pass out again at this rate.

Leo cupped her face with both of his hands and pulled her face toward his. "This is going to sound absolutely crazy, but have you ever tried staring at someone for more than a minute? Not a staring contest, blink as much as you want, but truly staring at them. No broken eye contact."

She took a deep breath. "Why on earth would I have *ever* done that?"

Leo shrugged. "It was a team-building exercise thing a year or two back." She tried to pull away and look at the finger again, but he held her face firmly in his hand. "Literally no one in the office could make it more than ten seconds without breaking down and laughing."

"This is not a laughing matter!" she whisper-yelled. "I am about to be harpooned!"

"Like I said, you already did that to yourself."

She shook her head. "This is different."

"Fun fact: the detachable part of a harpoon is called a lily iron. Kinda funny right? You can tell Lily that."

"I don't need this right now!" She looked at her finger. "I'm dying."

"Back to my suggestion, the staring contest is a distraction. The goal was to stare at each other for five minutes just to show that we can handle uncomfortable situations and not react. Sounds easy until you're doing it. So that's what we are going to do right now. The first person to break eye contact has to take the other out for breakfast for a week."

She looked momentarily shocked before her new resolve kicked in. "You wouldn't do that."

"Just give your hand over to the nice doctor lady and don't you dare break eye contact with me."

Sage gave her hand to the nice doctor lady who looked like she could do this in her sleep. She offered to count them down. "Three, two, one," she said before getting to work, likely thinking the pair shared a single neuron between them and it had clearly taken an early vacation.

Staring at Sage was uncomfortable. It was strange. It was fun. It was beautiful. Her eyes were a dark brown so deep he struggled to find her pupils. When she furrowed her brows and looked as if she were going to break, he threatened her with "Think of breakfast" and she got serious again.

It was stupid and it was dumb and she only winced a handful of times, but Leo brought her back to reality with words of encouragement like "french toast" and "bacon" and "cinnamon rolls."

They didn't even make it five minutes because two minutes later the doctor said, "All done." She left the room muttering, "Great, now I'm hungry."

The nurse gave Sage and Leo instructions on healing and how the stitches would fall out a week or so down the road and things would all be fine.

Leo considered staying at the ER because he was anything but fine. How could he casually ask the doctor "Is it normal to get all lightheaded and stupid in the presence of a beautiful woman?" or "Is it possible to leave part of your brain behind in a dream?" because he was all floaty again.

But food beckoned them and they stopped and ate their fill of pancakes, then game-planned on how Sage would ease into playing again after the swelling in her hand went down. She spent the rest of the day chatting with Jared and Lily and planning further, but not before giving Leo a quick (but full contact) hug and a heartfelt thank you. Without breaking eye contact. Leo nodded and said, "No problem." He watched her retreat up the stairs where she would no doubt be sequestered away in her office for the rest of the day.

Leo went to Tess's in hopes of a nap. He needed to find the piece of his brain he must have left in a dream because his mind was definitely floating around some-where between worlds and not at all here on Earth where it should be.

11

SAGE

The following week and a half passed in relative peace and quiet, post-hand-slicing incident. Oh, and she had seen Leo naked. *That* opened a can of crazy in her brain. She couldn't look at him without picturing *all* of him.

Sage slept horribly, her streaming the only thing keeping her motivated (that, and the intense sense of impending doom and failing at the competition). She spent a lot of time catnapping on the couch in front of the fireplace with Squash before an inevitable—now predictable—bad dream would yank her from sleep.

Overall, things were fine.

Which was why she nearly had a heart attack when she stomped down the stairs, early one morning, to find Leo in her kitchen, ransacking the cupboards.

She grabbed the nearest weapon and screeched like a banshee. A very normal reaction for someone to have, upon finding an unexpected pest in their home.

"What are you doing?" she asked, in her best banshee wail. She held up her umbrella—the aforementioned weapon—and shook it at him. "I could have killed you!"

"If you managed to stab me with that thing, I'd deserve the slow and painful death. However, since you have toothpicks for arms, I'm sure I could stop you. Or any other intruder."

Sage was working to calm her racing heart. "So, you admit it?" she seethed, stomping past him to loudly slam every cabinet door he'd left open.

"Admit what?" Leo asked.

"That you're an intruder."

"Nope." He hopped up on the counter like he owned the place. (Now, who had bad manners?)

And he had her cookies—*her* cookies—in his hand, munching away. "I just came in to give you a little surprise, since you decided to give *me* a little surprise."

"Those are mine." She snatched the sleeve from him to find that he had "generously" left her two Thin Mints. She stuffed them in her mouth.

"And, what surprise did I *graciously* bestow upon you?" She began her morning tea ritual.

"That little calendar surprise."

Sage froze. So, he *had* noticed. Well, shoot. She supposed it was a small comfort seeing that he still checked in on her instead of spending his days golfing away. Okay, so she checked his location occasionally. She was curious about what he did all day.

Leo made a show of wagging a finger at her like she was some naughty kid. "Didn't think I'd notice, did you?"

"I guess," Sage mumbled. "But it's not really a big deal."

Leo stood and made a beeline for her secret stash of cookies. How on earth did he find them? They were hidden in the backup teapot. She snatched them away before he had a chance to open them.

"Are you ever full?"

The mountain shrugged. "This is research. You can tell a lot about a person based on what they keep in their kitchen."

"And what have you deduced?" Sage wished she would take back the jab as soon as the words exited her mouth because Leo turned to her with a strange look in his eye, the look of someone solving a problem.

"You have a sweet tooth, obviously, but you are a seasonal girlie."

"Girlie?"

Leo physically shuddered. "Been spending too much time with Tess. Anyway, you hoard the seasonal snacks. Peppermint from Christmas. I even see some Pumpkin remains from October hidden away. I bet if I look hard I'd find some pumpkin spice latte mix or syrup or something."

Sage rolled her eyes and poured the boiling water into her tea, mentally making a note to find a better hiding spot for the pumpkin-spiced muffin mix and apple cinnamon syrup.

"Anyway, what do you want?" she asked.

"Unsubtle change of subject. I wasn't done yet." Leo grabbed a granola bar from the pantry and tore it open, resuming his post on the kitchen counter. "You like convenience food, but that doesn't always mean unhealthy. You like your frozen orange chicken and fried rice and those god-awful pizza rolls but you also like a prepackaged salad or a fresh one-pot meal. Easy. But you also hate driving in the snow and have tried meal delivery services, but you never liked those."

"How on earth could you tell all that?"

Leo shrugged. "Elementary. So why am I here? Ah yes, that little calendar update. I'm going with you."

"No."

"Not a request."

"I'll give you this whole package of Thin Mints if you don't go."

"Ah, negotiations. I like it. I accept." He grabbed the sleeve of thin mints she was holding and tore into them, shoving two into his mouth. "I can't believe you still have these. Don't they only sell them once a year? Oh, and I'm still going with you."

"You just said you accepted!" Sage snatched the cookies back and tossed a few in her mouth.

"Accepted the cookies, dear Subject. Don't negotiate with a terrorist."

"Should have known," Sage said. Well, the package was open, may as well finish them before they got stale. She dipped one in her tea and ignored Leo's horrified look. "Look, it's just a New Year's party. No big deal."

"New Year's was two weeks ago."

Sage shrugged. "Time is different in the online world I guess." In reality, there were too many scheduling conflicts for everyone with the whole new year and family obligations so The West Coast Streamer Showcase decided to host their annual meet and greet on January 18th. To tie it in, they had 18 different gaming-related companies showcasing their goodies and sponsored players (Sage and LilyTech included).

"Time is not a thing for you gaming type I guess."

"What's that supposed to mean?" Sage was not in the mood for this. She was actually looking forward to the event. She was finally going to meet some of the other gamers LilyTech sponsored, take some photos (which would get Jared off her back about curating content), and check out some new gear. There was an absolutely gaudy and unnecessary clicky purple keyboard about to hit the market and she *needed* it.

Leo went back to scouring the cupboards, clearly looking for something. "I just mean that you gaming folks have no regard for the hours of the world. You stream late, sleep in, you put last-minute things on the calendar. The rest of the world doesn't work like that and somehow there are enough delinquents out there to watch you and perpetuate this way of living." He closed the cupboard loudly. "Do you have *any* coffee in this place?"

"First you insult my line of work—"

"I did no such thing—"

"Then you demand coffee?"

Leo shrugged. "A man can hope. How's the hand?"

She was no longer wearing a bandage, the stitches had fallen out, and the bright scar was fading. "It's fine." She refused to look at him in case another flash of *all of him* decided to assault her mind. "And I refuse to have that bitter bean live in my house."

"You're like a bitter bean."

Sage threw up her hands. "I actually work hard, okay? Sure, the hours are weird but I think this disdain you have for my job stems from the fact that you don't actually *like* what you do and you are *jealous* that I actually found something I love to do and I get paid to do it."

"You're right on one count. I don't love this *particular* job. However, I do find great satisfaction in protecting people."

"You want to be needed, admit it."

Leo pursed his lips and turned away, scouring the fridge. "All I need right now is coffee. And an itinerary."

"Unsubtle change of subject but I am equally excited to get out of this conversation," *You rude and pompous person.* "So, I will send you the schedule of events. Luckily this one is in Portland so it'll just be a long day but nothing overnight."

"Those come later," Leo said, resuming the search of the fridge and now on his phone, presumably making additions to the calendar. "Like the big LilyTech conference in L.A."

"Right." She was also getting excited about that. The competition was looming overhead and she didn't feel totally prepared, but the grief was getting easier to deal with every day, and actually seeing people seemed to help. She had coffee with Tavy just the other day (she had texted Leo for that event and he deemed it safe enough to go alone) and Sage felt, dare she say, better? She felt more human. Less of a toad sitting on a log watching the world go by (while wrapped in a blanket). Life was starting to have some color again. And it was nice.

And she wasn't sure if the man in front of her added hues of blue or more shades of gray.

1 2

LEO

L eo picked Sage up, bright and early, the morning of the mid-January New Year's party. Sage had called him a few nights prior, asking him to reconsider going at all, bribing him with more Girl Scout cookies (he'd find those later). When he wouldn't budge, she moved to asking him to wait in the car. Then, asking him to wait in the lobby of the hotel. He let her complain for two minutes, before he threatened to hold her hand the entire time.

So, at "the ungodly hour of seven am" (Sage's words), she asked him what his cover story was going to be.

Leo whipped out a pair of the most hipster-looking glasses and a slouchy beanie (*thanks, Tess*). "I am your assistant, Bobert. But, you call me Bob for short."

"Funny," Sage said, her morning voice sounding more like a bulldog.

"You sick?"

"No," she said, rubbing her eyes, then berating herself under her breath for smudging her makeup. "I need tea."

"I need coffee."

The first agreement of their lives had just occurred. Leo pulled into the local coffee drive-through. He ordered something with "enough caffeine to cause a blue whale to have tachycardia" (again, Sage's words) and tea for Sage.

Then they were on the road again. The rain was persistent, and Leo was glad he'd opted to arrive a little early. Sage didn't seem in any mood to chat. At least for the first half hour. The last twenty minutes of the drive were filled with her word vomit.

"So, how am I supposed to introduce you?"

"As your assistant."

"Are you going to actually do assistant-y things?"

Leo scoffed. "Like what? I was just going to follow you around and hold your tea and stuff."

"But, like, you're going to look like you're supposed to be there, right? And does Lily know?"

"Yes, and yes." Leo sighed, dodging yet another crazy driver. "I just want to see what this is about, learn some of the lingo, and, maybe, chat with the other admin to see if they know anything you might not. Relax. It's not going to be weird. Why don't you want anyone to know you have a bodyguard, anyway?"

Sage paused for a long time before answering. "Any emotion I show, good or bad, is labeled as dramatic. Getting a bodyguard? That would go over as a completely delusional, 'pick me' type of thing. I don't want to deal with that."

"Even though you had a brick thrown through your window and several unsettling notes sent to you?"

Sage just shrugged. Leo felt out of his depth, just enough not to pursue the topic. Dramatic? Emotional? Those threats were real. How could anyone blame her for taking precautions? Didn't people know the statistics for violence against women?

He broke the long silence with a soft, simple comment: "I don't think getting help for your safety is dramatic."

"Thanks," she mumbled, continuing to stare out the window and twirl her fingers in her hand, until they reached Portland.

Once they entered the big city, she sat up straight and began checking her phone, over and over, rubbing her hands together like she needed something to keep her occupied.

"Nervous?" Leo asked.

"A bit," Sage said. It was a rare moment of honesty from her. "Haven't done an event this big in a while. It'll be fun though."

"Anyone I should be aware of? Anyone that makes you nervous?"

Sage shook her head. "No, I just know a handful of people there I think. I'm mostly excited to hear some of the talks and look at the exhibits. Just—" She sighed and rubbed her neck like it was sore. "Just try and act like you know gaming stuff. Don't embarrass me, please?"

Leo scoffed. As if he could be anything other than the cool guy there. More than likely he'd be the only one who had washed hair, clothes that fit, and didn't live in his mother's basement (he just lived in his sister's spare room).

When he parked, he donned the beanie and glasses. "How do I look?"

Sage rolled her eyes. "Like an absolute dork. So, I guess normal?"

She jumped out of the SUV before he could make a comment on her own attire, which was probably good because he didn't have much to say. She wore black jeans, practical waterproof boots, and a fitted purple t-shirt, with a gray flannel over it. Plus, a rain jacket. Really, it was the most practical outfit he'd seen her in other than the golfing outing they shared. It was strange seeing her in anything other than sweatpants and loungewear and no, Leo absolutely did not check out her body, he was merely noticing how nice she looked when she wore actual clothes. Completely unrelated, he decided black jeans were one of the most flattering things a woman could wear.

Her hair hung around her shoulders in loose waves and it was nice to see it in another style other than piled on top of her head. Though it was strange not to see the soft curve of her neck. (He would not be commenting on the soft curve of her neck and how delicate and soft it looked in the morning sun.)

Unfortunately, the rat still made an appearance on her bag. A giant print of the deformed rodent, complete with a crown of flowers.

Leo stepped into the cold parking garage and gestured

for Sage to lead the way. And she did, with strange confidence. She didn't look back once to see if he was following her. She probably was hoping to lose him with the speed she was walking. Fat chance. He even remembered to grab both of their drinks before locking the car.

The lobby wasn't too busy, but there were still a handful of people bustling about and getting things set up. According to the itinerary, the event didn't even start until one.

Leo followed at her heels, scanning the entrances and exits, making mental notes of where cameras were hiding, just in case he needed to review the footage later should an issue arise. Sage marched into the fancy hotel and followed the signs to the big ballroom (complete with a coffee bar) and into what was called the "green room."

"You can't come in here," a little dude with a headset and clipboard said. "Miss Moon doesn't have anyone on her guest list."

"How'd you know that was Sage?" Leo asked.

The little guy scoffed. "It's my job to know. Plus, I've been a patron of hers before she was even with LilyTech, but she doesn't know that."

The little guy blushed. *Actually blushed.* Did he have a thing for Sage? What backward world did he just walk into?

"Well, I am her assistant," Leo said. "I wasn't going to come today but things have gotten too hectic for her." He held up the two coffee cups as if to demonstrate that he was, in fact, needed. "If she doesn't have her morning tea you know she'll be a zombie the rest of the day."

The little dude acquiesced. "I just need your name, I

guess." Then he let Leo through. Tight ship they run, but not tight enough if any guy could simply talk his way in.

"The name is Bob. Please make sure to spell it with one o." And he brushed past the headset man into the green room (which was actually just a big white room—a disappointing discovery, really).

It took "Bob" a second to find Sage among the throng of people gathering around multiple couches and chairs. There were pastries, cookies, and coffee. He finally found her chatting with a few people and inserted himself in the conversation (because he had forgotten that he was supposed to be invisible) and handed her the tea.

"Thank you," Sage said, clearly surprised. "Uh, this is my assistant, Bob." She winked at the tall woman she was talking to.

"Nice to meet you, assistant Bob," the woman said. "I'm Lily."

Leo smiled wide. It was nice to meet the woman who had actually hired him instead of playing phone tag and leaving messages and emails to one another. Leo said as much.

Then Leo gently steered Sage away for a moment, telling Lily, "Just need to review something, I'll give her right back."

Sage protested for a step then gave in. Leo leaned in and whispered into Sage's ear just quiet enough that she leaned in to hear him. "Thought you'd lose me at the door, huh?" She smelled of lemons and grapefruit. Were those goosebumps on her neck? He was half tempted to pull the loose hair away to inspect this line of thinking.

Sage blushed. "No."

"Remember, when you lie, you gotta sell it. Be firm. And do something about that propensity to turn red."

"I do not—"

"Speaking of red. Little Man out front with the clipboard has a thing for you. A patron of yours. You should thank him. His name is Joey, according to the name tag."

"Wait really?" Sage asked.

Leo shrugged. "I am observant. And this is me blending in as your assistant, doing assistant-y things." He leaned in again, smiling as he spoke into her ear, despite his voice holding a very firm tone, like a father scolding his child. "But if you try to give me the slip or are otherwise unhelpful during this long and busy day, I will not hesitate to pull you from the event, citing rule eleven."

"That's not fair—"

"Do not tempt me, Sage. You might be cavalier about all of this, but I take security seriously, understand?"

Sage nodded, smiling, as if aware they had an audience. "We should have argued about this in the car and I am now coming to the realization that you decided to have this little...update in public so—"

"You wouldn't fly off the handle?"

Sage sighed. "So, I wouldn't respond with reason and put you and your arbitrary rules in a corner."

"Behave and we'll have no issue."

"Sure thing, *ass*-instant Bob." She downed her tea and handed him her now empty cup. "I'd like another. Black variety. Make it how I like it, please." She said it loud enough for the others to hear, spun on her heel, and returned to Lily.

Leo, despite being a self-titled expert in many things, was no expert when it came to tea.

It took him three (3!) times to get it right. And that was just the right tea bag. It took another four attempts to figure out she wanted a splash of cream, no sugar.

"Took you long enough," Sage said from where she sat. There was a maniacal gleam in her eye.

"I aim to please," Leo said with enough sarcasm to drown this whole dreaded green room.

Sage took a sip and she visibly relaxed, settling into the couch.

"Where's your fan club?" Leo asked because since he had been here people had been buzzing around her, mostly Lily and that Jared guy, but several other people came up to chit-chat and Leo had to fight down his rising annoyance. This little introvert who never left the house was actually popular? And well-liked? And people were interested in her?

To be fair, he had come to find several aspects of her life interesting, but none of that was directly related to her, exactly. He thought the business model she created was interesting. The love she had for tea was also interesting. But her fashion sense. Yikes. It was hard to get that out of his mind. He had seen her in nearly every shade of color and mismatched pajamas.

But now it was his turn to sit and watch the world spin by him. Sage, for being fairly easy-going on camera, was the same in real life. Apparently he was the only one who got to experience her venom, which was warranted for the first hour of their professional relationship, but he had since apologized! They had been working together enough, at least in a limited capacity, for months now. It was time she gave him some slack.

Still, this was a much larger event than he had initially thought. He needed to get things straight. Too many entrances and exits. To many people who wanted her attention. Too many people demanded her time.

Leo plopped on the couch next to her. "You need a safeword."

Sage choked on her tea. "A what?"

"A phrase that will let me know you're uncomfortable or feel uneasy. It'll help me know to be on alert or swoop in and get you out of that situation." He pushed the glasses up his nose, adjusting the beanie.

"Safeword just sounds so...dirty."

"It's a word used to make you feel...safe." Leo rubbed the back of his neck and smiled at a person passing by. He and Sage were relatively tucked away on a couch as other more popular (Leo assumed) guests arrived.

"Well, let's be fair, I never feel totally safe these days," Sage admitted.

"Okay, well do I at least bring some comfort or peace?"

Sage snorted. "You're...comfortable. In the way that a first-class airplane seat is comfortable. Like, better than coach but really, it's just what you have to deal with for a time. No one likes airplane seats."

"Thank you." Leo rolled his eyes. "I love being compared to airplanes. Now pick a *comfortable word.*"

"Filbert."

Leo scoffed. Of all the words to bring up horrid images in front of his eyes, Filbert and his accompanying parts would do that. "Why?" Leo said, not bothering to hide his disgust.

She smiled. "Because it makes you uncomfortable."

Mischievous Moon. Two could play that game.

"Great," Leo said. "My safeword is rat-dog."

"What?" Sage rolled her eyes. "You do not need a safeword!"

The pair chatting near them paused their rather enthusiastic conversation about graphics cards just long enough to raise eyebrows at Sage. She blushed and turned to Leo, whispering, "Why on earth do you need a...*special word?*"

"If I use it, you have a chance to gracefully exit the conversation or I will be the one to steer you away."

"Whatever." Sage downed the rest of her tea and handed her cup to Leo. "Thanks for that. I'll probably need another in a minute. Until then, I'm going to the bathroom. My panel is in ten minutes. You can probably just hang back in here. That would probably be best."

Oh, what's this? Sage being shy? Did she seriously not want him in the audience?

Too bad.

So sad.

He stood and followed her to the bathrooms on the far side of the green room. She said hi to a few people and made it through the crowd. For being so...what was the word? Borderline hermit-like at her house, she walked with poise and confidence. Her shoulders were back, she stood tall, she reached out and shook hands with a variety of people. When did she learn how to be so...charismatic? Wasn't that his schtick? Wasn't that his superpower?

Getting people to like him? Making conversation and social events easier to handle?

Now he was the weirdo on the outside.

Never one to worry too much, Leo soon remembered that the moment he stepped outside this conference, the world would be right again, and Sage would be properly classified as a nerd and Leo would be back in the saddle as the cool guy.

Not that he cared. High school Leo certainly would have, but that whole thing just feels...small.

Everything felt small now.

He scanned the room, pushing the strange thoughts of high school, who he was, and who he wanted to be (you know, just light-hearted musings while one had while waiting for their Subject to finish peeing but she was clearly emptying a bladder the size of an elephant because how did it take someone that long to pee?) when he spotted Jared making a beeline for him.

"Leo?" he asked.

"Yes, we met earlier," Leo said. "But Lily must have told you I am Bob today. You're the photographer?"

Jared gave a mock bow. "I am her social media manager and I make all the thumbnails and branding and yes I pretty much do the other creative side of things. Make sure everything is perfectly peachy and all that. So with that being said, where is Sage? I need her. I need to take some footage and content—"

"I'm right here," Sage said, walking up to the pair. She fiddled with her hands and when she noticed Leo glancing at her she shoved them in her back pockets. "I have like two minutes before they want us up there."

"Just peachy." Jared whisked her away.

When the photos were taken, and participants ushered on stage, Leo took the opportunity to slip from the green room and sneak into the auditorium. It was a madhouse. Packed. How had he let this get away from him? He had done some preliminary research but this event was much larger than he had anticipated.

She was one of two women on the stage (Lily was right next to her) and seven men. Though "men" was a generous term considering the varied states of these dudes. One looked like a teenager despite the fact a quick Google search said he was nearing forty. (Leo also did a quick Google search to see what his skincare routine was. Fun fact: turns out hibernating in a basement with no sun did wonders for the skin). Another guy had this long, stringy hair and it looked like the poor guy didn't own a comb. Or shampoo. And then there were a few that looked like total jocks, wearing shoes that were probably worth more than Sage's car (but to be fair, she would be lucky to get five hundred for that tin can, which is not a lot for a car but a lot for shoes). It was quite the eclectic mix and more than anything, Leo couldn't get over the fact that the people packing this room were eager to hear what they had to say. There was a palpable anticipation in the air.

Too bad it was all boring. They just had a few presenters talk about new gaming tech (Leo, a fellow techy guy preferred useful information) and then the floor opened for questions. There were a few of the contestants up there prepping to duke it out at the big competition, plus a few of their sponsors.

Even though watching paint dry would be more interesting, the crowd was entranced. They ate it up like this was the best entertainment of the year. Leo thought the panel was coming to an end when people were shuffling in their seats and starting to slip out into the aisles. Oh, but how wrong he was.

"We have set aside 45 minutes for the Q and A session," the host announced.

Forty. Five. Minutes. And that's when it became evident that the people weren't leaving, they were claim jumpers, trying to sneak in ahead of the line in hopes of asking their question.

The first guy to get the microphone to ask a question had this smug look about him like he was about to make a giant joke. Leo immediately didn't like him, it didn't help that he had a rather punchable face.

"This question is for Crickets. How do you feel about competing against novice gamers considering you're ranked by the old standards?"

There was a murmur through the crowd. Sage bit her lip and Lily leaned over to whisper something in her ear. Ah. It started to make sense for Leo. This was a jab at Sage, calling her unqualified for whatever metric they used to invite players into the competition.

Crickets gave a rather nice response, but not without throwing a few backhanded compliments. "I think it allows for media coverage and it adds a thrill. I'm not worried about the new standards, it's what the developers and the gracious hosts of the competition have set the bar at. I do fear the lack of equal standards will result in some boring play at times and quick eliminations."

There was some murmuring in the crowd and the host, before letting the next question be asked, turned to Sage, and asked, "Care to comment?"

Sage shrugged. "That question wasn't for me."

The host seemed to falter a moment but regained his ground. "How do you feel about the standards being shifted in your favor?"

Sage sighed, looking positively bored, except there was a slight tightening at her mouth and she only got that when she was playing and backed into a corner. Or when she was stressed. Leo scanned the room for refreshments because his Subject looked like she could use a calming cup of tea. Then he scolded himself. He wasn't really her assistant. He scanned the room again. Really, there was absolutely no threat here in this sea of sad, stinky teenage testosterone.

Sage finally responded. "The standards were not changed to let me into the competition. The standards were in place before the competition was even announced. Sure, I don't have as many hours of gameplay and the ranking Crick does, but that's probably because he's been playing before I could walk."

There was some snickering in the crowd like there was some giant inside joke between all of them.

Crickets even laughed and spoke into the microphone, "Yeah, yeah, I've been around the block a few times. You, little miss, have yet to complete a lap."

Sage laughed, but it seemed a little forced. "I guess that's because I don't like to spiral."

There was some joking and jabbing back and forth but Sage summed up the conversation with. "Look, I know the requirements for this competition are different, but so is everything with this new wave of gameplay and just the volume of new games and players. I don't think that makes me less deserving since they didn't make this rule because of me." She glared at the host. "I think it'll make for an interesting fight to the top."

"Or a bloodbath," the host said, stealing the small thunder Sage had managed to create.

It was sad. Even from the back of the room, Leo could see Sage deflate, just a bit. She was sitting tall and smiling but with each question, she shrank down just a little further.

While the guys were getting, "Do you think your history and success with playing *Welkin Wall* game include your success here?" or "Do you think just having a better understanding of mathematics creates a better strategy?" or "When is your new merch line coming out?" Sage was getting questions like, "What else do you do to increase your hand and wrist strength?" or "Do you think you'd play better if you had shorter nails?"

Lily seemed to be getting more disgusted by the minute. Finally, closing remarks were being made and it was a chance for the sponsors to plug their crap, but Lily went another route.

"Thank you for being here," she said. "I just want you all to know how honored we are to be up here sponsoring the only female player in the competition." There were a few hollers from the crowd. So maybe there were mermaids in the sea of stinking sailors. Lily beamed. "I just want to take a moment, not to plug our new line of remotes or headphones, but to recognize the tenacity of women everywhere. We have been tightlipped about some of the things going on with Miss Moon, but she wanted to let you all know she appreciates your support."

According to Sage's wide eyes, this was not something they had previously discussed.

Lily continued. "There is a unique challenge to being a woman in a man's world, and Miss Moon has done an excellent job. But here at LilyTech, we take security seriously. Between threats of violence, acts of violence, vandalism, and more, we have had to hire 24-hour security. Now while I'm sure our male counterparts have experienced the rogue fan, I doubt you know what it feels like to have your life threatened. To feel like you will be hurt. And because of that," Lily turned to the all-male panelists. "I ask you to donate to the DVRC of Oregon. It's time for change. Join me in this fight against the harassment of women everywhere."

There was applause and a few people balked at the story Lily was telling. But overall, it changed the tone of the closing remarks and went from "Look at me and look what I have" to "Look at us standing as a community" type of farce.

Sage looked absolutely livid by the time she was led down from the stage. Leo couldn't quite intercept her, so he hovered near as she and the other players were led to a backdrop of sorts and posed for pictures. Which lasted forever. Like seriously, how did she not die of a facial spasm or something? Leo couldn't even remember the last time he'd had his picture taken.

Still, that urge to get her a cup of tea didn't leave him, but he was not willing to let Sage linger by these strangers. He was glad for the decision. A creep masquerading as a fan got a little too close to Sage. She took what looked like an involuntary backward step into the backdrop, nearly tearing it from the wall. The man laughed and grabbed her arm, pulling her into him where he then wrapped an arm around her, his hand trailing down her backside—

Nope, absolutely not.

Leo took three giant steps toward the pair and grabbed the horrible man's offending arm by the wrist, twisting it. The man yelped. People stared. Leo did not care.

"Sorry dude, no photos for people that don't know how to keep their hands to themselves."

Leo didn't give the man a chance to protest and threw him (a little too roughly but who was there to tattle on him?) into the crowd. "Beat it or lose a hand."

The man opened his mouth for a moment but wisely closed it after taking a moment to size up Leo (who outweighed the guy by an easy fifty pounds).

Leo looked back at Sage just in time to watch her face go from surprise back to smiley and fun. She continued chatting with her fans (most of whom were female by this point). How could she act like nothing happened? How could she not be impressed by his quick actions either? Goodness, a small thank you would be nice.

It took five hundred years but eventually, the line died down and Leo ushered Sage back into the green room where he led her to the beverage table and made her a tea. He talked while he flicked through the basket of tea bags. "So explain to me, does the groping always happen?"

Sage groaned. "No. I am so embarrassed—"

"You have nothing to be embarrassed about other than the fact that you should have yelled 'pervert' or something so someone would have helped you sooner."

"Just. Stop." She rubbed her temples.

Leo wasn't going to let it go but he could tell this wasn't the time or place. Instead, he changed tactics and decided to focus on the other offending person. "What was Lily on about?"

Sage groaned. "I don't know! I think she just wanted to make a big statement, keep us relevant or something. But it's not like that."

"Like what?" Leo asked. He handed her the tea and she sipped it, eyes closing for a moment.

"I want to be relevant for the *right* things."

"Ah yes," Leo said. "Because donating to domestic violence campaigns is so horrible."

Sage gritted her teeth and spoke in a low whisper. "It's a great thing if you actually cared about that. But she is exaggerating my story all to get attention. And now I have to deal with the backlash of all those people thinking I am clout chasing and now they are going to examine every inch of my life to see if Lily was lying or if I am being dramatic. Lily, I'm sure deep down, she cares. But right now I am a paycheck to her."

Leo could understand where she was coming from.

She sipped her tea again. "This is really sweet."

"You needed it."

"What does that mean?"

Leo shrugged. "You're being sour so I added extra sugar."

She frowned at him and then peeked into his mug. "Is that coffee?"

"Of course, it is." Leo took an obnoxious slurp, glaring at a group of guys staring at Sage's backside.

"Why does it smell like a cinnamon roll?"

"Because despite having finally mastered your stupid tea order—"

Sage interrupted him with a laugh. "You butchered my tea."

"Whatever. It smells like a cinnamon roll because this stuff is burned and tastes like acid."

Sage took the paper cup from his hands with as much caution as she would a bomb. She sniffed it. "Seriously, why does it smell like a Pillsbury dough boy's fart?"

Leo was already itching for another hit. "You know I like my coffee black and fancy, but I had to get into this Bob's character. I've decided he has a blog talking about the latest flannels and matching beanies. He is a coffee snob wannabe and really thrives off of sugary drinks because he is too busy chasing you to get a proper meal. Here, try it."

She took the mug and sipped it slowly. Her eyebrows rose. "What on earth did you do to those poor beans?"

"I'll never tell. Just add it to your list of mysteries about me." He snatched the cup from her and took another sip. There was something...peculiar about taking a drink from where Sage's lips had just been. He'd file that thought under "Things to overthink later."

Sage seemed not to notice this hint of...strangeness.

"You're a 'get what you see' kind of dude. Not much mystery there."

Leo wanted to be offended but was more afraid she might be right. He crossed his arms over his chest, careful not to spill his coffee and careful to ensure his biceps were on display just right. Like it didn't look like he was trying (because he wasn't).

Sage made a show of looking him up and down. "I see a giant idiot."

"I can't help that you're visually impaired then."

She turned away from him. "Ready to go?"

"Don't you have somewhere else to be?" Leo asked, scanning his schedule.

"Not anymore."

"No?" Leo looked at the schedule again. "You have 'free time' written on the to-do list. And I remember correctly you were the one who told me not to deviate from the list."

"Ugh," Sage rubbed her temples and walked to the green room, plastering a smile on her face. "I just want to go home."

"No." Leo caught her in two strides and looped an arm through hers. She tried to pull away but he held firm. "Humor me. People don't interrupt people when they are walking around like—"

"Little girls ready to skip through the meadow?"

"Sure." His big biceps were definitely on display now. "People won't interrupt us if we look deep in a conversation."

"This looks so dumb. Like we are siblings about to take a photo shoot together at JCPenney or something."

Leo scoffed. "As if there was any way your genetics could be confused with mine."

"How does it feel to be the last Neanderthal walking this earth?"

Leo was saved needing to come up with a reply when his plan was blown to smithereens by a preteen girl walking up and interrupting them. So much for his looped-arm idea. So, it works on adults. Not kids.

"I made you this!" the little girl screeched. It was a little gift bag, and she held it out to Sage with such expectant eyes.

Should he look through it? Could it be poison? A bomb? Another threatening note?

Sage opened it only to pull out something much, much worse.

"I love it!" Sage exclaimed, leaning in to hug the girl. The girl looked back at the only sane-looking adult in the room and Leo assumed it was her mother.

Sage pulled out a canvas bag with puff paint art all over the sides. It looked quite abstract until Sage flipped it over and, to his horror, discovered it wasn't a bag at all. It was a hat. And he had a sinking feeling that she would proudly wear this out in public. And horrors upon horrors, it wasn't abstract art at all, it was a puff-painted portrait of the rat-dog, complete with flowers and little pumpkins.

Clearly, it was worse than a bomb. Worse than anthrax. Worse than a brick through the window.

This bucket hat was a danger to society.

Sage put it on her head with pride, posed for a picture, and stared up at Leo when the girl scampered off.

Leo shivered. "It frightens me."

"Good." A smile finally broke through her frown.

And so Leo spent the rest of the afternoon trailing behind Sage, taking photos when fans asked, and overall enjoying watching Sage in her element. He actually forgot to be annoyed and found himself enjoying the convention too.

What strange universe had he fallen into?

13
SAGE

Leo stuck to her like glue and Sage was exhausted from babysitting. Shouldn't it be the other way around? Wasn't her job to annoy him so much that he'd leave her alone?

Sure, she didn't leave the house much, but she occasionally went to coffee shops. Or met the girls for brunch when Tavy was in town. And the grocery store, which is the setting of her current frustration.

"These are horrible for you!" Leo said, reading the package of ramen she'd tossed in her shopping cart. They were in the local Mom and Pop grocery store instead of driving thirty minutes to the big city down the road. Sure, Sage wanted to go there. Target, Barnes and Noble, and a pedicure were calling her name, but the idea of Leo Camaro accompanying her to all those experiences made her want to rip her hair out.

"Please go away."

"No can do," Leo said, tossing a bag of trail mix into

the cart. "After that brick-through-the-window incident," he whispered the last words like they were some giant secret, "I have orders to keep both eyes on you."

"Your phone can do that."

"It tracks you, but it doesn't allow me to see what's going on around you. What if there are other baddies trying to cop a feel? Who will break their wrists for you?"

Sage groaned and hit the back of his heels with the cart. "How about I FaceTime you? Go home or wait in your fancy car and let me just do my shopping in peace."

"Absolutely not," Leo said. "I am here preventing serious death and destruction. You're welcome, by the way."

"What could you possibly be saving me from?" Sage asked, rubbing her temples. She had not been sleeping well. Sure, insomnia came in bouts, but she'd been playing more regularly and her stream analytics and views were rising like crazy. She was feeling the pressure.

"Those chips have radioactive ingredients and this cheese sauce, if you can call it that, is made of plastic."

Sage made a show of putting the items back. "There. Crisis averted. Now go home."

"Tess's condo is being fumigated for a cricket infestation." Leo then proceeded to tell her an entire backstory on that but it mostly involved Tess adopting some exotic frogs and spilling their food—*live crickets*—all over the kitchen floor.

"Ugh, then go hang out with your family or something."

"Can't do that. Mother is having her book club." Leo shuddered.

"And that's a problem because…"

"Because her book club consists of women of all ages falling over themselves trying to get my attention."

Sage snorted then paused. He actually looked disappointed. Like that was a real thing that happened.

"Scared the old ladies will objectify you to death?" Sage asked, trying to add some humor back into the conversation.

"No," Leo said, not looking at her but instead reading another ingredient label. "No, my mom just wants to set me up with one of her friend's daughters. She used to be covert about it but now she's borderline obsessed. I think she'd be happy if I found a husband at this point, so long as he was local."

"Why don't you? Sounds like a romcom in the making."

"I don't want to settle down here." Leo rubbed his eyes. "I don't want to settle. For anything. Or anyone."

"Is that why you have to be perfect?" Sage paused at the avocados, looking at Leo carefully.

"Nothing is perfect."

What had he just admitted to? He had a great mom and dad and family life for all she knew. Leo came from wealth. He was fit (she meant this in the most non-objectifying way—he was in good shape, okay?) and he had a high-paying job. But things didn't look so rosy now.

"What do you want?" Sage asked quietly, breaking the tension.

"I don't know," Leo said. It seemed like a confession. Then he went right back to scrutinizing what was in her cart, pulling out the radioactive chips again. "Seriously?"

he asked, all melancholy gone from his voice. Back to that arrogant know-it-all. "Fun fact, these chips were just banned in Canada due to their harmful ingredients. Do you want to grow a third eye?"

"That could be useful."

"No!" He tossed the chips on a shelf.

"You are unbelievable."

"I will not have you stocking the house with junk food. What am I supposed to eat?"

"It's my house! It's my kitchen! You're eating me out of house and home. Pitch in."

"Hey! I bought those Girl Scout cookies last week."

"With *my* money!"

He had been lounging on her couch downstairs when he hollered up to Sage (who was in the middle of a cozy gaming stream) to tell her there was an emergency at the front door. Sage, in her panic, leaped off the couch, and raced downstairs to see what on earth the problem was. She had thought Squash had tumbled off the couch and broken a leg or something.

No. Leo simply didn't have cash on hand to pay the Girl Scouts for cookies.

"Okay, so you chipped in," Leo said.

"And you ate them all!"

"Not true! The new flavor is trash. Those are for you."

"But they're trash!" They were absolutely horrendous raspberry-filled things.

This conversation was going nowhere and her headache was getting worse. He had been hovering for days. He literally only went home at night and only when he was certain the cameras were perfect. Sure, he went out and about sometimes, mostly the gym or running, but sometimes he forced her to go on a walk with him. He actually threatened to unplug the internet or something like that. She wasn't sure if he could do that but she wasn't about to risk it.

"Why are we out here?" Sage had asked when he dragged her from the house for a walk. All she had wanted to do was nap.

"Fun fact: walking increases blood flow to your brain and can improve mood. And because it's ten in the morning and you haven't seen the sun in probably two days."

It was annoying because he was probably right.

"It will make you feel better. You look like a car wreck."

"Classy as always."

The worst was that he *had* been right. She did feel better after a short walk in the cold sunshine. The jerk.

But she missed her space. She missed someone not eating all her food. She had to go grocery shopping more than ever now and this guy was *healthy*. Sometimes she just needed a plate of lukewarm pizza rolls and an energy drink to feel like a real human.

"I want the radioactive chips and I want my space and I want a pedicure." This time she stomped her foot and the few shoppers around them looked puzzled.

"You can go have someone fondle your feet whenever you want," Leo said, taking the chips out of the cart again. "Just put it on the calendar so I can join."

"I don't want you there!"

Leo rolled his eyes. "For a woman who puts her entire

life on the internet to see, you're actually shy about your feet? Come on, I've seen you at your worst."

"I'm not shy! And my whole life isn't blasted on the internet for everyone. And when am I really at my worst?"

"Each morning you look like you were fighting for your life and lost. Seriously, who hates sleep that much?"

Okay, so the nights were rough. She tossed and turned for hours on end. "I just want a pedicure."

"And you can have one."

"Alone. Please wait in the car."

"Sure." Leo shrugged. "I could do that."

Sage groaned. "But you won't."

Leo shrugged again. "Only one way to find out."

Sage stormed off, running over his feet as she passed him with the cart. "I'll just paint my nails at home for crying out loud."

"Oh, come on," Leo shouted from behind her. "Your toes can't be that bad!"

The stares she got made her want to die a little inside. "Go away," she whispered when he caught up to her.

"I read an article about pedicures once. It was actually about Latin roots and the study was 'pedi' but I digress. My fun fact is that pedicures are correlated with a boost in confidence. The competition making you nervous?" Leo asked, pulling out the other chips she had tried to sneak into the cart.

"No!" But maybe yes.

"Don't get your knickers in a twist."

Knickers? In a twist? That guy had a stick so far up in his butt it could scratch his brain.

She knew how to have a good time, she just hadn't

had a chance to let loose in who knows how long since he became her constant shadow. Maybe she was wound up a little tight, not that he needed to comment on it though. He was getting too comfortable, which was evidenced by him paying for and loading up the groceries. What a gentleman, the absolute butthole.

When they got home—no, rephrase. *When they got to her home,* she texted her friends.

> Sage: Clifford's?

> Tavy: For real? It's spring break, it could be crazy busy but I am SO down.

> Roz: Like you could get away from your parents, T.

> Tavy: I told them I'm meeting up with a study group. Should I pick you guys up?

> Sage: Yes, please! I have so much to tell you.

> Roz: good or bad?

> Sage: I'll let you know after I have a few shots of tequila in me.

Tavy didn't drink. Not that she didn't want to, but her coaches were strict. So strict that they would probably disown her if they ever found out that she ever set foot in a bar. She took a hit off of a vape pen once (just the fruity flavor) and nearly had a panic attack over the idea of her dad finding out. But she loved to dance and let loose until the guilt of not being a perfect princess crept in and ultimately consumed her alive.

Roz was a free spirit who knew how to let loose and was a great balance to the group. She would be the one with the loudest opinions about the whole bodyguard situation.

Sage wasn't totally sure why she had kept this little piece of information a secret. Maybe because she didn't want them constantly checking in on her about it? They were already amazing and called and checked in on her often after George passed, but life had been busy for all of them these last months because they all had new men in their lives. Tavy was secretly dating this total bad boy who her parents would absolutely hate. It was adorable. Roz has this rich older guy she's fake dating to impress her parents and help him out, and the fake dating was *definitely* turning into more real-life dating.

And Sage. Well, the only man in her life wanted to get pedicures to make fun of her feet and force her to take walks.

The sun had already gone down when Leo bid her goodnight, but not before checking the security cameras and announcing he was locking her in for the night.

Sage got dressed, topped off Squash's food and water, and waited on the couch for Tavy. She had asked her to park at the end of the street, and in no time, Sage snuck out of her own house out the back where she thought the cameras had the best chance of missing her and hopped in Tavy's car. In another ten minutes, they had Roz in the back seat. Perks of a small town.

Oh. And Sage had left her phone at home. *Oops.*

Clifford's was the only bar in town. The negative part of a small town. But, as far as bars went, it was a pretty good one. The lights were low, there was ample seating, and a giant space in the middle of the floor where line dancing took place every Wednesday and Thursday night. And luckily for them, it was a Thursday.

Sage felt a pang of guilt for not telling Leo where she was, but she pushed it away. This was her being spontaneous. This was her loosening up. This was her untwisting her knickers. Besides, she'd be back before he ever found out she was gone.

True to Sage's word, after she had a few shots of tequila in her (and some cherry-flavored thing Roz enticed her into drinking—which was absolutely foul) she spilled her guts.

"It's Leo Camaro," she cried when she slid into a booth, a little flushed from dancing.

"Wait what?" Tavy asked, sipping on her Shirley Temple, looking equally flushed. She loved dancing more than anyone.

"He's my bodyguard if you can call it that..." Sage mumbled the last bit.

"How on earth did that happen?" Tavy asked. They knew Lily sprang for security, but that? They gaped at her. For once, Roz was stunned silent.

Tavy pulled out her phone and tapped away on it. "Unacceptable. What's the company called?"

"Sentinel Security Agency," Sage said. "I already talked to Lily about it—"

"Did you tell her everything?" Tavy asked.

"Well, no—"

"If you did, maybe she'd be more willing to accommodate the situation." Ever the logical one.

"Is he the guy with a smile like the sunshine?" Roz asked through slurred words. So much for stunned silence.

"Roz!" Tavy yelled over the blaring music. "But yeah, he's always been good-looking. Too bad he's the absolute scum of the earth."

"Too bad," Roz said. "I mean, did he bring up, you know, what happened?"

Sage shrugged. "Sort of. I mentioned not graduating and he just apologized. The jerk!"

"I might need some clarification about that," Tavy said. "Isn't apologizing a step in the right direction?"

"He's only sorry because it's awkward between us." Her friends nodded at her, understanding the absolute jerk move. "And now *I'm* the bad guy because I don't want to give him a free pass?"

"So ridiculous!" Roz said. She slammed her hand on the table. "Another round for these sorry ladies. Let's drink our high school years into oblivion!"

Someone shouted "amen" from across the bar.

"Wait, look at this," Roz said, holding up her phone. A TikTok played. It was a short fourteen-second clip of a fight—if one could call it that. A man in a suit quite literally dove over a park bench to place his body in between a woman and a knife-wielding crazy person. Not only that, but the man in a suit managed to wrestle the bad guy into an armlock and subdue him, all while the crazy man (likely hopped up on drugs) thrashed about like a fish. It was professional. It was precise. It was brave. It was Leo.

"Are you kidding me?" Tavy gasped, grabbing the

phone for a closer look. "That's the wife of some mobster who was put under protection for testifying or something. I think this was actually a hit attempt or something. Wait. That's Leo!"

"Oh my gosh." Sage threw back another shot of that gross cherry drink. "See what I have to deal with? An actual professional who takes things way too seriously. She is a witness in some big case! I am merely a case of nerves. I get scared of shadows! I do not need this killing machine hanging around me."

"Well, according to the comments, he hasn't killed anyone I guess," Roz said in her floaty voice. "But people keep calling him Suit Daddy—"

All three made a face.

"And he's going viral on Booktok. I think this happened about a year ago too. Wild," Roz said.

"Just great," Sage mumbled. Would anyone recognize "Bob" as the Suit Daddy or was the flannel enough camouflage?

"I'm sorry," Tavy said. "This whole thing just sucks."

Sage sighed. "Yeah. I'm just ready for this whole competition to be over, then things can slow down. I mean, I was so excited about it but now it just seems like too much. Maybe I'll take a break for a few weeks and actually get the place in order."

"Oooh, I do love an organizing party," Tavy said.

"I don't know. I think it might be good to keep yourself busy. Might help with the transition to life without George," Roz said in a rare moment of wisdom. "Besides, that house is creepy. You could use a bodyguard for the ghosts at the very least. Still a bummer because he's hot."

And the wisdom was gone as soon as it came. Bless her buzzed little brain.

"Hot or not, I just need to make it through these next few weeks." Sage sipped on her tequila soda.

"You're tough," Tavy said. "I know you'll handle it. I mean, at least he's not staying in your house, right? Or making you move to a hotel or something."

"No, you're right. I need to stop being a wimp and get a grip."

"You're allowed to feel all the feelings," Roz said, sloshing her drink when she raised her glass in what was supposed to be a toast. Then she glared at Tavy. "That goes for you too. Relax a little. Feel things. That's allowed, you know. *Having feelings is normal.*"

"I do!" Tavy yelled. Then the conversation devolved into making fun of Tavy and her clean girl aesthetic and her strict parents and tennis, and then Roz managed to drag everyone to the dance floor and learn a new line dance which ended up being a tangle of limbs when Roz got her left and rights mixed up again.

Sage was beginning to relax and actually enjoy herself. Her friends *shouldn't* be her friends considering how different they all were, but it was a good balance and she didn't question it.

Watermelon Crawl was just coming over the speakers (and Roz was properly freaking out because they hadn't heard that song in forever) when a familiar face entered Sage's field of vision. Well, it wasn't exactly a familiar face. It was Leo Camaro, and he was looking...angry. More than angry, the guy looked *furious.* His jaw was clenched and he scanned the crowd with intensity, and when his eyes locked onto Sage he looked positively murderous.

"What the hell are you doing here?" Leo demanded when he finally reached Sage through the throng of people lining up to dance.

"What does it look like I'm doing? Knitting?" Sage tried to sound tough but there was something in the attitude of Leo that made her nervous.

"You have a lot of explaining to do," he growled through gritted teeth. Despite the loud music and the stomping of boots (and Tavy's sneakers, seriously who wore sneakers to go line dancing?) Leo's voice cut through the noise. "Come with me."

"Wait, what's going on?" Sage asked, letting herself be pulled from the dance floor. Despite Leo's anger, he wasn't rough with her, if anything, he was gentle as he guided her from the chaotic crowd, large hand on her lower back. But there was something different in the way he carried himself. This wasn't the almost bored security guard. This was a guy on alert. This guy meant business.

"Hey!" Roz called after them, dodging people and trying to make it through the crowds, having a much more difficult time than Leo had. It was like his anger emanated off of him and people gave him a wide path.

"Stop!" Roz called again, finally meeting Sage and Leo. "What do you think you're doing, Mr. Sunshine Boy?"

"What?" Leo asked.

"Yeah!" Sage said, finally gathering her wits. She wrenched her arm from his grasp with unnecessary force and stumbled back a few steps. "What's going on?"

"Who is this?" Leo jerked his head to Roz.

"I'm her best friend, so listen up buddy, you're not allowed to be mean to her." She leaned into Sage, attempting (and failing) to whisper. "Oh my goodness he really is cute though!"

Leo rolled his eyes. "Okay, Best Friend. Do you have a ride, 'cause I need to take this one home. Something came up."

"I'm her ride," Tavy said, joining the group.

"What are you doing?" Sage asked, slightly embarrassed as if a parent had caught her sneaking out or something.

"We have a situation," Leo whispered. "Let's go."

"Let me grab my bag at least."

"Your friends will get it, we need to go. Now. Besides, I know you don't have your phone or anything important in there." He had his hand around her arm again and was leading her out of the bar. Some part of Sage wanted to revolt and demand answers, but she also didn't want to make a scene...and this felt different.

Sage shook Leo off of her when they got to the parking lot but he kept his hand on her lower back, guiding her to the car like it was a dance and he was an experienced leader. He led her to his car and opened the door, ushering her in, and closed it promptly behind her. Leo hopped in the driver's seat and locked the car behind him. He stared out at the bar for a moment while inhaling a long breath. Then he let it all out, "What on earth were you thinking?"

"What is going on?" Sage asked, completely ignoring his question.

"Of all the *stupid* things you could do, seriously, what were you thinking?" Leo growled.

"I don't know what's going on, where are we going?"

"To the police station."

"What!" Her stomach churned.

"While you were out dancing the night away, a guy tried breaking into your house. I got the alert and managed to get there before he got away. I called the cops but got there first and held him until they came and took him away. You need to make a statement and press charges."

"Oh, my goodness," Sage mumbled. "Who was it?"

"Jimmy Slade."

"Who?"

"I don't know his background. I would have had a chance to do some research if I hadn't spent the last hour tracking you down. Now answer me, what on earth were you thinking?"

Suddenly embarrassed, Sage did what she did best: deflect. "Did that Jimmy guy want to, you know, hurt me?"

Leo paused for a moment, let out a sigh, and then said, "Jimmy Slade is a skinny kid, not even seventeen. Maybe weighs twelve pounds. I think he's a weird fan who managed to find out where you live. Now answer my question. What. On. Earth. Were. You. Thinking?"

"I needed to get out!" Sage said. "I wanted to go dancing with my friends, feel normal, you know? I didn't want you looking at my feet or making fun of my music or judging me for growing a third eye because I love those horrible chips!"

"Nothing about your situation is normal! There isn't

going to be a normal for the next few months for you! Why didn't you tell me where you were going?"

Sage leaned against the window, watching the moon reflect on the damp streets. "I don't know," Sage admitted. "I figured you had my location on my phone, isn't that enough?"

"That means nothing, especially if you don't have your phone."

"Oops." She meant it to be a snide remark, but instead, it just sounded like a pathetic apology. An admission of guilt.

"That's all you can say right now?" Leo was fuming.

"Well, I could say I'm sorry."

"Are you?"

"I'm not sure," Sage admitted. "I think I am. It was not very nice of me to ditch the phone like that. I do feel bad. Mostly I'm just confused and overwhelmed. I just want a break."

Leo scoffed. "Well, that is *definitely* not going to happen now. Clear out the guest room, Love. You officially have a roommate."

14

LEO

It's a good thing Leo bought AirTags like gum. That's how he'd found her at the diner those months ago. He'd stashed them all throughout her belongings (purses, tote bags, slippers, her car, he even slipped one on the rat's collar). Tonight, it paid off.

What on earth was her problem?

"What?" Sage squeaked. "You can't move in!"

"You have lost all *Alone Privileges.* Forever! You're grounded, Love." He wanted to pull over and grab her and—he didn't know what. He wanted to scream at her for being an idiot and at the same time he wanted to wrap his arms around her and squeeze her tight just to know she was really there and everything was all right.

Which was totally normal and a professional thing to do. Probably.

(And now he was here wondering what it would be like to hug her, to hold her close. Would she resist? Would she melt into him, also overwhelmed by what had happened? Would he get a chance to brush that soft spot on her neck?)

He snapped out of his thoughts and back to the woman sitting next to him.

Goodness, he had been so scared.

The alarm blared around ten thirty and it wasn't the normal chirp of a bird or squirrel crossing the camera. No. This was a full-on attempted break-in and Leo was out the door and careening down the road. He sent the automated message to the police department. (Sentinel Security Agency was pretty high up and part of his initial work when he came into town was to let the small-town officers know what was going on and set up a line of communication.)

Then he called Sage. A cold sweat rippled across his body when she didn't answer. He tracked her phone. She was *in the house.* In the house with whatever monster was crawling through the window.

He had tried again. Nothing. Then again. *Nothing.*

A deep dread settled into his bones.

He'd dealt with missing Subjects before. He'd had some that had run off, some who'd had their lines of communication cut, for whatever reason. Some threats created maddening chaos, but *this*? This was different. Leo was picturing Sage huddled in the bathroom, wielding a stupid plunger for protection. He even thought of the sad rat. No matter how close to death it already was, it still didn't deserve to leave this world being scared.

The ten-minute drive only took him four and he

barreled into the house, only fumbling with the key for half a second in his sweaty palm.

"Sage!" he bellowed. Nothing. Leo stormed out of the house, creeping around the corner, and found the cause of the blaring alarm. A kid, maybe a young adult, busy peeping into the ground-floor window around the back.

The shadow Leo cast over the Peeping Tom made the kid flinch and he tried to run away. It took Leo two steps to grab the intruder's coat and haul him into the porch light.

"I'm sorry," Sage whispered.

Her words brought him back to the present.

"What you did was unacceptable. I cannot do my job unless you do yours. I am so angry I am shaking." Not an exaggeration. Or maybe it was the drop of adrenaline. He turned off the car, the light of the small police station illuminating Sage's wide-eyed stare. "We are going to go in there where they will explain how a teenager managed to track down your address and wanted to meet up with you for a little chat. I don't think it was malicious. It was just creepy as hell and should serve as a huge warning to you that your creepy little mansion doesn't actually keep out the creeps."

Sage swallowed hard. "Do you know what he wanted?"

Leo shrugged. "He told the cops he just wanted to chat about starting up as a streamer or some crap like that."

Sage nodded. "But how did he find me?"

"I don't know. Probably because you blast your whole

life online. Wouldn't be that hard." He slammed the door and waited for her to get out, and led her inside the station.

The cop's rendition of the story made Sage blink in surprise despite the cop leaving out the fact that Leo had been the one to wrestle the kid into submission, not that it was hard, it just took one hard stare from Leo for the kid to wait on the porch step. Still, the cops should have mentioned that Leo was the one to detain him.

Sage opted not to press charges in exchange for the kid having to do community service. Leo wanted to be mad, but all things considered, it made sense. The teenager was creepy and weird in a hyper-fixated sort of way. Sage had practically begged Leo to let her avoid making public charges.

"Lily will ruin this boy's life."

"It's a man, albeit a small one, and it won't ruin his life." But Leo couldn't be sure of that.

"Lily will make it a big deal. Please don't tell her."

"I work for her. Not you. And you are in no position to ask me favors right now."

Sage nodded. "I know. I'm so sorry. I'll never do that again. I promise. Let's just get this taken care of quietly for everyone involved. *Please.*"

The plea sounded genuine. And to be fair, Lily annoyed him. And it was getting close to midnight. And he was tired. The adrenaline spike and subsequent crash were getting to him. So, he conceded.

It took them twenty minutes of driving in absolute silence before they pulled up to Sage's haunted mansion.

Seriously, why did it look so...ominous? During daylight hours the home boasted of character and proud craftsmanship that could never be replicated in today's modern architecture. Why in the darkness did it look like it had eyes and the porch was going to swallow them whole?

Probably because it was. The place needed some serious updates.

They plodded inside (and did not get eaten by the decaying steps) and once the door was firmly locked behind them, the pair engaged in a staring contest fit for the Guinness Book of World Records. (Fun fact: the longest staring contest was 40 minutes and 59 seconds.)

It was finally Sage who broke the silence. "I'll have to get a spare room ready—"

"Don't bother." Leo walked over to the plush couch and made himself at home. "We'll take care of it tomorrow. Right now, I feel like I could fall asleep on my feet."

"Leo, I—"

He held up a hand. "Just. Stop. We'll talk about it in the morning. Go to your room."

And for once she listened. He lay across the couch, trying to find sleep.

Wait, had she finally said his name?

The first thing Leo was met with the next morning (other than the labored breathing of the rat dog on the couch opposite of him) was the smell of coffee. The elixir of life was enough to rouse him out of the plushy couch. Seriously, the pillows and blankets were threatening to suffocate him and he vowed never to tell Sage how falling asleep on a mountain of impractical blankets gave him the best sleep of his life.

"You're up." Sage walked over to the couch, handing him a cup of coffee before sitting next to the rat.

"Thank you." Leo sipped the coffee. It tasted like dirt. He spit it out.

Sage raised her eyebrows. "I promise the gesture was meant to be a peace offering."

"Really? Looks like you are trying to poison me." Coffee grounds stuck to his tongue.

"I've never actually made coffee."

No kidding. "I'll show you. Seems like an important thing to know how to do—roomie."

She grimaced. Good. He was ready to torture her a bit. He was still not over her little escape last night.

"Roomie," she repeated. "Well, you are in the minority with us ladies ruling the roost." She patted the rat-dog's head. "So, let's go over the rules."

Leo sat up and almost took another sip of the poison. He set it on the coffee table gently, as if it may explode in his face if he were too rough with it. "Yes. Let's chat about some rules." He stood and walked to the kitchen, reheating the kettle on the stove, ready to make himself an actual pour-over. Then he saw the true abomination. The horror. The living nightmare he walked into.

"You used my pour-over *without* a filter?"

"A filter?" Sage joined him in the kitchen and hopped up on the counter to watch him. She gripped her mug of tea and took a sip. "I didn't know you needed one of those."

"Clearly. And I am not in the mood for an internal cleanse with these coffee grounds."

Realization hit her. "Oh. Yeah, that makes sense. So how did you find me?"

Leo made coffee (without the solid bits).

"Magic." Leo was not ready to admit that he had dropped AirTags around the house like candy at a parade. Luckily, she had brought a bag that he had slipped an AirTag into. Once he realized that Sage was not in the house after the attempted break in, he pulled out his app and scoured the fifty-plus (not an exaggeration) AirTags and found an outlier. At a bar. The rest was history.

"I don't believe in magic," Sage said.

"Can't reveal my secrets in case you decide to be a flight risk again."

"I won't," Sage said. "Look. Let's go over some ground rules now."

"Good. Rule one: don't be a complete idiot."

Then Sage droned on about how he'd have his own bathroom and not leave messes in the kitchen because of ants and if he wanted a fire to open the floo and a bunch of other nonsense. He quit listening when he got distracted by a coffee ground stuck in his tooth. He needed his toothbrush. And clothes. Really, he needed to grab all his things from Tess's house.

"Are we agreeing?" Sage asked, ending her monologue about...something.

"Until something needs to change," Leo said, avoiding actually agreeing with anything. "Now get dressed, we have errands to run."

"I am dressed."

Sage wore a pair of leggings and a long shirt that nearly went to her knees. And of course, it had an obnoxious purple tie-dye print on it with another familiar print of the rat-dog wearing a flower crown. Must be part of her branding. Which was ridiculous.

"You're a walking fashion faux pas."

"I would love for you to define faux pas."

Leo didn't dignify that with a response because he could not, in fact, define it and wasn't even sure he could spell it correctly enough to Google it.

Sage accompanied him to his house and waited in the car while he gathered his belongings. Luckily Tess wasn't there because he would have a tough time explaining why he came back at ten in the morning looking like he had a much better night than he actually did (with a girl who looked like she was wearing pajamas sitting in the passenger seat).

When he hopped back in his car (no he wasn't rushing because he was afraid Tess was coming home… he was just a quick person) Sage said, "The condo looks like a hospital."

He really couldn't argue. It was bright white with harsh lines and looked so…clinical. Still, he couldn't let her have any jab at him go by that easily. "At least the porch won't eat you."

"What?"

"Let's just get back. I want a shower, roomie. You've got dinner duty tonight."

.   .   .

It turns out that Leo would be taking over most of the dinner duties, which was fine. He didn't exactly feel like testing his stomach's resolve. He didn't expect it would fare well against an obscene amount of slightly charred pizza bites (apparently Sage thought she'd cook them the fancy way instead of in the microwave) and a pre-made salad with dressing that tasted mostly of syrup.

But cooking was a sword he'd fall on. He actually rather liked it. There was a quality about it that made cooking feel like a true escape. Maybe it was the giant windows pointing out to the yard or maybe it was just the ample counter space.

And so, another week passed in relative peace. Sage, for the last week, pretty much lived in her office, even falling asleep in there between streams and other projects. She occasionally came downstairs to flap the umbrella around while she let the rat do its business in the yard.

But Leo also discovered that she came down if he made something that smelled particularly delicious. And no, that's not why he was cooking every single night. He just liked cooking...though he had to admit that was a recent development, but what else was he supposed to do while cooped up in this house? Fix the porch? He'd ordered the lumber already. Repair the sticky bathroom door? Done. Run twelve miles a day? Pretty much did that, sometimes more. Bury his nose in his computer and updating and perfecting the cameras and software Sentinel Security used remotely? Every single day.

Maybe she was right. Maybe he did need a hobby. Something to learn. Something to improve his mind. He could practically hear her shrill voice whispering in his ear, "Hobbies are supposed to be relaxing. Something you're allowed to be bad at and do for fun."

The thought of her whispering in his ears gave him the tingles and he decided to run a half marathon as a distraction.

Cooking was the only thing that really seemed to entice Sage out of her little cave and Leo had to admit that it was nice taking care of his Subject (what? It was in the job description) and he had to admit he was starved for conversation.

Today's dinner menu consisted of seared pork chops and roasted broccoli and, right on schedule, Sage closed down her stream with her signature, "Thanks, everyone! I'll see you tomorrow, go pet a puppy!" (Yes, he had her stream playing in the background. He needed to keep tabs on her.) Moments later she was casually walking down the stairs in her simple black t-shirt (only a small print of the rat on it in the corner pocket) and grabbed the umbrella, squawking as she walked out the back door, flapping the rainbow material around so her dog could "pee in peace" which seemed totally backward considering the song and dance Sage performed.

Once inside Sage commented on how good "something smells" which was her line to try and act casual, like she just *happened* to be down here and so she "may as well have a bite to eat." Leo could see right through it. And he didn't mind one bit.

"Made you a plate," he said, sliding it to her usual spot at the counter. Sure, there was a formal dining room down the hall with a big oak table, but it was covered in old vases and art. Sitting on the barstools at the counter felt better for both of them. Less formal. They could both tell themselves this was just a happenstance occurrence and not a routine they'd cultivated over the last two weeks of forced cohabitation.

"This is good," Sage said. "When'd you learn to cook?"

"The barracks actually," Leo said. "I had a little kitchenette and after a bout of food poisoning, I was skeptical of the mess hall. After the second time, I was sure there was something off about the food. Third time I never went back. I am a proud student of YouTube University."

Sage laughed. "I say you graduated with honors. I too, am a student of YouTube. I learned how to change out the graphics card because of a video. It mostly worked. I think I am more of a B Student and actually not that great with the guts of the computer."

Leo cocked his head. "I can fix that pretty easily, you know. PCs are kind of like Legos in the way they are built."

"You know computers?"

Leo snorted. "I am pretty much the IT guy for the agency. As much as I love lounging around here with your rat all day," Sage pointed a butter knife at him but he was undeterred, "I actually do a lot of work for the company remotely. Mostly tracing hacks, fixing tech issues, you know the drill."

Sage glanced at his computer, which still had her stream up despite it already ending. "That part of the duties?"

Leo stabbed at his plate. "As much as I love listening to white noise, which your voice has become pretty close to, still a little shrill and squeaky, I actually have a filter on, monitoring the comments, seeing if there are any red flags I need to chase down."

"Sure," Sage said, chewing and looking around. "Why do I smell eggs?"

Leo made a show of looking at his watch. "That would be the quiche. Needs another ten minutes."

"Quiche? A weird thing to have for dessert."

"That would be for breakfast. The more your mouth is full, the less talking you do."

"You know, there is a mute button on that fancy computer of yours."

"But alas, not for real life."

Sage rolled her eyes. "So, catch any baddies waving red flags?"

"You have quite the eclectic mix in the chat, that's for sure."

Sage just shrugged. "It pays the bills."

"You keep saying that. Do you actually like pandering to these people?"

Sage bit her lip. He touched a nerve. "I don't pander to anyone. I actually like streaming and chatting. I get to have fun and get paid for it. But sometimes the weirdos come in, and sometimes people I don't really like join the group. There's not much I can do about it."

"Doesn't it get to you?"

"No." She looked down at her broccoli.

It was a lie. He didn't push it.

They finished eating in relative silence. Sage did the dishes while Leo ignored his mother's phone call and checked the cameras. He chased down a few leads, getting absorbed into the world of IP addresses and locations (which he had to admit was fascinating).

They mumbled goodnight to each other despite it only being eight and Sage went to her office where she streamed a cozy game because "she couldn't sleep" and Leo watched the stream from his bedroom downstairs, where he also couldn't sleep.

15

SAGE

Okay, so it was really annoying having Leo around, but it was also... somewhat convenient. She'd probably put on a few pounds since he moved in, which was probably good considering she had been sporting a gaunt appearance since George died.

But goodness gracious he was also annoying. He constantly hounded her about what her schedule was going to be like for the day and made no effort to hide how annoyed he was with her "go with the flow" mentality.

She was putting in some serious private gameplay time for *Welkin Wall.* She wanted to give herself the best shot of wowing everyone. Other times, when she was not buried in a game, Leo would drag her to that god-awful, fancy golf course and make her look like a fool by encouraging her to hit some balls. Though, he'd lost some of his zeal since she'd pointed the club at his own balls and threatened, "Those are my next target."

And, okay, *fine*. It *was* nice watching him come in after one of his long runs. He was usually shirtless by then, wiping sweat from his brow, his muscles on full display, and he was flushed, and—

He was just nice to look at, okay?

She could appreciate pretty things. So, it wasn't weird that she'd track his location and peek out the window when she saw him come back down the road home, so she could catch a glimpse of his final sprint.

They took nightly walks together to end their day. Crazy how a little bit of time moving outside could melt the tension away. Not that she'd ever admit to Leo that he had been on to something. He was already too puffed up. He didn't need an ego boost. If she said, "Yeah, you're right," his head would explode, and Sage didn't want to be an accessory to manslaughter.

It was on one of those nightly walks that she asked him about his running.

"Why do you do it? It seems miserable."

He scoffed. "I signed up for the Portland Marathon so I need to train for it."

She kicked a stone across the sidewalk. "Yes but why did you sign up for it? Why was it a goal? A thing you wanted to do?"

"It seemed like a good idea. A challenge."

She tried not to show frustration but failed. "Okay but why? Do you like checking off boxes of personal challenges? What next? A mountain to climb?"

He seemed to pick up on her frustration. "Why does everything have to have meaning? Sometimes we just do things. And I like to conquer challenges so yeah, maybe this is one of those things. Fun fact: only one percent of the human population has ever run a marathon. I want to be in that one percent."

"You seriously need a hobby."

"I have running as a hobby."

This time, Sage scoffed. "No. You decided it was a challenge to be conquered. Hobbies are for fun. They're relaxing. It's giving yourself permission to be bad and do the thing for the sake of doing the thing."

It had been a point of contention. During their forced proximity, Sage had commented how Leo needed more to do in life than working out, physical therapy exercises, and reading self-help books and articles.

He took a turn kicking the rock across the ground. "My hobby is not letting my brain turn to rot."

Then an argument ensued about the freedom of being bad at something and hobbies and how society tried to monetize them—and Leo pointing out Sage had done just that—and Sage pointing out that she started watercolor painting with Roz for fun and then it devolved into an argument about whether or not her latest watercolor was a scene of a gruesome murder or a lovely red rose. It was a red rose, obviously, but now she couldn't unsee the murder scene, the jerk.

But other times, in the rare moments they weren't arguing, things were quiet. Things were...nice? No, not nice, but there was a strange level of comfort. Like the other night, for example. It was late. She couldn't sleep—not out of the ordinary these days—so she went down to the den, cozy blanket in one hand, Squash in the other, and turned on a movie. A classic. *Ever After* (again). George used to love that movie.

Then Leo walked in wearing sweatpants and a baggy shirt. He looked equal parts exhausted and wired.

"Can't sleep either?" he asked.

Sage nodded.

Then Leo left and Sage turned the volume down a smidge, wondering if she had woken him up, but five minutes later he came back to the den with a sleeve of Oreos and a mug of tea for her (vanilla chamomile—her evening favorite) and a protein shake for him. He just handed her the mug and set the cookies between them when he sat down. They watched the entire movie like that, sipping their drinks and dodging each other's fingers as they reached for the Oreos. And when the movie was over, Leo simply got up, said, "Night" and left her alone.

And how dare he look so good in those sweatpants? It was a cliché.

She went to bed and dreamed of libraries, English accents, Quiche, and sweatpants. Wait, how had he known what tea to make her?

"Hi, hello?" Sage asked the unknown number that had called her not once, not twice, but three times.

"Hi, George?"

A lump formed in Sage's throat. "Sorry, I think you have the wrong number."

"No," said the male voice. "This is a number George left me. I know he passed on—"

"So why are you calling?" Sage couldn't keep the frustration out of her voice. She was lying on the couch in the den, flipping through Netflix and trying to decide what to watch. (She would eventually pick *50 First Dates* again so why was she even bothering to look?)

"I found out through the grapevine that you inherited George's estate. I believe we met. You were his nurse? I am Ralph Emmerson. I own a gallery in Portland and was in contact with George about a piece. We had discussed my purchasing of a painting—"

"Sorry, the estate is still in the works of having everything transitioned into proper names and all that legal stuff," Sage lied. "And I am not planning on liquidating any assets until July at the very earliest." It sounded so posh and formal. It was a script Tavy gave Sage after she began receiving calls from people wondering why George had suddenly ghosted them all and left several business deals unfinished.

"Well, George and I were very close to an agreement. Only missing a bill of sale at this point really—"

"Did he give you the painting? Or did you give him any money?" Sage rubbed her temples. She hated this whole business thing. Tavy said she'd help over the summer and get it all squared away. She was put together and smart like that. Roz would bring the snacks.

"Well, No," Ralph said. "But for all intents and purposes–"

"I'm really sorry," Sage said. "But we'll chat in July."

She hung up, adding a new contact of "DO NOT ANSWER UNTIL JULY" and flung her phone across the couch.

"Who was that?" Leo's voice said from the doorway behind Sage. She nearly jumped out of her skin. Goodness, he was like a creepy shadow.

"Just a guy interested in some things."

"A guy?" Leo looked a mix of confusion and curiosity. "Some things?"

She decided to play with that. "Yes, I do have the attention of males from time to time." Even if it is just for old paintings. But why had she phrased it like that? To get a rise out of him? "Now go away. I have work to do."

"*50 First Dates* is work?" he asked.

"It's refilling my creative well."

"Good grief," Leo murmured, walking away. "Get a hobby."

She rolled her eyes at the echo of their earlier argument. She yelled "You get a hobby!" because that was a very grown-up response, apparently, just like making snide comments hoping to get a rise out of him. Plus it was nice to stare at his backside as he walked away.

Days later, they were forced into his car on a two-hour journey. Sage would be testing out some gear she'd be using for the competition, taking photos with Jared, and other mundane stuff at LilyTech headquarters.

It was her turn to pick the music, because, yes, their music taste was so wildly different, they had to take fifteen-minute turns, coming to that compromise like four-year-olds.

It didn't help that he was already more annoyed with her than usual. He had told her to be ready to leave at eight sharp. She was not ready, though she had tried to be. And they were out the door ten minutes later than they were supposed to be, which wasn't that big of a deal until they were half a mile away and she made him turn around because she forgot her bag with all the clothes Jared requested she bring for outfit changes.

And then when they were on the road again (now thirty minutes behind schedule) she had begged him to stop at the only coffee drive-through in town. She bribed him with paying for his order, which had enough caffeine to send a moose into cardiac arrest. She told him as much.

"Please. Maybe my coffee will kill me and put me out of my misery."

So, he wasn't a Celine Dion fan. Naturally, Sage put Celine Dion's greatest hits for her turn of picking music.

"If you play one more song of hers I swear you will never make it to your precious meeting because I will be turning this car around and calling Lily to explain that you had a medical emergency."

Sage sighed. "And you call me dramatic. What emergency would I be having?"

"Busted eardrum because I will turn her winging up so loud that it will blast both our eardrums. I won't have to listen to her scream anymore and you will never get the pleasure of hearing Drake again."

"Seems like a perfect solution all around." Instead, she played Billy Idol and they both seemed satisfied for the time being.

"You come down here much?" he asked once he had enough caffeine in him to be human again.

"Maybe once or twice a month. I don't really mind it. Sometimes I go down on the coast for a prettier drive even though it's longer."

"A lot of my friends went to school out here but I never made it over this way much," Leo said.

Sage looked out the window, watching the passing trees. The green would never get old. "Did you go to college?" she asked.

Leo shrugged. "Dad was a military man. I scored high on my ASVAB so I got into the Marines at a decent level. Got my bachelor's in biology before my leg got blown up."

Sage turned to look at him. He looked fine for having gone through such an...ordeal. Leo patted his right leg. "It acts up sometimes, but they thought they were going to have to amputate and a physical therapist with God complex said he could fix me and he was right. I was discharged, medically, but was hired on at Sentinel Security before the rehab was even done. Been studying for the MCAT and will just have to go to med school a different route instead of through the military."

Sage paused for a long moment. "Did you ever—"
"Kill a guy?"

"No!" She held up her hands. "I seriously do not want to know the answer to that. I was just gonna ask if you ever went to therapy, like real therapy, for what happened?"

Leo shook his head. "Not needed."

"Everyone needs therapy."

"Do you?"

Sage was quiet for a long moment. "I did. Maybe I still do." She cleared her throat. "But not for your hand in my life. We all have crap going on." She went to therapy to deal with the abandonment of her mother, for having a chaotic life, and learning how to handle it. George was the one who forced her to every appointment. They'd go together and meet up after and he always, always, treated her to tea at his favorite sushi place, though he forbade her from eating the oysters there, but gave everything else a thumbs up. Green tea hasn't tasted the same since George left this earth but she kept trying anyway.

She must have been silent too long because Leo asked, "Did you ever go to college?"

"I never even graduated high school. But don't worry, I know how to use the Pythagorean theorem and the difference between *there* and *their.*"

Leo scoffed and licked his lips. Was he uncomfortable? Did he think less of her for not having that piece of paper that basically said, "Congrats! You jumped through the ridiculous hoops of the American education system."

"Well good. I guess the University of Oregon has gone downhill since leaving the Pac-12. A fun spot to hang out though." Sage was impressed with his change of subject. It actually felt like he was trying to be nice.

"It's just another big city. You didn't have to drive," Sage said. It was kind of nice not having to deal with the freeways and she could live her passenger princess life. She'd never been one of those. She drove George everywhere. She practically knew every location of every flea market, secondhand store, and antique shop because of it. Those were always his favorite places. If he had been here now, he'd have gone with her down to the big city. They'd make a day of it. He'd smile while he sat on his little chair at LilyTech and try to give Jared some fashion tips, and when they were finished he'd insist he found the best sushi place and they'd go and he'd critique everything and mutter to himself when the chef couldn't speak Japanese. Then critique the green tea. After that, they would find a shop or two and spend time looking at bad art and he'd buy the worst painting because "It will haunt my dreams, anyway, may as well have it close enough to berate when I need to."

She was *not* going to cry thinking about green tea and bad art.

Leo scoffed. "It's my job to drive you around. And I want to see this LilyTech office in person. Should be an interesting change of pace."

He wasn't wrong. When they pulled into LilyTech, Sage was whisked away to the "content area" and Leo and Lily chatted for a bit. He was probably giving her an update about safety and protocol. Maybe getting more information about the competitions and all that junk.

Several photos and outfit changes later, Jared gave a small sigh and said, "This should work for a month or two. Don't give me that look. You wouldn't have to come and do this so often if you actually took some content and filmed stuff like you said you would."

He had a point, but did he have to be so smug about it?

Finally, they got to the fun stuff—getting fitted for new gear. Headset, controllers, even a new chair that would be the big unveiling for LilyTech at the conference. It had a wide seat, so you could—*get this!*—sit *cross-legged.* Sage squealed with delight when Lily showed her.

Leo looked confused. Probably still working out the difference between *there* and *their.*

Then a strange thought crossed her mind. Could he even bend his legs like that? How had she not known that he had been through...that? An explosion? Where did that happen? Sure, she noticed the occasional limp and him icing it but she chalked it up to a running injury or something. Why did her chest get tight thinking about that?

The day at LilyTech came and went and Lily waved to Leo and Sage as they walked out the doors, yelling, "Keep my girl safe, Camaro!"

Leo waved back. "She's in excellent hands."

She was in the hands of an annoying know-it-all.

"So," Leo said when they got into his truck, rubbing his hands together. "I am starving. I looked up a local spot here. Supposed to have the best sushi in town, and get this, they even boast to have the best green tea in the city."

"No!" Sage yelled.

16

LEO

"No!" Sage yelled.

Okay, so definitely not the reaction Leo had been expecting. Seriously. He had gone out of his way to look up green tea and what made it good and the best spot in town. He had several new fun facts to casually share with her now. And he thought for sure she'd be into it, even if there was sushi involved. He could admit it was an acquired taste, and she had the palate of a toddler.

"They have cooked options there. Noodles and stuff."

Sage looked out the window and quickly wiped her eyes. "It's not that." She sniffed and blinked away—was that a tear—and sniffed again. "I love sushi. And green tea. But that used to be our thing. George and I. And we..." She sniffed again. "Actually, it's fine. It's just sushi. And tea." Her voice cracked on the last word.

"Eh, I've actually lost my appetite for fish." It was a lie. He had been practically salivating after fresh salmon nigiri. Maybe some black cod. "But it would be a shame to leave the city on such a beautiful day. You need to get out. Live a little. Be spontaneous. I know you don't have any streams planned for today."

"I could do a pop-up stream?"

"Or you could go on an adventure with me."

"I'd rather get a root canal." But there was a gleam in her eye. Was it curiosity?

Leo rolled his eyes. "What's something you've wanted to do down here that you've never done? Something you wouldn't have been able to do with George since he was... older?"

Leo must have said the right thing because Sage cocked her head and seemed to be considering his proposal. "Do you have a rain jacket?"

Leo snorted. "It's Oregon. Obviously I have a rain jacket with me." He pulled it from the back seat.

"Okay same," said Sage, thinking. "I have an idea but it might require some driving. I think you'll be into it because it's outdoorsy and stuff and I'm sure you'll jump at the chance to show off how in shape you are. I'll probably fall on my face. If we do this, you have to promise not to make fun of me."

"I'll do my very best." It was the truth, though his best was just a notch above the "will laugh at literally anything" level.

She blew out a breath. "You ever heard of Thor's Well?"

"That's on the coast, which is like forty-five minutes from here." He said it with a flat tone despite the fact that, internally, he was rather excited about this little excursion. But she had to work for it. It never hurt to have a few "get out of jail free" cards in the back pocket.

"I know, but the little city is just north by a few minutes. We could go over there, grab lunch, and then hike down to see it or vice versa depending on the tides."

"You got a deal, but on one condition."

"You're the one that asked me to be spontaneous!" She pulled her legs onto the seat and sat cross-legged. "I am losing my spontaneous spirit."

Best not to push his luck. "You haven't even heard of my conditions!"

"What?" She was on the verge of backpedaling.

"You pick where we eat." He turned on the 4Runner. "I can't handle another emotional breakdown over tea."

Her face lit up for half a second, then she rolled her eyes. "You haven't seen anything close to an emotional breakdown, trust me."

He handed her the phone, already open to Google Maps. "Just put in the address here."

She did and set the phone up on the stand. "Ya-chat?"

"It's *Yaw-hats*," she corrected.

"How the hell is *Yachats* pronounced like that?" Leo asked. "English is stupid."

"At least we can finally agree on something," she said. Little did she know they'd be fighting over who was better, Whitney Houston or Mariah Carey, for the rest of the drive.

They bundled up, Leo in his black rain jacket and Sage in her purple waterproof shell. The hike down to Thor's Well was pretty easy, actually. They had opted to hit the well first since the tide seemed to be in their favor.

Sage only fell on her butt twice. The first time Leo helped her up with only a hint of a smile. She glared daggers at him. The second time she fell he didn't hold back. Maybe it was her undignified squeak or the fact that the mud actually made a *splat* sound as her butt connected with the ground.

"Ugh. At least I have a change of clothes in the car thanks to the entire wardrobe Jared made me bring."

"Yeah," Leo said. "What was up with all those flowers?" At one point, a dozen different flower arrangements came in and Sage looked absolutely murderous when she was told to pose with them all.

Sage wore the same murderous look now. "Jared's idea. To be honest, he's trying to push boundaries to increase my social media growth, which was doing fine on my own. Sure, not as aesthetic or streamlined but good grief, he didn't have to stage a remake of all the condolence flowers people sent after George's passing."

Leo's stomach dropped. "They sent flowers to your house?"

"I have a P.O. box! I'm not an idiot," Sage scoffed, which turned into a squeak as she slipped over a rock. Leo walked behind her after she insisted she lead because he was taking "Goliath steps" and she was convinced he was going to leave her behind. He settled for a hand reaching out behind her, ready to grab the back of her lilac rain jacket when she slipped on the wet rocks.

"So Jared," Sage continued, "he was all like, 'just pose with them so we can use them next year and so you can maybe post some stories on gratitude and stuff' and he was totally fine using George as content!" She slipped and

Leo shot out a hand and grabbed under her arm. "I wish I could fire him." She shook Leo off without even thanking him. Her cheeks were red, likely from the wind and the cold, but her neck was also pink. Was that a blush?

"So, fire him."

"It's a lot like trying to fire you," she said.

Leo barked out a laugh. "Yeah, good luck with that."

"Yeah, good luck with that," she mumbled.

Thor's Well was magnificent. The giant hole in the rocky landscape sucked in the waves crashing against the wall, shooting it up like a geyser where it turned to a pink mist against the sunset backdrop. It was beautiful, the sound was heavenly. The constant bashing of waves against rock was like the very heartbeat of the earth. Everything stood still to listen to the rhythm. The birds were quiet. The trees were still. Even Sage stopped her endless chatter. They stood next to each other for what could have been minutes. Hours? How long did a sunset last? Because they stood there until the last rays of the sun dipped beyond the ocean's horizon, and then the spell was broken.

"It's amazing," Leo said.

"Yeah," Sage said. "It really is."

Then an unearthly scream pierced the stillness. Sage jumped into Leo. "Get it!"

"What is it?" Leo asked, heart racing, just because the sound had been so startling and not because Sage was pressed against his side, her hand over his chest.

She grabbed his arm and pushed it out in front of them. "Use your guns and get it!" She turned and looked at the narrow trail leading back up the hillside. "Actually, let's just run!"

"Yeah, you're right!" he said, mostly because he wanted to see her try to run up that slick mess. He wasn't about to tell her it was just a lonely fox looking for a date.

The spectacle did not disappoint him.

Only when she nearly face-planted and turned back to see if he had followed her the two feet she'd managed to make while running like a cartoon, she scowled. She took stock of him standing there without a care in the world. Then the fox screamed again and her scowl turned to actual fear. Her face paled. Her eyes darted to the darkening tree line. And that wasn't in his job description. He was supposed to make his Subject feel at ease.

"It's just a fox trying out speed dating," Leo said. He tried to look sincere, but his face must have betrayed him because she flung the mud sticking to her hands at him.

"You are such a jerk, Leo Camaro."

"What? It took me a minute to figure out what it was. But for the record, in an actual emergency, you're going to be following me, not the other way around, Love."

She glowered. "Fine. Just lead us out of here. I want to change and I am starving."

Leo led them out as best as he could, thankful the moon was full and the night was clear enough. He really had been lost in that sunset. It wasn't like him to lose the light like that. Luckily the trail wasn't long and was well-marked. There was only one casualty.

"My shoe!" Sage yelled while she watched it tumble down the ravine with resigned sadness. The kind of acceptance only a true Oregonian could have about losing a battle to the mud and thick tree roots.

"Good thing you have extra clothes in the car."

Sage sniffed. "I loved those things."

"Should have had them laced tighter."

"They were Velcro."

Leo balked. "Then you deserved it. Now hop up. Parking lot is just up here."

"Up?" she asked.

"I know it's a two-letter word, but surely you can use context clues to help you define it."

"I'm fine." She took two steps and hissed. "It's like ice." She stood on one leg like a muddy, purple flamingo.

"Just hop up."

She must have been really cold because when Leo crouched, she reached over and gripped his shoulders and hiked her legs up around his waist. Were her hands always this small? No wonder LilyTech needed to exist if people had such small hands. And for literally lounging in a chair twenty hours a day, she had decent strength. He looped his arms under her legs and shouldered her on like a backpack, his shoulder hitting her chin a little too hard.

"Sorry," he said.

"I bit my tongue."

"Don't bleed on me."

"No promises."

The rest of the short walk went in silence, save for a final scream of that bachelor fox. Maybe he could return with the rat-dog and they could work out some sort of platonic friendship.

When he deposited her at the 4Runner he said, "It's unlocked. I'm going to go see a monkey about a tree."

"What?"

"You know, gonna go tell the racehorse hello?"

"Excuse me?"

This woman was dense. How did she field sexist and borderline abusive comments from strangers all day and come up with witty replies just to be lost with a euphemism about peeing?

"I'm going to take a leak and will be gone long enough to give you plenty of time to get in the car and change." He gave her a lazy salute and turned toward the woods, but not before catching a blush. A real deep red rose up her cheeks. She practically glowed in the dark.

"Oh. Right. Okay."

True to his word, he gave her ample time, but he was still within earshot. The fox only screamed twice. The first time he hadn't been ready and nearly watered his shoes, the next time the animal sounded so desperate that he considered inviting the thing to come back and eat the rat-dog.

Meet. Of course, he meant *meet.*

He hollered to Sage as he walked back, "You decent?"

"To my standards, yes. To yours? I don't know, you might vomit."

He hopped into the car and tried to suppress his repulsion.

"I'll clean it up!" She promised. "I feel like I got a muddy baptism. Your car is an innocent bystander."

Leo chucked a little, storing his muddy jacket in the

back seat. She had sure done a number on it. How was there a footprint on the ceiling?

"No big deal. Your outfit though." He hissed through his teeth.

"I wasn't about to put on jeans in the car! That's like trying to put toothpaste back in a tube."

Her outfit was adorable. But she wouldn't ever hear that from him. Tight leggings that flared at the bottom, a cropped sweatshirt (with the dog on it, of course), her hair in a loose braid to the side, and a pink beanie made for a cute "I am comfortable in my own skin" type of vibe. It suited her.

He reached out and touched her cheek with his thumb. She paused, looking at him wide-eyed before he realized the gesture could convey something else. "So much mud," he quickly said.

How was her cheek so soft?

"Whatever, it's not like we're going anywhere fancy." She turned to her phone, which only illuminated her beet-red face. Did she...feel uncomfortable in his presence? No. They had created an equilibrium of sorts these last weeks. A carefully cultivated balance of "I'll stay out of your way if you stay out of mine." *Unless I am making your tea and you return the favor later by making my coffee just the way I like it. Unless I pick up that weird tea you like when I see it at the store. Unless you offer to chop veggies while I cook your favorite soup because you feel a cold coming on. Unless we are sharing Oreos and watching one of the best romance movies ever. (What? Drew Barrymore was the queen and Ever After only proved as much.)*

Yes, they had a great, totally business-like equilibrium thing going.

Nothing out of the ordinary.

Leo was a professional.

Sage cleared her throat. "You like clam chowder?"

In hindsight, that question was the first mistake of the night.

They opted to drive a little south to hit Mo's, arguably one of the best places to grab a piping hot bowl of clam chowder, just to realize that the line was out the door and the wait was hours. Leo admitted he was tired, and it was clearly the opening Sage needed because she suggested a place down the street. She was likely equally tired but didn't want to be the one to prevent him from getting (what he thought) was some well-earned clam chowder. He had carried a damsel in distress a hundred yards on his back, after all. Quite the gentleman and those gentle-manly (emphasis on the *manly*) gestures deserved a piping bowl of soup.

They walked into Sunshine Palms and ordered "two of the biggest bowls of clam chowder you've got," Leo said.

Walking in was mistake number two.

Ordering clam chowder was mistake number three.

They agreed that it was hard to determine if the clam chowder was halfway decent because they were so hungry or if it was just halfway decent.

Sage sighed. "It's no Mo's." But she ate it anyway.

"Beggars can't be choosers," Leo agreed, finishing off his bowl and ordering more garlic bread. (That was mistake number four.)

They resumed their musical debate, this time over who was better: Kenny Rogers or Jimmy Buffett, which they eventually decided was incomparable, especially when the stern-looking waitress came over and handed Leo the check. "It's a wonder you two are still together considering all this bickering."

It was Leo's turn to blush.

Sage insisted on paying since it was her idea for clam chowder. He tried to slip his card over hers but she caught it and threatened to flush it down the toilet. She had an unusual look of excitement in her eye, so he actually believed her threats this time.

They agreed not to discuss music for the rest of the two-hour drive home to keep the fragile peace between them intact.

Instead, the pair quarreled about the best movies of all time and were surprised to find their tastes overlapped a little. Still, there was plenty to argue about until they hit about that forty-five-minute mark when Sage paused her yammering about "the chaotic beauty of *Water World*" to ask Leo to pull over at a rest stop or gas station or *something* so she could use the bathroom.

Normally this would have been great ammunition to remind her of her childish way of living life and the whole "you should have gone before we left" type of lecture. Leo had a few fun facts about the dangers of public restrooms, but he also had to use the bathroom. Bad.

He wasn't a fan of rest stops, but the churning in his stomach was growing and Sage didn't seem to complain about the shady rest stop right off the freeway. He insisted on clearing the bathroom stall before he allowed her to enter (which she did with a little extra pep in her step).

"I'll be in the next one. Wait for me out here," he called as he dove into the bathroom next door.

A trained professional wouldn't have left his Subject like that. Instead, as he was busy unleashing his bubbling gut into the toilet (from both ends) he was grateful the thick walls prevented her from hearing what were likely inhuman sounds echoing from every orifice.

His insides screamed at him.

His phone lit up with a text and he was barely able to read it through the shakes overtaking him.

Sage: I might be a minute. Lady issues.

He vomited into the little trashcan next to him. (That's why garlic bread was mistake number four.) Bullcrap. There was no way she was having "lady problems" unless she counted the involuntary cleanse they both took in the form of risky clam chowder as a "lady issue."

Leo: If you're having lady problems, call me the matriarch of Mother Nature then.

SAGE: I'm like a broken frozen yogurt machine in here.

Leo tried to laugh but it turned into a gurgle and then a groan.

LEO: I think my insides have turned to lava.

It took about ten minutes before they both braved the outside world, looking at each other's shoes, both red-faced. They tried to make it to the car to press on like the soldiers they were, but they both bailed and sprinted back to the lavatories as fast as they could while squeezing their cheeks together. At least Leo hoped Sage was also doing the undignified half-run to the bathroom. He hadn't even waited to see if she made it into her own stall before diving into his own.

Some hardened security guard he was.

After yet another ten minutes, they both agreed that they had nothing left in them and could brave the hour-and-a-half drive back to Sage's home.

That was mistake number five.

But before mistake number five turned into mistake number six, Leo pulled over to a small but quaint hotel.

It looked as if Sage was going to put in a word of protest, but she grabbed her stomach, gagged, and hopped out of the car to vomit.

He guided her in as best as he could across the parking lot and pretty much pushed her into the lobby, where he parked her in front of a trash can. She held onto it as if it were the most precious thing in the world.

The clerk at the front was a little confused by the sense of urgency behind Leo's request for two rooms, and they *had* to be adjoining, and they *must* have two separate bathrooms. *Now.*

She clicked away at the computer, which felt more

like the ticking of a bomb the longer it went on before she produced two room keys.

Leo and Sage grabbed them and darted toward the stairs.

"You forgot your credit card!" the woman called as Leo disappeared into the stairwell, dragging a woman as green as her namesake behind him.

"I'll grab it in the morning!" he yelled. If he survived the night.

His stomach laughed at him. That tell-tale wave of nausea and accompanying cold sweat washed over him.

Sage got the keycard stuck in her door trying to pull it in and out before she just followed Leo to his room and disappeared through the door connecting their rooms.

"See you on the other side!" Leo called, trying in vain to add some humor to the situation (which was hard to do when he was dying).

His answer came in the sound of Sage retching.

17

SAGE

She would have been humiliated if she could feel anything other than a cold sweat and nausea (accompanied by every liquid spewing from her body).

She stood in front of the sink and splashed cold water on her face. Her phone buzzed.

LEO: Are you alive? Pound the wall twice if yes. Once if no.

SAGE: or I could just text you back.

SAGE: Yes. I'm alive. Barely. I assume you got hit with the same poison.

LEO: I'll never eat clam chowder again.

SAGE: For once, I agree with you.

After one more bout of vomiting—which eventually turned to dry heaving—she found herself lying on her bed, staring at the fan. The room was small enough that she could swing a leg over and nudge the curtains open. The stars looked like they were pinpricks in the night sky and there was a secret world going on behind the curtain of darkness.

Were they really going to stay the night here? She didn't have pajamas! She didn't have clothes. Her toothbrush!

She screeched.

What about Squash!?

Not two seconds after her unintentional scream, Leo burst through the door, though "burst" was a generous term. He more like shouldered the door open, face wet, like he too had been enjoying a moment in the sink's cold water.

"What is it?"

"Squash!"

"What? A spider?"

"No!" She was frantically tapping on her phone. "I need someone to let her out and feed her! She'll be fine alone for the night, but she needs the sweater, the thick fleece one since she gets so cold at night. "Ugh—" She swallowed down a gag. "Tavy is at a tournament and Roz is painting at a destination wedding thing in Spain." Sage sniffed.

Leo leaned against the doorway. "Relax. I've already got it taken care of."

"You what?"

Leo turned white as snow, took two giant steps into her bathroom, and emptied his guts into the toilet. How did he have anything left to give as an offering to the porcelain gods?

"What about Squash?" she asked again. She tossed him a water bottle she'd grabbed from LilyTech and had stashed in her bag. He caught it with ease and took the tiniest sip.

"I called Tess in between bouts of vomiting and she's on her way over."

"But it's locked!" Sage's stomach was nauseous for an all-new reason. Squash needed her pill with her food.

"Your backdoor has an electronic lock on it now, remember? I installed it a few weeks ago. I'll unlock it remotely when she calls me. I already gave her the instructions about where to find the coat and what pills to give the animal. She's in good hands. My sister has always loved rodents. Mom and Dad never let her get a rat of her own."

Sage sniffed, too sick, or too relieved to push back on the rodent comment. "And she knows how much food to give her?"

"A scoop and a half with a splash of water. Got it. And I told her it would be okay to hang out and cuddle if she wanted. She'd use my room, don't worry."

"Really?" Sage sniffed again, fighting the rising churning in her stomach. "She'd do that?"

"Yes," Leo said, quickly backtracking to his own bathroom. "She's an animal person!"

A warm, fuzzy feeling overcame Sage for a moment. He had thought of her dog before she had. He had taken care of it. Those fuzzy feelings were taking root somewhere, but she didn't have long to dwell on that because her stomach made her sprint to the bathroom and eke out another tribute to the porcelain gods.

An hour later (or more? Apparently time ran differently when your guts got turned inside out) Leo knocked on the door.

"I haven't heard any more inhuman sounds coming from your side of the wall. Are you okay?"

Sage was lying, once again, on the bed, staring at the overhead fan. The glow of the two lamps on the nightstand was her only light. She was actually almost able to doze off except for the occasional stomach twist or bout of nausea. It had turned into a mental game and she was determined to win.

"Go away and leave me to die."

"I have dinner."

She nearly barfed at the thought of food. "Go away."

"Are you decent? I'm coming in." He cracked the door and peeked around, apparently deciding that her lying prone on the bed was invitation enough for him to come in. What was it with this man and his serious lack of boundaries?

"I come bearing gifts." He tossed a Gatorade and some saltine crackers on the bed. "Dinner of champions. Also, my sister says Squash is doing great and is snoring on her lap while they watch The Bachelor."

Sage smiled a little and reached around on the bed, trying to find the crackers before she gave up. "Where'd you get these?" she asked.

"DoorDash. There's a Walmart up the street. I also conned the driver into buying us pajamas even though that wasn't really on the list of things to purchase. But a great tip was worth not having to sleep in muddy clothes that reek of vomit."

"You miss too?"

"Backsplash." He shuddered.

She pushed the crackers away. "Sorry I asked."

He tossed a bag on the bed. Inside was a pair of simple, knock-off sweats trying hard to look like Lululemon, but a little too crooked to pull it off. Still, oh-so-comfortable.

"They didn't have pink or purple so I got you green to match."

"Match what?" she asked. Her eyes were brown.

"Your skin tone, though it's looking more normal now."

She threw a cracker at him.

"You don't need to get revenge on me. Walmart already did that." He pulled out another matching set, much larger than hers, also green. "We'll see if a women's double XL will fit."

Sage snorted and pulled the tags from her sweatpants and sweatshirt. "Wait, did they not have men's?"

Leo shrugged. "I don't even know. I just am thankful that I won't have to sleep in jeans. Normally commando would work for me, but I don't want to tempt your feminine wiles with—"

"Forgetting boundaries and giving me a show?"

"You already got that with a side of teapot." He shook his head. "You gonna be okay for the night?"

Sage nodded. "Might take a few field trips to the commode for various reasons, but I think I will survive."

"I left that place one star because negative stars were not an option. You owe me big time."

"I'll pay you back for the new fashion faux pas and the hotel accommodation."

Leo sat on the bed next to her, reaching for a cracker. "Not because of that. I'm writing it off as an expense, just to see what my boss has to say. You owe me for picking the world's worst restaurant."

They argued about whose idea it was for several minutes before Leo politely excused himself to vomit and Sage took the opportunity to sit on her personal throne and continue her slow transformation into an out-of-order frozen yogurt machine.

She showered and changed into the bright green outfit, thankful the hotel had some complimentary soap and the softest towels ever. Her hair wasn't going to recover from air drying and not having a hairbrush, though.

When they later reconvened in Sage's room, Sage couldn't suppress a smile. "Wow," she said, scanning his outfit up and down. Clearly he'd had the same idea and his hair was wet and messy and he smelled of fresh, generic soap.

His outfit was not nearly as flattering. The green sweatpants were taxed to the limit. The sweatshirt was nowhere to be seen and instead, he had a towel slung over his shoulders. She tried not to linger on his bare chest too long, but it was right in front of her face. *Right there.* But when her eyes met these too-tight hot pants, she laughed.

"Shut up," he said, using the corner of the towel to tousle his hair. "The alternative was just a towel. Or I put on my muddy jeans and get your bed all gross." He said it as he climbed onto the bed, snatching the remote from where it rested on the bed.

"Go away. You have a TV in your own room," she reminded him. *Don't stare at the naked chest. Don't stare. Too late. How could he eat so much and yet stay so fit?*

"It's not working," he complained. "But I know they got a Bourne movie on. All hotels do."

Was it hot in here? She should crack the window and get some air.

"I want to go to sleep," Sage lied.

He called her on it. "Unless you uncovered some trick to make your stomach behave, something tells me you won't be sleeping anytime soon. Best to ride this wave with the feast of crackers, electrolytes, and Jason Bourne."

Well, she couldn't argue with that logic.

He sat on the other side of the queen-sized bed, up against the headboard. It was a respectable distance, the crackers and Gatorade were a perfect barrier between them. It was still strange having another (half-naked!) person in her bed. She'd never had a "boy sleepover" and this was not what Sage had in mind when she was a giggly teenager who couldn't even say the word "boyfriend" aloud without combusting into flames.

How times have changed.

How far she'd fallen.

Her stomach rolled and for once she knew for certain it wasn't anxiety, it was just the cold, hard reality of food poisoning.

Leo leaned his head back and sighed. He looked like crap, and she was certain she didn't look much better.

They had these cool matching outfits, though. It was also kind of convenient that his sweatshirt was too small. Silver linings.

She didn't have the energy to try to steal the remote back and in the end, he paused to see what Indiana Jones movie was playing and never turned to the next channel. So, there they were, eating crackers in her bed, sipping Gatorade like champagne, and watching *Indiana Jones and The Raiders of the Lost Ark* with heavy-lidded eyes, screaming stomachs, and spinning heads.

At least Thor's Well had been incredible. But at what cost?

Later, when she was bent over the toilet, retching up those crackers, she vowed to never be adventurous again.

S age woke to a pounding on her door. "You in there?" a now familiar voice asked.

Sage made a strangled sound.

"Great!" Leo called. "Complimentary breakfast ends in thirty minutes. I'll go down for seconds with you. I suggest something light. And I have a surprise for you."

"No more clams," Sage muttered. She felt like a sponge left out to dry. Her tongue tasted of blue Gatorade and salt and when she shook out her hair, crumbs littered the floor. The spot Leo had claimed next to her was empty, which was a relief, but there was definitely a Leo-sized imprint. How long had they been there watching Indiana Jones? They had finished the first movie just to grunt in amusement when the next movie conveniently started playing.

"No clams," Leo pounded the door again. "I've been up since the sun and have decided we need a redo of yesterday. Just get dressed. Shower. Do whatever you gotta do but be ready in thirty minutes. You won't want to miss this."

He sounded excited. He was all giddy. What could be a do-over of yesterday? Another short hike to the beach and a breakfast that *didn't* end in violent spewing? That did sound like a dream, but she wasn't quite willing to risk a bite to eat just yet.

She showered, pulled on the sweatpants she'd slept in, and for good measure, the matching sweatshirt. They were only a few floors up but she swore she felt the building sway with the frigid and ferocious breeze. Or maybe she was just lightheaded. Probably the latter.

She brushed her teeth (thank you DoorDash driver), downed some water, and knocked on the adjoining door.

"Camaro? You decent? I'm ready."

He swung the door open before she was done speaking, wearing the brightest smile, showing no indication of how close he was to death the previous night. He opted to wear his muddy jeans, leaving the hot pants on the floor. Probably for the best. They were a single broken stitch away from giving her another free show.

Great. Now she was wondering what underwear he wore. If any.

Great, she could feel her face heating. Get it together, Sage!

She scowled at his pretty face. "You bounce back well."

He shrugged. "Some carbs will do that. I grabbed you

a bagel. Got you strawberry cream cheese too." He wiggled his eyebrows and thrust the paper plate with the bagel on it toward her.

"Why strawberry?" What she meant to ask was "How on earth did you know that was my favorite especially since I never have it in the house because I'd just eat it straight out of the tub and I do not need that temptation lying around."

He smiled. "I just know."

His smile really was like sunshine.

Sage suddenly felt the urge to run her hands through his perfectly messy hair. Instead she looked at the bagel. Was she just really hungry because she'd emptied her stomach completely last night or was she still nauseous? He must have known about her internal conflict because he said, "The first bite is the scariest, the second bite is the most satisfying."

She took a leap of faith and discovered he was right. That bagel really hit the spot. She ate it as they walked to his car. She was ready to go home and take the longest nap of her life.

"So, what's the surprise?" she asked. "That the sun is shining and we survived the night?"

Leo shuddered. "A miracle. And most miracles deserve to be shouted from the rooftops but I would appreciate it if we kept this epic tale of survival between us."

"I wish to forget the events of the last fifteen hours, please."

Leo nodded. "Great, because I have something

amazing to show you. Something that will blow the memories of last night down the toilet."

"No reminders of toilets, please. I can still hear the clams mocking me."

Leo started the car. "Well, it's not clams we'll be meeting today, Love."

Ten minutes later Sage screamed, "Whale watching?" She turned to him as he basically pulled her kicking and screaming from the cab of the SUV. "Are you insane? Haven't our stomachs endured enough?"

He set her in front of him and gripped her shoulders. "Miss Moon. This is a once-in-a-lifetime event. There is a pod of humpback whales not even a quarter of a mile off the coast here. The sea is absolute glass. We will never get a chance to see these creatures like this again, probably ever." He pulled the hair from the side of her face, exposing her neck to the chilly air. Why were his hands so big? Why was he looking intently at her like that with that little furrow in his brow? Did she have something in her teeth? Why did he smell so good?

She tried to take a step back but his hand held her firm. Then he caressed her like he was familiar, *familiar,* with her. Like touching her neck was the most natural thing in the world. Goosebumps erupted down her spine. How dare rough hands be so gentle?

Then he leaned in, eyes serious, pulling a rogue hair away from her eyes, using his thumb to caress a sensitive spot on her neck.

She wanted to step away again, but she also wanted to lean in because he smelled...good? Why would hotel soap smell so good on this man? It must be the salt air. Must be the near-death experience of losing every liquid in her body that forced a new perspective on beautiful things in life. And why was he so close? And why did she want him closer?

"There," he said, taking a step back and releasing her from that...moment.

"What?" she raised a hand to her neck where he had been caressing her neck. Leo grabbed her hand and pulled it away. "It's a Dramamine patch, just in case. But I am told there is nary a wave to be seen. Still, it's better to get some anti-nausea medicine in us before we start." He placed a patch on his own neck.

"Leo," she groaned like it was a curse. "It's the ocean. Of course, there are going to be waves."

"If you throw up I'll make dinner for a week and do all the clean-up."

He pretty much already did that. He was kind of a good cook and it looked like he realized this might be a useful bargaining chip. But she wasn't one to fold so easily.

"Two weeks."

"Deal."

In the end, it didn't matter, because it was the best trip of her entire life.

There were whales jumping and splashing and they were so close she swore she could smell the krill on their breath. There were only a few passengers and the crew was so knowledgeable. Baby whales showed off and even dolphins decided to join the group. Apparently this was one of the last migrating pods of the year and they were sure making a show about being late to the party.

The sea wasn't exactly glass, and more than once Sage found herself caged between Leo's arms, his large body behind her acting as a wall while they skimmed over a few rogue waves. She tried not to linger when their bodies collided but he was warm and it felt nice and she may have "accidentally" let her body rest against him a moment longer than she should have. She was probably still suffering from food poisoning symptoms. It was the only explanation.

Leo and Sage actually enjoyed their time together, which was probably the most shocking event of all. They didn't even argue about music or books or movies. Instead, they marveled at the whales, debating (in a friendly sort of way) which whale was cuter, which one was cooler, and what type of whale they would both be. (Sage would be a beluga because she talked a lot and Leo would definitely be a whale shark because he was such a poser but he was okay with that answer because they are "definitely the best looking" type of whale.)

After several hours of slowly chugging behind the beautiful creatures, the tour headed back to the dock, waving goodbye to the whales as they jumped and played in the sea.

Once they got back to land, Leo trotted into the little gift shop, buying them both (matching) sweatshirts that said, "Someone thinks I'm Whale-y Cute" with a map of Florence, Oregon on the back. They had gotten soaked due to a rogue whale getting a little too close and splashing sea mist all over the onlookers and Sage wasn't too shy about admitting how cold she was.

Sage cracked up when Leo tossed her the sweatshirt,

but she was more than happy to rid herself of the damp Walmart special she was wearing in exchange for the whale sweatshirt. "Thanks," she said, "It's a good look." She stared at Leo who kind of rocked purple.

"I'm your assistant, aren't I? Bob needs to stay true to the purple brand."

Sage laughed and looked out the window, letting her mind wander. Today had been one of the best days, and it had nothing to do with her "brand" at all.

Oh, and she did get seasick and barfed all over the side of that pretty little boat (RIP strawberry cream cheese bagel) but in the end she considered it a win because Leo promised homemade pasta for dinner.

The days after their "food-poisoning-turned-epic-whale-adventure" rebound passed in a blur. Sage was busier with gaming and streaming than she'd been in the last month. Was it because she was suddenly *very* aware that a man was living with her, making delicious food, *and* that he smelled nice? Maybe.

But, she was also a very busy woman. Okay.

But, still, Leo Camaro was in her house, making her pasta and tea, and being... nice? Sure, he was still a brat, but he *was* kind of funny. *And*, she'd caught him being nice to Squash; he'd even offered to flap the umbrella for her when Sage got stuck on a call! It was quite the sight to see from her office window, but he had the technique down perfectly, and Squash was spared being an appetizer for the hawk (at least for another day, Leo had to remind her).

They had found sort of a routine between them. And that was scary because Leo fit into her routine well. And she didn't need someone changing things up on her when she was busy trying to find her new routine without George.

So, yeah, she might have been a little distant.

She might have skipped dinner once or twice, in order to squeeze in more gaming. That had been her plan for this evening, too, but there was something different about the scent wafting up from the kitchen. It wasn't Leo's regular cooking. Sure, Sage smelled grilled asparagus, steak, and were those mashed potatoes he was making?

But, *this* particular aroma... it was something else.

She quickly logged off her stream (it had been an unscheduled pop-up anyway) and nearly broke her ankle on the stairs on her sprint to the kitchen.

"She's alive!" Leo yelled. "What? Was I being too loud again? It's not my fault your mixer is so old it's practically become a fossil and I have to whisper sweet nothings to it just to get it turned on—"

"Quit seducing the kitchen equipment and tell me what that smell is!"

"First off," Leo patted the old kitchen mixer with a gentle softness, "she likes it when I talk pretty to her. And secondly, what you are smelling is tender hanger steak cooked to perfection—"

"The tea." Sage nearly cried.

Leo smiled, pushing the tin and a steaming mug toward her. "Happy birthday."

Scratch that. Sage cried.

18

LEO

"How'd you know it was my birthday?" Sage sniffed. "And the tea."

Leo rolled his eyes. Emotional little thing. It only took the tiniest of digging to find out Tavy was away at another tournament and Roz was hired to do a live wedding painting three hundred miles away.

And that was it. Those were her friends.

"The tea," Leo said, copying her exaggerated tone, "was quite tricky to procure considering there is only one manufacturer and they no longer sell retail and only sell wholesale to a few select establishments."

"Yeah," Sage said. She opened the tea tin and inhaled. "I have been rationing the last bit I had for months."

"I am aware. Quite the sad sight to see." She occasionally opened her old tea tin of tea, took a deep sniff, smiled, and put it in the far corner of her tea cabinet. He'd only seen her make one cup and that was after a particularly rough day of streaming, when the bots and spammers were particularly gruesome.

"Where did you get this!"

Leo shrugged. "I have my ways. Mostly sweet talking to the ladies at the club." That was grossly simplifying it. He pretty much begged, borrowed, and flirted his way into nabbing a tea tin for his tea-loving Subject.

"This—" She sniffed again and opened the tin, inhaling the tea leaves. Then she capsized his world for a moment because she set the tin aside, took two steps toward him, and hugged him. Like actually wrapped her arms around him and squeezed. It was like a real embrace and for a moment he considered reciprocating, wrapping his arms around her and pulling her even closer so he could smell her hair (what? It smelled like strawberries).

So he did. He allowed himself a moment to hold her close. But only a moment. Then he remembered he was a Professional. And she was his Subject. So, he peeled his arms away and settled for patting her shoulder like he would pet the rat-dog.

"You're welcome."

She took a step back and grabbed the tea tin, holding it close to her in one hand, like a baby on her hip, while she pulled the mug toward her. "Tavy and Roz are out of town." She sniffed again. "Cutting onions?"

"Yes," Leo lied.

"Ah, figures." She wiped her teary eyes again. "We normally do something but not this year. I mean, we'll go out or something when they get back but this—"

"You're welcome. Now, let's eat."

"I can't—" She looked upstairs. "I told another

streamer I'd pop into their game. Another practice match. You know how it goes—"

He did. She had been busy, downright avoiding him if he thought about it. Part of that delicate balance between them was him cooking and them hanging out for just a little bit so he didn't go insane in this creepy house by himself. He even started talking to the rat. He was slowly running out of home improvement projects. He updated the system of the agency's computer tracking several times over, so much so that his boss asked him to slow down so the other servers could catch up. Plus, in between the arguments over dumb stuff (like really, why did she have to be team orange when tangerines were far superior, and don't even get him started on her Smash Bros opinions), they could have some fun conversations.

"No," he said. "Go for it. Have a good stream."

But divine intervention was on his side and just as he finished his last words, the power went out.

"Hello?" Sage yelled.

"The power went out, I didn't evaporate!" Leo said, grabbing his ringing ears.

"Where are you?" she shouted again.

"Good grief, right in front of you." She smacked his chin with her mug. "Ouch. Yes, right there. Just stop moving." He rummaged around one of her many junk drawers and pulled out a flashlight and shone it in her face. She took a step back into the stove, shrieked, and ran into him.

"Ouch." She rubbed her backside.

"Just stop moving for two seconds!"

"What about Squash!"

"She's already mostly blind. This is her normal life."

"I think the power went out."

"Shocker." Leo rolled his eyes so hard he hoped she'd hear it. "I know you don't have a generator so it looks like a candlelit dinner and some good old-fashioned conversation for your entertainment tonight, birthday girl."

Squash found them in the dark but tumbled down the stairs in the process. The rat bounced well and showed no signs of injury and was more than happy to twist under Leo's feet in hopes that he would drop a piece of steak (which he did, the poor thing didn't have much to live for so who was he to deny the thing it's last meal?) and Leo finally got the food plated and candles lit.

All in all, it looked pretty cozy, especially after he got a fire roaring in the fireplace. It felt like the final goodbye to winter, the final fire of the season, and tomorrow any remaining snow and ice would melt and be replaced by flowers.

They sat on the floor, using the coffee table as their table.

"This is so good," Sage said, chomping down on another piece of asparagus. "You'll have to teach me how to do this so when you're gone I can still have some sort of vegetable in my life."

Leo rolled his eyes. "Love, that is cooked in butter and prosciutto and topped with parmesan. It's not exactly the best thing for you."

She held up an asparagus with her fingers. "So, this is just a vessel for the good stuff."

Leo laughed and started in on his steak. He was lucky the lights went out after he had finished dinner, otherwise he'd be cooking by candlelight and that didn't seem nearly as fun. What *was* fun was seeing Sage illuminated by the glow of the fire, a gentle smile on her face, and the tea tin next to her. She touched it every so often, as if to make sure it wasn't a dream and that he had really gotten her the elusive and favorite tea of hers.

"I can't believe you did this," she said, whispering to the tea tin. She pointed her fork at him. "You must tell me your secrets!"

"Cannot. I need some bribing power in the future considering how long this job is going."

Her face faltered. "Yeah, so strange. But the competition will come and go and everything will be okay. You'll go back to your big fancy D.C. statesman and actually have some real action."

Leo scoffed. "I'd say that you have given me enough of a headache. And the agency called and asked me to come out for a high-profile oil guy flying in next week."

"Oh?" Her face was hard to read, but her eyes jumped from the fire to the asparagus, to his eyes, and back to the fire.

"I said it would be too much of a hassle to train a new guy to take my place here." It was true. The call had caught him off guard and while he had been yearning for some action, something to keep his mind sharp, he'd also fallen into a routine here. He hadn't had one of those in years. It wasn't domesticity, but it was nice knowing what his day-to-day was going to look like. Sure, it got a little old at times, but he had the umbrella flapping job to keep him busy and he went on the hunt for Filbert the other day when his caregiver lost him. (Filbert had been wandering the local orchard picking up apples to feed to the ducks at the pond and had gotten a little turned around.)

But maybe, deep down under his (impressive) muscle and hidden behind his heart was a small piece of him that wanted to spend more time with this woman.

"Too much of a hassle?" Sage prompted.

Leo shrugged. "Told him there were certain demands the Subject made that would be difficult to train on such short notice. I'm very deep undercover so it just wouldn't do to have a new person jump into that role."

"Bob is very well established."

"Plus, I think I am in a few of your social media photos and people have begun to speculate about my role."

"True," Sage said. "Wouldn't want people thinking I already fired my assistant, Bob. Not good for the brand image."

"Exactly." Leo nodded. "It would just unravel the whole balancing act we have created. So, I am afraid you are stuck with me until you win this competition thingy."

Sage nodded, biting back a smile. "I appreciate your sacrifice in the name of maintaining the balance."

"To the equilibrium," Leo said, raising his water in a toast.

Sage clinked her mug against his. "The equilibrium!"

Except Leo's equilibrium was slipping. Tipping. Totally off-kilter. The balancing act was getting harder to maintain.

What was this thing he was feeling? Admiration, dare

he say...fondness? No, this was Sage. There was no room for these...emotions.

It must be the asparagus. Stupid of him to have an aphrodisiac on a date. Except it wasn't a date, *obviously*. It was a birthday dinner. He was only being nice. But he could have made the table nicer, like added flowers and some music. And music would lend itself to the idea of dancing. Dancing was always fun and definitely the sort of thing one might do at a candlelit birthday dinner in the dark...

This was clearly the asparagus talking.

He was always sensitive to substances. It's why he didn't drink, he didn't like feeling floaty or out of control. It's why he didn't take allergy medication, even the non-drowsy stuff would put him in a slumber. Now he had to cross asparagus off the list because it, too, was making him feel floaty. His head was in the clouds and he had trouble focusing on anything other than the stunning and beautiful (the asparagus's words) woman in front of him.

Sage sighed, sipping her tea, leaning against the couch. "Thank you for this." She gestured to her now empty plate. "And this." She lifted her mug. "It's silly that tea could bring me to tears but it was the first tea George made me after a panic attack. I know it's more of a placebo than anything, but whenever I feel nervous or on the edge of losing it, this tea just feels like the perfect medicine."

"I'm like that with watermelon."

Sage snorted. "What?"

Leo shrugged, leaning back, and smiling. "Not necessarily moved to tears but watermelon was always served at picnics and family events. I had cousins and places to escape to, outside and sunshine. And there was always watermelon. Takes me back to simpler times." The words poured out of him and suddenly nothing sounded better than a cool, crisp watermelon slice.

"I don't have cousins. Just Cherry."

"Your brother." He wanted to add "the jailbird" but held his tongue.

Sage nodded. "Yeah. We were close until he went off to join the circus."

Leo laughed. "I was like that with my sister but I felt like she and I actually got closer when she decided to do something crazy and be a stunt double."

Sage laughed but shook her head. "No, I literally mean he joined a circus. He was a pretty good juggler I guess. Swords. He's only missing two fingers now."

Leo couldn't help but raise his eyebrows. "Well then. Here's to crazy siblings and tea."

Sage beamed and sipped her tea, closing her eyes and letting her head roll back. It was like she was in this intense moment of joy and Leo suddenly felt hot and uncomfortable as if he were intruding on a private moment but he couldn't stop staring at her face and the way the glow of the fire made it light up.

It was definitely the asparagus making him crazy.

They sat like that for a while, enjoying the crackling of the fire. Squash even found her way to Leo's lap, nearest to the fire and circled up next to him. Sage looked on in complete awe and maybe with a hint of jealousy.

"What can I say?" Leo whispered (he didn't want to

scare the rat away and have it accidentally scurry into the fire in its blind state). "I am the rodent whisperer."

"They can always find a leader in their own kind," Sage said.

Before he could respond she grabbed their dishes and set them in the sink, returning with a carton of ice cream. "Since the power is out, we should probably not risk this melting."

"You know it could last a long while in the freezer as is so long as you don't open the door too many times—"

"It's a sacrifice we must make!" She tossed a spoon at him.

There was something special about sharing a tub of ice cream with Sage. It put them on an even playing field. Neither one was trying to prove their job was important to one another. Neither one searching for the next sarcastic thing to say. Just staring into the glowing fire, scooping ice cream. This was something friends might do. Close friends.

That dang asparagus was making him floaty again.

And when the ice cream had been consumed and the candles died down, they bid each other goodnight (Sage did the initial bidding). Only then did it occur to Leo it was time to do some research.

Turns out asparagus isn't an aphrodisiac after all.

L eo woke with a harsh reminder that asparagus hadn't actually betrayed him but instead, it was his own...emotion. Most people had several of those things (feelings) but Leo prided himself on only being able to feel one thing at a time. It made him sharper. More focused. Which was an issue when his head continued to go all floaty when he smelled strawberry shampoo lingering on the couch or heard laughing upstairs. He needed to get his head in the game. So, he texted her that he was going on a run around the neighborhood after he checked the perimeter and power problems.

She liked his text which almost seemed worse than a simple "K" but he was determined to outrun this feeling (undefined at this moment in time).

Admiration was a normal thing.

And he was a little starved for friends. Sure, he had a few he kept in contact with, he even got a chance to meet up with some old buddies during his stay here, but it was all surface-level. His closest friend was Tess, and she seemed to be hiding something major from him anyway, so how close were they really?

After walking half a block, he decided he was warm enough (maybe it was just the pent-up energy) and he took off down the street. His legs burned. It always took his bad knee a few blocks to go from an agonizing pain to just a dull throb. He was almost there.

Today's podcast was all about revolutions. Specifically the moons that revolve around Jupiter. But he was stuck on the root word here. Revolve. Everything revolved around something. Someone. Why did Sage's face pop into his mind?

His life always revolved around someone else. First, it was his parents. Making them happy. Keeping the peace. Then it was the military. It seemed like a good thing to do.

His dad had been a career man and had done well for himself. Military and then medicine. But that exploded. Literally.

"Sorry Dad, the idea of going through med school just to kill myself as a doctor makes me want to take a long walk off a short pier" just didn't seem like the right move to make, especially considering he had no idea what he actually wanted to do with his life.

Sure, he was good with technology, but where would that take him? Did he even enjoy living out of a suitcase? He'd done it for years now and it just seemed...normal.

He shook the feeling of frustration away and moved on to feeling confused. Where was he going in life?

Around the block again, apparently.

A new feeling overcame him. Curiosity. Why were all the porch lights still on in the neighborhood? Why could he hear the hum of heaters in the early morning? Why were there glowing windows? And most importantly, why was their house the only one without power? (Later, he would reflect upon his use of "their" in that thought—as if he were some domesticated pet, or something. He had no time at present, however, since he was being a macho sleuth.)

It only took him a few minutes to discover the source of the issue. The breaker box lines had been cut. Early this morning, when he'd gone to check on the breaker box to flip the switches, in hopes of getting the power back, he'd been so lost in his feelings (of admiration—not any other nonsense, like... *liking*), that he had totally missed—just feet away—the severed lines.

He needed to Get. A. Grip!

A professional didn't act this way. A professional didn't get floaty and goofy over a candlelit dinner and a gamer girl. She was just an adult teenager trying to avoid hard work. But, deep down, he knew even that wasn't true. She had a business mindset and, yeah, it was kind of cool that she got to live out every teenage boy's fantasy of playing games all day.

There he was. Getting all... floaty again.

It only took a few minutes to call the right people to ensure that the power would be restored and lines repaired, but it was still unsettling.

Someone had been outside. Someone had been there. And why hadn't his blasted cameras caught it?

Leo decided not to tell Sage what had happened. He explained that someone would be coming out to fix the lines and she could just work from her phone. She chatted with Jared and Lily going over the plan for the next (quickly approaching) gaming event. She was sequestered in her room (avoiding him maybe?) and didn't come out much so he was spared having to explain why her house was the only one on the block getting work done to it.

He checked the cameras. And double-checked them. Then put in a formal complaint to the company that set them up and acquired his own cameras (with his own money) to actually get them working right. The stream was better, clearer, and more accurate. For having such a techy brain, he was letting the protocols of the agency stand in his way of good quality. It felt good to get back into the headspace of a tech guy and to get back to the gritty part of protection work. No more of this making dinner and watching movies and domesticated-type life. It was back to business.

Now if only he could figure out a way to anchor himself to the floor...

The following days passed in a blur and Leo was kept busy running and prepping for the next gaming event. He had secured nice connecting rooms at the hotel where the event would be held. This one was a much larger convention, kind of like a comic con for gamers, and Sage was expected to be on several panels. It was going to be a busy weekend for sure, and he was doing his due diligence to know the place inside and out. As her bodyguard. Not as her personal assistant, though he was now realizing the line between the two blended often enough to get confusing to anyone looking in at their weird partnership.

"You were really going to drive by yourself?" Leo asked as they boarded the plane.

Sage shrugged. She wore jeans (practical) and a sweatshirt with the LilyTech logo (finally something not dog-related). "I was going to take two days and maybe take Squash with me. But the vet recommended she stay home."

Leo nodded. "It would be a shame for it to die abroad."

"Shut up. Roz is stoked to have her at her place." Roz

loved Squash but was very adamant about not staying in the "house that could eat people" by herself.

"Where are you going?" Leo asked as she continued down the aisle of the busy plane.

"To the seat Jared booked for me?" Sage said. She hoisted her overstuffed backpack on her shoulder and held her tote bag in front of her (white with patterns of pumpkins and Squash). She frantically pulled out her phone, probably looking for her seat.

Leo shook his head, lifted the backpack off her shoulders, and put it in the overhead. "We fly first class, Love. I already changed your ticket."

"What?" she squeaked.

Leo gestured for her to sit next to the window and she slid in, open-mouthed, glancing around like she was a naughty kid about to get in trouble for trespassing.

"For being such an anxious traveler, I'm surprised you didn't see your boarding pass changed." Leo shoved their bags overhead and took the aisle seat.

Sage opened the window. "Jared booked the ticket weeks ago. I just had it memorized..."

"Nervous traveler?"

Sage shrugged. "More like inexperienced. I've seen lots of the country, on four wheels. Not in a maze they call airports."

Leo closed his eyes, willing the throbbing in the back of his head to go away. "It's like a second home to me."

"What is?"

"Airports."

Sage sighed. "Do you like that?"

"Sure." He wasn't sure if it was the truth.

The trip went in relative peace. There was some minor turbulence which surprised Sage, as evidenced by how she grabbed his arm for a moment before quickly correcting herself and grabbing the armrest. (He allowed himself a brief moment to get all floaty at her touch. It was allowed, since he was literally floating in the clouds, after all.)

"Fun fact: most plane crashes occur during take-off and landing. Odds are in your favor here."

She answered him with a withering glare and refused to speak to him the rest of the flight. (She clutched his arm during the landing, so not all was lost.)

The Uber to the hotel was quick and short. They both retired for a little afternoon nap before heading down to the Friday night dinner a few of the sponsors were putting on.

He laid down for what felt like two minutes and was woken with a startle by Sage knocking on the door connecting the room. "Leo?"

"Here," he said, sitting up. "Is there a problem?"

"No, no. I just wanted to give you this." She handed him a black ice pack wrapped in a thin towel. "I got it from the concierge downstairs. It should help with that headache."

"Headache?"

She was already retreating back to her own room. "You're not the only one to observe things. I noticed you don't take pills, I have some if you need them—"

"No."

She nodded. "I figured."

She had? Was he that easy to read? Did he really have

a sign on his forehead that said "Hi, I had a bad injury and took too many pain pills and it took me nearly a year to taper off of them and sometimes I still think about them years later and I can't even handle Tylenol because the temptation to take more than I need is still there?"

Instead, he just muttered a quiet, "Thanks."

"You looked like you needed some relief. Ice on the front of the neck. It helps with migraines. It cools the blood before it circulates around your head. At least that's what the doctor told me when I needed help for George."

He nodded. "I'll give it a go. I have my alarm set. Don't leave the room again unless I'm with you. You might not be worried about your safety but I—"

"I know, I know. You don't want to get fired."

"Glad we have that established." That and he really wanted this event to go smoothly for her. She had been stressed about it for the days leading up to this. It was becoming more and more apparent that this "little niche side of gaming" wasn't so little after all.

"I'll be up in an hour to go to the dinner thing with you."

She sighed. "Got it." She stepped through the door and closed it as she spoke the last word.

"Sage?" Leo called.

"Yeah?" she asked through the door, muffling her voice.

"Thanks again." He was already lying down, wrapping the long, cool ice pack around his head and neck.

"Just start feeling better and be ready to play the part of Bob."

"At your service."

He might have imagined it, but he thought he heard a laugh from behind the door. And he got all floaty again. This time it was because of the headache and not at all because of the idea that she was paying as much attention to him as he was to her.

19

SAGE

S age was more than ready for the LilyTech welcome dinner. Her stomach was ready for fancy steak and the appetizers she couldn't pronounce. Plus, she knew almost everyone at the table. It was fun to hang out and recharge after a day of travel. Leo looked like crap, which was hard to do considering how fit he was. (What? It was hard *not* to notice with the way he was always hanging around. And how he took his shirt off in the yard after his runs to do his pushups...and how those pushups just looked so effortless...) The flight looked like it took all the wind out of Leo's sails and she was *not* weird for noticing that. She knew a migraine pulling into the Pain Station when she saw one.

But he looked better now. Leo laughed and joined in the fun, still he constantly scanned the small crowd. He wore a name tag that said "Bob" and assumed the personality of a dopey but semi-competent personal assistant.

He was like a cute blonde Labrador that could retrieve tea.

"So, Bob," Alice said, chewing on her straw. "Sage tells me you've been pretty helpful these past few weeks."

Sage choked on her rice.

"That's a lie," Leo—Bob—said. Then he winked at the table. "I am the *only* reason she gets anything done!"

The table laughed.

Alice sighed and elbowed her boyfriend, Andy. "Would be nice to have a man around to get all my crap together."

Andy threw an arm around Alice. "Honey, you'd need four assistants to keep up with your tornado." Alice only shrugged and laughed. "But what do you do most of the time?" Andy asked, directing the question at Bob.

Sage internally screamed. Andy had unknowingly set up Leo with the perfect lineup of insults and backhanded remarks. He could talk about how he had to fetch her dog from under the porch when she fell through the rotted stairs (and then fix the rotted porch) or how she begged and begged him to take her to Taco Bell for a Crunch Wrap Supreme because she *needed it* and how he only agreed if she joined him for a walk outside "so you can actually remember what that glowing orb in the sky is." She had looked up and asked, "What?" He groaned and pretty much yelled, "The sun, you idiot! You need some vitamin D before you turn your insides to liquid with Taco Bell."

She had joined him and it was actually a lovely walk.

Or Leo could tell the table about how half his job was

cooking for her. Or how he spent a few days a week corralling Filbert and guiding him back to his house and cooking for him too after the state forgot to send out a caregiver.

Or Leo could talk about the night Sage screamed and Leo frantically raced into the den where Sage had spilled cherry juice all down her front and on the floor and it looked like a crime scene. He had helped her clean up and even done her laundry because he was certain she would forget his very detailed instructions for getting the stain out.

Instead, all Leo said was, "I pretty much drive her around so she can do stuff on the road. Book tickets. Fulfill merch orders."

Okay, now he was being *too* modest. How dare he actually do his job well and make her feel valued and important? That wouldn't do. She cleared her throat. "He's being too nice. He's also a fantastic cook and I bribe him into making me dinner from time to time."

Leo rolled his eyes but smiled anyway. "Despite her creepy house, the kitchen is massive. A chef-wannabe's playground."

"Is that what you want to do?" Iris asked.

Leo scoffed. "In another life maybe, but I'm content for now."

But it made Sage wonder. What did Leo want to do? In life? At work? She had been so focused on herself, trying to get herself in order, that she hadn't even bothered to consider what her uninvited roommate had plans for. Not that it mattered. When this was all over, he'd go back to Washington to protect some prince or something and she'd go back to watching her rom-coms alone without Leo's most recent pastry experiment. Or his low snore when he dozed off. Or the smell of cedar and cologne. She could smell it now on him. Outdoorsy and refined and—

"What?" Leo whispered.

"What do you mean?" Sage hissed.

Leo's eyes darted around the restaurant. "You're leaning in like you have a secret. Something making you uncomfortable?"

Only you and in a whole new way. "No, sorry. I was just—"

"Guys!" Iris said, downing the rest of her soda. "We gotta get going." Iris was another gamer sponsored by LilyTech. She severely burned her hand in a fire and it had essentially melted together. Sage wasn't proud of the fact that it took her some time to get over the queasy feeling she got when she saw Iris's scarred hand. Sage could almost feel the discomfort and pain. Iris was one of the models and gamers used to show off some of Lily-Tech's gaming controllers, which could be formed and created for anyone's needs, even Iris, who had limited use of her fused digits. She mostly stayed in the cozy gaming niche.

"Going where?" Leo asked.

"Time to let loose!" Sage said. Leo booked horrified as if she had just thrown a bomb on his plans. To be fair, it had been a last-minute invite, and Sage really did want to go so she figured blindsiding him in front of a group was better than arguing about it in the stairwell.

Now she felt bad.

"And what does this group of gamer geeks do to let loose?" Leo asked, glaring at Sage but she was trying not to notice.

"Trivia!" Iris exclaimed.

Leo sighed. "Good grief."

Sage smacked his shoulder. "Be nice! I might just give you the day off tomorrow!"

He grumbled, "Like I'd ever let that happen with these crazy people surrounding you."

Andy looked offended for a moment, then got the joke. "Not much of a gamer yourself?"

Leo shook his head. "Not my thing."

They were edging too closely to work-related topics and good ol' Bob was about to blow his cover, so Sage grabbed Leo by the arm and stood them up. "And your job has just begun. Tonight, you are our driver! To the Tavern!"

Leo drove her, Andy, Alice, and Iris to a cozy tavern with a wild night of trivia gearing up. Seriously, some of the teams had matching shirts. Sage was almost jealous. Leo gave Sage an eye roll as if to say, "This? This is the wild night of partying for you?"

But he also looked mildly intrigued. Dare she say even amused? Like the posh prince was actually having fun in a strange little tavern with a giant sign above them displaying their team's name (Gamer Girls).

"I'm not even a girl!" Andy complained.

"You're on our tab and our guest so be thankful we're considering you an honorary girlfriend here." Alice kissed his cheek and gathered up the flier with the rules on it.

It was simple. Press the button on the table when ready to answer. It would let the host know the order of tables to question their answers. Easy peasy.

And Bob was the star of the show.

"Fun fact: elephants are the only mammal that can't jump."

How did this guy know so much about everything? Iris asked him as much, pouring him another celebratory lemonade for another round won—all thanks to Bob.

Bob just shrugged. "I read a lot. Articles are my favorite. Kinda on a sea animal kick right now. Did you know beluga whales can live up to sixty years in captivity?"

"Weird," Sage said. "Now do whale sharks."

Bob shrugged. "They're posers."

The table laughed and Sage couldn't help but notice the sparkle in Leo's eye. Was he poking fun at himself? Did they have a little secret inside joke? Why was she getting all warm and fluttery?

Bob played his part well. Too well.

"In which city was Beethoven born?"

Answer? Easy, Bonn, according to Bob.

"What is a duel between three people called?"

A truel, duh. (Seriously, how did he know this stuff?)

And for the tie-breaking questions, what is measured in "Mickeys?"

Leo thought for half a second before slamming his fist on the buzzer.

"Final answer?" the announcer asked.

Leo shrugged. "Pretty sure it's the speed of a computer mouse."

"Correct!"

And the crowd went wild. Lemonade was flowing, backs were slapped, and Sage had to dodge a million "Where did you find this guy" questions.

"To Bob!" Iris yelled, wrapping an arm around Leo. Sage bristled and decided not to dwell on that unpleasant feeling, instead, she ordered another round of iced teas and beers, smiling at the table.

They eventually made it back to the hotel, high on their victories.

She dreamt of Bob and trivia and maybe a little bit of Leo.

The following day was a blur of panels both as attendee and panelist. Sage even hosted an event. It was chaos, and Bob was right by her side all day handing her water, bringing her snacks, reminding her of certain names, and even taking pictures for some fans. He acted like a real-life secretary. A butler and a bodyguard all rolled into one. He was rather smug when he snuck into the green room where Sage had explicitly told him he wasn't allowed because she had been afraid he'd embarrass her. She'd been right of course, he sweet-talked his way in when she gave him the slip and he thought it wise to announce that he had finally found her and handed her some juice to "get that coal train moving again."

She wanted to die of embarrassment. He leaned in close, his whisper tickling her ear. "Don't sneak off again or it'll be worse. I'll make up some nonsense about a meeting with your parole officer and then your fans will really go crazy."

Her skin tingled. His whisper tickled her skin and his breath smelled of minty toothpaste. Goosebumps erupted across her skin and she tried to regain her focus, but she was flustered. "Hey. But that's—"

"An effective threat I will carry out. Jared may kill me for the scandal but that's okay. Maybe I'll drop hints about a secret boyfriend instead."

She nearly choked on the pomegranate juice.

"Easy," he exclaimed, snatching the bottle away from her and thrusting a napkin into her hands. "I spent ages getting that stupid cherry juice out of that stupid shirt of yours and now you want a repeat performance. Good grief."

"Well quit smothering me and maybe I could actually breathe."

He rolled his eyes and asked, "Black or green?"

"Green please." There was a strange comfort in knowing that Leo would be back in about two minutes with a cup of tea prepared exactly how she liked it. Was that friendship or was that him just doing his job? Or was there something more to the way he handed off the tea, hand lingering just a moment too long on hers? And was there something more to the gentle way he said, "Good luck, you got this," every time she was about to jump on stage?

She hadn't been lying. It *was* getting harder to breathe around him and she needed to Get. A. Grip.

Leo returned with the tea. It was perfect. Of course it was. He whispered, "Good luck, you got this" as she was called to the stage, taking her cup from her, fingers grazing over hers. Ugh, why did he have to do that? Things were far less complicated before he arrived and filled her brain with his...presence. His habits. Just him.

The interview went fine. Everything was fine. She was in control of her feelings and not falling into a comfortable rhythm with Leo. She wasn't at all worried about what life would be like when he left for his next job. She wasn't worried that she'd miss his cooking and foodie snobbery and movie nights and the smell of his cologne and those long quiet walks around the neighborhood that she had gotten used to.

Okay fine. She was a little worried about it.

But everything was fine.

And speaking of fine...the suit Leo packed. How dare he look so good in gray?

After the final panel, she was whisked away to her room where she frantically tried to figure out how to put on the needlessly strappy and complicated gown Lily had sent to her room for the event tonight.

Tonight was a Big Deal. She had it written in the calendar as "Fancy auction gala thing for Children's Hospital" and on paper, it seemed like a great event. It was a fancy live and silent auction with some of the most successful and connected businesses invited. LilyTech had gotten started in the orthopedic and pediatric centers, fitting mobility devices. Now they were leading the way with inclusionary gaming devices and empowering women. Sage felt a little weird about being included on the guest list. But Jared had explained it well to her, "You're the money maker this quarter! You've brought in a lot of new revenue and advertising. You're important to the company. You're a peach!"

She didn't *feel* important. Well, important in the sense that she knew she was important to the company in the way that computers were important to businesses. She made them money and was valuable, but if she burned out or broke down, they'd just get another computer. Another person.

Sage sighed at herself in the mirror. It really was a lovely satin dress, a deep blue so dark it was almost black and she wore silver hoops and a matching necklace. Her shoes were simple black heels and though she wasn't used to wearing them, she knew she'd be sitting for most of the night anyway.

It would be fine.

And circling back to that subject of fine...

"Ready?" Leo asked as he opened the adjoining room door.

"I guess." She smoothed out her hair. It was in loose curls and hung down her back. She was already itching to throw it up in a bun. She hated the way it tickled her face.

"You look..."

Wait, did he just? No. He didn't just check her out. And yet, was that a little redness creeping into his cheeks? Did she catch him in the act?

She totally did. And now she didn't feel so awkward in the dress after all.

"I look ready to go?" Sage filled in for him.

"Exactly." Leo cleared his throat. "It's going to take us

about twenty minutes to get to the venue. I have already checked in with the staff and we will enter through the back door. There is an upper floor, but there is no reason for you to go up there. There are two main bathrooms on the primary ballroom floor. You may use either, but do not, under any circumstances, go into them unless you check with me first and I escort you—"

"Surely I don't need your help with that!"

"To them. Get your mind out of the gutter." Leo checked his watch. "And don't go anywhere without informing me first. There are a lot of people going to be there today and while the clientele does not look like they're the vandalizing type, there's enough public around and enough cracks in security that someone could slip in relatively easily."

"I think you are being paranoid." Sage didn't say it with much conviction though.

"It's my job to be paranoid and to keep you alive."

That sobered her. "You don't really think there is a threat on my life, do you?"

Leo didn't meet her eye.

"Leo, what is it? What do you know?"

"It's nothing." Leo opened the door and ushered her out. "No need to freak you out."

"Well, now I am properly freaked out!"

They walked to the stairwell and Sage took the stairs awkwardly enough that Leo grabbed her hand and placed it on his arm. She didn't have enough time to appreciate his bicep because he said, "One of my co-workers had a similar job going on down south. A stalker from the lady's work. Despite the obvious security, the stalker tried attacking her at church. She's okay, my buddy is a little beat up, but she's okay too."

"Wait what?" Sage's heart dropped to her stomach, which was a shame because she would really like to be focusing on his muscular arm and cologne right now. She should be imagining herself as a princess being led down the stairs in her pretty dress, not imagining her own murder, darn it! *Way to ruin her momentary fantasy, Leo.*

Leo swallowed hard. "The agent had been on the job for months. I'm not saying she got complacent, because I don't think she did. But the stalker got bolder. And if that could happen to her—" He took in a deep breath. "I take my job seriously and I won't let anything happen to you, alright?"

"Alright," Sage said, taking in a deep breath. She was supposed to be hyping herself up for a night of socializing with fancy people. Instead, she spent the car ride over thinking about all the people in her life who would want to do her harm. Mom? Who knows where she is, she took off years ago like a fart in the wind. Brother? Prison, and despite how smart he was, even he couldn't orchestrate a prison break. Probably. And then there was Jason...

"Leo..."

He glanced at her briefly while making a slow turn into the ballroom's parking garage.

"I have a confession. I think."

He put the rental car in park. "I don't think I'm the right person for that."

"Don't be mad."

"Please don't tell me you forgot something vital at the hotel and we need to traverse the nightmare that is

Downtown L.A. to go back there. I mean, I'm Bob, your charming and brilliant assistant, in *public*. In private, I am not."

"Yes, *so* charming."

Leo growled. "Watch it. You're confessing something."

"There is a guy that is going to be there tonight, probably not at our table, but, uh... he kind of hates my guts." Sage wrung her hands in her lap. She felt a tension headache coming on. She wanted to rub her eyes but that would ruin the professional make-up artist's handiwork and Sage, despite living like a nocturnal raccoon at times, was not keen on looking like one.

Leo gave her a hard stare. The silence threatened to choke her, so she pushed on. "He asked me out a while ago, and I rebuffed him. It was sometime last year, and we did some streams and, honestly, I was interested in him. We kind of flirted, and people thought we were going to get together, but when I actually met the guy? There was absolutely *no* chemistry, so I kind of let it fizzle out. I guess he hasn't gotten the hint that I'm not interested, because he still drops my name occasionally."

"No, he most certainly got a hint. But he's a dumb guy and, when a beautiful woman shows him an ounce of attention, he'll do anything to keep it. What's his name?"

"Jason Jones."

"Lovely," Leo said, in a way that conveyed that this was actually not lovely at all. "Just a new migraine-inducing mental backflip I have to do on the fly. I'll figure it out." He was tapping away on his phone. "He'll be here tonight?"

"Probably." *Definitely.* "I saw him at the hotel. I really

didn't think he'd be at the convention. He wasn't on any panels or anything, so I assumed… "

"I can't do my job if you're not honest with me!" He let out a breath. "This is serious, Sage."

"Well, I never felt comfortable telling you about it before. I never felt comfortable letting you in on anything before. But now… "

"Now that I've explained to you that this is real life, and real-life bad things *can* happen, you decide to take me seriously?"

Sage threw up her hands. "Now that I actually trust you!"

"You didn't before?" He looked hurt.

"Trust you to do your job? Yes. Absolutely. Trust you to take what I said and not twist it and make me feel like a total idiot. No."

Leo let out a long breath and for once Sage decided to stick to her guns and keep her mouth shut. Silence could be a powerful weapon. He finally spoke. "I'm sorry I made you feel that way. I'll be the first to admit I have been a jerk, especially at the beginning when neither of us was too excited about the task at hand. But I'd like to think we have made professional and personal progress. So, thank you for telling me about this Jason guy."

Sage blinked back the water pooling in her eyes. "Thank you. I know you take your job seriously. I feel guilty for not having been more honest with you."

Leo smiled his easy smile, checking his watch. "I meant what I said. He's a dumb guy. And you are a beautiful woman. But you're also a pain in the neck."

She didn't even have time to respond because he

jumped out of the car, circled around, and opened her door, offering his arm to her. "Bob, at your service."

She laughed, leaving the awkwardness in the car. Still, she had been hoping for a little more Leo and a little less Bob tonight.

What. Was. He. *Thinking?*

And you are a beautiful woman? How cliché could he get?

But it wasn't really a cliché if it was true. She looked elegant, refined, yet, still so... Sage. She carried herself with her usual energy in that incredible (no doubt, expensive) dress, which hung off of her like a waterfall.

Great. There he went, making comparisons to nature like some love-struck idiot. Next thing, he'd be writing sonnets about her.

Get it together!

Right. She carried herself with the same confidence in this dress as she did in sweatpants back at home. In a world of fake, two-faced people, she was a breath of fresh air.

Okay, so he has so far compared her to air and water, what next? An earth metaphor? Maybe how she set his blood on fire? Good grief, he needed to get his head out of the clouds and firmly back on the ground. Floating was getting easier, the longer he spent with her.

"What are you thinking?" she asked, breaking what he supposed was the awkward silence he had created.

"Floating." He cleared his throat.

"What?"

"Back door is this way." He led them through the door and back halls, trying not to think too long and hard about the way her delicate hand felt on his arm. He wanted to hold that hand. He wanted to go on one of their sunset walks and hold her hand and say nothing at all. Simply enjoy the feeling of her hand in his.

He was *feeling* feelings, and that simply would not do. No.

He had work. And with her new revelation of a spurned crush (lover was much too harsh a word) he had some new background checks he had to complete on the fly. So much flying today. He hadn't meant to fly off the handle at her but, goodness gracious, she didn't realize how serious this actually was, especially after what had happened earlier at her home. He'd talk to her about it. Maybe on the plane. The situation was under control at this point anyway.

He navigated them straight to the double doors of the foyer. Sage made a move to go in, squaring her shoulders and ready to stride in. He grabbed her upper arm.

"I'm sorry," he whispered. He didn't mean for his voice to go all husky. "For raising my voice like that. It was uncalled for, and you didn't deserve it." He rubbed the goosebumps along her arm with his thumb and stared at the place where his thumb met her skin for a moment too long. He cleared his throat and released her.

She looked taken aback, eyes slightly wider, her mouth parted. She caught herself, answering, "Accepted. And, I'm sorry for holding out on you. That wasn't right of me."

Holding out on him? She had no idea how much she held from him. He wanted to know more about her. More of what she liked and hated, her favorite foods (other than fluffy pancakes and tea). He wanted to know her dream vacation destination. He wanted to know her deepest fears and her guilty pleasures.

Well, shoot. He found himself yearning for a change.

A man could dream.

"Apology accepted. Now, shall we?" He plastered on a grin, swung open the doors, and ushered her in.

He really didn't have time to play the goofy identity of Bob right now. He was busy scanning the crowd, looking for people that shouldn't be there. He lingered in the foyer, scanning the crowd for this Jason guy. He'd had a moment to pull up his profile and it only took a twenty-dollar tip to the doorman to confirm that, yes, Jason the Jerk was in the building. A guest of an official invitee, so there was no throwing him out.

At least not yet.

Still, if this Jason dude tried anything, then Leo would be more than happy to throw him through the doors like a cartoon character.

He and Sage meandered to the giant ballroom where patrons dropped off their coats at the tables and made their way to the other side where a very exciting cocktail hour was taking place.

"You going to be okay?" Sage asked.

"Okay?"

"I mean, I know you don't drink, and I didn't know if it was a problem for you—"

"I don't drink because it's nasty and makes me feel sick just smelling it. Teenage Leo did enough drinking and partying to last a lifetime." Leo suppressed a shudder.

Sage laughed, grabbing a glass off of a tray passing by her. "I don't drink often. But when I do it's gotta be stupid expensive stuff that tastes like juice." She sipped the pink drink and made a sour face. "This is not it."

She was being nice to him, offering him an olive branch after their little spat in the car.

"We all have our vices. Mine were pills. For a time."

"Ah." She nodded like it was no big deal. They both knew it was. Confessing an embarrassing secret, an addiction (despite being recovered from it) was intimate. "We all have our struggles. You don't need to tell me."

"But you noticed," Leo said. How had she noticed?

"I notice a lot of things, too."

"So, you've said. How?"

Sage dropped her glass off on a tray passing by. "You work out a lot. You have a limp sometimes. I notice on our walks now, only when you've done a long run though. And you never take anything for it. You ice religiously and use my heating pads when you think I won't notice—"

"I resent that accusation."

"But you don't deny it. I think the Hello Kitty heating pad works the best."

"It does," Leo admitted. When had they gotten so familiar?

Sage laughed. "You have protein powders and gross pre-workout—"

"You've tried it?"

She shuddered. "Once. You're healthy, but not *that* healthy. You still eat Oreos and steal my Girl Scout cookies. I just figured there was a history... pain is complicated."

"Pain *is* complicated," Leo said. "Bad car accident in high school got me started. Then a pretty gnarly training accident first year in the military. Got dependent on the opiates. They had no business giving me enough to kill an elephant. And now even Tylenol feels like a hit. And I know myself well enough to want another. And another. And then something stronger." He took a deep breath and rubbed the back of his neck. Why was it so hot in here?

Sage placed a hand on his shoulder. "So, you found a solution that works for you. And you stuck to that. And your life is better for it. That's all that matters."

"And you?" Leo asked because the conversation was flowing and he didn't want it to end. Dang it, he just wanted to *know her.* "Any secrets you've been hiding other than your Jason guy? Addictions you want to get off your chest? Dark skeletons in your closet you want to shed some light on?" It would have sounded so serious if they weren't grinning at each other.

She thought for a moment. "I am terrified of dying alone because I know if I do, it's my fault."

Before he had any time to react to that revelation (not that he had anything on his silver tongue to say) Sage was whisked away by Jared who "Just has to introduce her to some VIP people."

There was a definite feeling of *lack* on his arm now that she was gone. It was soon replaced by Iris. It wasn't the same. She was talkative and friendly at the dinner last night and smiled at him like a friend she'd known for years.

"So," Iris said. "Are you aware that you're dating Sage, or is that just happening in her head?"

"Wait, what?" Leo took a break from scanning the crowd (lingering a little too long on Sage's back—okay fine her backside) and turned to Iris. "What does that mean?"

Iris snorted, wrapping her arm around his in an exaggerated way that could only scream, "This is a platonic type of physical touch, because I am being so weird about it."

Iris gestured to Sage. "I asked her if you were single. Sage sputtered a bit before answering, but basically came up with a weak non-answer. Something along the lines of you're talking to someone and aren't exactly available right now."

"She did, huh?" Leo felt himself puff up a little and told himself to simmer down. He didn't, of course. This was Big News, and he was allowed to stand a little taller (and broader) because of it. Goodness gracious, was he a bird, ready for a chance to do a crazy dance to impress a lady?

How far the mighty have fallen.

"Took me a minute to figure out that the woman in question you were talking to had to be her." Iris released his arm and grabbed a champagne flute, giving a mock cheer in Leo's direction. "Congrats. I've never seen her smitten before. But to be fair, I mostly spend time with her through a screen. Be nice to her."

"I'm her assistant. Of course I'm nice to her." That hadn't always been true, but he didn't need to elaborate on that right now.

"You know that's a standard she has, right? Pretty sad. After a terrible blind date, we talked for a bit about it. I asked what she wanted in a guy, you know, asking what her standards were. She just looked defeated and said she only wanted someone who was nice to her."

"That is... "

"Pathetic?"

"Profoundly sad," Leo said.

Iris walked away, calling over her shoulder. "Just be nice to her. Also, I know your name isn't Bob."

"Great," Leo mumbled to himself.

Sage and Leo reconvened for dinner and Leo only had to break Sage away from one man who seemed a little handsy, but it turns out he was Italian and that was "just how they are," according to Sage. Interesting. Leo considered doing one of the DNA test things to see how much Italian ancestry he had and figured he should start tapping into that particular cultural side.

Dinner was an extravagant affair. The important tables were introduced quickly. The announcer had a charismatic quality that allowed the room to laugh and relax—which was the point, considering they dove straight into the auction. Vacations, motorcycles, art, and everything in between, were auctioned off, the charming emcee angling for more dollars each round. Lily bid on behalf of LilyTech.

"What?" Leo asked Sage. "Not into Greek vacations?" He gestured to the package being auctioned off.

Sage snorted. "I have never been out of the country. I swear I have traveled more than anyone, but only within the boundaries of the states. I should really get a passport."

Leo's eyes widened. "Yes, you really should." Especially since—if given the opportunity—he'd whisk her away to Italy. (You know, for his newly developed cultural side.)

Jason sat with the CEO of the hospital. Apparently, this Jason Jerk was his nephew, and he pulled some strings and was a last-minute addition to the table. Leo couldn't help but notice how Jason's eyes also scanned the crowd, settling on Sage more often than he'd like.

When the live auction finished and dessert was served, the tables in the lobby were opened to the public for the silent auction part of the evening. Sage took her time walking out there, Leo trailing behind her.

But he wasn't the only one.

"Well, well, Miss Moon... Fancy seeing you here!" Jason said, intercepting Sage who had been busy reading a sign on a table.

Sage faltered for a moment but then gave into a side hug. Leo stood close, ready to intervene, but Sage seemed at ease. She smiled and chatted with him and this Jason guy accompanied her around the foyer as she looked at the tables and placed some bids.

It was evident that Jason wasn't carrying any weapons (other than an unfortunate haircut). It had been an intense part of his training protocol, and the weight of the suit jacket and pants was even, there were no bulges or anything to warrant suspicion. Still, the guy seemed sleazy. His eyes lingered too long on Sage. It was like he was trying to undress her with his eyes, and the way he licked his lips? Disgusting. Sage wasn't a meal to be had.

But, if she were, Leo supposed she would taste divine. Like sweet cherries with just the right amount of tart.

He loved cherries.

Still, Leo and Sage had discussed this. Leo would only ever intervene if there was a reason to. And so far, there wasn't a reason.

The pair posed for some pictures and Jared looked like a kid in the candy store. He captured so much content of the pair, muttering, "Finally, something people can speculate about."

"What does that mean?" Leo asked, making the social media manager jump.

"Oh, the 'will-they-won't-they get together' tension was pretty good for the brand. Jason has a massive following outside of Sage's circle, so the overlap is nice. You should read some of the gossip sites. People are spec-ulating. It was good exposure."

Leo scoffed. "Exposure." That was something he'd never be able to understand. She lived her life online. At least he once thought so at first, but being with her, doing life with her, it became clear that she was wholly transparent with her audience about *certain* aspects of her life. Not everything though. She was a complicated person with a complicated life, and she managed to make it seem like her fans were friends. She made it seem like she had her life on display.

But did her fans know that she cried every time she watched *50 First Dates?* Because Leo did.

Did her Patreon members know that she could taste the difference between green tea brands? Because Leo did.

Did her subscribers know that she always—*always*—turned her face to the sun, the moment she stepped outside? That she squinted at the rays like it was a secret greeting between her and the light? Because Leo did.

Did her fans know that she had a fear of heights?

A fear of poison ivy?

And of splinters?

And frogs?

And the dark?

And needles?

Because Leo did.

Instead, all he could respond to Jared was a simple, "Right," despite knowing how wrong he was.

In a blink of an eye, the silent auction was over. The guests were ushered back into the ballroom where the tables had been cleared, the open floor already littered with a number of people dancing, too elegantly in Leo's estimation. This wasn't *Pride and Prejudice* (the 2005 version—which Sage had proudly proclaimed was the best adaptation; Leo was forced to agree). Still, he found himself ready to put on his waltzing shoes. Too bad Jason was already in the circle, swaying with Sage. She looked stiff and awkward as she glanced at Leo.

She looked at him again.

Then again.

No, this wasn't her admiring his well-fitted suit (thanks to Jenson always insisting they pack an expensive suit for emergencies). No, this was her asking for help.

It was a nice thing to be needed. Almost the same sensation as being wanted.

Leo wasn't two steps away from the pair when he heard a strained laugh come from Sage. "I love candied nuts. And filberts. Have you had *filberts?*"

"Excuse us," Leo said in a way that did not convey he was the least bit sorry to be interrupting the pair's slow dancing. He gathered Sage to his side, arm around her, and escorted her to the table of drinks. Sage quickly released herself and dove for a glass of water.

"What happened?" Leo asked.

"He's just—" Sage took a deep drink of the ice water and then refilled the glass. "Ugh, he's just a creep. But not enough to call him on it, you know? If I said something about a small comment he made, he'd say I was being too serious or took it the wrong way. That I was too prudish. So, I let things slide, because maybe I was reading too much into it. But, *ugh!*" She drank some more water and held the cup of ice to her throat. "He's just a creep. Too many small comments and I just had enough. He tried to grab my butt. Maybe. His hand kept sliding lower and lower, and I tried to step back to create some space." She was blushing now. Embarrassed, and... was that shame?

"Hey," Leo said.

She looked away, staring at the punch like it was the most interesting thing in the world.

"Hey," he said again, reaching out and taking her chin in his hand, pulling her face toward his. He waited until she made eye contact with him. Tears welled in her eyes.

"I just wanted to dance—"

"He made you uncomfortable and that is *his* fault. You did nothing to warrant his advances. You are not to blame here."

"Is there a problem?" It was Jason, coming to check on Sage like a dog who'd lost his bone.

Leo rounded on him. "Give us space, so we don't have to make a scene."

"Do you want to take this outside?" Jason asked, puffing up.

Leo cracked his neck, because he wasn't immune to the posturing that males had to do. Plus, it looked dang cool.

"Look, kid," Leo growled, in such a low tone that Jason actually leaned in a fraction to catch his words. "Take a hint and take a hike. I do not want to see you so much as *look* Miss Moon's way, let alone attempt to talk to her. The niceties are done. You blew your chance. Move on. If you do not respect her boundaries, I will personally escort you out. And yes, I *do* have the authority to do that."

Jason looked to Sage where she shrank back half a step but nodded.

"Maybe we should take this outside after all," Jason said.

Leo shook his head. "First rule of fighting is to always look at your opponent's shoes."

Jason glanced down at Leo's feet. "What do you mean by that?"

"These boots are Italian leather. Hand crafted and fitted perfectly. See a scratch on them?"

Jason shook his head and crossed his arms over his chest.

"I've had them for three years," Leo said. "It's because I refuse to run in them. I refuse to do anything but wear them to nice events where a scuffle or skirmish is least likely to happen. So why look at your opponent's shoes? Well, if they are not prepared to run, they are prepared to win. You, on the other hand," Leo made an exaggerated show of looking down at Jason's shoes. "Those sneakers are quite the fashion choice for an event like this. But at least you're prepared to run. So, tell me. Do you still want to go outside?" *Do it, punk. Say yes. Give me an excuse to hit you.*

He deflated some. "Sage, is this what you want?"

"It's what I wanted when I asked you to let me go four times."

"You said you wanted to dance!" Jason said, all bravado out of his voice. He was just a whiny kid.

"A dance!" Sage hissed. "I love dancing. Actually dancing. Not getting felt up by a total stranger—"

Leo cut off what she was about to say by extending a hand and ushering Jason toward the nearest door. "Take a walk and find a new dance partner when you're ready. Also, just a word to the wise, never pick a fight with a guy in flip flops because that is definitely a guy who does not plan on running." And like a good boy, he actually left.

"That was a mistake," Sage said, rubbing her temples. "I need Tums. I am going to have heartburn with this stress."

"Why a mistake?" Leo asked.

"He's going to look you up. Your cover is blown. I know it."

Leo couldn't care less. Sure, Bob was all fun and games on trivia night, but he preferred being Leo. "Dance with me?"

She lit up like the sun for the briefest of moments before doubt flashed over her. "I'm actually a terrible dancer, and your shoes—"

"Cost me a whole forty dollars at the mall."

"What?"

Leo shrugged. "I do have nice Italian shoes. Just not these. But faux leather is easier to wipe off blood."

"Has that happened before?"

Leo shuddered at the memory. "Oh, yes." The dry cleaners were *not* happy with him.

She took his hand, which was still extended out to her. "I really do love dancing."

"I know."

"But I really am bad at it."

"I know that too."

But still, they danced. It was an easy sway and Leo showed her a few steps that she quickly caught onto. They danced in circles, because she wasn't totally certain how to reverse her steps, despite Leo trying to lead her. She laughed when she stepped on his shoes and whispered a quick "sorry," before she stepped on him again.

He didn't mind. It was hard for his feet to hurt when he was floating ten feet off the ground anyway.

The live band was impressive with their choice of music, light and airy—yet, clearly curated—pieces to create movement and a comfortable dancing atmosphere for any skill range. Some people swayed back and forth, some actually waltzed in small circles.

"How come you know how to dance? Like a fancy dance?" Sage asked.

"Parents are rich and go to events like this all the time. They love throwing money around for charity instead of doing actual work. Just kind of grew up knowing how, I guess." That, and Great Aunt Betty forced him to be her dance partner for every little thing. That woman had the energy of a hummingbird.

A comfortable silence followed, and Leo was content to focus on the feeling of her hand in his. He'd wanted this. Had been thinking about what it would be like to hold her hand in public without a second thought. This was doing nothing to stop the growing fantasy in his brain. He imagined kissing that spot on her skin, right where her neck and shoulder joined. It was just open and staring at him in that strappy gown. It would be so easy to lean down slightly and brush his lips over her. She might let him. He found himself leaning in, smelling her signature scent of strawberry and green tea and something else he'd come to know as just her. Something that only people close, people intimate, knew.

Did she close the gap, or did he pull her closer?

That spot on her neck teased him.

"Ask me again," she said, leaning in so her whisper could be heard over the music and crowd. Her breath tickled him. The physical reality of her being *right there* and her lips so close brought him crashing back to earth.

"Ask you what?"

"To forgive you. Ask me again."

This was real. Too real. Was this crossing a line? No. No, it couldn't be. It was just burying the high school hatchet. Closing a door on the past. It wouldn't be crossing a line unless he kissed her.

Which he wouldn't.

Probably.

He caressed her hand and closed his eyes for the briefest of moments, giving his brain a moment to join his body.

He took his hand from her back and brushed a hair from her face. He wasn't willing to let go of her hand just yet. He squeezed it tight as he spoke. "Sage, I am so sorry for what I did. I can't make excuses for my behavior. Just know that I am so sorry for what happened and what it did to you."

"Just ask." Her voice cracked.

"Will you forgive me?"

"Yes."

21

SAGE

She never slept well in hotels. Maybe it was the impending nightmare about clams that woke her up. Or maybe it was because she dreamed Leo Camaro was kissing her by the ocean, and she woke with a start.

She touched her face where Leo had last night, letting wild thoughts of Leo being hers cross her mind. She told herself she could dream about him until the morning alarm went off. A quick glance at the clock told her she had exactly twelve minutes to fall asleep and dream about him again. She didn't. Instead, she let her mind wander and relive last night. They danced nearly every dance together. He held her close. Not intimately, but definitely more than a bodyguard should.

The alarm blaring in her ear was about as welcome as a crab in a kiddie pool.

But life goes on.

And she needed to get it together. Leo was leaving after the competition. This was just a job to him. She had to focus on the *game*, not the Leo-leaving thing. She did what every person did when they felt overwhelmed: chalked her feelings up to stress. Nothing specific, obviously. Definitely nothing named Leo.

They rode to the airport in silence and Leo took care of returning the car and checking them in. The early morning seemed to have surprised him as much as it had surprised her. She couldn't wait to get home to Squash and take a long nap. She was peopled out and needed to recharge alone.

"First class, again?" she asked with a laugh. Goodness, she'd been awake for almost two hours and still had a raspy morning voice.

"I will never cosplay as a sardine in a can." Leo took the aisle seat, and she watched the sunrise through the takeoff, enjoying the peace and quiet of the clouds and low hum of the plane's engine.

That was before Leo dropped a bomb on her.

"Something happened," he said quietly. "Yesterday. I didn't want you to worry, because I handled it, but... someone broke into your house and ransacked it. Everything has been handled by the police, but they have no leads. Messed up your house, but it doesn't look like anything was destroyed. Don't worry."

"Don't worry?" she seethed. "Did you bring this up while we were on the plane so I couldn't throw a hysterical fit because what. The. Heck. Is. Happening?" She wanted to tear her hair out. She had just had one of the best weekends with Leo—*er* best weekends of her career—and this is the way it ends? "What do you mean there are no leads? You have like five hundred cameras!"

"I know!" Leo rubbed a hand through his hair, looking equally as exasperated. "I know, I know. As soon as I got the notification of an intruder, I contacted the police. They took almost 20 minutes to get there! Had I been there I would have apprehended the guy in twelve seconds."

"What took them so long?" Wasn't having a security presence supposed to stop this?

"I guess they read the address wrong. Essentially swatted the wrong home."

"This must be a joke."

Leo shook his head. "It's not. They did a quick scan for prints, but after I sent them the surveillance video they stopped because the guy was masked and wearing gloves. No physical evidence I guess."

"Did this guy destroy my home?" Come on George, I know you're up there. Kindly help me get this crap in order. Go haunt the bad guys or something.

Leo said nothing, just popped open a small bottle of Tums and handed her one. She took it, already feeling the bile rise into her throat. "Looks like your house is a mess but nothing was destroyed. I handled it, but I wanted to warn you that we were going to be walking into a mess. I've already contacted Roz, and she'll keep Squash another night so we can work on getting the mess cleaned up. No need to confuse the poor girl."

"That bad?" Sage asked.

"Let's just wait until we get back to assess everything."

It was that bad. The mess was truly awful. It was like this madman got off on dumping drawers and dressers of things. George's room got hurt the worst. Everything was in disarray, paintings pulled out of their frames, but not torn or destroyed. His closets had been thoroughly cleared out, and his things scattered over the floors. Her tech had been left alone. Pretty much everything upstairs had been.

"This doesn't make any sense," Sage said.

She got a text from Lily.

Lily: Heard what happened. Let me know if you need anything. Send pics to Jared. People need to know that you are being harassed and we take this seriously.

Ah. Yes. Another chance for content. She didn't need a pity party. She needed a brigade of maids to help her clean this up.

Leo looked at it and smiled. "We can get this done in a few hours."

She tried to laugh but it came out more like a choked sob.

"Hey," he said, tossing his duffel bag onto the couch, clearly realizing a moment too late that it had been turned over, so the bag crashed onto the floor with a *thump*. "Chin up. I'm putting on the tea and coffee and we'll start one room at a time. Chef's choice."

"Living room," Sage said, rolling up her sleeves. An object in motion stays in motion, and she was not about to sit down when her house needed attention. She wanted it to feel like home once again. "Then the den. I want a movie night tonight."

"Now, you're talking."

"*50 First Dates*."

"Now, you lost me."

"Ugh, fine." She had been on a bender with that movie and probably needed to pump the brakes. "*Mad Max?*"

"Again?"

"It's my movie night and you're the one crashing it. I get to pick."

"Pick a good one and I'll make that popcorn you like."

"Wait really?" He made this popcorn with coconut oil, sea salt, and a dose of secret seasoning. It tasted amazing, but he rarely made it, because he hated cleaning up the pot of coconut oil after.

"Pick a good one."

"*Burnt.*"

"The cooking one with Bradley Cooper?"

"Figured an amateur chef could appreciate that choice and I am definitely angling toward some popcorn."

"I accept. Consider me bamboozled by your perfect scheming. Except, you're sad, so I would've made the popcorn, no matter what movie you picked," Leo said, walking over to the upturned couch, kicking his duffel bag away, and pulling the velvet green couch back on its feet. He only grunted once. It was solid oak wood. At least, that's what George had told her.

A real sob burst through her this time.

Leo's eyes went wide. "Okay, okay! *50 First Dates* it is! Popcorn on the house."

"I can't go through George's room. I already did it once, and it was horrible. Now, I have to do it *again*." She quickly wiped tears from her face. She couldn't be faced with his favorite sweater still hanging over the edge of the bed where he'd left it or how that last painting he bought was still sitting on his dresser while he had been waiting to find the perfect frame for it. The room smelled like him and had his fingerprints everywhere. It made her forget that her only family-like figure was gone, and it made her think she'd turn around and see him and get to hug him and play chess with him and discuss tea and birdwatch and the world would be right again.

Leo walked over to her and pulled her into a hug, fierce and strong, and it was like she was transported out of her own house, to a world that smelled of Leo. She was surrounded by him. She squeezed her eyes shut, face pressed into his sweatshirt. "He was in my home. My space."

"I know," Leo said. "I know, and I'm sorry I couldn't do anything about it."

"It's not your fault." She sniffed and another sob rattled her. She wrapped her arms around him and squeezed. "I want to feel safe in my own home and this just feels like a violation."

He rubbed her back in slow circles. "I know, I know." He pulled her back, so she was looking at him. "But I need you to know that while I am here, you are safe. Nothing will happen to you. Know that while I am here you are safe."

She nodded, ready to crumble under the sincerity of his words. "Okay. Okay, you're right." Time to get serious. She didn't have time to cry.

"George's room can wait. Let's get the part of the

house where you live set back to normal before you open that wound again, deal?"

She nodded, wiping her tears away, suddenly embarrassed. She broke away from him and the world felt colder. The embrace had lasted maybe thirty seconds, and she decided that it could never happen again. She was going to like it too much. She was going to get used to him. His presence. His comfort. And it would be a harsh withdrawal when he left. They were platonic roommates. Occasional friends. But this was a Working Relationship. Period.

True to his word, Leo made her tea just the way she liked it—which is a totally normal thing a roommate would do—and they got the living room sorted and made decent headway on the den before Sage called it quits and turned on *50 First Dates* (again). Leo joined her, quoting the movie as he made his entrance with a giant bowl of steaming popcorn.

Drew Barrymore was waking up in the Arctic when the reality that Sage was going to have to go up to her own room where a stranger had been and go to sleep like nothing happened crashed over her. How was she supposed to relax knowing that someone had lurked around in her room? Maybe even sat on her bed. Maybe he was still hiding under the bed.

Relax Sage. The police cleared the place.

There were no monsters under the bed. At least not real ones.

But anxiety often manifested itself into apparitions and she quickly clicked on *Burnt,* hoping the foodie inside Leo would be interested enough to stay for a movie encore. It was.

"Now, you pick a good one," he said, staring at the screen with a smile on his face. He settled into his side of the couch. Yes, it was perfectly normal for platonic roommates to have their preferred sides of the couch...

"I'm grabbing some water, want anything?" she asked, with renewed determination to venture into the dark living room and kitchen without flinching at the shadows.

"Water would be great."

She returned a moment later bearing sparkling water for him because she knew that's what he had meant. Another thing a totally platonic friend would know, obviously.

They watched the movie in silence, other than the occasional chirp of Leo's phone where he would confirm that it was just an email and not an alarm for the cameras.

Bradley Cooper was finally leading his team of chefs to success and Leo made a move to stand up. "Good pick. Makes me hungry."

"You going to bed?" Sage asked, trying to keep her voice normal. She must have failed because he looked at her and cocked her head.

"You going to watch another?"

"I was thinking Never Been Kissed?"

"A classic." He leaned back into the couch. "You're not going to go up to bed, are you." It wasn't a question.

Sage took a shuddering breath in. "Stay with me?"

He kicked off his shoes. "Just turn on *Ever After*. You know you want to."

She did. And so, she started the movie and felt the winding anxiety coiled inside her relax a little. Leo breathed in deeply and slowly when he slept. It felt like she was invading his privacy staring at him so intently while he slept, but she couldn't help it.

At some point he startled himself awake, adjusted from his sitting position, and laid across the couch, his head toward her, only six inches away, legs hanging off the end of the couch.

He could have left. But he didn't. She stretched out on the chaise, willing herself to sleep, knowing she had a full day of streaming ahead of her. *Ever After* ended in its happily ever after and she started it over.

She closed her eyes, but sleep evaded her like a roadrunner hellbent on outrunning a coyote. Just as she drifted off, she woke herself up, sitting upright and looking around the dim room. Her friends Dougray Scott and Drew Barrymore were still bantering on the screen, keeping her company among the sounds of Leo's breathing.

By the third time of her jumping awake, Leo let out a long sigh. "You're safe," he mumbled. "Restart the movie, lay down, close your eyes, and try to sleep."

She laughed nervously. She thought she had been quiet. As soon as she curled up on the chaise, Leo reached his hand out and clasped hers, holding it tight. "I'm right here." He didn't let go even as he slept.

Sleep never really did come for Sage, but now it was because she was simply distracted by the rhythmic sounds of Leo breathing and the weight of his hand in hers.

Yes, totally something platonic roommates would be doing right now.

T here was nothing left for her to do, considering the situation. Butterflies had taken up residence in her stomach. Stars floated in her eyes. And that simply would not do. She had a competition to win! She didn't have time for boys.

Well. *A* boy in this case.

Actually, a man.

Because yes, she could grant him that title, given all that he had done for her and his crisis management style.

Also, no *boy* would have shoulders that broad, and muscles so well-defined, and—

She mentally slapped herself. *Enough.* She stretched the hairband on her wrist and snapped it against her skin. It stung and was just enough to pull her from her day-dreamin' and dilly-dallyin' and back to reality.

She couldn't be wasting time thinking back to his naked chest, water dripping down his neck, his well-defined abs, and... the pink teapot.

What was happening to her? She wasn't the daydreaming type! She was the escape into another world of games to disassociate and recharge, not come up with fantasies and "what if" scenarios pertaining to her *very real very* serious life!

And yet, the daydreams lingered. She thought about what it would be like to have him stay in town. Have a standing taco Tuesday night. Have him hold her hand on their nightly walks.

Speaking of. She stopped those strolls, all in the name of streaming and putting more hours into gaming. Which was kind of true.

The competition was five matches, the bottom five contestants of each round were eliminated until only the top five players were left. She was one of twenty-five vying for a spot in the Top Five. Five simple matches.

Easy, right? Right.

The days passed mostly in the same manner. Except they didn't have any more movie nights. Sure, she would have liked to, but her late-night streams were edging into the territory of early morning hour streams by the time she was finished. She needed to get her sleep schedule back in order.

Leo was there, living in her house, but she never saw him.

And it was weird to admit to herself that she might actually miss him.

They didn't eat together anymore. She usually ran late or bribed herself with food, promising herself if she ended on a solid match she could go down and eat. By the time that usually happened, it was well past eleven and there was usually a plate left for her in the fridge.

Squash was her constant companion, and, at times, Sage almost forgot Leo was even there. Still, for some reason, life didn't feel any better. And the conversation with Lily didn't help.

"Hey girly," Lily started. She sounded far and away like she was doing four different things while being driven around. "I just wanted to check in and see how you were doing."

"Fine. Have you caught any of the streams? I'm not doing too bad. Might play anonymously to practice, though, mess around with a few things—"

"That's great. Any more incidents?"

"Uh, no." The few weeks that had passed since the whole "someone broke in and ransacked the place" issue.

"Oh good, good. Look, I think you are going to rock the competition. And then, you can say goodbye to your little Bob guy."

"Oh?" The word nearly got stuck in her throat. "He's moving on?"

Lily muttered something to a driver and Sage could hear the tapping away of emails and a siren blare past. "Huh? Yeah, honey, once the competition is over, there won't be any need for him."

The code wasn't complex to decipher—it basically said, "Hey, the marketing part of you having a bodyguard won't really be necessary after the competition, so you'll be fine on your own again, right?"

"Okay," Sage said.

"What? I thought you'd be happy to have your space back, you introvert. He actually requested another agent to take over his job, but they couldn't on such short notice. They're busy people. Luckily, the competition is almost here. Just another two weeks for him is all."

Sage forced out a laugh. "Yeah, right. Sorry, just distracted. Been playing like crazy lately." He'd requested another job? Why did that make her stomach twist?

"Glad to hear it. Keep me posted!" Then she hung up.

What would her life look like without Leo in it? Probably the same, just a bit dimmer. She'd do the same things, maybe even try to keep up the walking routine. But there would be something missing, and she hated Leo for that. The super, perfectly platonic—*not at all romantic*—roommate.

She already missed him, and he was sitting in the same house.

Ugh. She needed to focus.

The chat was disappointing today. Her regular mods couldn't keep up with the comments and bots spamming the chat.

lorenzi12#!: Show us your boobs.

Block.

blokeazz: Chaz is going to absolutely murder you at the competition.

rewd1e: Shut up and play.

She blocked some other outright vile comments. There was no need to put up with threats to her life over a game, especially since they were probably 12-year-olds hiding in their private school dorms.

gordie9a9: She's blocking people.

gordie9a9: Can't handle the pressure, babe?

gordie9a9: It's a free country you know.

gordie9a9: Freedom of speech.

"And I have the freedom to block people. Protect my peace and all that," Sage said, highlighting the comments for the stream.

BobFilbert123: Hey, @gordie9a9 Does your mom know you talk to ladies like that? Phyllis would be so disappointed.

gordie9a9: The hell? How do you know my mom's name?

gordie9a9: This isn't funny.

BobFilbert123: You also have a cat named Spider.

gordie9a9: Are you hacking me rn?

gordie9a9: Seriously dude wtf?

BobFilbert123: Not hacking so much as using the skills my mama gave me. Speaking of mamas, yours was just emailed a screenshot of your filthy comments. Maybe hop off and start explaining yourself, kiddo.

gordie9a9: left the chat

Sage laughed. "I should make you a mod." She swore she heard the signature chuckle of Leo rumble from downstairs. "I'm gonna do it," Sage said to the chat. "I don't know who you are, Bob Filbert," a lie, obviously, "But you sound like a good guy."

BobFilbert123: Fun fact: in the 1600s filberts soaked in honey were thought to cure coughs.

"Lovely," Sage said.

And BobFilbert123 went on the block, responding to, and threatening to call the parents of, unruly kids in the chat. It was strange to know he was in her house, watching her, yet, at the same time, she didn't really mind him joining her in this world, either.

LiL8TE: Girl, I love your thick hair, but you have got to try a middle part. You look so old with a side part.

She laughed. "No offense, but I just can't get behind taking fashion advice from people who weren't around during the low-rise jeans era or the early 2000s and who are actively trying to make mullets a thing."

The bantering with the chat continued and she

finished another few matches, playing for fun and not necessarily to show off her skills.

The stream was coming to a close, and she tried not to be disappointed when she couldn't find Bob in the chat. She ended with her usual "go pet a puppy" and Squash wave, ignoring the new wave of spam demanding she take off her clothes or start an Only Fans since she was "only good at being looked at" and "sucked at playing" and "needed to get a real-life" and to "quit being a pick me."

She sat in silence and leaned back in her chair, taking her headphones off. There was a soft knock on the door.

"Yeah?" Sage asked, rubbing her temples. It was either a tension headache coming on or her headphones were too tight.

"I brought you some snacks." Leo opened her door and hovered in the doorway like he was waiting to be invited in. He held up a plate.

"Why does it smell… "

"Like crap?" he asked. "Because this is your favorite crap."

She was going to say, "Amazing." The scent of pizza bites, Cheese-its, and other junk food filled her office. "But why?" she asked.

"I wasn't too clever with my username, and I figured you put it together—"

"Bob."

He chuckled. "Yeah. Well, some of that stuff was just vulgar. Awful. More than normal. Thought you could use a little pick me up."

More than normal? How often was he lurking in her streams?

"Wow," she said, "thank you." She stood, grabbed the plate, and sat on the fluffy couch in the corner of her office.

He smiled, nodded, and turned to leave, pausing when she blurted out, "I've missed this."

Leo turned back to her and leaned on the doorframe. "Me too."

"Why did you want to leave this job?" she asked. It felt vulnerable. Like she was admitting that maybe she had been too harsh and that maybe, despite all her bravado, she wanted more. It felt like she was asking why he wanted to leave *her*.

He raised his eyebrows and plopped down into her gaming chair, spinning in a circle. "Who told you?" Leo stared at the ceiling.

"I heard it from Lily. She was cagey with details. Look, I'm sorry if—"

"I can't be objective with you." He sighed, running his hands through his hair, finally pausing and making eye contact with her. "I had to stop while I was ahead."

Sage sighed. It was a lot. She was careening off a cliff and Leo was doing everything he could to keep them from both falling over. She just wanted to let go and see where it went.

They would crash and burn. No other way around it.

"Thank you for your professionalism. But is there a chance you are overthinking it?"

Leo chuckled. "Maybe. But I'm a by-the-book kind of guy."

"I know. We'll be careful. Professional." They were dancing around *The Forbidden Topic*. And they both knew it, and both agreed not to say the quiet part out loud. She sighed again, leaning into the couch. "Care to join me?"

"Afraid it'll go too far?" he asked, eyebrows raised, smirk on his face.

Yes, she thought. "No," she said.

He sat on the couch and only made fun of her horrible food opinions a few times until she finally admitted that her palate had seriously been elevated and that was totally due to Leo's influence. His smug face had been missing these last few days.

"Now, care to join me?" he asked, stealing a pizza roll from the plate.

"Join you?"

"On a walk."

And the walk was just a walk. Simple and normal and it felt too much like falling back into a comfortable routine. She chose not to think about how this routine was hurtling toward an ending. How this couldn't be routine because this wasn't *real life.* Instead, she pretended it was.

22
LEO

Keeping his head on earth was far more difficult than he initially planned. Sage was getting under his skin. This job was getting harder by the minute, and not just because she was distracting his every waking (fine —some dreams too) thought. The event was going to be a logistical nightmare. After conferring with some of his coworkers, the agency decided to fly out two more body-guards to help with security.

Leo had his bags packed and loaded in the car and was busy triple-checking the rental car and the arrival of his counterparts, Suey and Willis. The pair would be meeting at the hotel a few hours earlier and reviewing the entrances and exits and would update Leo's plan if there were any changes to the layout or location of events.

The plane ride was totally uneventful except for some mild turbulence that made Sage grasp onto his forearm like a cat trying to escape a bathtub. He obviously pretended his initial jump was because she had grabbed him "hard enough to break skin" and not at all because her touch was like an electrical shock and he needed a moment to recover.

"Sorry," she laughed, removing her hand quickly and glancing out the window. The plane lurched again and she grabbed his forearm again. "My bad." She removed her hand a little slower this time, staring at his forearm. Thank goodness he had rolled up the sleeves because there was nothing like feeling her warm hand on his exposed skin.

The "fasten your seatbelt signs" popped up and a little announcement about how they were hitting a slight patch of weather and that everything was fine but to expect bumps for the next half hour or so. The plane jumped and this time Leo caught Sage's hand and held it in his own.

"Fun fact: your brain is trainable. So just pretend you're used to it. You can trick your mind into being a confident traveler."

She laughed a little and looked out the window at the thick clouds. It was like they were in a sea of gray.

"This is weird," she whispered and tried to pull her hand away.

He held her tighter, stroking the top of her hand with his thumb. "Just pretend it's not."

She held his hand even after the turbulence was long in the past.

. . .

They finally got into the rental car, which should not have been that complicated, but nothing could be simple when the pressure was on, could it? He glanced at Sage. Yeah, nothing would ever be simple again.

He dropped her off at her room, introducing her to Suey. "She'll be in the adjoining room. I'll be down the hall. Let me know if there is anything you need, but Suey will be with you for most of the competition and meet and greets. Willis and I will be doing the perimeter checks and video surveillance."

"Oh, so you're not going to the welcome dinner?"

Was it just him or did she seem...disappointed? He smiled at the thought and he must have given too much away because Sage crossed her arms, now on the defensive. "No, I won't," he answered. "I have, you know, a job to do."

She deflated a little. "But you've always done the job with me..."

Suey took the cue, but not before giving Leo some serious side-eye and went to her own room.

Leo leaned on the doorframe, looking down at Sage. "You actually gonna miss me hanging around?"

She scoffed and leaned against the other side of the door. "I just got used to having Bob around."

"Dang, I was hoping Leo would suffice."

She shrugged. "Maybe I'm just nervous. Or maybe I do actually like you sometimes, on the rare occasions you're nice."

He grabbed her hand. "Is this nice?"

"What do you mean?" She laughed.

Then he pulled her into himself for a hug. A real hug.

He enveloped her, wrapped his arms around her, and just squeezed. It was more contact with a person than he'd had in years and it nearly made his brain short-circuit.

"What are you doing?" she asked, slowly wrapping her arms around his waist.

"I am attempting to be nice. The whole comforting thing. Something like a friend would do." Except a friend wouldn't be smelling the side of her neck, a friend couldn't be rubbing circles with his thumb on the small of her back, a friend wouldn't be imagining what life with her would be like.

"Nice, huh?" she choked out against his chest. Her arms slowly came up and met around his middle, returning the embrace

"Is it working?" Leo asked. "I could tell you all the benefits of hugs and their calming powers?"

"Please don't ruin this moment of peace with a fun fact or an 'I read an article' moment."

And so, they stood there, for minutes? Hours? Years?

Clearly the measurement of time was different when someone finally, *finally,* got a chance to wrap his arms around the girl he wanted but couldn't have. Time couldn't be broken into seconds or minutes, it was too precious to be considered measurable.

Eventually, she let go and stepped back. "Thanks," she said, taking a deep breath. "I guess I am on edge a little bit."

"From the threats or the competition?" Or something more, he wanted to ask.

"I'm not sure," she said.

There was a pause that lasted exactly eight seconds

(because pauses were measurable in the normal unit of second—unlike overdue strictly but not strictly friendship hugs) before Leo's body reacted. His brain couldn't stop him (it wasn't really his fault, his brain was still floating around in the clouds due to the whole "being nice" thing). Leo leaned down and pecked her on the cheek. "Good luck, Love," he said because honestly everything else he wanted to say was stuck in his throat.

So, like a man, he turned around and walked away because he was *aloof. He was strong. He was emotionless.*

His slow and steady retreat had nothing to do with the fact that his legs had turned to jelly and he was incapable of thought because his lips had lightly grazed the softest cheek in the world.

He glanced up. He really needed to find his brain if he was going to make it through this weekend in one piece.

23

SAGE

Sage touched her cheek. Then her other cheek. Then she went and took a shower, because how else did someone handle an existential crisis? One simply had to stand under the cascading water and contemplate their life while staring at the white wall, obviously. Sage didn't make the rules of life. She just followed them.

He'd kissed her! On the cheek but still, he'd *kissed her*. And it was *nice*. It felt... normal? Totally ordinary, like it was something they'd done a hundred times, like it was the most natural thing in the world... like they were a couple that did couple-y things.

What a jerk.

She needed to focus! Not get all weird about a boy.

Except, he wasn't a boy. No. She'd been admiring his muscle and lean body from afar and tonight she got to touch him. She got to wrap her arms around him, and felt his wrapped around hers, and *ugh*.

She was a sucker for muscular forearms. And for

someone who took care of themselves. Someone who valued their health and fitness and made *her* want to do the same thing. She liked someone who exercised their minds and had "fun facts" about what they'd learned—especially, if they were on a sea animal kick.

It didn't hurt that he was nice to look at, too.

Sage shook her head, banishing the images of Leo and a pink teapot that flashed across her mind.

Suey was nice. She was a professional and the assistant façade fell away with the crisp uniforms with the agency's name embroidered on the chest.

Oh. And the fact that they had guns.

Whispers swirled, but nothing could outweigh the buzz of excitement at the impending competition.

Players, sponsors, commentators, and other influencers all enjoyed the welcome dinner, and Sage did her best not to appear absolutely on edge with her nerves.

This was really happening. This competition had been an *idea* for so long, it was strange to actually be here, doing the thing.

Lily looked to be high on life and was totally milking the whole bodyguard thing. Jared was insufferable, but he always was.

The event went off without a hitch, save for the nerves trying to fry her alive. She chatted and ate *wayyyy* too much cheesecake. She couldn't help but glance around the giant room, hoping to catch a glimpse of Leo. She never found him.

When she returned to her room, she got ready for bed and lay awake for far too long.

Her phone buzzed.

LEO: Heard you ate all cheesecake.
Please tell me it was horrible otherwise I
shall die of envy.

SAGE: I must admit it was subpar. The
risotto though…might have been better
than yours.

LEO: I will not dignify that slander with a
response. But if I were you, I would
probably make a comparison about how
their sorry excuse for rice looked more
like oatmeal and mine is always a work
of art.

SAGE: Good thing you didn't have to
dignify that with a response. Everything
okay?

LEO: All good. Just wanted to wish you
luck. So here it is. Good luck.

SAGE: A man of many words.

LEO: Goodnight, Sage.

She didn't sleep a wink.

The morning came with texts of "good lucks" and "you've got this" and a "make us proud" from Lily.

Sage wanted to vomit. Instead, she put on her race day outfit of black jeans, simple boots, and a classic (but extremely soft) t-shirt that had Squash's signature face embroidered on the front and all her sponsors on the back. She actually curled her hair and let it fall in loose waves around her, not that it would last that long. She'd no doubt throw it up in a bun when the stakes got higher. The higher the bun, the better she played, apparently.

Suey knocked on the door to let Sage know she'd be walking her down for the first meet and greet and introductions as soon as she was ready. The event started at eleven sharp.

Suey was a tall and muscular woman in her forties and she was clearly a no-nonsense sort of gal. She waited outside the door like a real bodyguard, which, of course, she was, but it was so weird to think even now she had guards—multiple—keeping an eye out for her. This felt real.

Suey gave Sage a nod when she exited her suite. "Ready?" Suey asked.

"As I'll ever be!" Sage said with all the bravado she wanted to feel but just...didn't. This was supposed to be fun! This was supposed to be exciting! So why did she feel like her limbs were trying to each run away in a different direction?

Suey paused at the elevator, looking at her watch. "Says we are to go to the second floor where we'll convene in the green room."

"I actually prefer the stairs," Sage said, pointing down the hall.

Suey shook her head. "Leo was specific that we do not deviate from the plan."

Speaking of her source of annoyance, Leo trotted up, looking just as wired as she felt. "Hey, glad I caught you," he said to Suey. "Forgot to mention stairs are acceptable."

Suey raised an eyebrow as if what Leo had said was ludicrous.

"Hey," Leo said, raising his hands in defense. "Small concessions, alright? Unless you'd rather be wearing her morning tea on your shoes?"

Suey glanced at Sage. She just shrugged. "I don't like small spaces."

"Stairs it is."

Suey fit her earpiece in place. "I'll wait by the door," she said. Did she just wink at Leo? Or was that for her?

"Hey," Leo said. "Things are going to be crazy today for both of us. And you and I both know this job is going to be over as soon as you win this competition—"

"If," Sage said.

"You're going to do great and I wanted to give you something so you knew I was thinking about you. A good luck charm of sorts."

"A gift?"

And then he leaned down and kissed her. It was soft, and his hand rested on the side of her cheek. How is it that she felt his thumb brushing against her cheekbone when his lips (his lips!) were pressed gently against her own? He smelled of cedar and soap and mint and—and it was over just as soon as it happened.

Her stomach lurched. Butterflies were nothing compared to the chaos happening in her blood. She was acutely aware of the heat between them, more than likely emanating from the flush quickly rising from her chest to her face.

"Good luck," he whispered, before leaving one more peck against her nearly open mouth. And like a freaking movie scene, he walked away.

Was that a strut?

Wait, what was happening?

Suey opened the stairwell door. "Ready, Miss Moon?"

"Not even a little bit," Sage said, walking through the doors, fingers brushing over her lips.

They didn't make it to the second floor. They didn't even make it three floors down before a side door opened and everything went black.

The last thing she heard was a yell, a scuffle, and the *thump* of Suey hitting the ground.

20px

24

LEO

She tasted like strawberries. She smelled like citrus. She was sunshine on his winter day. He was floating high as a kite and didn't even care that he had turned into a driveling poet. Should he write her a sonnet?

He could barely wipe that goofy grin off his face when he met up with Willis, who gave Leo the current reports of the tech reviews. He'd check on Sage in the green room in about ten minutes, then immediately plant himself near the stage in the giant room where the whole shindig would go down.

Leo checked his phone for alerts. Nothing. All clear. Things were going well and Willis even mentioned how he had underestimated the scope of this event and how he'd let Jensen know how well Leo did.

"Jenson mentioned you asked for a replacement on this job a few weeks back," Willis said as they walked the hall toward the security lounge.

Leo shrugged. "I feared I could no longer be impartial... "

Willis nodded. "Part of the job, kid. I think there's some psychology behind it, you know? Like, we get paid to *protect*; it's natural for instincts to take over and turn it into something it's not. You're young now, so it feels like a romantic gesture—you know, throwing yourself in front of a bullet for her. Eventually, you'll grow old like me and every young woman will feel like some daughter, or niece. How'd Jenson react to that little request?" Willis laughed like he knew the answer.

"He pretty much told me the same thing."

Willis clapped Leo on the shoulder, "Like I said, it's the psychology of it all."

Leo had his doubts. He fully accepted this was more than just a fleeting feeling when he impulsively decided to kiss her. He wished he'd done it sooner. How many kisses had he wasted these last few weeks, all in the name of professionalism?

Once Willis settled in front of the camera screens and monitors, Leo opted to pop into the green room early, just so he could lock eyes with her. Did she feel the same way about the kiss? He wasn't normally that forward, but when he got the call this morning that, after this job, he'd be flying to D.C. for a new job, he couldn't wait another second. He'd had to do *something*.

Tomorrow was another problem for another day.

The second-floor conference rooms were abuzz with excitement. There was a palpable energy in the air. There were media crews—the *news?!*—gathering interviews from social media managers, fans, and influencers. This was a *Big* Deal. Leo found himself wishing he had been a little more kind, regarding his "hobby game" attitude. This was well beyond that. He scanned the growing crowd for any sign of Sage.

"Leo!" someone screeched, running toward him. "Where on earth is Sage? She needs to go on for introductions in like two minutes!"

"She came down here fifteen minutes ago."

"She's not here!" Lily said, opening her arms to the crowd in an exaggerated manner, as if to say "Look, idiot. A Sage-less sea."

"Jared?"

"Texted me that he's going to try her room and maybe the actual event center." Lily sighed and ran a hand through her long hair, looking more haggard than normal despite her professional pencil skirt and heels. "Where on earth is she? I guess if there was a threat to her safety, I could go up and explain that. Good grief, where is Jared? He needs to be documenting this too," Lily said, tapping away at her phone.

"Willis—"

"Camaro," Willis's voice cut through the chatter. "Come to the eastern fourth-floor stairwell now. Sage is gone. Suey is okay, but I just called in a medic for her. What the heck happened?"

Leo couldn't hear the mumbled response of Suey through the earpiece. Leo ran to the stairwell, ignoring the "Leo? Leo, what's happening? Is Sage in trouble?"

Willis spoke to Leo in the earpiece. "I'm taking Suey out the back. She has a little gash on her head but she's not thinking right. Looks like someone hit her over the head. Likely concussed."

"And Sage?"

"Gone," Willis said. "A guy came out of the stairwell and grabbed her, then another from the Janitor's closet behind Suey and blitzed her."

Leo's stomach dropped. Two attackers? "Report this to the authorities, take care of Suey, then scour the cameras."

"On it."

Leo pulled out his iPad, and the map of all the AirTags he'd planted on Sage lit up the screen. Now, it was just a matter of finding the outlier. Why hadn't he shoved a tracker in her shoe? There were at least a dozen back at her house. There was one pacing back and forth —obviously, Squash trying to get comfortable on the couch.

There was one in the car they parked at the airport.

A handful in the hotel, likely her room.

But there was one on the move. It was on the far side of the hotel, a dot blinking quickly across the screen. But where? It couldn't tell him the depth or height! For all he knew she could be on the forty-first floor or in the basement.

He wasted a precious moment notifying the building security and Willis of his suspicion that Sage was likely still in the building.

"We need to do a grid search," Willis said over the radio.

"I know!" Leo said, working hard to keep the rising fear from rising to his throat and strangling him. He stared at the map, willing the tracker to move. Just a little. Something to give him an indication of where she might be. That's when he noticed another tracker, unmoving, but definitely where it shouldn't be.

Why on earth was it by the pool?

"Start at the top and the 22nd floors. Everyone, work your way down. I'll start in the lobby and meet you."

"Understood,"

Willis said. "Security is already on the move."

Leo ran, dodging people left and right, jumping over a suitcase in the foyer. He looked like a madman.

The pool? There were a ton of people out there, but why would Sage have come this way at all? She wouldn't have. She hated the idea of being sunburned and would never go out in the highest UV index, unless she *had* to. So why—

He skidded to a halt when he saw it. Her signature tote bag. It had Squash painted on the front with little pumpkins floating around the rat-dog. Why on earth was it lying near the—

And that's when it hit him. The parking garage. Instead of taking the stairs or elevator down to the parking garage, they must have used the car entrance beyond the gate to the pool.

Leo switched radio frequencies "Security—"

"Here."

"Check out the south parking garage entrance and exit. I need eyes from the last—" he glanced at his watch, "Half hour. Anyone on foot?"

"I'll check, but you know that the outside cameras are not the quality you're used to—"

"Just check."

Leo raced down the ramp. Apparently, this was just an exit and there was no need for an attendant. Just his luck. He scanned the busy lot. His service was going to be terrible, but something told him there was merit to the parking garage theory.

2 5

SAGE

She was blindfolded, and more than anything else, she had her hands tied behind her back. Based on the tight, thin plastic, she guessed zip ties. And they were quite effective. Not one TikTok video showing young women how to escape really did any justice to how hard it actually was when your whole body was shaking with fear and adrenaline.

All she remembered was standing in the stairwell as Suey fought with someone. Then she had her arm wrenched behind her while a guy pressed a gun to her back, commanding her to not make a sound. He led her to the ground floor and out to the pool deck, which was nearly empty that early in the morning. He jostled her through a gate and then she passed out.

No wonder her head ached. Did she inhale that sleep drug or something? Or did she simply forget to breathe and panic-passed out?

She smelled pine and leather. New car smell.

317

"Hello?" Sage asked. "Let me go and we can pretend this never happened. Honestly. No one would believe this anyway."

"We all know that's not true."

She nearly shot through the roof when the raspy voice next to her spoke. Was there a skylight? Maybe she could have burst through with that thick skull of hers. That would have been a better escape plan than whatever delusion told her she might be able to talk herself out of this one.

"Who are you?" It was worth trying at least.

"No one."

The voice seemed so familiar, yet so foreign. It was like seeing a person and not remembering their name but knowing them. Maybe she could talk her way out after all.

"Who are you?"

"Shut up!" the voice yelled.

Okay, so maybe no talking out of this. She was obviously in the backseat of whatever car this was. Her fingers were numb.

"How much time do you think there is?" an unfamiliar voice asked. It was a deep, menacing sound. It turned the blood furiously pumping through Sage into ice. It was one delusion to think she could take on one person, a totally different scenario to take on two.

"What is happening here?" Sage asked. Any bravado evaporated from her voice the moment her voice wobbled on the last word.

"Drink this," the raspy voice next to her said.

"Why?" Sage asked. The sound of liquid pouring into

a glass met her ears. The scent hit her then. Tequila? Vodka? What was this? A little cocktail hour before her murder?

"Just drink it and everything will be perfectly peachy."

"Wait, what?" She knew that voice, that annoying phrase.

Perfectly peachy.

"Jared? Jared is that you?" Sage asked, twisting her head, hoping the blindfold would come flying off. "What is going on?"

"Not Jared," the not Jared guy said in a totally Jared voice.

Sage actually relaxed a little despite the whole blindfold and numb fingers situation. "I know it's you. And come on, are we really in your car?"

"Ugh, fine."

And the blindfold slipped from her eyes and she was face to face with Jared, who held a shot glass full of clear liquid toward her. "Salut. Now have a drink."

"What, why?" Sage struggled with her hands. "Untie me. What time is it? Who is that guy?" She jerked her head toward the driver's seat where a large man sat. She only saw the back of his head, but this dude was clearly beefy and strong. Who else could have taken out Suey and her? Certainly not Jared.

"Take a drink and I'll tell you."

"The competition," Sage whispered. She could practically feel the blood draining from her face and pool in her toes.

"The competition will go on without you," Jared said,

tapping away at his phone. "The service down here sucks."

"What is going on!" Sage tried to shoulder the door open and the stranger in front reached over the center console and squeezed her knee, *hard.* "Ow! Okay, okay, I'll stop!"

"And drink this," Jared said, holding up the shot glass.

Sage nodded, and Jared held it to her lips. She contemplated spitting it in his face, but the large man in front glaring at her evaporated any notions of being brave. At least for now. Hey, maybe some liquid courage was what she needed.

Jared helped her drink the shot, and he quickly poured another.

Sage coughed and sputtered. "Is that Everclear?" She was going to be toast if she had another shot of that jet fuel.

Jared shrugged. "Not fancy but would a woman falling headfirst into a stress-induced bender really care?"

"What are you talking about?"

Jared slapped the phone down on the console. "You want to know what's going on, Sage? This is me saving both of our careers. Do you know that? Did you know that Lily wasn't going to keep you around unless you got top three? And we both know that isn't going to happen."

"What time is it? I can still make the competition." She could feel her heart beating in her ears. Her head felt like it might explode.

Jared was undeterred. "Of the twenty-plus people competing, you'd be lucky, *so* lucky, to make the top ten.

And me? Well Miss Moon, you sure don't make my job easy, do you?"

"What do you want from me?"

"It was my job to catapult you to social media stardom, influencer status, but getting content from you is like pulling teeth. My job with you is so freaking impossible. I'm not meeting the metrics Lily wanted and I could see the writing on the wall. You'd be out a sponsor, and I'd be out of a really well-paying job. Let's be honest, we both can't afford that."

"So, what does that have to do with burning a hole in my stomach?" Seriously, Everclear was only good for stripping paint.

"We know you are going through it. The grief of losing your Grandpa Joe—"

"George—"

"Right. And the stress of the, you know, threats, which were absolute gold. So glad Lily latched onto that and gave me the green light to elaborate on the whole bodyguard thing. Really pumped up my numbers, but I needed more. Something bigger. And what better than a whole 'cool girl hitting rock bottom' moment?" Jared asked.

"That isn't real life. This isn't a girl-sitting-on-the-couch-in-her-underwear-smoking-a-cigarette-while-drinking-scotch moment. This isn't Hollywood. That's not what's happening here. I'm sorry I've been…difficult. It's been a hard few months but—"

"It's not enough. People need more. They need some tangible way of seeing your fall from success. They love an underdog story but they love a hot mess even more."

Sage was putting it together. Slowly. Was her mind moving in slow motion because of the Everclear in her system or the adrenaline come down?

"You," Sage gasped. "You were the one sending those letters? Trashing my place?"

Jared shrugged. "Me or my cousin." He pointed to Scary Guy up front.

Scary Guy waved a hand and winked at her from the rearview mirror.

"To drum up some pity for me?" Sage asked. The words threatened to choke her. "All for clout? Social media sympathy? You're sick. This is my life you are messing with."

"And I promise it will all be worth it. You and I both know you won't make top ten, but you most definitely could next year. So, what's better than an underdog story?" Jared pushed another shot of the paint stripper toward Sage's mouth. "Think about it." He was growing excited. He had this mania about him, a Cheshire cat grin and wild eyes. "You're going to miss the competition, accept that. You might embarrass yourself by stumbling back to the hotel, but people will see you. They'll put two and two together. I'll announce how you choked on the pressure and grief and how sorry you are but you're doing better. Next year will be your redemption. Lily might even approve of you going dark for a little bit, two months off social media type thing, really get people curious about what's going on in your life. Some might speculate rehab."

"My life isn't a drama you can manipulate! I was

prepared to place mid-level. I was just excited to be here, to have this opportunity!"

"I'm not finished yet!" Jared barked, shoving the glass into Sage's face. He pinched her nose until she opened her mouth and he poured it in. Sage coughed most of it up and it dribbled down her chin. Jared sighed. "Look, Lily won't drop a player like this, especially with all that attention on you. Even she knows how bad it would look for her brand to drop you at your rock-bottom moment with the mystery stalker still on the loose. I am guaranteeing you and me another year of work. She'll pull the 'we always support women and will stand by her in these trying times' card and be forced to stand by her word. You'll come back next year better than ever and crush the competition. The timing isn't right for you this year, but next year is yours. Now drink up." Jared checked his watch. "We have time to kill. I'm not going to 'discover' you down here until the tournament is nearly over. Then we'll stagger into the lobby where I'll help you to your room. People will see you. They'll take photos. Just be prepared for that."

"I'll tell them everything."

Jared scoffed. "Oh honey, do you really think anyone would believe you?"

26

LEO

His heart thundered in his chest. His stomach lurched. He prayed he was doing the right thing by chasing this wild theory. There was a fire escape close to the pool. Maybe she was smuggled out that way?

The marathon training was coming in handy as Leo circled yet *another* level of the parking garage. He wasn't tired, if anything his muscles were electrified. Leo channeled his panic into focus. He only had two more levels of the parking garage to check, and he was growing more anxious with each step.

What if he was wrong? What if he'd wasted ten precious minutes being out of service underground, away from his team?

But that's when he saw it. A car parked in the far corner, lights on, running. He glanced at his map. Perfect match to the lone tracker.

She was right there.

That had to be Sage.

She was only mere feet away from him.

Leo didn't have to think. He reached behind him, pulled out his gun, and flipped it in his hand. He used the butt of the weapon to hit the window. Once. Twice. The third hit shattered the glass, spilling over the driver, who was still fumbling with getting the car into reverse. Leo's training created a muscle memory in him, and he opened the door from the inside (ignoring the glass shards cutting him—like any hero would) and pulled out the startled driver enough to slam the door on his head. Once, then twice.

Problem solved.

"Leo!" Sage screamed. "It's me! Sage! Back here!"

"I am well aware of that!" Leo flung the back door open and pulled her to him, immediately retraining his gun on the assailant in the back seat.

"Jared?" Leo asked, his chest heaving.

"Ow, ow, my hands," Sage said. She was tucked safely behind Leo. Despite wanting to wrap her in a bear hug, Leo held Jared's gaze. Jared blinked twice and then opened his car door to dash out the other side.

Leo would deal with that rat later. He turned his attention to Sage, grabbing her face in his hands. "What happened? Are you hurt? What did he do to you?"

Sage sniffed. Then she smiled. It was the best sight in the world. "Oh my gosh, how did you find me? Do you have anything to cut these?" She turned around, and he found the issue of her zip-tied hands. Her fingers were slightly purple.

He was guiding her up out of the car park toward an exit, trying his radio. When he finally got a signal, he let the team know the Subject was safely recovered, Jared was on the run, and an unconscious guy was hanging out in the only car in the basement of the garage.

"We'll get scissors at the front desk. The police are going to want to talk to you—" He was in grave danger of kissing her again.

"What time is it?" She looked at Leo with wide eyes. "Oh my gosh, please tell me it hasn't started yet."

"Seriously? You're thinking about a game right now?" Leo glanced at his watch. "Match started ten minutes ago." And the opportunity for an impromptu "I saved your life" embrace had officially left the table of opportunities.

"I can still join! I can join, as long as I'm not past fifteen minutes late. There won't be a penalty!"

"Other than the huge time delay! Sage, what is going on?" He held on to her arm as he guided her inside, reassuring himself that she was okay. She was here, and she wasn't going anywhere.

And why did she smell like nail polish remover?

They made it to the lobby, where he made quick work of cutting off the zip ties around her wrists, ignoring the stares of the people lingering as he rubbed blood back into her hands. Definitely just aiding in her finger recovery and not at all because Leo felt the need to hold her hands and make sure she didn't slip away again.

She was here and she was okay, and she wanted to go play video games despite just being held hostage for the last half hour.

"I *have* to go in," Sage said, dragging him behind her as she made her way to the giant room full of nerds and geeks and computers and everything else. She was sure going to make an entrance. But when didn't she?

He couldn't ignore how she was beautiful and successful and charismatic. And, for being stuck inside all the time as a borderline hermit, she could hold an audience with her authentic chatter. Her laughter made him melt. Her eyes made him want to do a silly dance just to keep them on his. Her smile was the best sight in the world.

And right now, she had a wicked and determined look on her face: eyebrows furrowed, eyes darting toward the door, and jaw clenched.

She talked as she ran. "I know this doesn't make sense, but if I don't go, *they* win. I swear, it'll make sense when I explain it to you. Just trust me."

People were starting to recognize her. Murmurs spread through the crowd as she paused at the door to the tournament.

"We need to find Jared, and who was that in the car? The police are here—" Leo paused in front of the door. "But I trust you." The giant double doors separating them from the competition seemed to loom over them.

"Thank you," she said. Then she reached for his collar and pulled his face toward hers. She kissed him. It wasn't the gentle kiss he'd given her earlier.

He pulled her into him, returning her kiss with the weight of a thousand "almost" kisses from these past months. This kiss had the taste of revenge, fire, tenacity, and... Everclear?

He released her. "Sage, are you drunk?" He kissed her

again, wrapping his hand around the back of her neck, and pulling her in close.

After what was definitely not enough time for their lips to properly get acquainted, she pulled away. "It's a long story," she said, as breathless as he felt. "But no, I don't think so."

"How do you feel?" he asked, touching the side of her face, ignoring the open-mouthed stares.

She let out a long sigh. "A little lightheaded. A little floaty."

Leo rolled his eyes. "Welcome to my life."

27
SAGE

Floaty? Welcome to his life? *Doesn't matter right now.*

Sage needed to focus if she wanted a chance of not coming in dead last. So much for top five. She could be content with the top ten. Top half. Anything but dead last.

She opened the door, took a deep breath, sprinted across the room to her station, and dove into her other world. And in this world, it was an even playing field. And she was ready to fight back.

She blocked out the sounds of the commentators, pretended she was at home with Squash snuggled in her lap, and did what she did best. She played. She talked to herself like she would if subscribers were watching (and quickly pushed out the thought that people were actually *right there* watching her play) and she scraped by in the first round, but she had to pull out her secret move to do so.

Through a lot of trial and error, Sage had learned how to attach to the armor of other players and bounce off of them. This was supposed to be her Big Final Move—the last-ditch effort to pull her out of trouble. She was supposed to use this later in the competition, not at the very beginning. But time was not on her side and she was backed against a wall (literally). But she squeaked by.

She had a whole ten minutes to collect herself before the second round started. Lily barreled through the roped-off section to the "arena" of sorts. It was the first time Sage got a moment to look around. It was a long, long table spanning the length of the room with gaming setups surrounding each side. Giant screens covered the walls, allowing everyone's gameplay to be broadcasted.

Then there were high-rise bleachers surrounding the perimeter of the room, clearly the first two rows of seats blocked for VIPs, commentators, and support staff. Speaking of other players, they leaned back in their chairs and either drank their energy drinks (were you really at a high-end gaming event if not at least five people were sponsored by some energy drink with questionable ethics and ingredients?) and others were stretching and chatting with their managers or sponsors.

"Where were you!" Lily screeched. She sounded like an absolute wreck, which was strange because she was smiling. A camera flashed at the eliminated players being ushered to a green room where they would conduct some interviews and statements.

Let the speculation begin, Sage thought.

"I ran into some issues with Jared," Sage said, not even able to wrap her head around the whole thing.

"Why do you smell like you just made moonshine in a bathtub?" Lily asked, still smiling. "Pose real quick."

Sage defaulted to her smile and leaned into Lily, who was squatting next to her while a photographer snapped a picture.

"Here," a deep voice said, thrusting a mug into Sage's hands. "Drink this. And I got this for you too. You know, for the whole moonshine debacle. Don't want people talking more than they already are."

Leo handed her a pack of bubble gum. "Mr. Camaro, I demand to know what is going on! You told me she was missing, and the police—" she hissed the last words.

"Good luck, Love." Leo winked at Sage, ushering Lily back to the section for sponsors.

"I thought you had to talk with the police?" Sage said it too loudly and only realized this after the fact when several heads turned her way.

"How did you—" She held up her mug of perfectly prepared tea.

"I can multitask." Leo winked and adjusted his earpiece. Then he turned into the serious bodyguard— not the guy who made her tea just the way she liked it. Leo left the room as quickly as he entered. Willis sat next to Lily, scanning the crowd much like Leo always had.

And with two sips and a piece of gum, she was thrust into round two. Then round three. Then the fourth. She made it to the fourth round! Top ten! If she played her map correctly, she could scrape into the top-five round.

Except she didn't.

The other players were just too good and she didn't have enough experience. She was just outgunned.

It was a solid defeat with some amazing gameplay. She stood when the round ended, smiled along with the other eliminated players, waved to the photographers and live-streaming channels, and made her way to the green room. Surprisingly, she couldn't wipe that grin off her face. She had really done it. It was a failure, but one of the best because she finished in seventh place, higher than her initial goal. *And* she had done it off the heels of just being kidnapped!

Take that, Jared.

She had a million questions thrown at her.

"Why were you late?"

"What happened?"

"Why were the police here?" another commentator asked.

"How do you feel like you performed despite the news swirling about you on social media?" someone asked.

"Are you dating one of the cops? There is a photo of you making out with a man."

"Is that why you were late? A little love rendezvous that went too long?"

Ah, finally a question she could answer. She cleared her throat. "Uh, well, I am not totally sure what is being said about me on social media at the moment, but I assume there is a lot of false stuff going around." Lily nearly caused a scene with how fast she jumped onto the stage and stood behind Sage, leaning over her shoulder and nearly yelling into the microphone about how there was an incident, the police are looking into it, and there cannot be any comments made as "it is an active investigation at the moment but LilyTech is here to support our gamers" and all that other crap.

Sage had won. Well, she had won her own little goal and that was all that mattered to Sage right now. And the fact that Leo, despite talking into his earpiece and with different officers, kept looking in her direction, tracking her through the room. Every time their eyes met he smiled. And Sage couldn't help but swell with pride. No, that wasn't it. Excitement? No, that wasn't it either.

Affection.

More questions were asked, and more were answered with non-answers. Overall, the interviews ended when the final match was set to take place. She joined her Lily-Tech crew (minus Jared) and watched the finalists compete. It would have been amazing being at that final five table, but in the end, how could she be mad about the outcome?

When Crickets won (not totally unexpected but still annoying) Leo whisked Lily and Sage away to a small room where they answered questions with the police. The police informed Sage that both Jared and his cousin were in custody and "Yes, absolutely we would like to press charges!" Lily exclaimed.

And that was it.

It was all over.

Case closed.

So why did she feel so...bummed?

The biggest event in her career and it was over just as it began.

Leo and Lily chatted in a quiet corner and paused their conversation when Sage joined them.

Lily sighed and turned to Sage. "Take a breather. I am so proud of you. Not the outcome we wanted, but we can use this. I sent a dress up to your room earlier. Hair and makeup will be up at five, so let's say we meet down here at six? Good grief I need to hire a photographer to get some photos since Jared decided to screw us over."

Oh yeah, being kidnapped and held against her will in a basement and forced to drink poison was totally inconvenient.

Sage and Leo took the stairs to her room. "Willis is up there if you need anything. I have to get back down there and answer some questions and file some reports for the agency. I'll pick you up at six."

"Pick me up?"

Leo cracked a grin. "Gotta have a final farewell event with your assistant, Bob, right?"

Sage smiled back. "I think I'd prefer to go with Leo."

Sage had to hand it to Lily (and maybe Jared's hand in this). The dress was impeccable. It was a deep red, silky material with a halter neckline and low back. The color was the exact shade of the primary planets in the background of *Welkin Wall*. The hem of the dress had gold stitching—cute little stars and designs were also motifs for the game. Her hair was pulled away from her face and fell down her back in gentle waves. It was a great look and Sage, despite not being one to wear dresses often, felt confident in the gown.

She stared at herself in the mirror, admiring the make-up. The artist had given her a smoky eye very reminiscent of the 2016 trends and she would likely have to endure comments from her younger subscribers pointing out this fact. The red lip matched the deep gown perfectly and complimented her hair. It was bold and beautiful and she wiped it off with a towel, smirking at her reflection.

She opened the door before Leo could knock. He looked surprised for half a second and then smiled, taking her in. He didn't even try to hide how his eyes roamed her body.

And now she was certain she was blushing as red as her dress.

"You're beautiful," Leo said, voice not much more than a whisper.

"That's not something Bob would say."

"You wanted Leo."

She smiled. "I do."

"Worried it'll go too far?" He reached out and grabbed her hand, intertwining his fingers with her as he spoke.

She looked at her hand in his. "Terrified," she whispered.

"But we could pretend."

"Pretend?" She looked up at him. He really was handsome.

"Pretend I'm not on the clock. Pretend that this is normal. For my last day on the job, we can pretend that going too far isn't wrong."

She wanted to ask if it was wrong. Was it wrong to want him? What was too far? Where was the line?

Instead, she just reached up and grabbed the back of his neck, pulling him gently to her lips. If they were going to pretend, she could confess later that she was a method actor or something.

He kissed her back, leaning over her and pressing her against the door, wrapping a hand around the back of her neck, angling her face toward him. This wasn't a gentle kiss like before, this was a thousand kisses funneled into one. Her body could barely keep up with the sensation of his body pressed close, his lips over hers, his thumb stroking her cheek *and oh my goodness, was it hot in here?*

Leo's radio beeping broke them out of the moment. They laughed. Leo rested his forehead against hers. "I think I am terrible at pretending."

"Me too."

He stepped back and clicked off the radio, removing the earpiece. "Well, I doubt anything I do tonight will change my fate. I'm either getting fired for having my Subject kidnapped under my watch or a pat on the back for recovering my Subject. Word from Willis says my boss man was surprised this job ended with a bang like it did but was nevertheless impressed by how I handled it. Glowing review from Lily too, so I'm hoping for the latter."

"There is still one more day for me to get you fired," Sage said, still holding one of his hands.

He pecked her on the lips. "I've wanted to do that for so long." He kissed her again. "Let's see if word of my fraternizing with a Subject gets back to the boss man. Maybe I'll get fired after all."

"Would you really lose your job?"

They walked toward the stairwell. "I have other plans forming. I can't be James Bond forever," Leo said. "But making out with a Subject is definitely against the rules. So are a lot of things. It's a gray area."

Sage shrugged. "Well, you were deep undercover as Bob. And maybe my fans are right."

"Right about what?"

Sage couldn't help but smile. "That I might have a thing for my assistant."

28

LEO

That dress was a red flag walking. A sign that said, "don't come any closer, because every ounce of professionalism will go out the window."

He was never good at listening anyway.

Leo got to indulge in holding her hand and dancing with her, without second-guessing a touch of her bare back. How was someone allowed to look so gorgeous while simultaneously being the biggest nerd in the world?

That spot where her neck met her shoulder taunted him with every dance. It teased him, begging for his lips to graze over the soft skin.

Alas, he was forced to be a gentleman when he *really* wanted to be a randy teenager, sneak out of this place and—

No. This was her night to shine. He could play the part of the perfect gentleman.

Well, a gentleman who refused to let her dance with anyone else, but it was clear she didn't mind. They had a lot of catching up to do. When did his frustration turn into infatuation? Hard to tell when it all flipped.

He pretended this was normal, that he had the privilege of being with her every day, and this was just another day in his life with Sage.

He wanted to do life with her.

Which was terrifying considering his whole career path really wasn't conducive to families, relationships, or even friendships.

Family? With her? Maybe.

Relationship? With Sage? Absolutely.

Friendship? That couldn't be where it ended.

"What are you thinking about?" Sage asked.

He twirled her on the dance floor where others were simply swaying. The ballroom was decked out and everyone was wearing some motif, some homage, to *Welkin Wall.* There were photographers and interviewers and someone streaming from every table. It was like Comic-Con for computer geeks. Lily was over at the table conducting unofficial interviews, trying to head off the damage about Jared that was likely already leaking.

Leo turned his attention back to his favorite Subject. He *wanted* to say "I'm thinking about a life with you." Instead, he turned on his work brain, because there was something niggling at the back of his mind. "I'm just thinking about Jared. Obviously, he was insane. Out of touch with reality. Delusional."

Sage shivered. "Sick."

"So why did he ransack your house? Why did it look like he was after something?"

"Because he is delusional and now in jail and won't be bothering me anymore?" Sage didn't look like she believed her words.

"It just doesn't make sense," Leo said, trying not to kiss her again.

He failed.

Sage kissed him back. She raised her hand and then looked to be second-guessing herself and then plunged forward anyway and ran her fingers through his hair. If he had been a dog, his tail would be wagging.

Was he so touch-starved that a hand through the hair was enough to make him melt?

"Sorry," she laughed slightly. "I just wanted to do that. Ever since you fell asleep on the couch watching *Ever After.*"

Leo rolled his eyes, hoping above all hopes that she'd do it again. "Sorry I'm not like that Prince Charming with locks long enough to donate."

"You've always had nice hair," Sage said. "Want to know a secret?"

"Always."

"I thought you were handsome. Back in high school, I loathed you. You were mean and crass and a total jerk. But even I had to admit that your thick hair and stupid long eyelashes were nice to look at."

He puffed up. "You were into me back then, eh?"

"Ugh, no."

"You just said you admired me!"

"Like the way someone admires a strange piece of art."

"Am I a strange piece of art to you, now?"

Sage shook her head. "A fun fantasy."

"I can make fantasies come true, you know."

They both laughed. "That was bad," Sage said.

"Terrible," Leo admitted.

"Like a line out of a cheesy romance novel."

"I have one though."

"A cheesy romance novel?" Sage asked. "I was wondering what you were reading on the plane."

Leo shook his head. "A fantasy," he whispered.

"What is it?" Sage asked after a heartbeat.

The music changed to something even slower, and they made no move to leave the dance floor. Or toward the bar. Or to the cars outside, where people were beginning to disappear into the night in search of more cantankerous fun.

"I want to kiss you," Leo whispered, lifting a hand to stroke her neck. "Right there." He ran a hand over that spot on her neck. "I want to kiss it so bad."

"So why don't you?"

"Because I think it might push me over the edge. Take this game of pretend too far."

"Would that be bad?" There was hope in her eyes and Leo knew he was about to crush it.

"I leave in the morning."

"So do I." Sage chuckled, growing slightly uncomfortable with the pause.

Leo took a deep breath. "You're flying home. I'm flying to D.C. to protect a congressional nominee."

"Oh."

"Oh," Leo said, still stroking that spot on her neck.

"I guess now will be your only chance, then," Sage whispered, barely heard over the music.

Leo needed no other invitation. He dipped his head and gently brushed his lips over her neck.

Goosebumps erupted across her skin, and he smoothed them away just to kiss the spot again and make them reappear.

She melted into him. He held her close, and they danced and swayed and walked around the hotel's garden courtyard until they tried to bid each other goodnight, but kept coming back to each other for one last kiss. The final moment of pretending.

They paused at Sage's hotel room door. On the precipice of something culminating these last few months. The edge of the cliff they had been teetering on for far too long. He wouldn't make the first move. This was just pretend after all, and he had to pretend to have an ounce of self-control. He had to pretend he was a gentleman. He had to pretend that he could kiss her goodnight and be able to turn around and pretend this never happened.

But he wanted to spend the final hours of this night showing her all the ways she had driven him crazy, to explore every inch of her, to kiss that spot on her neck a thousand times, to enjoy her presence in real life instead of just in his imagination.

She grabbed his hand and pulled him through the door.

And when the early rays of the morning sun tried to poke through the curtains, Sage's head lying on his chest, Leo whispered, "I don't want it to be pretend."

"Neither do I," Sage replied.

But in the end, that's all it was.

29

SAGE

The sun shining on her face pulled her from sleep. She had vowed she would stay awake the entire night, determined to make the most of their game of pretend. But in the end, she had fallen asleep against him. And—ever the professional—Leo had returned to his room sometime in the early morning hours, effectively ending the most perfect game of pretend.

The morning was bleak. The buzz of excitement had finally left the building, and most people were in one of three camps: sleeping in and hopefully sleeping off the hangover, still out partying, or up early to catch a flight at the unholy hour of seven am. Sage and Leo were in the latter category.

Lily (in camp one) had sent a text to the pair of them at two in the morning stating she was so happy to have worked with Leo and the agency and that though the job was finished, she would use them again in the future should she require their services and bid them both a safe trip.

They silently made their way through airport security, avoiding eye contact and careful not to brush too close to one another, in case their bare skin might touch and ignite some explosion of the tension growing between them.

She couldn't help but rub the spot between her neck and shoulder that his lips had found a thousand times last night. She caught him looking at her hand on her neck once but quickly averted his eyes.

Last night didn't happen. It was all pretend. They agreed to treat it as such. She was also not delusional. All good things had to come to an end.

When they checked their tickets, Sage realized this was goodbye. He'd be heading to the terminal on the south end, and she'd make her way to the gate at the north end.

He must have realized this too. "If it's alright with you, I will send Tess over to grab my things. It's just a few toiletries and a pair of shoes or two." He patted his suitcase at his side. "I pack light."

"Always ready for another job?"

"Part of the job," he said.

Her voice was scratchy. A lump was stuck in her throat. She needed a soothing, calming mint tea. But finding peace and quiet in an airport was about as likely as finding a four-leaf clover in the desert.

"Well, thank you for taking care of... this job." She wanted to say "me," but that felt too vulnerable.

"It was fun, you know, despite the whole kidnapping thing."

Sage laughed, but it didn't sound real. "Right, other than that minor detail."

"Sage, I—"

"It was good reconnecting. Thank you for your professionalism." With that, she turned and walked toward her gate.

She tried to remain distracted on the flight, but failed, so she caved and bought wi-fi so she could spend the entire flight on social media (super healthy), responding to comments, posting, and overall engaging with the community more than she had in the last few months.

It didn't help calm her racing mind.

Roz picked her up from the airport (along with Squash). Roz had been incessant in her questioning of the "You got *kidnapped*, for crying out loud!" experience.

And when Sage had updated her on everything—other than the whole "let's pretend to be together for the most perfect night" thing—Sage convinced Roz to spill her news. They chatted about all of Roz's updates regarding her fake dating situation, painting at a Spanish wedding, and her other drama.

"So, what are you going to do?" Sage asked, because she *certainly* didn't want to have to answer the same question. Best to keep Roz talking.

"I don't know!" Roz said. "It's all a mess."

"I know the feeling," Sage mumbled.

"Well, what are you going to do?" Roz asked, taking a turn way too fast and slamming Sage's head against the window. "Sorry."

Sage rubbed her temple. "I don't know. Probably do some more chatty streams. Maybe go live on IG. Get some new merch branding done. Anything to shift attention away from the whole Jared debacle."

"I meant about Leo."

Sage shrugged "His sister is coming to grab his stuff—"

"That's not what I mean."

Sage tried to look dumb, but she was afraid she only came across as guilty. "What are you talking about?"

Roz only rolled her eyes. "Okay, be that way. I won't pull it out of you. That's something you gotta work on. Speaking of work. Wanna do an eBay party?"

Sage groaned. "Some other time. Next week? Next month? How about next year?"

Roz came to an abrupt halt in front of Sage's home. She patted her shoulder. "Whenever you're ready."

The trio of friends had decided to throw an eBay party where they would scour the house for things Sage didn't want to keep and list them, making a little profit for a girls' trip. Sage had the idea of using the money for something fun, but the girls were hesitant, at first. Until the first day they came over to help clear away George's things and realized how big a task it really was. "Well, crap," Roz had said. "We'll all need either a vacation or therapy after this job."

Tavy had snorted, "Why not both?"

Sage stared at the old house now. *Home.* Despite all the changes these last few months—the pain in her heart after losing George, and her strange housemate-turned-friend-turned... something-else-turned-stranger again—

this house still made her chest feel warm. It was her place. Her sacred refuge.

"Thank you," Sage said.

As soon as she laid her head down on her pillow, ready to take the world's longest dissociation nap, her phone buzzed. She was not proud of how she grappled for it. The phone clattered to the ground, and she pounced on it like a cat.

It was just a notification that showed Leo had stopped sharing locations with her. A text followed shortly after.

> LEO: A local guy will be by on Thursday at three to disassemble and remove the cameras. Don't worry, they are all disconnected.

Sage simply liked the text, threw her phone across the room, and tried to sleep. It's what any rational person would do.

She allowed herself to mope for the rest of the day. She rotted in bed, watching trashy TV and TikToks while replying to more comments. Lily must have slept off the hangover because she texted Sage letting her know that the activity on social media is most helpful considering the firestorm LilyTech still had to handle with the whole Jared thing.

Yeah, the whole Jared thing.

No big deal.

He was in jail.

He wasn't going to get her.

She was safe.

So why did she still feel uneasy?

Little bit of trauma, she thought. Tomorrow she would get out of bed and clean the house. Everything was better when she organized and cleaned. It was a big house and it would take her all day, and that would be great because she wouldn't be able to let her mind wander to Leo, busy in D.C. or wherever. She wondered if he would come back this way for the marathon he'd signed up for. Would he let her know he was back in town?

Morning came and she almost reneged on her promise to clean, but she could hear George's voice in her ear. "Happiness comes from our actions. So make tea and make yourself happy!"

Right, George. Absolutely right.

She made a big pot of tea and got to work tidying the kitchen. Clearly Leo had made himself home here because, despite her rather infrequent use of the pots and pans and other utensils, they were not where she originally kept them. She wiped down her teapots—she had seven, which was a totally normal number—and glared at the little pink teapot. It mocked her. She stashed it in a cupboard. One day she'd be able to look at it the same again—maybe when she could look at it without being reminded of Leo, which would be rather hard because last night Sage had been determined to memorize every inch of him.

She was a mess.

She sipped her tea and filled the sink, ready to start wiping down the cabinets when the doorbell rang. She nearly jumped out of her skin. Sure, she had Shania

Twain blaring, but she wasn't that loud. How had she missed the sound of someone driving up?

She grabbed her trusty golf club—sitting conveniently next to the front door—and swung the door open, ready to attack. Squash grumbled from the couch.

"Oh hey," said the stranger walking up the porch steps. "I'm Tess."

"Oh." Sage lowered the club and swung the door open more. "Hi. I'm Sage."

Tess laughed. It sounded a little like Leo, and it made Sage's throat constrict. "I know," Tess said. "I'm here to grab Leo's things."

"Oh, right." Sage stepped out of the way and allowed Tess in. "I guess you know the way since you stayed with Squash. Thanks for that, by the way."

Tess snorted. "Leo gave me the redacted version of events but even that sounded awful."

Sage groaned. "I still can't even look at any kind of soup without my stomach tensing."

Tess paused at Leo's doorway. "Leo's a fantastic cook, which is sad clam chowder took you out. I have a feeling he won't be making that any time soon. It's my favorite. "

"I have to admit I'll miss his cooking," Sage said through a choked laugh. *And his fun facts, the way his wet hair would curl at the ends, the way he'd bark out laughter when Filbert said something inappropriate, and the silhouette he'd cast against the fireplace...*

Tess leaned against the four-poster bed, staring at Sage. "He's cooked for you?"

Sage snorted. "Yeah. I mean, he lived here for like two months."

"Did he ever make the popcorn?"

Sage could feel her mouth salivating at the thought. "With the coconut oil? To die for!"

"I have to agree." Tess tossed his clothes into a bag. "Thanks again for letting me steal your time. I gotta run to the post office if I'm gonna make it before they close. Weirdest break-up ever," she mumbled the last bit to herself.

"We weren't—" Sage cleared her throat. "We aren't. It was a job for him, you know?"

Tess paused at the front door. "Sure it was." She winked and slung the bag over her shoulder.

With the last bit of Leo's presence officially out of the house and en route to D.C., it felt like the whole thing was behind her.

Sage decided to mope around for the rest of the day feeling sorry for herself.

30

LEO

Bleaker1212: Crawling back to the game after a week with your tail between your legs, huh?

bleaker1212: Speaking of between your legs...

A2ZBT: Let's see 'em.

4k2summit: Heard you choked on the competition. Was it Crickets?

bleaker1212: I have something you can choke on.

Good grief, could these guys be any more piggish? What did one call a group of swine? Ah, FILBERTS (Foul Insects Love Berating Everyone Because They Suck).

It was three in the morning. He had to be up in four hours, yet here he was, watching Sage play *Welkin Wall*. It was strange knowing she was also awake at this ungodly hour.

He knew he shouldn't. He knew it wasn't appropriate. But Leo couldn't help but jump into her streams and watch like some creep. (He wasn't—obviously. He just liked to daydream that Sage was talking to him, that he could smell her strawberry shampoo and green tea—you know, like a normal person. Not weird at all).

Currently, he was stalking her. Really, stalking was such a strong word; he was merely checking in on her, because something still just didn't sit right with Leo. Jared was a total creep (unlike the lurking Leo) and a danger (Leo liked to figure himself dangerous but would settle for menacing at the moment), but some things simply didn't add up.

Why trash her house?

Why ransack George's room?

He let the questions simmer while he responded to comments.

bobfilbert123: oh no, @bleaker1212 I just had to text your mama all about your profanity and hatred toward women. She didn't seem too happy.

Leo had gotten good, really good, at using some programs and doing a little coding for himself over the past few months. When Sage had been streaming, he had been practicing being a menacing (and dangerous) presence online. It piqued his interest, and he found himself wishing he had more time to dedicate to learning about cybersecurity. He even floated the idea of some continued education to the agency and maybe heading in that direction.

Leo blocked comments and waited for the bots to simmer down and eventually the chat found the right audience again. Sage babbled on about how Squash had a tumble down the steps but was otherwise unharmed (apparently her face had always been that crooked) and Sage talked about how she tried to make cupcakes for Tavy's birthday but they were too salty and didn't rise.

Sage's face flicked over the comments, reading and pulling some up between matches. Was her smile because his username popped up on the screen?

"I miss popcorn," she mused to the camera.

hunnymama98: Just make some.

misterymIn: Is it on your Amazon wish list? I'll order you some if you respond to my DM.

Sage rolled her eyes at some of the comments, chatting about popcorn and when Leo's name popped up on the stream (well, his alter ego as online personal Bob Filbert) he swore her breath hitched. She quickly recovered and laughed. "I like homemade popcorn. With coconut oil and extra salt."

And then she dove back into the game, leaving Leo hungry for more.

This particular job and new Subject were fairly easy. There was a lot of driving around involved and a lot of waiting in cars. While Leo hadn't been slapped on the wrist or anything because of the last job and the whole, you know, Subject being kidnapped thing, he was given a few meetings where he had to reflect on what went well and what didn't. (All parties agreed that the Subject being kidnapped was the shining moment of what *not* to do.) But still, the Agency seemed overall pleased about the fact that this job took up only one of their agents and was a great use of his time.

Now Leo was paired up again, this time on car babysitting duty. A glorified driver of sorts.

Whatever, it allowed him to people-watch from the side of the road, next to the giant courthouse while his sleazy Subject was inside.

He answered Tess's call on the first ring, putting her on speaker while he continued to wait. He checked his watch, another two hours watching the doors for his Subject.

"What's up, sis?" he asked, trying not to sound bored out of his mind.

"Why do you sound like you haven't slept in days and are stuck inside a vacuum?"

Apparently, he failed. "I'm currently being blasted with air conditioning because I have the wonderful job of not being on point for this job and I am tired. Because no, I haven't been sleeping."

Tess snorted. "Okay, Bob."

Leo raised his eyebrows. "What do you know about Bob?"

"More than you think." Tess yawned. "Anyway, I just wanted to let you know that I mailed your box, and I just want to know when you'll be back?"

Leo scoffed. "Miss me already?"

Tess snorted. "Hardly." Which meant yes, she did. "But I'm heading off to Croatia for a month or so for a job."

"A movie?"

He heard the smile in her voice. "Mhm. Action. Long days. All the fun."

"You have to tell me the title."

Tess laughed. "I'm pretty sure the titles they gave us for set stuff are fake. But got some big names in it. If I meet Judy Dench I'll have her sign something for you."

Leo laughed. Tess sounded excited, which was fun to hear because she was so painfully even-keel about everything. She made him look like the excitable one. (Which he wasn't, of course.)

"Why do you want me home then?" Leo asked.

"Oh, I have some plants that need watering..."

"Liar."

"Sage misses you. And I like her. You should keep her."

"Shut up."

"She's funny. Kind of sad in some ways, but so are you." Tess ordered coffee from what sounded like a drive-through. "But actually if you do come back this way, will you set up a security camera? I should probably know that I don't have a squatter in the condo, you know?"

"I'm not going back. Probably not for another few years. Maybe for Christmas."

Tess just sighed. "That's what I say, but there is something about home that keeps me coming back. I *should* move to L.A. It would be a good career move, but I just can't. So I pay to have a vacant condo I can come home to and that's fine. You just gotta accept the same fate."

"What fate?"

"That there is something about Hollandsway that sinks its claws into people, dragging them back home. It's less painful to resist the pull, promise."

Leo sighed. "It's never felt like home." Well, not until recently.

"That's what I said. Yet I keep coming back."

Leo needed to shift this conversation out of dangerous waters. "Well, you're going to Croatia, maybe you'll find a hot foreigner and fall in love and stay there. You can fly tours."

He could practically hear her shudder from across the country. "Never. Just letting you know my apartment is open for you when you decide to come back," Tess said.

Leo laughed. "Thanks, Tess. Keep me posted so I know that you're actually alive, ya know?"

"If I die, you'll be the first one I call." She laughed at her own pathetic joke. "Give Squash a smooch from me!"

"If I ever kiss that dog I will die on the spot due to some unknown disease."

She hung up.

Leo touched his lips, remembering the feeling of Sage and the taste of her, remembering the scent of her. He was a lost puppy ready to return home.

The problem was he couldn't be sure where home was anymore.

He was left alone with his thoughts (a dangerous game really) until his Subject emerged and Leo drove him home. He had the evening off (the pros of having a Subject who required at least four security agents) and he spent his time like any rational person would: running for miles on end on the treadmill, chasing that runner's high that was supposed to clear his brain.

All he got was a throbbing knee, sweat in his eyes, and more confusion.

. . .

The phone ringing startled Leo awake. He glanced at the clock, for half a moment worried he'd somehow slept through dinner (he had—a travesty). He hadn't slept through breakfast (fantastic) and was even more delighted to find it was Sage calling him.

"Hey," he said in his best "I am totally casual and my heart is not beating out of my chest right now" voice.

"Hey, sorry to bother you—"

"Never a bother," his voice went husky on the last word. So, clearly he failed at the whole nonchalant thing. But maybe it was the right thing to say because her voice went from tense to soft.

"I'm just a little concerned. The cameras are still up and stuff. Can we maybe postpone the guy coming to get them? And can we maybe turn them on? Or can I buy them since they are already installed?"

"Sage, what is going on?" Leo tried to keep the panic from his voice. Radio silence for three—*three!*—days, and *now* she had the audacity to call him out of the blue and freak him out? Kind of rude, but he'd rather hear her voice than not at all.

"It's fine, I think." Sage sighed and he could imagine her sequestered in her office, rubbing her temples, a plate of long cold pizza rolls on her desk. "I just think there's a car rolling around too often to be normal. And I think someone tried to get in at one point when I was gone. Like, they were maybe looking for a key or something. The flower pot by the front door was moved and stuff and—"

"Do you feel safe there now?" he asked.

"Yes."

"Sage Moon, I swear I can feel your lack of eye contact right now."

"Because there is no eye contact. We are on the phone!"

"Don't make me FaceTime you to confirm that you're lying to me."

"I feel…" Sage let the moment hang in the air. "I feel unsettled. Something is off."

"Can you go to Roz's? Or Tavy's?"

"I think so."

"If not, then Tess's apartment is open and you can crash there."

Sage sighed. "I'll go to a friend's. Something just feels wrong. I called Lily to ask what I should do, but she tried to be reassuring with the whole 'Jared is behind bars and I promise we won't hire any more felons or crazy people' type of thing."

"I'll call the company. They are technically contracted with the Agency so I might be able to pull some strings. I'll see if I can get them to turn them on."

Leo went to work calling the appropriate people. Jenson, the big boss man, was first on the list. Leo explained the situation. Once Leo finished what he thought was a very succinct but well-fleshed-out synopsis (Jenson had the gritty details in a report on his desk) he paused, waiting for Jenson to give him the green light.

"Leo, I think we need to have a chat about where all of this is going…"

It's going on a one-way ticket back home, that's where it's going. Instead, Leo said, "What do you mean, sir?"

"I mean I can tell that your passion for this line of work is manufactured. There is more out there for you."

"I'm sorry, sir. Have I done something wrong?"

Jenson laughed. How could he be laughing at a moment like this? He needed to give Leo the green light to do something about Sage *right now.*

"Look Leo, you have shown more excitement and interest in all the computer stuff we've been struggling with. By the way, we just hired two new IT guys who should be able to handle everything from now on."

"Oh, great," Leo said. "I fail to see how that is relevant to Sage's case right now. Do I have permission to contact the company to turn on the cameras?"

"Yes, sure. Give them a call and turn them on. Do what you need to do. But Leo, this is a favor to you, understand?"

"Yes sir."

"No, I don't think you do. This is rather unorthodox but I understand where you are coming from to a certain degree. I have two other guys heading your way to relieve you of this job. Take a week's sabbatical—"

"But—"

"Not a discussion. Not a suggestion. Not a punishment."

"Sir—"

"I have an offer heading your way later this afternoon. Give it a read-over on the plane or something. Let me know your thoughts."

"Plane? Offer? Am I being transferred?" Could they even do that?

"I assume you are going to Miss Moon's to check on

her. Give my proposition some thought. Get your head out of the clouds."

Leo ran a hand through his hair. "Sir, I have been trying to do that for the last three months."

Twelve hours later Leo was back in Hollandsway. Maybe Tess had been onto something about the pull it had on people.

Leo was relieved (fine—and disappointed) that Sage was not at her house when he waltzed through the unlocked (unlocked!) door. There was no sign of the rat dog despite Leo listening closely for a gurgle that was supposed to be a bark. The house was calm and empty and quiet. No sounds of chattering from her office, though Leo checked her office to be sure, lingering in the doorway. It smelled of lemonade candles and Sage and looked like a bomb of purple pillows detonated.

It felt like home.

He wished he still had her location shared on his phone.

Where was she? Did she make it to Roz's? Or was she at Tess's? She never did text him to confirm she got out of the house.

But that's when he heard it. The telltale squeak of the backdoor slowly opening. The hinges, despite the obscene amount of WD40 Leo had used on them, were too old and decrepit to be brought back to life. Now he was grateful for the unintentional alarm bells ringing.

The sounds of heavy footsteps floated up the stairs. Leo rounded the corner, hoping to tiptoe down to the first floor unseen. He could take the steps two at a time, making sure to step on the far edges of the stairs to avoid making them creak.

The footsteps grew quieter. The intruder made their way deeper into the house. Leo's heart beat with calm intensity. Adrenaline wasn't part of the equation yet, which meant he was focused and in control. This would be a quick subdue and a simple car ride to jail. His training created muscle memory and his brain was on autopilot. He was a professional. This was his job.

But why did he feel embers of anger? Why did he feel personally attacked by this unknown intruder? Probably because he made his girl nervous.

His girl.

Keep your head out of the clouds, you moron.

By the time he reached the bottom stair, he was prepared to make his presence known and subdue the creep. Instead, the front door burst open and the lights flicked on and a sea of "get out of here" and "Who are you" and "What do you want" and "Squash, attack!" burst forth. Leo was suddenly blinded by a rainbow umbrella flapping in his face along with a stick hitting his knees.

"He's in George's room!" someone called. It sounded like Sage. "There are two of them!"

"Two?" another familiar voice said, holding the umbrella weapon (with dangerous precision). "We only spotted one. Abandon mission?"

"Mission?" Leo, not about to be bested by a now familiar umbrella, grabbed the weapon (because that's what he would label it in his report) and thrust it aside, blocking a rather well-timed slash of a cane across his chest with his arm. "Filbert?" Leo asked. "What on earth are you doing here? Is that Sage's robe?"

Filbert wore a pair of yellow boots and a floral robe that barely covered Filbert's own *filberts*. "Don't worry, Sage! It's only the Blondie Boy!"

Sage, who was nowhere to be seen, called from down the hall. "Fil, we messed up!"

A crash and then a small yelp followed.

Leo leaped into action, racing down the hall toward George's room. Sage was standing on the bed, backed against the headboard, brandishing a closed umbrella at a figure looming in the corner. It was clearly a tall, but lanky man, wearing a ski mask, holding Squash in one hand. Not that intimidating of a figure, save for the gun leveled at Sage.

"Sir, you need to back off now," Leo said, pausing in the doorway. Filbert joined him, gasping slightly when he took in the scene. "Just take a hike. This doesn't have to get ugly."

"I need the painting," the masked man said. He wiggled the gun at Sage. "I know it's here. Where is it?"

Sage swallowed, opened her mouth, and then swallowed again, clearly too terrified to talk.

"We moved all the paintings of value to a temperature and moisture-controlled storage unit in Portland," Leo lied. "Isn't that right, Sage?"

Her eyes were watery and her face pale. She nodded. It was a lie, but at least she held on to some eye contact for a change.

The masked man uttered several expletives but didn't lower the gun.

"I have valuable vases." Sage gulped. "In the closet there. Please let my dog go." She lifted a shaking hand and pointed to the large walk-in closet, holding a closed umbrella to her chest.

Leo took three giant, but slow steps, into the room. The gun shifted and pointed at his chest. Leo held up his hands. "Just helping the lady from the bed. We'll leave you to it." He reached out to Sage and gripped her cold and shaking hand. He had to pull her toward him harshly enough for her to break her terrified and frozen state. She managed an ungraceful step off the bed and nearly tripped on the umbrella clutched in her hand.

The masked man gestured to the doorway where Filbert stood.

"Head out." The masked man lifted the dog in his arm. It gurgled, which was the only indication that it was sleeping and not dead. "I know you love this animal, so it comes with me as insurance."

Sage, who had been shaking like a leaf next to Leo, must have gotten a surge of bravery because she stiffened. She stood taller. She looked ready to fight, which was the last thing Leo needed her to try.

This was supposed to be simple. Now he was a hostage with a senile old man, the woman of his dreams, and an elderly animal spawned from the depths of some unknown place.

No amount of training prepared him for this.

Well, if you can't beat crazy, may as well join 'em.

In a flash, Leo grabbed the umbrella from Sage and threw it at the masked man like a spear. It hit him square in the chest and he broke the eye contact long enough for

Leo to launch himself over the small bed and tackle the masked man into the wall behind him.

"Get Filbert out of here!" Leo yelled. He really did not need another umbrella to join the mix.

Leo grappled for the gun with one hand and scooped up Squash with the other. The masked man was clearly no athlete because he tried in vain to kick out Leo's legs. He made decent contact with Leo's bad knee (just his luck) but one well-placed shoulder check into the man's chin subdued him for long enough to toss the animal on the bed behind him. Squash landed with a fart and a grumble. The sound of Filbert's rubber boots pounding the hardwood behind Leo told him that he had not fled as he had commanded.

"Good grief, get out of here you three!"

"You're Ralph Emmerson. You wanted to buy a painting—" Sage gasped.

"Sage, I swear if you don't leave right now and call the police I will never let you out of my sight again!"

He glanced back long enough to see Sage grab Filbert's hand and pull him from the room. He swore he heard her mumble, "Is that a promise?" and they fled outside.

It took about two seconds for Leo to get the masked man, Emmerson apparently, wrestled into submission. They waited on the porch and about a minute later sirens and lights came down the tree-lined road.

It took a little bit of questioning, but Leo eventually pieced together the puzzle.

"So let me get this straight?" Leo asked once Emmerson was in the back of the cop car. Leo looked at

Filbert, Sage, and the confused cop."You didn't take my directions to go to a friend's house—"

"I beg your finest pardon," Filbert interrupted.

Sage shrugged and then nodded like it was true. "I went to a friend's house, like you said."

Filbert nodded, tamping the end of the umbrella on the ground. "It was my idea to set up the trap."

Sage shrunk back, looking a little sheepish.

"Excuse me, a trap?" the cop asked. He looked exasperated, and he wasn't even the one held at gunpoint.

"Yes, sir!" Filbert said. "Miss Sage here told all her innerweb friends that she was going to be gone all weekend. And that the house would be totally empty. We figured that bad egg would be watching and waiting for a prime opportunity to break back in. That photographer fellow—"

"Jared," Sage added, petting Squash who was asleep (or dead) in her arms.

"Yes, Jared. He was crafty but we figured there was another man wanting a piece of the pie. Thank you for that by the way," Filbert said.

"No problem." Sage looked to the cop and very earnestly added, "I brought Filbert a pecan pie yesterday."

"Right," the cop said. He looked more confused with each passing moment.

"Anyhow," Filbert went on, unwrapping the robe and flashing everyone in his attempt to tighten it around his waist. "We had a stake out. Which was why the pie was so nice. We about polished it off by the time we saw the sneak attacker go in the back."

Now it was Leo's turn to be confused (more than normal). "I came into the house by the front door! Which was *unlocked,* thank you very much!"

"Well, we couldn't see the front door from our hiding spot!" Sage said. "Oh, this is a mess."

"You have no idea." Leo wanted to grab her by the shoulder and shake her and ask, "What on earth were you thinking?!" He also wanted to kiss her. He decided he'd settle for kissing her when this was all over. Then a firm talking to and then more kissing, obviously.

Filbert cleared his throat. "We were set up in the tree house—"

"Excuse me?" Leo asked.

"There is a treehouse—more of a birdwatching set up in the woods out back. We used that as our lookout."

"Dear heavens, this report will be the death of me," Leo whispered.

"Tell me about it," the cop said, rubbing his forehead.

"We can't see the front door from the bird platform out back. I thought I locked the front door and that would force someone around back. But I guess it didn't lock up. Oops."

"Oops?" Leo asked.

"Anyway, we saw the Ralph Emmerson guy go in. Of course we didn't know it was him at the time, but we figured we'd shake him up a bit," Filbert said, looking rather pleased with himself.

"And you figured that before or after you called the cops?" Leo asked, sarcasm etching every word.

Filbert stood tall and pointed the umbrella at the cop. "We did call. I raced home while Sage kept a lookout and called you folks. Nearly broke a toe, I was racing so fast. Do you know what I got?"

"What?" the cop asked.

"I got a 'not again, Filbert' and then I got the 'do you need me to call the state, Filbert?' and then the cherry on the pie was the lady gal told me to call the non-emergency line!"

The cop shifted uncomfortably. "You know how often we get calls from you, Fil—"

"So we decided to be the ones to take care of it!" Filbert saluted the sky. "We figured we'd bust in and—"

"And what?" Leo asked, staring at Sage. "What did you think would happen?"

"Honestly, I thought it was another weird fan. We'd scare him off and that would be the end of it. I was going to call the cops on my cellphone when we got inside since I didn't have any service out there, and then we went inside and *you* scared us!"

"I scared you?" Leo asked, arms crossing over his chest. He had been the hero!

"You were much bigger than the man we saw and then we figured out there were two and there wasn't supposed to be a gun involved!"

Leo ran a hand down his face. "You're killing me here." But he was also still preening over the fact that she had called him big. Obviously in an intimidating and macho sort of big way. He flexed his muscles to prove that point again.

Sage groaned. "This was not supposed to go this way. It was dumb but it also seemed like a good idea at the time. I was just scared and tired of living life scared."

Leo softened a little. "Fear makes us do stupid things."

Sage nodded, hanging her head. Filbert patted the top of her hair and then Squash's head, whispering, "There, there. It's all over kids." Then he tapped the umbrella on the ground and said, "If that's all, I've got a slice of pie calling my name back home." He tipped an imaginary hat and walked away, whistling as if this were the most normal thing to have ever happened. Like it was just another Tuesday.

The cop scratched his head. "Are you alright?"

Sage nodded. "I think so."

"I'll make my reports. I'm assuming you want to press charges."

Sage nodded.

"All right. You'll be hearing from us. Have a good night. I'll send someone to pick up Filbert tonight."

Leo patted the cop on the shoulder. "That won't be necessary. We'll take care of him. I'll call the state for services."

Cop shook his head. "Whatever you say."

Sage and Leo watched the cop drive off and they stood together in silence for a few moments before Leo pulled her into him, wrapping his arms around her tightly.

"You absolute idiot," he whispered into her hair.

She was here.

She was okay.

She was stupid and perfect and in his arms and everything was right in the world again.

Sage sighed, wrapping her arms around him. "Fun fact: I missed you."

TWO YEARS LATER

SAGE

"Tess, I swear this is totally unnecessary and honestly terrifying!" Sage screamed into the headset.

Tess looked at ease in the helicopter, like she was ready to start driving (flying!) with her knees. She shrugged. "Leo asked if I could pick you up!"

"In a car! I am pretty sure he meant in a car!"

The last two years had been a whirlwind. Essentially the agency offered to pay for Leo to go to school and get a degree in cybersecurity. He fast-tracked the program and was on a contract with the agency heading up the new cybersecurity side of things. It was a big decision, but Leo ran for hours, clearing his head and making a list of pros and cons. In the end, he'd said it was an easy decision. Sage felt like home. And this job allowed him to be home.

And now Sage was en route to watch him walk across the stage.

Tess laughed. "We'll just land in the overflow parking lot."

"How is this legal?" Sage squealed, staring at the treetops below her. She was flying in a glass bubble with just metal blades and physics holding her up.

"I got permission!" Tess said. "I know a guy who can pull some serious strings for almost everything."

"Sounds like a famous—"

"Ah, ah, ah!" Tess smirked. "No questions. I signed an NDA anyway."

Sage's heart jumped into her throat. "Just park this thing before I puke."

"We call it landing."

The duo got several stares as they exited the helicopter and sort of jogged toward the bleachers of the university. They found their seats, both ignoring the gaping faces of those who had seen them land in the back parking lot.

"I can't believe he did it!" Tess said, pulling out her phone to snap photos of the crowd. "My baby brother graduating!"

Sage cocked her head. "Wait, he always told me he was older."

Tess shrugged. "We are ten minutes apart. But our parents never did say who was older. Afraid it was going to foster unhealthy competition. Little did they know that it would only fuel the flames of sibling rivalry. But I'm totally older. The golden child crown belongs to me." She snorted. "That's a lie but it's fun to believe."

Tess fit into her life as perfectly as ice cream complimented apple pie. She was fun and full of life and her off time in Hollandsway was never long enough.

Leo bought her condo from her and she was happy to be the proud resident of the spare room in exchange for not having to pay a mortgage.

Plus Leo was secretly convinced Tess was dating some movie star and he didn't want her name on a mortgage if there were some crazy fans out to get her or something. Can't take the security agent out of Leo.

"I see him!" Tess stood and pointed, waving. "Yes! Go baby bro!"

She could practically feel his eye roll from where they sat.

"See, I'm totally the oldest. It's the eldest's job to embarrass the younger ones."

They watched Leo walk across the stage, grab his paper, and sit back down. It was kind of anticlimactic (as Leo had warned her it would be). He wanted to skip the walking across the stage thing, but she had convinced him to go, a physical representation of the change and exciting moves he was making in life.

And for the first time in a long time, Sage wasn't so terrified of change.

LEO

Over the last two years, Leo had managed to buy the condo from his sister, run two marathons, kiss Sage five million times, take her golfing (it was a beautiful disaster), take Sage hiking (also a disaster), and live life lighter and happier than he had ever thought possible.

Oh, and he walked across the dumb stage and got the dumb paper that only said, "Your actual diploma will be mailed to you" and all of that jazz. When Sage had been pretty insistent on him walking for graduation, he took the opportunity to have his own little surprise planned.

After the shenanigans were over, he finally found the pair he was looking for (quite the challenge in the sea of people). He hugged his sister and kissed Sage, immediately shedding the stupid cap and gown.

"Ready?" Leo asked.

"Your chariot awaits," Tess said, a maniacal gleam in her eye. Sage looked clueless, which was a good sign. At least Tess could keep a secret after all.

They wandered through the crowd and made it back to the helicopter, which had a small group of people staring at it.

"Good grief," Tess said. "I thought we'd landed far enough away for people to overlook the whole helicopter in a parking lot situation."

Sage snorted. "Good thing I skipped lunch."

She was looking a little green. Maybe this wasn't a good idea after all. Leo pushed the thoughts away. He'd gotten the wise counsel of Roz and Tavy. This was a good plan.

They hopped into the helicopter and Leo couldn't help feeling a little smug. He wondered how long it would take Sage to realize they were not heading home.

About half an hour, actually.

"Wait, is that the beach?" Sage asked.

Tess nodded and began to take the helicopter down, landing softly on the sand ten minutes later.

"Where are we?" Sage asked, laughing as Leo helped her out.

Tess waited in the cockpit, a goofy grin on her face. He probably looked just as giddy. He couldn't help it. He was going to freaking sweep Sage off her feet like the romantic guy he was. A little smugness was allowed.

The June air was crisp and the sun was perfectly above the horizon. Sunset was another two hours away but that golden hour was fast approaching.

Sage must have had some sort of inkling where this was going. She allowed herself to be pulled toward the water with Leo and then they did one of their favorite things.

They walked and talked.

"What are we doing here?" Sage asked, holding his hand and leaning into him as they walked along the hard sand.

"Watching the water," Leo said.

"Mhm, right." He could hear the smile in Sage's voice. She allowed him to yammer on about life. How grateful he was to have been given the opportunity to go to school and have a clear direction in life. How excited he was to help people. How he already tracked down a scammer that tried to swindle his other Aunt Betty out of ten grand. About how much he was excited to finally replace the roof on Sage's home this summer. How pleased he was that the stain they'd used on the porch held up over last winter.

And when he was done rambling and found his

courage again (not that he ever lost it, it had simply taking a quick vacation in the clouds or something) he turned her so she faced the sun and water.

She was stunning. Her dark hair was in a messy low bun. She wore a long skirt with a slit in it and a simple t-shirt and it was gorgeous.

It was Sage. She was a mystery to him still yet he felt like he knew her better than anyone else in the world. There wasn't enough time in this lifetime to uncover all her little quirks and hopes and dreams and everything that made her so uniquely Sage.

Was he rambling in his head? Why was she staring at him like this? He was supposed to be telling her all of this and speaking his thoughts aloud.

"I love you," he choked. *So much for romance.* May as well lean into the whole middle school declaration of love type of thing then. "I think it started here. On the beach. At Thor's Well. I feel like I got to see a secret part of you that no one else does and I haven't been able to get enough since."

"I love you too," she said through a smile. It wasn't new.

They had told each other before. But only in serious and quiet moments. They were more precise with their words, saving the *I love you's* for precious moments.

Except for Squash. Sage had no problem pouring the declaration over the animal and Leo had vowed never to be jealous of the attention the rodent got.

Well, now or never. The waves crashed behind him. The sun made her glow. The breeze fluttered around them. He got to one knee. "Will you let me love you for the rest of your life?"

Her face was a mix of elation and joy. She bent and kissed him. She kissed him slow and then fast. He grabbed his face with her hands. And then he tackled her.

Tackled was an intense term, but it was the most accurate way to describe how he swept her legs out from under her and she crashed onto him. There really was no other word to describe being bowled over by a sneaker wave and the force of which pushed one into their fiancé (Leo decided that was going to be his new favorite word).

Sage coughed and sputtered as the sneaker wave retreated back to the sea just as quickly as it came.

"Ah!" Leo shouted in a manly way and not at all like a surprised pipsqueak screech that was still echoing off the trees behind them.

"The ring!"

She wiped sand from the side of her temple and managed to avoid a total faceplant because Leo had graciously broken her fall with his body.

They stood and sort of coughed.

"Your face!" she snorted. "It's bleeding."

Leo pinched his nose. "Must have been when you kicked me. I think your foot is still in my spleen."

Sage laughed again, untying her elegant bun and tying her hair up into a sandy knot on her head. "Must have been when you decided to headbutt my knee!"

He reached out and brushed some sand from her eyebrow. "I love you."

"That was a terrible apology. I love you too."

He pulled out the ring and slipped the band over her finger.

"It's beautiful," Sage said. She leaned into him. He wrapped the free hand not pinching his bloody nose around her. "Can Squash be a flower girl?"

"Anything for my girls."

After the bleeding stopped and they had sort of cleaned themselves up (okay fine, they got cold) they meandered back to the helicopter where Tess sat waiting. She squealed when she saw them and gushed over Sage and the ring.

"I finally have a sister!" she cried. Then she took in the state of the pair. "Is that blood?"

Leo rolled his eyes but wiped the remaining evidence away with his sleeve. "I fought a bear and won and now we have a wedding to plan."

Tess screeched again and hugged him. "I can't wait!"

The three got in their seats and just as Tess was lifting off the ground she said, "I called Mo's. They said I could land in the field next door. Anyone care for a bowl of clam chowder?"

ACKNOWLEDGMENTS

Honestly, this is my favorite part of the book to write because it gives me a chance to simmer down and reflect on all the people who helped make this book possible. That reflection is so important because it gives me that boost to move forward with other projects, blotting out all the negative aspects of writing and publishing (looking at you, Word Doc crashes).

I always have to thank my husband, Malachi. You are the reason I get to take risks with my work and the reason I get to pursue writing. You are my biggest cheerleader despite not being into the whole words-on-a-page thing. You carve out time for me. You sent me out on writing dates by myself, encouraging me to let the flow state take over and just "not worry and get stuff done." Also, I am not sorry that I shamelessly stole your line—the "Will you let me love you forever" line. Yes, folks. That was real life. *(Swoon.)*

Thanks, Jess. Because of you, this book took four times as long to write, but I wouldn't have it any other way.

Special thanks to Lolli. You would take Jess almost every Friday and give me uninterrupted hours to sit and cram my week's worth of writing sessions into. This book was written because of your patience and willingness to take a crazy eight-month-old off my hands!

Thank you to my AMAZING critique partners. Victoria, your feedback is always so valuable. Your friendship is even more precious. Thank you, Chris Kenny, for your help in the initial stages and helping me with the whole techie side of things and making sure I wasn't writing total fiction when I didn't want to be—seriously, the whole "insert mumbo jumbo about computers here" note was fixed because of you!

Thanks to my little sister, Cassidy! You were the most excited about me taking a leap into a different genre, and your listening to me word-vomit an outline at you was most appreciated, as were all your notes!

Special thanks to Jahsh and Kendra (and Adalee) for their excitement for everything in my family's life, and for hanging with Jess, and just being people who push me forward.

Special thanks to my dog. (He can't read, so hopefully an audio version will get to him at some point.) You got to hear me talk out my ideas. All I know is that you are grossly underpaid. Love you though.

Thanks, Ignite Coffee—you fueled my writing sessions. I can't thank you enough.

Now for more of a serious note. This book was partially inspired by a friend of mine in college. Without giving away too many details, she had a stalker. The police didn't take it seriously. Her life was a living nightmare for months until the stalker tried to break in. There is no excuse for the fear and anxiety women are forced to live with. If you want to support women in many different scenarios, please consider donating to the Oregon Coalition Against Domestic and Sexual Violence.

ABOUT THE AUTHOR

Bethany Joy is the penname to Bethany Votaw, a short story and thriller author. She wanted to try her hand at writing something cute and fun in order to give her mind a break from the dark and heavy stuff she's been known to write. And she likes it here. She might stay awhile.

Bethany got her start writing in college when she would write little short stories on notecards when she should have been paying attention to the physics equations instead.

Oops.

Now she's an author so everything works out in the end.